131104

A Garland Series
Foundations of the Novel

Representative Early

Eighteenth-Century Fiction

A collection of 100 rare titles
reprinted in photo-facsimile in 71 volumes

Foundations of the Novel

compiled and edited by

Michael F. Shugrue
Secretary for English for the M.L.A.

with New Introductions for each volume by

Michael Shugrue, *City College of C.U.N.Y.*
Malcolm J. Bosse, *City College of C.U.N.Y.*
William Graves, *N.Y. Institute of Technology*

The Voyages and Adventures of Captain Robert Boyle

by

William Rufus Chetwood

with a new introduction
for the Garland Edition by
Malcolm J. Bosse

Garland Publishing, Inc., New York & London

The new introduction for the

Garland *Foundations of the Novel* Edition

is Copyright © 1972, by

Garland Publishing, Inc., New York & London

All Rights Reserved

Bibliographical note:
*This facsimile has been made from a copy in the Beinecke Library of Yale University
(IK C426 726)*

Library of Congress Cataloging in Publication Data

Chetwood, William Rufus, d. 1766.
    The voyages and adventures of Captain Robert Boyle.

    (Foundations of the novel)
    Reprint of the 1726 ed.
    This work has also been attributed to Benjamin Victor and to Daniel Defoe.
    Includes The voyage, shipwreck, and miraculous preservation of Richard Castleman, gent., with a description of the city of Philadelphia and the country of Pennsylvania.
    1. Voyages, Imaginary. 2. Pennsylvania—Description and travel. I. Victor, Benjamin, d. 1778. The voyages and adventures of Captain Robert Boyle.
II. Defoe, Daniel, 1661?-1731. The voyages and adventures of Captain Robert Boyle. III. Castelman, Richard. The voyage, shipwreck, and miraculous preservation of Richard Castleman, gent. 1972. IV. Title. V. Series.
PZ3.C428Vo 5 [PR3346.C3]   823'.5   79-170565
ISBN 0-8240-0558-9

Printed in the United States of America

Introduction

William Chetwood was well known in his day as the prompter at Drury Lane. As a bookseller he incurred the displeasure of Alexander Pope, who suggests in The Dunciad Variorum *(11, 159) that Chetwood was a henpecked husband. As an author Chetwood wrote a group of plays and a history of the contemporary stage, though he is better known today for his travel and adventure stories.* Voyages, and Adventures of Captain Robert Boyle *(1726) is a trove of literary devices used in popular fiction of the period. It is also a capable narrative, featuring dramatic escapes and deliverances, an appealing love story, and a likable protagonist.*

Traditionally a picaresque hero is orphaned and badly treated by the people with whom he has to live. Robert Boyle is no exception. Apprenticed to a watchmaker, he is bullied by the man's adulterous wife, then tricked out of his inheritance by a wicked uncle and sent to sea. Captured by pirates, which is the common fate of fictional eighteenth-century traveler-heroes, Boyle reaches Morocco where he displays the inventive skill of an English artisan by building his master a complicated fountain that inspires awe. Boyle helps a beautiful European woman escape from the Mohammedan harem, and together they are rescued by a French ship. Falling in love, they consummate their passion after an exchange of vows which are "spiritually" legal; then they are separated by her maid's treachery. Boyle resumes his travels, first in Morocco, then in Italy and

INTRODUCTION

the West Indies, from which he returns to England rich enough to buy an estate and to settle down in well-earned retirement. After rescuing a woman from an attacker and a child from gypsies, Boyle is shocked to learn that the woman is actually his wife, who earlier had been reported dead, and that the child is the issue of their brief union. In his new-found happiness the hero delivers a brief, pious homily in the style of Defoe; loose ends of secondary plot are tied; and the novel draws rapidly to a close. This précis only suggests the complications which arise in the pell-mell narrative.

Throughout his adventures Robert Boyle never succumbs to lust and greed, although he is pragmatically acquisitive and resourceful, an Englishman confident of facing the dangers and marvels of life. During the story, various life styles are thrust upon him: child-victim, sailor, slave, engineer, lover, traveler, merchant, and landowner whose recovered family promises him an old age of love and stability. To run his hero through these many changes of status and occupation, Chetwood employs situations and patterns which were standard fare during this literary period: interpolated stories, reversals of fortune, captures at sea, journeys to exotic lands, bizzare coincidences, disguises, intricate flashbacks, and romantic separations.

Although Boyle observes a strict standard of morality, there are always people in his midst who are capable of theft, rape, and murder. His ability to retain a sense of humanity in the face of violence and misfortune gives the novel an edifying tone similar to that in Robinson Crusoe. *On the other hand, Chetwood persistently taps some popular veins of sensationalism: sexual assault, battle at sea, murder of revenge.*

INTRODUCTION

Sometimes his fiction reflects the callousness of the age; for example, he permits his hero to witness a brutal castration without more than a slightly amused response. Chetwood manages to concoct an often heady mixture of instruction and entertainment by weaving into The Voyages of Captain Boyle *many of the literary patterns found in Defoe's successful novels and in the more extravagant fiction of Eliza Haywood and Penelope Aubin.*

In addition to that full-length novel the 1726 volume included a novella, promisingly titled The Voyage, Shipwreck, and Miraculous Preservation of Richard Castelman. *It is a slight performance whose inclusion was perhaps justified by its American setting. Chetwood swiftly transports his hero across the Atlantic and shipwrecks him in the New World where Castelman becomes an enthusiastic guide through the wilds of Carolina and the streets of Philadelphia. Some of the misinformation is amusing; Castelman describes a rattlesnake encountered in a Carolina swamp: "I believe it was near six Yards in Length, and as thick as a lusty Man's Thigh" (352). During his sojourn in Philadelphia the narrator, who remains a shadowy figure without the appeal of Robert Boyle, dutifully records the names of streets: "The chief are Broad-street, King-street, and High-street, tho' there are several other handsome Streets that take their Names from the Productions of the Country" (363). The travelog ends with Castelman's return to England from which he claims he will never roam again.*

Malcolm J. Bosse

THE VOYAGES AND ADVENTURES OF Captain *Robert Boyle*,

In several Parts of the World.

Intermix'd with

The STORY of Mrs. *VILLARS*, an *English* Lady with whom he made his surprizing Escape from *Barbary*;

The HISTORY of an *Italian* Captive; and the LIFE of *Don Pedro Aquilio*, &c.

Full of various and amazing Turns of Fortune.

To which is added,

The Voyage, Shipwreck, *and* Miraculous Preservation, *of*

Richard Castelman, Gent.

With a Description of the City of *Philadelphia*, and the Country of *Pensylvania*.

LONDON:
Printed for JOHN WATTS, at the Printing-Office in *Wild-Court*, near *Lincolns-Inn Fields*. 1726.

To the Right Honourable

Sir *William Yonge,*

One of the Lords of the Treaſury, and Knight of the moſt Honourable Order of the *BATH.*

S I R,

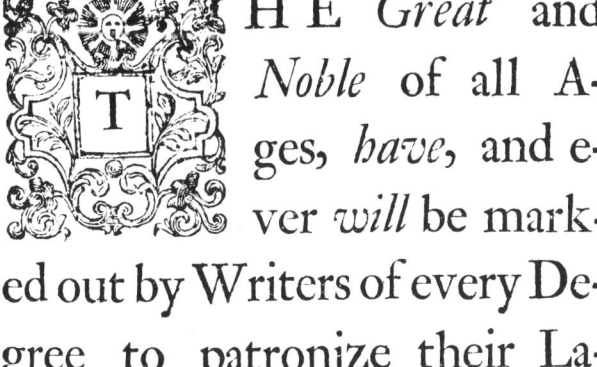

THE *Great* and *Noble* of all Ages, *have,* and ever *will* be marked out by Writers of every Degree to patronize their Labours:

Dedication.

bours: And as Publick Fame (though sparing of her Favours) has distinguish'd You in an Age of *Politeness*, *Wit*, and *Learning*, among other eminent Virtues that exalt the Mind, and dignify Human Nature; I am sufficiently justify'd to the World in the Choice of my Patron: But must depend on your known Candour, for thus presuming, without your Leave. Yet I have this for my Excuse, Exalted Merit is free

Dedication.

to the Confideration of all Men, and where Excellencies fhine, every Man has a Right to admire.

Though Praife is the juft Due of Merit, and all the World would join with me while I grew warm in yours, yet as I know your Nature more enclin'd to *deferve* than *receive* it, I fhall eafe You of that Pain, and in Silence wonder, where Words muft fail.

Dedication.

The People of *Mexico*, every Year, offer'd something to their *Emperor* in Token of *Vassalage*; and frequently, among Things worthy the Notice of a *King*, he receiv'd even Sacks of common Earth, from those Persons who could not afford a nobler Offering: But *they*, like *me*, did what was in their Power, with an Expression in their Language, which signified, *I would it were more worthy of your Acceptance.* I am assur'd

Dedication.

fur'd from your Goodnefs to find Pardon for this Freedom, though I add to my Prefumption, by fubfcribing my felf,

Your moft Obedient,

Humble Servant.

THE
PREFACE.

HE *following Sheets are a Detail of Fortunes I have run through for many Years; and however extraordinary they may appear, I shall give you the Circumstances for Truth. Yet this I must own, they lay by me undigested, and I had never any Intention to make 'em publick, if an old Asquaintance had not taken my loose Papers from me, and declar'd, if I would not digest 'em, he would.*

The

The PREFACE.

The Shipwreck of my Friend Mr. Castelman, *the Dangers he underwent, together with the Descriptions of* Pensylvania, *and* Philadelphia *the Capital of that Country, I hope will not displease the Reader. There are no Embelishments, nor one Step out of the Road of Truth. I believe every one that knows him, will give him the Character of a Person of the greatest Probity; as the Post he is in will sufficiently testify.*

THE
ADVENTURES
OF
Captain Robert Boyle, &c.

WAS born at a Sea-Port call'd *Boston* in *Lincoln-shire*. My Father was Captain and Owner of a Merchant-Ship that traded to the *West-Indies*, but was cast away homeward-bound upon the Rocks of *Silly*, and but one Man sav'd of his whole Crew. My Mother and I were at an Aunt's in *London* when the unhappy News of my Father's Death arriv'd.

I was too young to feel my Loss; but my Mother's Grief soon broke her Heart, and left me a poor helpless Orphan not ten Years of Age. It's true, I had a tender Aunt that was in pretty good Circumstances, who took Care of my Education. I soon learnt to read, and write a good Hand; I understood a little *Latin*, and was perfect Master of the *French* Tongue, which I
B   had

had been learning from my Infancy; my Mother being born at *Paris*, where my Father marry'd her very young, and brought her to reside at *Boston*.

By that time I had reach'd Fourteen Years of Age, my Aunt told me it was Time for me to think of some Trade, desiring me to chuse what I lik'd best, and she would provide for me accordingly. Said she, If I might advise you, I would have you study the *Law*, under the Tuition of your Uncle ———; But I told her I did not much care for any Calling that must owe its Prosperity to the Misfortune of others. And at last I chose that of a Watchmaker, as imagining my self to have a good mechanical Head. Accordingly I went upon Liking (as they call it) and my Master and I agreeing very well, I was bound with the usual Forms, and found civil Usage from him, in respect of my Birth and the Misfortunes of our Family.

My Aunt paid Forty Guineas (which was reckon'd, at that Time, a great Price; but he was one of the Top of his Business) and besides to find me in Cloaths and other Necessaries, during my Seven Years Apprenticeship.

The first Half Year we agreed very well; but within that Time my Master had married a Wife of a pretty good Fortune, and a large Share of Ill-nature. In a Month's time she began to tyrannize over my Master, as well as me, and soon prov'd, as the Saying is, *The grey Mare to be the better Horse*. She brought it to that Pass at last, that I was obliged to go on all her halfpenny Errands, and carry her Book to Church of a *Sunday* after her. I bore this tolerably well, but not without complaining to my Aunt, who advis'd me to make my self as easy as I could, for she fear'd Speaking would do no good.

Captain Robert Boyle.

I went on this Way for a whole Year, and then to compleat my Misfortunes, my poor Aunt died of a Dropsy. This indeed was the greatest Shock of all my Life; for while she liv'd I felt no want of Father or Mother. She left me 800 *l*. and my Uncle —— to be my Guardian. I shall forbear mentioning his Name, not out of Regard to him, but of his Children, who have prov'd a sweet Grafting from a sour Stock, and as good as he was base.

My Shrew of a Mistress continu'd her Ill-nature to me, and one Accident made her prove outragious.

My Master had a vast Trade, and vented a great many Watches beyond Sea. One Day he had a large Parcel of them to go on Board a Ship bound for *Lisbon*; the Vessel lay at *Deptford*, and my Master was pleas'd to take me along with him in the Boat.

Before we were got to *Limehouse*, my Master call'd to Mind that he had forgot a Silver Watch that he had purposely made for the Captain of the Ship. He landed me at *Ratcliff-Cross*, and desir'd I would be expeditious in going (for the Tide running downwards I could get to the *Exchange* sooner on Foot than by Water against the Stream) then to take Boat at *Billingsgate*, and follow him to the Ship.

I ran almost all the Way, and I believe got to the *Exchange* in half an Hour. When I came home, I found no Body in the Shop but my Fellow-Prentice, who inform'd me my Mistress was above. I went immediately up Stairs for the Watch (for my Master told me he had left it in his own Room, being he had wore it several Days to prove the going of it) but found the Door shut. Standing a Moment to consider, I heard a Man's Voice speaking to my Mistress, in a low Key, and I foon underftood by their Dialogue that Love was the Subject they talk'd of. I liften'd fome Time, till I found they had left off Difcourfing, and were enter'd upon Action.

Now at the Head of the Stairs the Maid had left a Step-Ladder, that fhe had us'd in the Morning, in nailing up fome Valens to the Windows in the Dining-Room, and there being a Glafs over the Chamber Door, I had a great Mind to fee who it was that was doing my Mafter's Bufinefs in his Abfence. Thereupon I fixt the Ladder very foftly againft the Wainfcot by the Door, and up I got; but leaning towards the Window in order to fee into the Room, my Weight made the Ladder flip, and the Top fliding againft the Door burft it open, and in fell I into the Room, Ladder and all, with no little Noife.

The loving Couple were mightily furpriz'd you may be fure, and were in fuch a Fright that they had forgot what they were a doing. But I faw enough to convince me that my Mafter was in a fair way to get to Heaven purely upon my Miftrefs's Account.

After our Surprize was over, and every thing put in Order again between the Gentleman and Madam, I ventur'd to tell her my Errand. She gave me the Watch with a hearty good Box on the Ear, and told me fhe wonder'd how I had the Affurance to come up without Knocking; but, added fhe, I believe you rather came upon fome knavifh Defign, and had intended to rob your Mafter, if I had not been in the Room with my Phyfician, that came on purpofe to fee how I did.

It was plain enough what Phyfic fhe was taking, yet I made my Excufe to her that I went to remove the Ladder, and it fell out of my Hand

Captain Robert Boyle.

Hand againſt the Door and burſt it open; but I told her I was ſorry I 'had diſturb'd her, made my Honours and walk'd off, taking no Notice that I had ſeen any Thing. I took Water at *Billingſgate,* and follow'd my Maſter.

In the Boat I began to ruminate with my ſelf, whether I had beſt keep this Accident a Secret, or diſcloſe it to my Maſter. At laſt, with many Pro's and Con's with my ſelf, I reſolv'd to acquaint him with it; partly to be reveng'd on my Miſtreſs for the Blow ſhe ſtruck me, and on the other ſide not to let my honeſt Maſter be kept in Ignorance of her Uſage of him.

When I came on Board, the Captain commanded me (with my Maſter's leave) to ſit down at Table with 'em. We din'd heartily, the Wine and Punch went merrily round, and my Maſter, the Captain, with two more that were Paſſengers, began to be in high Mirth; when Word was brought that the Captain's Lady (as the Meſſenger call'd her) would be on Board in an Hour to take her Leave of him. My Maſter upon this Meſſage began to be merry with the Captain; I wonder, ſaid he, that you Seafaring Men will venture upon Wives. Why ſo? reply'd the Captain. Why ſo! return'd my Maſter, Becauſe in my Opinion it ſhould put you in Mind of *Cuckold's-Point* as you went by Water: Your Abſence gives 'em ſuch a Conveniency, that I believe few let ſlip the Opportunity. Why, anſwer'd the Captain, mayn't your Wife, even now, be doing you the Favour; has ſhe not Time enough, d'ye imagine? The Thing's ſoon done; and if they have an Inclination, Watching and Reſtraint will do no Good: Many an Alderman has been cornuted while upon *Change*; and I knew a Parſon's Wife that ſeldom went to Church, but took

Time by the Forelock, and while the Husband (good Man) was taking Care of his Flock, the good Woman at Home was at her Occupation with her Gallant, a rich young Farmer. But the Parson one Afternoon being taken suddenly ill with a Giddiness in his Head, was convey'd Home before he had begun his Work, and there soon found the Occasion of his Pain; for he had been breeding Horns, as Children breed Teeth, a little unkindly. But however, the Parson having Witnesses enough of his Promotion in the Herd of Cuckolds, went to Law with the Farmer, and recover'd 500 *l.* Damages; and yet he has been heard often to say, that his Wife's Tenement was never the worse.

This Story occasion'd some others much to the same Purpose: At last my Master and I, (the Tide being turn'd,) took our Leaves of the Company, and wish'd 'em a good Voyage. Coming by *Cuckold's-Point*, my Master cry'd, *Robin*, why don't you pull off your Hat to the Gentleman in the Window yonder? I pull'd off my Hat very orderly, but saw no Body; at which my Master fell into a great Fit of Laughter, and cry'd I had been very courteous to the Horns. I then, understanding his Meaning, told him, that it was only for marry'd Men to shew their Complaisance that way; and, being a little piqu'd at the Affront I thought put upon me, said I believ'd most marry'd Men were, or would be in the List of Cuckolds. Why, how now, Sirrah! reply'd my Master, d'ye think I am, or shall be a Cuckold? Why truly, said I, Sir, I have but little Reason to believe my Mistress a Saint more than any other Woman; and to inform you farther of what I have seen to Day, I beg you would be pleas'd to go to some Publick House, that we may not be observed

served by the Watermen. My Master's Colour began to change upon this; and being very impatient to be inform'd of what I knew, order'd the Waterman to land at *Ratcliff-Cross*, and wait a while.

We went to the *Ship* Tavern and had a private Room, where I declar'd to him the whole Truth. After many Questions and Answers between us, I soon found he believed all that I told him, for he turn'd as pale as Ashes, and the Tears stood in his Eyes. I then was sorry I had disclos'd it to him, remembring the inimitable *Shakespear*,

He that is robb'd, not wanting what is stole,
Let him not know't, and he's not robb'd at all.

After some Time being silent, my Master broke into many extravagant Words, and threatning Actions; and at last I ventur'd to tell him, I thought him in the wrong to grieve at what could not be called back, and I wonder'd the World should unjustly cast upon the Man the Ignominy which was properly due to the Woman for her Licentiousness.

After some Time he began to be more calm, and made me this Compliment; *Robin*, said he, I have observed in thee a more than common Understanding, Pr'ythee tell me in what Manner I shall behave my self in this Affair. I thank you, Sir, said I, for your good Opinion of me, and, were it my own Case, I would not take any Notice of it till I found her in the Fact, or such Circumstances that even she her self could not deny; and for these two Reasons, 1. Whenever it comes to an open Rupture you'll have but an uneasie Living; and 2. that she may take it into her Head to deny it, and then the whole Weight of her Anger will fall upon me; and truly, said I, I have too much of her Ill-nature already to bear any more with any manner of Patience.

My Master resolved to follow my Counsel, and intended to make his Wife believe he knew nothing of the Matter.

My Master could not imagine who this Gallant should be, by my Description, for I had never seen him before. We went to our Boat, and so Home. When we came in, my Mistress ask'd my Master if *Robin*, meaning me, had been telling him any Stories. Stories, Child! answer'd my Master, what Stories? he has told me nothing. Nay, no great matter, said my Mistress, but I gave him a Box on the Ear this Morning, when he came back for the Watch you had forgot, and I did not know but he had made some Complaint; but I am sorry for it, and will make him Amends one Time or other. This she said so loud that I might hear.

The next Day when my Master was gone to *Change*, she came up into the Work-house, as we call'd it, up three Pair of Stairs, and took an Occasion of sending my Fellow-Prentice on some concerted Errand. When he was gone out she sat down upon his Chair, and look'd me in the Face for some time. Well *Robin*, said she, I am very much oblig'd to you, that you did not take any Notice of the Accident that happen'd Yesterday to your Master; and to make you Amends for your Silence I give you this Broad Piece to buy you a Pair of Gloves, with this Promise, that you and I will never disagree again. I receiv'd her Money, and told her I should never take any farther Notice of it. She call'd me good Lad, and left me.

My Master had not always an Opportunity of talking with me at home, so he appointed me every *Sunday* after Sermon in the Evening at some Tavern or other, that we might talk about the matter. At our first Meeting I told him the Story of the Broad Piece, and the Discourse my Mistress and I had together. I shew'd him the Money, and he soon knew the Piece to be his Wife's from the particular Fairness of it, being the same he had some time ago given her for a Pocket-Piece.

Now, said he, *Robin*, I am fully convinc'd of the Infidelity of my Wife; for notwithstanding your former Story, I had some faint Hopes it might have been a Tale of thine, rais'd out of Malice to thy Mistress, from her indifferent Usage of thee.

But now to find out this Spark, that I may reak my Vengeance on him first; for, to own my Folly, *Robin*, I must tell thee I can't find I shall ever be able to hate this ungrateful Woman. Some time after, my Master was pretty well convinc'd that his Wife had been with her Spark to the *Mulberry-Garden*, and my Master had discovered who he was; he prov'd to be a young Attorney of *Clifford's-Inn*. The next Thing we consulted about at our weekly Meeting was how to give 'em an Opportunity of pursuing their Amour at Home. In Order to this, my Master gave out to my Mistress that he should be oblig'd to go as far as St. *Margaret*'s in *Kent*, to look after some Goods, that were landed there in order to avoid paying Custom for them, and he fear'd the Affair would not be so well manag'd if he was not present.

The *Tuesday* following was chose for the Day of his setting out. My Master gave me publick Orders to go to several Places in his Absence, to look after the Workmen (for there are several Trades belonging to the making of a Watch). On *Tuesday* Morning my Master got on Horseback, in Order (as my Mistress and the rest of the Family thought) to pursue his Journey: But he went no farther than *Islington*, and return'd, putting up his Horse again; and went strait to the Place of our Rendezvous.

As soon as my Master was gone, my Mistress call'd me up to her, and ask'd me if I had Time to step a little Way for her. I told her 'twas impossible, being I had some Work to finish that I was oblig'd to carry out immediately. Then she begg'd I would call her a Porter, which I did, and one of my particular Acquaintance, one well to pass in the World; for a City Porter in those Days was a very beneficial Employment, there being then no Penny-Post-Office. I told him what he should do, that he must go to my Mistress and receive the Letter, and then to an adjacent Ale-house, and wait till I came to him. Accordingly he receiv'd the Letter, and went to the Place I appointed. I did not let him wait long, but order'd my Matters as if I was going about my Master's Business, and went to the Porter. From thence I took him along with me to my Master, where we open'd the Letter, and found it as follows;——" Dear *Tom*,
" it's an Age since last I saw you; the Cuc-
" kold's gone out of Town for a Week, there-
" fore meet me at the Old Place by Six this E-
" vening." Here we were at a Stand, for we could not imagine where the *Old Place* was, unless the *Mulberry-Garden*. At last we resolv'd to send the Porter to the Spark, and bring the Answer to us, to see if that would give us more
Light

Light in the Affair. Accordingly he went, and return'd with his Billet; we made bold to open it, and found it contain'd these Words,—" My " Life, I don't think the old Place convenient, " being a Brother Lawyer has discovered some- " thing of our Intrigue; therefore I'll wait on " you before the Time, that we may concert " Measures accordingly. I am glad your Beast " is out of Town; we'll add another Antler " to adorn his Brow, assoon as I have the Hap- " piness to see her who shall eternally com- " mand yours.——

When my Master perceiv'd that the Scene was to be open'd at his own House, he began to demur: But after keeping Silence a little Time, he spoke to me to this purpose. *Robin*, this Letter has in some sort confounded our Design, for what I intend to act I would not, if it could be avoided, put in Execution at home, for fear it should make too much Noise; for, added he smiling, tho' a Man has the Misfortune to be a Cuckold, yet he would not have all the World know it. I told him I was glad to see him so merry upon the Occasion, but begg'd he would not keep the Porter any longer, for fear of some Accident. He thank'd me for my Care, seal'd up the Letter again, and sent him away with it. When the Porter was gone, my Master order'd me to go home again, and observe how Matters went there, and as soon as ever the Spark came, to send the same Porter back to him with this Notice, *That the Work was ready to carry home, whenever I thought fit.*

I had not been at home a quarter of an Hour ere my Gentleman came in a Coach; he went up Stairs, but did not stay a Moment, came down again, whisper'd the Coachman, and drove into *Cheapside*. I was at a loss how to behave my self, but

but my Miſtreſs order'd another Coach to be call'd. When I found that, I ſent for the Porter, and told him ſecretly that he muſt dog that Coach let it go where it would, and be expeditious in bringing me Word. My Miſtreſs came down in her Hood and Mask in her Hand, and went off in the Coach. I look'd after her as far as I could ſee her, and obſer'd the Porter to jump up behind the Coach. I immediately went to my Maſter, and acquainted him with the Buſineſs. He hurried me home again, for fear the Porter ſhould wait for me, and order'd me to bring him, when he came, to the *Pope's-Head* Tavern, becauſe he would be nearer home.

The Porter did not return in two Hours: He told me that the Coach drove to *York* Stairs in *York* Buildings, and there they got out and took a Pair of Oars; he went in another, and follow'd 'em till they landed at *Lambeth*, and dog'd them into the *White-Lyon* Inn. There he ſtaid ſome time, to ſee if they intended to go from thence; he walk'd into the Kitchen and drank a Mug of Ale, and in a little time one of the Waiters came in, and told the Cook the Gentleman and his Wife had beſpoke a roaſted Fowl and ſome Fiſh for their Dinner, and had ordered clean Sheets to be put to air, for as ſoon as they had din'd they deſign'd to go to Bed, being the Stage Coach was to call them up at One the next Morning.

I did not think it altogether ſo proper to take the Porter to the *Pope's-Head* to my Maſter, but went alone, where I found him with another Gentleman, a Stranger to me. When I had given him an Account, we took Coach all together and drove to the Horſe-Ferry, *Weſtminſter*, took Boat and landed at *Lambeth*. We all went into the *White-Lyon* the back Way, and I went

to

to the Drawer (as we had before concerted) and ask'd if there was not a Gentleman and a Lady that did defign to lie there all Night to wait for a Stage Coach in the Morning; he anfwer'd in the Affirmative, but added they were that moment gone to Bed, that they might be the better able to rife in the Morning. I ask'd him which Room they lay in, for that I had Bufinefs of great Confequence to communicate to him. Why that Room up one Pair of Stairs, anfwer'd the Drawer, and pointed at the Door. Well, faid I, fetch me a Pint of Wine, I'll drink a Glafs, and then go and wait on them.

The Drawer ran down for the Wine, and in the mean time I beckon'd my Mafter; up Stairs we went, I fet my Foot againft the Door, burft it open, and there we foon perceiv'd the loving Couple playing at *Rantum Scantum*. I fhut to the Door again, and ftood Guard that no One fhould enter. My Mafter laid faft hold of my naked Gentleman, and with the Affiftance of his Friend threw him upon his Back, clapt a Piftol to his Breaft, and fwore he would fhoot him if he offer'd to ftir or cry out. Then my Mafter's Friend took out a Box of Inftruments, and, with a Pair of Sciffars for that purpofe, foon depriv'd him of what *Senefino* and feveral *Italian* Singers want, as well as our Spark. The Thing was done fo fuddenly, that I believe my Gentleman hardly knew his Lofs till he felt the Blood trickle about his Legs. He made feveral Attempts to get up, but to no purpofe. My Mafter told him he had better be quiet, for fear he fhould be worfe ferv'd, (but in my Opinion that could hardly be.) The Surgeon (for it prov'd my Mafter's Friend was no other,) had all his Implements about him; he manag'd his Needle, his Plaifters, and Salves, and finifh'd my
Gentleman,

Gentleman, and would have had him gone home something lighter than he came, but he prov'd so weak with Loſs of Blood and the Pain together, that he fainted away.

My Miſtreſs had hid herſelf behind the Curtain, and did not ſo much as ſay one Word; but in all her Concern ſhe took Care to dreſs herſelf, and when ſhe had done ſhe ſat upon the Bedſide next the Wall, and ſeem'd to be in deep Diſcontent.

We had got my Gentleman to himſelf again by the help of the Drawer, who ſoon found how Matters went. When we had done, my Maſter ſaid to his Wife, Madam, I muſt confeſs I was to blame to diſturb you in your Diverſion, but I own my Fault, and will endeavour to mend it by leaving you together to ſolace your ſelves, and ſo I take my Leave.

Upon this we march'd down Stairs, paid for our Wine, and went to our Boat that waited for us, and landed at the *Still-yard*. My Maſter was very uneaſie all the Way home, and we could not get one Word out of him. He went up Stairs, lock'd himſelf in his Room, and remain'd alone ſeveral Hours. I would have been willing to have diverted his Melancholy, but did not well know how I ſhould go about it.

Near ſeven a Clock in the Evening he call'd me up Stairs, and aſk'd me if I had heard any thing of his Wife. I told him no. Nay, ſaid he, if ſhe has any Shame left, ſhe will hardly attempt to come home again in haſte. After ſome time he went out, and did not come home again till twelve a Clock. He aſk'd me ſtill after my Miſtreſs, and underſtanding we had no News of her, went to Bed.

The next Morning he order'd me to ſend the Porter to *Lambeth*, to learn how they behav'd
themſelves

themselves when we had left 'em. He return'd, and told my Master that the Gentlewoman went away as soon as she found we were gone, and left the Gentleman there, who was so weak that he remain'd there still, and had sent for several of his Acquaintance.

In the Afternoon my Mistress's Mother came to my Master, and they had a long Discourse, and afterwards went out together. But I was never more surpriz'd in my Life, when he came home the same Evening with his Wife and Mother. He vouchsaf'd to tell me the next Day that his Wife resolv'd never to be guilty of any Fault again, and by her Submission and the Intreaties of her Mother, he had resolv'd to take her home once more. Sir, said I, if you can forgive her, no one else has any thing to do with it. But, added I, I fear I shall feel the Effects of her Displeasure. No, answer'd my Master, that was one of my Conditions with your Mistress, that she should take no Notice to you of past Transactions. And truly she kept her Word, for she would not so much as look at me.

She continu'd very reserv'd for a great while, and never went out but to Church of a *Sunday*.

In the latter End of the same Year my Master began to be out of Order, and the Physician advis'd him to go into the Country for the Air; and accordingly he took Lodgings at *Hampstead*, where my Mistress us'd to go twice or thrice every Week to see him; and my Master told me (when I went of a *Sunday* to wait upon him, to give him an Account of the Business of the Shop). that his Wife had been so tender of him in his Illness, that he verily believed he should never have any Occasion to blame

her

her Conduct again. I told him I was as well pleas'd as he was.

About a Week afterwards my Miſtreſs went in and out very often, and ſeem'd to be very buſie, giving Orders to my Fellow-Prentice for taking her a Place in the *Hampſtead* Coach as uſual. This happen'd on the *Tueſday*, and I ſaw her no more that Week.

When I went to my Maſter on the *Sunday* following, he ask'd me if my Miſtreſs was out of Order, being he had not ſeen her ſince the *Monday* laſt. Nor I ſince *Tueſday*, ſaid I, but I thought ſhe had been with you, for ſhe took a Place in the Coach in order to come to you that Day, and ſent out ſeveral Bundles to be carry'd; as ſhe uſually did when ſhe was coming to wait on you.

My Maſter was ſo confounded with what I told him, that he did not offer to ſpeak for ſome time, and the Sweat ran down his Face like Drops of Rain. At laſt, ſaid he, *Robin*, I fear all is not well! My Wife has certainly undone me. Come, hope for the beſt, ſaid I.

Well, my Maſter reſolv'd, weak as he was, to go for *London* immediately. We took a Coach, and ſoon got home; and there to our great Sorrow found my Miſtreſs had robb'd my Maſter to the Value of Five Thouſand Pound in *Bank* Notes and Money, with Six and Thirty Gold Watches and Seventeen Silver Ones, beſides her own wearing Cloaths. My Maſter at this Loſs ſunk down upon his Bed. I went and fetch'd ſome of his Neighbours and Friends to comfort him, while I ran up and down like a Madman, to ſee if I could get any Tidings of the Thief.

I went to give Orders at the *Bank* to ſtop Payment, but to my great Sorrow found the Money had been receiv'd four Days before. I
came

Captain Robert Boyle.

came back to acquaint my Master with my ill Success, and found him alone and gone to Bed. When I told him I could not hear any Tidings of my Mistress, and that the Money had been receiv'd, he cry'd, *Robin*, it is not the Money that grieves me, but the ill Usage of my Wife; 'tis that has got to my Heart, and never to be remov'd till Death. I sat up with him a great while, till he told me he began to be sleepy, and ordered me to retire; but as I was going from him, he took me by the Hand, and bid me good Night. I found by his Pulse that he was in a Fever, and begg'd I might call a Physician; but he said he should be better on the Morning, if not he would send for one. Finding him willing to rest, I left him and went to Bed.

As soon as I wak'd in the Morning, I put on my Gown, and went to see how he did; but found him so weak and faint that he had not Strength enough to lift up his Head. I was immediately running to fetch a Physician that liv'd hard by our House, but my Master call'd me back, and told me it was too late, for, said he, I feel my last Moment approaching. He order'd me to sit upon the Bed by him, he took my Hand in his, which burnt like Fire, and said, *Robin*, my Wife has kill'd me; I could have born any other Misfortune with Temper; if thou ever shou'dst see her, tell her from me that I forgive her, and that I beg she would reform her Life; but also let her know that she was the Death of me. I told him I would not have him talk of Dying for an ungrateful Woman that did not deserve the least Regard, but to chear up his Spirits and let me go for a Physician. No, said he, all Physic or Counsel comes too late;

I've that within which baffles all their Art,
Sure Means to make the Soul and Body part,
A burning Fever and a broken Heart.

He had no sooner repeated those Lines but his Speech fail'd him, his Eyes clos'd, and he expir'd only with a Sigh.

I must confess I was inwardly shock'd, and the Spirit of Revenge rose in my Soul against the barbarous Cause of his End.

When I had a little recollected my scattered Thoughts, I went to a Cousin of my Master's that liv'd in *Cheapside*, and desir'd he would come and take Care of his Affairs. For my own Part I could not compose my self for two or three Days: At last I went to my Uncle, and desir'd he would let me have Twenty Pounds to buy me Mourning, (for I did intend to wear Black, that my melancholy Outside might conform with what I felt within) out of Respect to my Master's Memory. Mourning, *Bob!* answer'd my Uncle, Why if thy Master's Friends won't give it thee, 'tis my Opinion thou ought'st not to think on't. Yes, Sir, added I, I think it my Duty; for tho' my Mistress us'd me ill, my Master always was civil to me. But my Uncle told me in plain Terms that I should not have a Farthing. I told him I wanted but my own; but he reply'd, when he thought I was of Years enough to manage my Money my self, perhaps I might be trusted with it, but at present he would take Care of it for me.

I was very uneasy at this Affair, for it began to look as if he intended to cheat me of it, and I did not stick to tell him my Sentiments in a civil manner, but to no purpose. I left him with a very heavy Heart, and came home. I
went

went to Bed in the utmoſt Confuſion of Thought; yet notwithſtanding my Diſcontent, ſlept 'till Morning. I got up about ſix a-clock, with a ſcurvy Idea of my future Fortune. About eight, my Uncle's Man brought me a Letter from him, in which he begg'd my Pardon, and told me it was only to try my Temper. The Man gave me ten Guineas by his Order, and farther told me that his Taylor would be with me immediately to take my Directions; and accordingly before the Fellow was gone he came, took Meaſure of me, and told me he would be ſure to bring my Cloaths home by twelve a-clock the next Day; and he kept his Word with me.

In the mean time I had provided my ſelf with every Thing elſe with the Money my Uncle had ſent me; and the ſame Evening waited on him to return him Thanks. *Bob*, ſaid he, I had only a Mind to try your Temper, and I find thou art Father's own Child, a Chip of the old Block.

He would have me ſtay to ſup with him, and among other Diſcourſe he ask'd me what I did intend to do now my Maſter was dead, for he did not ſuppoſe I was Maſter of my Trade enough to follow it. I reply'd, I knew enough to recommend my ſelf to any other Maſter without paying any more Money. My Uncle reply'd, I needed not be in ſuch haſte, but take ſome Time to conſider of it, and in the mean while I ſhould live with him and be heartily welcome. And to make his Actions agree with his Words he gave me five Guineas more for Pocket-Money, and gave Directions for me to be with one of his Clerks, a good-natured young Fellow, that was a School-fellow of mine.

I was very glad of the Occaſion, living with my Uncle in great Tranquility the ſpace of a Month,

Month, and all the time he seem'd to be very fond of me, never denying me any thing that I ask'd him.

One *Sunday* Morning before Church-time he call'd me to him, and (after many Professions of Friendship) ask'd me if I had never done any Business for my Master out of the Watch-making Trade. I pretty well guess'd at what he meant, and answer'd him in the Affirmative. Very well, said he, I must send you as far as *Gravesend* to-morrow about the same Affair; and if I executed my Commission dextrously, he told me it should be the better for me.

The next Morning I got up, and my Uncle sent me with a Letter into *Pall-Mall* to a Client of his, and returning with an Answer, found him taking his Leave of a Gentleman that look'd like a Sea-Officer. As soon as their Compliments were over, my Uncle dispatch'd me away to *Billingsgate*, and gave me Instructions what to do. I was to enquire for a Ship call'd the *Success*, Capt. *Stokes* Commander, at *Gravesend*, and then to follow his Directions.

As I was talking with my Uncle, my Bedfellow thrust a Book into my Pocket, and told me that would divert me in the Boat, if I had not Company that I lik'd. I did not much regard what he said, but went about my Business, got into the *Gravesend* Boat which put off upon the Instant, and had the Fortune to light of good Company, and one young Man that was going to the same Ship as I was.

We were very merry all the Way with little Stories we told among our selves. We got on Board the *Success* about two a-clock in the Afternoon, and the first Person I saw was the same Man that I found with my Uncle in the Morning. He took me by the Hand, and carry'd ry'd me into the Cabin, and set a Piece of Ship Beef before me. When I had din'd, he inform'd me my Things would be on Board immediately. I told him it was very well; not suspecting any thing. Afterwards the Captain went out, and left me alone in the Cabin: I got up, and looking out of the Cabin Window, found the Ship was under Sail. At first I began to be surpriz'd, but yet was so ignorant that I thought we were sailing up the River. While I was ruminating on the Matter, the Captain came and told me my Things were ready for me, whenever I wou'd. I went out; but how was I surpriz'd when I saw my Trunk that I left at my Uncle's with all my Cloaths in it! I was in such Confusion that I had not Power to utter one Word for some time. At last, recovering out of my Surprize, I ask'd him the Meaning of what I saw! Meaning, Child! reply'd the Captain: Why, what's the Matter? would you go such a Voyage as we are upon without Necessaries? What Voyage? return'd I. Why, to *Virginia*, reply'd the Captain. At that Answer I sat me down upon my Chest and burst into Tears, and had such a Combat in my Mind that bereav'd me of the Power even of thinking for some time. The Captain indeed did all he could to comfort me: At last I fancy'd it might be only a Jest; but to my Sorrow found by all their Discourse it was but too much in earnest.

The Captain declar'd that my Uncle had bargain'd with him for my Passage, and that I was to be deliver'd to a Relation I had in *Charles-Town*, upon the Continent of *America*. I ask'd the Name, but he told me one that I had never heard of before.

When I found I was certainly betray'd by my barbarous Uncle, I fell upon my Knees, and begg'd begg'd the Captain to put me on Shore, and I would find some Means to pay the Sum he was to have for my Passage. He answer'd, he was too well paid already to let me go on Shore again; and further added, I had nothing to do but to make my self easy, for I was not likely to set my Foot in *Europe*, till I had first seen *America*.

I found it was to no purpose to intreat any further: It is true I had no Aversion for the Sea, but rather an Inclination; and if my Uncle had made any Proposals to me concerning such a Voyage, and properly prepar'd, 'tis ten to one if I had not accepted it. But in this manner to be kidnapp'd, for it was no better, and then the Dread of being parted with as a Slave when I came thither, shock'd me prodigiously. But being naturally of an easy Temper, eight or ten Days pretty well wore off my Apprehensions, and I began to be contented with my wretched Fate. I set my self with all my Diligence to learn the Mathematicks, as also the Work of a Sailor, and quickly attain'd to some Knowledge. I soon ingratiated my self with most of the Crew, who instructed me in all they knew.

I mention'd a Book my Uncle's Clerk put in my Pocket, as I left the Chambers that Morning I was trepann'd, which for the first three or four Days I did not remember; but putting my Hand in my Pocket to feel for something else, I took it out, and found in it a Letter directed for me, which was as follows;

Dear Bob,

WHen you went to St. James's *this Morning,* [supposing I would have read it the Day I receiv'd it] *I overheard my Master discoursing with a Captain of a Ship, and I learnt that he*
intends

intends to send you to Virginia. *I could not understand the Particulars, but enough to know the Bargain is made. My Friendship to you and the Barbarity of your Uncle obliges me to give you this (I hope) timely Notice. I shall leave the Management to you; but whatever Steps you take, I am not to be in the Question: and I thought of this way to acquaint you with it, fearing I should not have the Opportunity of speaking to you. Farewell till I see you again, which I hope in God will not be long.*

A. M.

This Letter made me curse my Fate again; for if I had had the good Fortune to have read it before I was on Ship-board, I might have prevented my Uncle's Design: But it was my Destiny, and therefore I submitted to it.

We met with nothing in our Voyage till we came near the *Canaries*: When one Evening we heard several Cannons fir'd, as we suppos'd two Leagues from us. Our Captain alter'd his Course, in order to avoid a Rencounter with an Enemy; for our Ship carry'd but ten Guns and twenty Men, besides Passengers. But notwithstanding the Captain's Care, as soon as ever the Morning dawn'd and the Fog was clear'd up, we found our selves within half a Mile of a Rover of *Barbary*. We were all mightily surpriz'd, for the Gally made up to us with Sails and Oars, being to Windward of us. Our Captain advis'd us to surrender immediately, but the Sailors were for fighting, and were confirm'd in their Opinion upon Sight of another Vessel bearing down upon us, whom they knew to be *Spanish* by her Colours. All our Guns were immediately brought to the Starboard Side, and every Body ready to engage, Passengers and all who were willing to preserve their Liberty.

The Rover by this time was juſt upon the Starboard Bow, and prepar'd to board us. We had ſome Hand Granadoes on board, with ſeveral other Stores for our Fort at *Charles-Town*, and a Gunner as one of our Paſſengers. He ordered ſeveral Men into our Main-Top with Granadoes, and follow'd himſelf, and as ſoon as ever the Gally came near enough, our Men at the Helm bore away, and fir'd our Guns upon him, which rak'd 'em fore and aft, and did much Execution. Our Gunner above in the Top threw in upon them with his Granadoes, which we could perceive put them into much Confuſion. But all this would not have avail'd, if they had not perceiv'd the *Spaniſh* Man of War bearing upon us. They did not make any farther Attempts to board us, but they fir'd their Cannon and gaul'd us with their ſmall Arms.

I had gotten a Musket on board and had diſcharg'd it as I thought, for it flaſh'd in the Pan, and the Noiſe of the other Pieces deceiv'd me. I charg'd again, but then found by the Rammer that my Piece had not gone off. However I was reſolv'd to fire it: I ſtood upon the larboard Gunnel juſt upon the Forecaſtle, to be as far from the Enemy as I could, and fir'd my Piece; but being double charg'd, and a ſtubborn Jade, gave me ſuch a Bang that threw me over the Side of our Ship; my Foot hung in the Fore Change for ſome time, but ſtruggling (with my Head downwards) to raiſe my ſelf up, my Foot diſentangled, and I fell plum into the Sea.

Altho' I had learnt to ſwim in *England*, yet the Fright, the Smoke and all together took away my Underſtanding, and I found by my Struggling that I had got within ten Yards of the Rover, and ſhe that Inſtant bearing away before the Wind, they did me the Favour to ſtun me

with

with a Stroke of one of their Oars, and took me on board them.

They row'd with all their Strength, and the Wind being in their Stern, they infenfibly left the *Succefs*, who flatted their Sails and laid by till the *Spanifh* Ship came up with her, and then we could perceive 'em both making after the Rover.

The Captain of the Corfair was an *Irifh Renegado*, and as foon as he was out of Danger, he fent for me into the Cabin, and ask'd me feveral Queftions concerning our Ship, where fhe was bound, and who I was, (for he took me for more than a common Sailor, being I was not in a Sailor's Habit.) I told him my Story, as I have related in the foregoing Sheets. He fhook his Head, and, with a Smile, faid I was very ready at a Lie. Sir, faid I, I am fo far from lying, that I jump'd overboard on purpofe to come to your Veffel rather than to ftay with them, chufing to be a Slave nearer home, than to go I don't know where with the Knave that trepann'd me: And to convince your Honour of the Truth (for I *honour'd* him much) here's the Letter which my Uncle's Clerk flipp'd into my Pocket in a Book, (for by good Fortune I had the Letter and Book in my Pocket when I fell overboard.) At reading the Letter he was convinc'd, he faid, of my Sincerity; and thou fhalt fee, added he, notwithftanding the bad Opinion is held of us *Renegado's*, that you fhall fare the better for your Confidence in us. Sir, return'd I, this Accident may convince you that I thought very well of your Honour, for as foon as I faw your Honour upon Deck giving Command, I thought you had the Look of a Gentleman; (tho' by the By he had a damn'd *Tyburn* Face.)

I clarkt him up so well (with *your Honour*) that he began to fancy himself a Hero indeed. He order'd my Chains to be taken off, (for they had done me the Favour to provide me some assoon as ever they had got me on board) and told me that if I would turn *Mahometan* I should have Command under him. I answer'd him, I hop'd he would give me some Time to consider of it. Ay, ay, Time, thou shalt have half a Year's Time to consider of it, return'd the Captain. He carry'd me out upon Deck, and told my Story to his Crew, who were mightily pleas'd with the Relation, and saluted me after the *Moorish* manner, by bowing their Heads, and clapping their Hands across upon their Breasts.

There were several other *English Renegado's* that were Officers in the Galley, but most of the common Sailors were natural *Moors*. The Captain told me that he did design to make for *Sallee* with all the Expedition he could, for he had engag'd with a *Spanish* Man of War the Night before, and had suffer'd very much in both his Vessel and Crew: but he told me he would soon be out again, for he had another Vessel ready in *Sallee* Road to put out to Sea. We had before Night lost Sight of the *Success*, and *Spanish* Man of War, that had so luckily freed her from the Infidels Clutches; and we steer'd for *Sallee*.

Ten Days after we discover'd the *African* Shore, within five Leagues West of *Sallee* Road; and the Wind favouring us, we anchor'd in the Harbour by Six in the Evening. The Captain went ashore, but ordered me to remain on Board till the next Day.

I must confess I began to have some Hopes of seeing my own Country again, but yet did
not

not know how to bring it about; however, I resolv'd to trust Providence.

The next Morning my Master sent for me on Shore, by a young *Renegado* Sailor born at *London*, whose Christian Name I learnt was *Francis Corbet*, but had exchang'd it for *Mustapha*; a good intelligent young Fellow, and one that was a perfect Master of the Mathematicks. The Reason why he did not accompany the Captain in this Voyage, was a violent Fever when he set Sail. I ask'd him why he could forget the Saviour of the World to turn *Mahometan*; he told me that he was only one from the Teeth outward, and he thought it better to trust God with his Soul, than those barbarous Wretches with his Body. I thought it was a pretty free Declaration to one that was an utter Stranger to him.

As soon as we were landed, I had the whole Town of *Sallee* staring at me; for the Captain of the Rover had taken Care to spread my Story among 'em; and I had as much Respect shown me by the People of the Town as he had. He took me home to his own House, and us'd me with much Civility for a Week or ten Days; during that time he had carry'd me twice or thrice to his Country House, about six Miles up the River. It was a very pleasant Place, situated in a little Wood, with the River running round it, and no approaching to it but over a Draw-bridge. At this House his Wives liv'd, for I was inform'd he had several.

Observing his Garden, I told him it was but indifferently kept. He answer'd it was for want of a Gardener, none of his Slaves understanding that Art. I offer'd him my Service, but told him I did not pretend to be a Gardiner, but I was assur'd I could soon make Amendment to it,

with

with the Help of some of his Servants. He order'd me to take as many as I thought fit, and, added he, because I am impatient to see it in a better condition, I'll leave you here. I told him I begg'd to be excus'd now, because I should want several Things for my Designs. If it be Tools, said he, or Seeds of all Sorts, I have 'em here. Upon which he carry'd me into a little House, meant for a Green-house, where I found every Thing that was wanting, with a large Quantity of *European* Seeds and Roots. I told him I was satisfy'd there was every thing that I should want. The Captain order'd me a Bed to be made in the Green-house, and an old Eunuch, that understood *French* very well, to wait on me, with a strict Order that I should have every Thing I ask'd for, but I was not to approach the House in his Absence upon any Account. I told him I had no Curiosity that way, and did not doubt but I should show him something that would please him the next time he came, which was to be in 20 Days.

As soon as he was gone I went to Work, (for Gardening was what I always took delight in, both Theoric and Practic.)

I drew out Plans, order'd my Workmen, and in six Days time brought it into some Form. I perceiv'd in the middle of the Garden a Puddle of Water, which I gave Directions to be drain'd, and found that it had been formerly a Fountain, but was only choak'd up with Filth by Neglect. I ask'd the old Eunuch if he had ever known it to play, and he answer'd in the negative, neither did they imagine it to be any such thing; for his Master had bought the Estate of an old *Spanish* Renegado four Years before, and he told him it had been a Fish-Pond. I examin'd about the River, and found the Head of the Pipes stopp'd with Rubbish, which I clear'd, and by degrees the Water work'd thro' into the Fountain, and out again thro' another Conveyance. I observ'd that there had been Figures upon it, by the Pipes; I ask'd my Eunuch if he had ever seen any such things: He told me there were several lying in a back Yard on the other Side the House. I went with him, and found four small Figures of *Tritons*, and a *Neptune* in his Chariot drawn by Sea-Horses. I order'd them to be brought to the Fountain, and fixt them on, (first stopping the Water) and then letting it loose again finish'd my Fountain, which plaid admirably out of the Shells of the *Tritons*, (which they seem'd to blow with) from the Nostrils of the Horses, and the Trident of the *Neptune*. The Workmen were astonish'd to see with what Expedition I had compleated it, and imagin'd I had dealt with the Devil. The next Morning the Eunuch came to me before I was up, and desir'd I'd give him the Key of my Chamber, and be contented to be a Prisoner till he came to me again. I was a little surpriz'd, and ask'd him the Reason: He told me he could not give me any, being it was beyond his Commission. Accordingly he lock'd me in, and went away. I began to ruminate about this Accident, but could not imagine the Cause: I had no Way to look out towards the Garden, being the Windows of the Green-house look'd over the River into the Wood, and the Back which fronted the House had only painted Windows for Ornament, not Use. In about two Hours my Eunuch came and releas'd me, and we din'd together. I us'd all the Rhetoric I was Master of to find out the Secret, but to no Purpose; he only added that I must be in the same Condition again the next Morning. This was still

more

more furprizing, and I began to think by Degrees I fhould entirely lofe my Liberty. The old Eunuch imagining my Thoughts, affur'd me there was no harm meant to me. This Afternoon was my laft Day's Work, and in three Days more I expected the Captain. About an Hour before Night I perceiv'd another Eunuch of the Houfe talking earneftly with him that us'd to attend me, who immediately came to me, and told me he muft beg me to retire to my Chamber that Inftant; upon which I readily obey'd, knowing it was to no purpofe to contend.

I was upon the Tenters to know the Reafon of my Confinement: Whilft I was employing my Thoughts about it, I heard the Voices of Women. It furpriz'd me at firft, but I foon found that was the Reafon of my being made a Prifoner. When the Eunuch came to bring me my Supper, I told him he need not have made fuch a Secret of what I was lock'd up for, for I had found it out; and then told him that I had heard Women's Voices in the Garden. Did you? (faid he, furpriz'd) I'll take Care they fhall keep their Tongues within their Teeth for the future. He faid no more, but immediately went out, and foon return'd, and told me I fhould hear no more of them. I was confounded with this odd Proceeding, and my Curiofity began to be more and more rais'd.

When I was left alone, I began to examine my Room where I was, to fee if I could find ever a Peep-hole; and by good Fortune found one made by Time and ill Weather under the Pent-houfe. I upon the inftant of my Difcovery made all the Ufe I could of it, and foon perceiv'd three Women in the Walk with their Backs towards me. They were in a *Turkifh* Undrefs, dress, with their Necks bare: One of them above the rest seem'd to me to have a better Shape and Air than commonly the Women of *Morocco* have. I don't know what came over me, but I seem'd impatiently to expect their nearer Approach. At last my Desires were answer'd; for assoon as they had spent some Time at my new Fountain, they directed their Steps towards my Confinement, and when they were near enough, I could distinguish them to be three handsome Women; but one of 'em that seem'd to be very melancholy, surpass'd the other two, at least in my Opinion. She seem'd to be about twenty, fair to a Miracle, and much like an *Englishwoman*. She did not seem to converse with the other two, but follow'd them with an Air of Contemplation; and I could observe her sigh often. I never till this Moment had the least Regard to any of the Female Sex, no more than good Manners and Decency requir'd; but I found myself in a Moment full of aching Tenderness for this strange Woman. Though I had no time for Thought till the Ladies were retir'd, I then began to reason with my self, and found Love like Destiny was not to be avoided; and the more I thought, the more I was plung'd in this tormenting, yet pleasing Passion. Yet I thought it was very odd to fall in Love, considering my Circumstances. I had nothing to hope, and all to fear: I was poor, a Prisoner, and a Stranger, far from my native Country, in want even of Necessaries, and, to compleat my Misery, sunk in one Hour an Age in Love. Every new Thought seem'd a Thorn to torment me; yet notwithstanding all these Difficulties, a Beam of Hope would now and then shine thro' the thick Clouds of Despair, and encourage me to love on. From this Thought I began to think with Reason (if a Lover can be call'd a reasonable Creature) how I should manage my Passion. I began to reflect the *Moors* were jealous of their Women even to a Degree, and did not in the least doubt but my *Irish Renegado* had learnt that Part of their Manners. At last I pitch'd upon an odd Expedient: I determin'd to shew to my Captain an utter Detestation of all Females, (and in truth the Usage my poor Master met with from his Wife, very much lessen'd the Regard I ow'd the Sex) and try what that would do. This Thought seem'd to give me some Satisfaction, and assoon as the Eunuch came to release me, I begg'd he would sup with me that Evening. He accordingly promis'd me, and came immediately with my Supper, and brought under his Garment a Bottle of excellent *Greek* Wine. I must confess I was surpriz'd and pleas'd; for as I knew the *Moors* are restrain'd from Wine, I did not expect any there. The Eunuch told me, smiling, that he had brought that Cordial to make me Amends for the Loss of my Liberty; for though, added he, *Mussulmen* are not allow'd to drink Wine, we very well know you *Europeans* seldom eat without it; and our Master (meaning the Captain) is not so strict a *Mussulman* but he drinks much himself, and procures privately great Quantities for his own Use. I told him, I thought *Mahomet* order'd his Followers to abstain from Wine, because an immoderate Use of it generally turn'd to immoderate Passions; but to take it sparingly gave Health and Vigour to the Body, and Chearfulness to the Spirits. He agreed with me in my Sentiments, and show'd he approv'd of them by drinking to me. Notwithstanding my Endeavours to hide the Trouble of my Spirit, my kind Eunuch took Notice of a Concern in my Countenance,

nance, and chear'd me up with repeated Glasses; and imagining my Confinement caus'd that Alteration, told me he would not have me take to Heart the small Abridgement of my Liberty, for assoon as his Master arriv'd, I should not be restrain'd any more; for the Cause would cease, by the Confinement of the Ladies to their several Apartments. I told him, with a seeming Joy, that I should be mightily pleas'd when that should happen, for I abhorr'd the Sight of them; Women were my utter Aversion, and had been from my Infancy; and that Aversion was aggravated by the Knowledge of their Perfidy; and I thought it the greatest Curse could fall upon that noble Creature Man not to be born without them. Upon this I told him the Story of my Master and Mistress, and several extravagant Tales of my own Invention, which painted that beautiful Part of the Creation in the Colour of the Devil. My Companion prais'd me for slighting the Sex, and back'd my Stories with as many of his own Knowledge. Between our familiar Talk and our *Greek* Wine, he began to be very loquacious: He told me, his Master, after the Mode of the *Moors*, had several Wives, beside a Captive that he had lately taken, that seem'd averse to his Passion, and all the Rhetoric he was Master of could not prevail. He did not know, he said, what Countrywoman she was, but she spoke very good *French*. I imagin'd this could be no other than that sweet Creature I had seen: I chang'd Colour; but to put it off said, A Pox take all the Sex, don't let's talk of them any more. I am afraid, said he, you love to converse with the Men, and that makes you slight the Women. I did not immediately understand him, but he soon explain'd upon it, and then I was no longer ignorant. I told him

him it was of such a beastly Nature, that I was of Opinion those Persons that us'd it should be treated worse than Beasts. Why, reply'd he, it is so common here that 'tis reckon'd only a Piece of Gallantry. Well, said I, I hate that Action, even worse if it be possible than the Sight of the Female Sex. The old Man and I parted like two Friends; but before he went, I told him he need not give himself any great Trouble to lock me in for the future, for I would take Care of my self. Well, well, said he, and shook his Head, I believe I may trust you. As soon as he was gone I went to Bed, not to Sleep, for I had Thoughts enough about me to keep me waking. I began to conceive a great deal of Hopes from my Dissimulation. I spent the whole Night in thinking of a thousand Expedients to forward my Designs, till I had thought of so many that they were all confus'd like a Skein of Silk pull'd the wrong way. At last with the Fatigue of Thought I fell asleep till Sun-rising, nor awak'd till I heard Voices in the Garden. I ran immediately and barr'd my Door on the Inside, for fear of being discovered at my Peep-hole, huddled on my Cloaths, and ran up; where I saw my lovely Charmer reading in a Book, walking by her self in the Alley that led to my Prison. The other Women were got about the Fountain, admiring the playing of the Water. She drew nearer me; but what was my pleasing Surprize when I heard her repeat the following Lines in *English!*

—— *My Grief lies all within,*
And those external manners of Laments
Are meeely Shadows to the unseen Grief
That swells with Silence in my tortur'd Soul.

I must confess, the Transports I felt were beyond Expression: She had such a Softness in her Voice, and yet so musical, that it made my Blood thrill thro' my Veins. In short, during the time I beheld her, I was in such an Ecstasie, that all my Cares were forgot. She turn'd up the Walk again, but I follow'd her with my longing Eyes till she was out of Sight: I then turn'd them into my Imagination, and there beheld her still.

I was convinc'd she was an *English* Woman, and kept in her Restraint against her Will. I soon resolv'd with my self to find some Expedient to let her know I would serve her all that lay in my Power, if she was dispos'd to accept it.

I had staid so long fixt at my Peep-hole, that the old Eunuch knock'd at my Door, which soon rouz'd me from my pleasing Thoughts, and put me upon another Task, which was to dissemble. I suffer'd him to knock twice or thrice before I let him in; at last I open'd the Door, when he had call'd to me to give me to know who it was: Assoon as he was enter'd, I began to exclaim against him in a friendly manner; said I, You promis'd me Yesterday that I should not be troubled with the Tongues of those Female Devils, and I have been so plagu'd with them for an Hour together, that I was oblig'd to shut my Door, and run up Stairs to be free from the Sound. He smiling told me, the Fumes of the Wine which he drank over-night had drove it out of his Thoughts, but he would be sure to give them a Caution to hold their Tongues for the time to come: But then, added I, I may be surpriz'd by them when I little expect 'em. No, said he, I'll take Care to send, or bring you Word when they are dispos'd to walk in the Garden again. I thank'd him for his Caution. He told me he did defign to come and dine with me that Day, for, added he, I fhall not have another Opportunity a great while, for the Captain has fent Word he'll be here to-morrow without fail. Accordingly he came with a roafted Pheafant, and fome boil'd Rice, attended with another Bottle of *Greek* Wine.

Notwithftanding my new Paffion, I eat and drank heartily; but my Eunuch got almoft tipfey, and the Fumes of the Wine getting up into his Head, he defir'd he might repofe himfelf on my Bed for a while, which I granted him; well knowing if he had been found out, we might both have fuffer'd for tafting the Juice of the Grape. I had much rather he had gone within the Houfe to have flept, for I could not even think to the purpofe while he was there: But he foon got into a found Sleep, which I found out by his Snoreing. I then ventur'd to take Pen and Ink, and wrote the following Lines.

To the Englifh Lady.

Madam,

I Have obferv'd your melancholy *Air*, and other *Circumftances*, fpeak you a Prifoner here. The Perfon that writes this is your Countryman, and tho' in the fame Diftrefs, yet has a Heart and Hand to do you Service. I flatter my felf it will one Time or other be in my Power to effect our Liberty. If you have no Thoughts that way, I am perfwaded you have too much Generofity to do one a Prejudice that would venture any thing to ferve you. You know the Confequence if this Note fhould be difcovered, therefore I beg you would deftroy it affoon as you have perus'd it; and if you will favour me with an Anfwer, with your Sentiments of what I have wrote, you'll find a String hanging on the North Side of the Garden Houfe, to which if you fix your Letter, I shall be ready to prevent Discovery of what may hurt you, and him whom you may freely command.

I had not the Conveniency of Sealing-wax or Wafer, therefore I folded it up, and directed it *To the* ENGLISH LADY. When I had finish'd, I began to have odd and confus'd Notions of the Success of it: Perhaps, said I to my self, she may be contented with her Fortune, or be afraid to hazard any Attempt towards her Liberty: She may also imagine I am set on purpose to betray her, and therefore to shew her Innocency may discover me to the Captain. I was in a hundred Minds: Sometimes I resolv'd to burn the Letter; but at last Love prevail'd upon all my Reasons to the contrary, and I resolv'd to try the Success of it the first Opportunity.

In reasoning with my self, and writing my Letter, I had spent three Hours, and therefore I thought it high time to awake my Eunuch, who started up frighted out of his Senses. When he had recover'd himself, he thank'd me for breaking his Rest, for he was assur'd he was wanted within. And he nick'd his Time to a hair, for before he was got half way the Walk (for I immediately got up to my Peep-hole) I saw the Ladies at the farther End. He talk'd to them some time, and then left them, to go into the House.

They saunter'd about the Garden a good while, till at last two of them sat down by the Fountain, and the *English* Lady continued her Walk towards my Apartment. Now my Blood ran its swift Course, and the whole Frame of my Body felt violent Emotions. I thought this was a fair Opportunity, and yet was fearful to make Use on't. But mustring all my Spirits, I ventured,

D 3   and

and when she was within twenty Paces of the Green-house, I darted the Letter, and by good Fortune it fell in the Middle of the Gravel-Walk, so that it was almost impossible to miss on't; but had it happened otherwise, I had time enough to run down and take it up before any one else could discover it. She continued her Walk, and when she came at it, she kick'd it with her Foot, once or 'twice, and at last took it up. She was reading in a Book, as she was the Day before; I could perceive her open it, and spread the Note upon her Book, so that no one could tell but that she was reading. It is not possible to express the Anxiety I lay under all this while: But I began to be a little more compos'd, when I observed her tearing the Letter into very small Pieces, and scattering them in several Places of the Garden. She had not walk'd far, but she return'd, and view'd the Green-house with a great deal of Regard, and, to my Imagination, wanted to come to the North Side of it, as mention'd in the Note, yet seem'd fearful; often looking back, and not fully confirmed in her Resolution, at last went unwillingly to the rest of the Ladies. This gave me some Hopes that she received the Letter kindly, and that I should hear from her soon.

I observed she sat by the Fountain very intent upon her Book, which did not much please me. In about a quarter of an Hour, she got up, and came towards the Green-house again. When I saw her coming, I ran down Stairs, and fix'd a Packthread to the top of the Window, for fear if she should take Courage, and come to that Side, not seeing the Packthread, she might be startled, and persuade her self there was nothing in't. I had plac'd it, and got to my Peep-hole before she had reached the South Side. But

coming

coming close to the Wall, I could not see her by reason the smallness of the Hole cut off my Sight. But in less than a Minute I discover'd her walking back again, and sometimes turning to view the Place of my Retirement. Assoon as she had got to the Top of the Walk, (for I had not Power to stir before) I went down, and pulling in the Packthread, found a Piece of Paper ty'd to it. I unty'd it with a great deal of Expectation and Impatience, and found these Words wrote with a Pencil, upon a clean Leaf of a Book (which I suppose she had torn from that she had been reading in.)

I Was much surprised when I perused a Note, I found in the Walk of the Garden, as believing it directed to me. I confess I am a Person in Distress, but know not how to take the Word of a Stranger, and one I never saw, who perhaps is no more than a Spy upon my Actions, and what the Note contained may be by Order of him who pretends to tyrannize over me, because I am in his Power; and seeks this Way to find out my Inclination, for Pretences to use me worse. Therefore I'll expect a farther Assurance in half an Hour from the same Place. And I'll take an Opportunity to convey my real Sentiments back again.

The Joy I felt at reading this Note cannot be express'd in Words. I sat me down and wrote the following Answer.

MAdam, to tell you my Motive to serve you, may convince you of my Sincerity, which I'll let alone till I have the Favour of speaking to you, if ever I am so happy. You have heard, no doubt, of the Person that the Master of this House brought from Sallee, who is the same that is willing, and proud to serve you. By him that dy'd upon the Cross for our Sins,

Sins, I am sincere in what I write to you; and if I cannot serve you, it will be the greatest Grief can happen to one who shall ever be yours.

R. B.

When I had wrote this I went to the usual Place, and saw my Charmer very near me. I threw it down as before; she readily took it up, and walk'd back again, tearing the Note when she had read it, as she did the former, and went into the House. Just as she was got within the Gate the other Eunuch came out (not my friendly Eunuch) and as he was walking along, I observed him picking up the Pieces of the torn Notes. If any one had observed my Countenance at this Action, they might have discovered the utmost Confusion there. I thought we were certainly undone, and could not tell how to behave my self. I sometimes repented of the Affair, but yet I always found my Concern was more for her whom I lov'd, than for my self. Assoon as he had pick'd up all he could find, he return'd, with my hearty Curse, and Wishes that he might be obliged to swallow them down his Throat for a Penance.

I don't know when I should have recovered out of my fit of Confusion, if the Sight of my Bliss had not done it. She went to the Fountain, sat her down upon the Margin, and spent some time there, then rose and made to my Apartment; she took two or three Turns with a Book in her Hand, but at last went out of Sight, as before. I staid till I saw her in the Walks again, and then ran down, where I found another writ with Ink, as follows.

Captain Robert Boyle.

I Am convinc'd of your Sincerity, and shall wholly rely upon your Endeavours to help me. If we succeed, and get our Liberty, I have it in my Power to reward you when we arrive in England. As we are two unhappy Persons, I should not be displeased to see the Man that I own an Obligation to, even in his Intention to serve me. I have Liberty enough, I mean as far as my Bounds, and am not over-closely watched. The Captain who took me Prisoner has hitherto us'd me very civilly, and is only Troublesome when he tells me he loves me. I have kept him from being too violent, by shewing him a little Civility sometimes, but how long he will continue within the Limits of Modesty I can't tell. 'Tis that makes me dread his Presence, and the sooner I am out of his Power, the sooner I shall breath the Air of Content, which is the Wish of

Your humble Servant.

At the reading of this Paper, my Heart ran over with Contentment; and had it not been for the Fear of what would happen about the Pieces of the Letter that were pick'd up by the cursed Eunuch, I should not have known how to have contain'd my Transports; but the Thought of that, like Water on a Fire, dampt my Joy. I past my Time between Hopes and Fears, till my Eunuch came to sup with me. I had torn my Letter into many Pieces, and had dispos'd of all the Fragments that had any Writing on it, but two or three small Bits that were vacant of Words lay under Feet. As soon as ever my Eunuch spy'd them, he pick'd them up, and said, I did not do well to tread upon Paper; for, added he, if *Achmat* had seen you (meaning the other Eunuch) he would have been in a strange Passion. He has chid the Lady that my Master brought home last, very severely, for throwing
Pieces

Pieces of Paper about the Garden, well knowing it could be only she that had don't, because the rest were all *Mahometans*, and know the Virtue of it. I ask'd the Reason of all this Bustle, about a Thing we *Europeans* put to the most servile Uses. He told me with some Intreaty at last, that all true *Mussulmen* have a great deal of Regard for Bits of Paper, because the Name of God, or their Prophet, may be wrote upon it; and they have a Tradition, that when they are called out of Purgatory at the Day of Judgment, to be Inhabitants of the ever-blessed Mansions, there will be no other Way to come to their Prophet *Mahomet*, but over a large red-hot Iron Grate, which they must walk over Barefoot. And therefore, upon the Instant as they are going to step upon the Grate, all the Pieces of Paper they have pick'd up during their Residence in this World will run and place themselves of their own accord under their Feet, so that they will be enabled to get to their Prophet without much Difficulty. This whimsical Story set my Heart at Rest, and we sup'd chearfully, emptied our Flask of Wine which held two Quarts, and took our Leaves. I went to Bed, and felt such a Calm in my Mind, that I did not lye long awake, but continu'd sleeping till ten a-clock the next Day. I was surpriz'd, and vext I had rested so long, when I consider'd perhaps that I had lost Sight of my Love. I dress'd my self, and took a Walk in the Garden, finding the Coast clear as I thought. The Sun being pretty warm, I retir'd to a little Shade made by a few Lawrel Trees; but was much surpriz'd to find her that was ever in my Thoughts, sitting under the Shade in a thoughtful Posture. She turn'd her Head at the Noise I made in approaching her, and was running away. I pluck'd up (with much ado) Courage

rage enough to speak to her; Madam, said I, I would not have you be under any Apprehension. If I had known you had been here, I would not have disturb'd you. I will only inform you, that I am the Person that has vow'd to serve you to the utmost of my Power. Sir, answered she, I am not at all displeas'd at this Interview which is merely Chance; on the contrary I am pleas'd to see the Person whom I once hope to be obliged to for my Liberty, and wish we could often meet, that we might consult about the Means. Madam (answered I) if you'll condescend so far, I don't doubt but to find Opportunities enough. I told her of my Plot with the Eunuch, and I had some Hopes it might produce something. She approv'd of my Design, and my Conduct hitherto. She added that she would take hold of all Opportunities to walk in the Garden (where I had inform'd her I could see her without being seen) and so we parted for fear of being discover'd. She went into the House, and I went back to my Dwelling, and in less than half an Hour the Captain arriv'd. He came to fetch me to Dinner, and told me I had work'd by Magick, or I could never have done what I did. He told me he thought himself much obliged to me, and that I should find it. I answered him, I was convinc'd it was but my Duty to serve him with every thing in my Power, and that if he pleas'd I would make farther Improvements. He made me a great many Compliments his way, and declared he would leave it to my better Judgment.

By this time Dinner was ready, and I was ordered to sit down at Table with him, (for tho' he had turn'd *Mahometan*, yet he eat as we do in *Europe*, not on the Ground upon Carpets as the *Asiatics* and *Africans* do.) We had our Dinner dres-
sed

sed after the *English* Fashion, and we drank plentifully of his *Greek* Wine. He told me he had a Dispensation from the *Mufty* to drink Wine, and smil'd. I answered I believed the Crime was pardonable by *Mahomet*, if it was drank with Moderation. For my Part, I don't think (said I) Religion consists in Castigation and Penance; and I am convinc'd that an upright Man, let him be *Jew*, *Turk*, or Christian, may find his Way to Heaven. We had several Discourses at Dinner about Religion, but I soon discover'd the Captain knew very little of any; and I am of the Opinion there's very few of the *Renegado*'s think of Religion: Their Motive to change is Ease and Interest. But this is a Digression.

When Dinner was over, we walk'd in the Garden, and I show'd the Captain what Improvements I had design'd to make. He approv'd of every thing I said, and inform'd me that he had heard from *Mirza* the Eunuch my Abhorrence of Women. But he advis'd me to keep my Sentiments secret, for when you abjure (said he) the *Moorish* Women will make you feel their Resentments. But 'tis odd, continu'd he, that one of your Youth and Make should take such an Aversion to the Female Sex. I told him I had very good Reasons for my Hatred, and even my Mother was odious to me, tho' she brought me into the World. Well but, added the Captain, Time and a Fair Face may make great Alterations. I told him I was very well assured I should carry my Resentment to the Grave. I fancy (said he) I have an *English* Woman, a Slave of mine, that I have lately taken, would make you change your Sentiments, if you saw her. Sir, answered I, I would be willing to stand the Tryal to convince you of the contrary, tho' I would as soon look upon a Serpent with my Will. Well,

Well, said he, I have not learnt the Strictness of the *Moors*, in keeping Women without being seen; or if I had, your Aversion to them would convince me I have not much to fear. He desired me to walk a-while in the Garden, and he would be with me again immediately. Upon this he left me, and went into the House, and return'd in five Minutes. Come, said he, I have order'd my Women to walk in the Garden, and you and I will abscond behind these Lawrels, where we may see them, and not be seen. We had not sat long, before we could perceive three Women coming towards us. The two first were very handsom, a little inclining to Fat, one seem'd to be about thirty, and the other twenty one according to my Guess, and not so fair as our *English* Women; but the third was she I look'd for. All my Circumspection could not avoid my feeling a sudden flow of my Blood rise into my Face, which my Captain observ'd. Well said he (when they were walk'd out of hearing) I have taken Notice of your Disorder, and perceive your real Aversion is unsurmountable, which I am not sorry for, being it will add to your Liberty. I have no Occasion to have you confin'd when they walk in the Garden, for I fancy (added he laughing) you'll shun 'em fast enough. Just, answer'd I, as I would a creeping Snake, unless it were to destroy 'em, and that the Regard I have for you would prevent. The last (said the Captain) is your Countrywoman, one that I took in a Ship (my last Voyage but one) bound for the Island of *Zant*. I lik'd her so well, that I refused her Ransom that amounted to five hundred Pounds, and her Charms have overcome me so much, that I would willingly enjoy her with her own Consent, for Compulsion palls the Joy. I have given her twenty Days to consider on't, and when that

Time's

Time's expir'd, if she will not consent, I am resolv'd to force her.

Lord (said I in a seeming Passion) how can you take such an extraordinary Trouble for a thing that does not deserve the least Regard. If the rest of the World were of your Mind (said my Captain) the Women would have but a scurvy Time on't. Now 'tis to me amazing (reply'd I) that Men should take Pains, live hard, and run all Hazards, to come home, and spend all the Fruits of their Labour on such Trifles, that perhaps have not the least Tenderness for 'em, especially in these hot Counties where Women are given to be amorous, and yet have but one Man to sometimes a Dozen of them and more; when perhaps a dozen Men would hardly satisfy one Woman. Why (reply'd my Captain) that's the Reason they are so strictly guarded, we pretty well know what they expect. Now, if I had not had this Aversion to Women (I return'd) I have a Secret without Witchcraft, to make a Woman doat upon a Man. How, said the Captain, have you such a Secret? if you'll let me know it, I will not only give you your Liberty, but amply reward you besides. Sir, said I, I thank you; but as for disclosing the Secret, it is what I never can do; yet 'tis in my Power to prepare you a chymical Liquid, which put into White-wine will do the Business, though it will take up a great deal of Time, and be very expensive. As for the Expence, reply'd the Captain, I shan't value it. But in how long Time can it be done? Not under one hundred Days after Projection, answer'd I. Upon this he paus'd some Time; A hundred Days is a great while, yet I think 'tis better to wait for her Consent than to force her. So far (said I) I think you are in the right; and further (added I) you may continue her

her Affection, as long as you think fit, by now and then adding some of the chymical Drops into any Liquid she shall drink, after she has taken the first Prescription.

The Captain seem'd mightily pleas'd with my Project, and ask'd me what the Charge would be. I answer'd, I fear'd it would be about two hundred Pounds in this Country, tho' it would be much cheaper in *England*, where the things that I should want were easier to be had; but I told him I could not give a just Account of the Charge, till I saw the Prices of the Things I shou'd want. I told him I was afraid I should find it a difficult thing to get a *Still*, for that was the first thing I should want. He answer'd me, he did not question but I should easily procure every thing I wanted for Money, and he would take care I should not stand in need of that. He farther told me that several *Jews* in *Sallee* had all manner of Drugs, and he believ'd every thing else that I should want. (For fear of the worst) I told him, I should not want my Drugs these fifty Days, tho' I should want the *Still* immediately, and Liberty to go into the neighbouring Woods in the Night-time, being there were several Herbs that I must gather by Moon-light, and when the Moon was in its Full, in the Increase, or Decrease, according to the Nature of the Herb I wanted. He told me I should have all the Liberty I required, not doubting I would make any wrong Use of it. I told him, to be more secure, he might send who he thought fit, to guard me. No, return'd he, I'll leave you to your self. But you may take who you will with you of my Servants, if you want their Assistance. I told him I should stand in need of some of 'em sometimes. Well, said he, you shall go up with me, and take what Money you have Occasion for.

for. So accordingly we went into a little Closet, where was a strong Box, which he open'd, and took out two hundred and fifty *Spanish* Pistoles; said he, if there is not enough, you may have more. I told him I was assur'd there was too much. Well, said he, we'll reckon after the Affair is over. And because it will be so long about, I'll e'en take another cruising Voyage, that I may not think the Time tedious. I was very glad to hear him say so, because I should have the better Opportunity to work my Design. Tho' I dissembled my Joy, and told him I should be sorry for that, for I should often have something or other to give the Woman he design'd me to work upon. Well (said he) *Mirza* shall take your Directions. Upon saying this he call'd *Mirza* to us; *Mirza*, said the Captain, you must observe this Person's Orders; whatever he commands you to do, you must obey with as much Exactness as if you were serving of me. This he told *Mirza* in the *Moorish* Tongue, but explain'd it to me in *English*. *Mirza* also told me in *French* the Commission his Master had given him, and farther added, he hop'd I would often command him to visit the Wine Cellar. I told him we would not want. I advis'd the Captain to let me go to Town, to enquire for the Still as soon as possible, and to be known to those People that sold the Drugs. Why if you will (reply'd the Captain) we'll go immediately; upon which I consented. He ordered a Horse to be sadled for me, and I went into the Green-house to prepare my self; and luckily for me I did, for I found a Note fixed to the String, which my fair Correspondent had taken Opportunity of leaving, when she walked in the Garden by the Captain's Order. The Contents were as follows.

SIR,

SIR,

I Take this Opportunity to acquaint you that the Tyrant Captain is arriv'd, and has given me twenty Days to confent to his abominable Love. I hope you will believe me when I tell you it has almoſt taken away my Senſes. The Time I fear is too ſhort for us to effect our Liberty; and if we do not ſucceed before the fatal Day, I ſhall be the moſt miſerable Wretch the Earth contains. Let me hear from you, and if you can give me the leaſt Glimpſe of Hope to lull my Sorrows, fail not to chear the Heart of

Yours.

How lucky was it for me to find this Note! It might have fell into the Captain's Hands, and then we had been in a fine Condition. I had Time to write but a ſhort Anſwer, which I threw on the Ground, and pull'd in my String; it was this, *Hope every Thing: Write no more till to-morrow.* I lock'd my Door, and took the Key with me.

When we were on Horſeback, our chief Diſcourſe was concerning Charms, Philtres, and Witchcraft. I convinc'd him there was not any ſuch thing in the World; and my Compound was the only thing that could do what was defir'd. He ask'd me if I my ſelf had ever try'd the Experiment: I told him more than once; and related the following Tale to him off hand.

There liv'd in our Neighbourhood a rich old Man and very amorous, but deformed to the laſt Degree: He was round-ſhoulder'd, broad-fac'd, bleareye'd, ſhort-noſed, and his Mouth as wide as his Face was broad; a pretty Object as one ſhou'd ſee. This old Gentleman fell in Love with a very pretty Woman, a Mercer's Daughter over-againſt him, but seem'd to be the very Offspring of Pride, and nothing less than a Lord shou'd be her Husband, being well assur'd her Charms would conquer every one that look'd upon her. She could not bear the thoughts of the old Gentleman, and whenever he talk'd of his Passion treated him so ill that he was almost distracted. I went to visit him one Day, as I often us'd to do, for before his Love-Fit he was wont to be very good Company, and would make as free with his Deformity as any Body else would do; but I found him now in such a Condition that I began to pity him. I us'd all the Arguments I was capable of to bring him to Reason, but it was the same thing as to stem a Torrent. At last I call'd to Mind this Elixir, which I had never try'd before this Occasion; I was pretty well convinc'd of its Virtue from what I saw it was compos'd of, though the chief Ingredient is calcin'd Gold.

This wonderful *Arcanum* was found out by an Uncle of mine that had studied the Secrets of Nature sixty Years. When he was dying he call'd me to him, and gave it me in Writing, with the most sacred Conjuration that I should never reveal it, nor cause it to be wrote till I thought my last Hour near, and to destroy that which he gave me in ten Days, for fear it should be found by Accident, and that ten Days would be sufficient to imprint it in my Memory; I give it into your Hands, said my dying Uncle, because I find thy Understanding exceeds thy Years, and thy Aversion for Women will never let thee make an ill Use of the valuable Secret; and further added, that the Charge would deter me from doing it upon any slight Occasion. I took it from him with a sacred Promise not to disclose it, till on my Death-Bed; for if my Uncle had recover'd recover'd I muſt have deliver'd it up to him again: But he expir'd in half an Hour.

I ſo far pitied the old Gentleman (and alſo having a Deſire to try the Experiment) that I told him I had it in my Power to make the Lady as fond of him as Love could wiſh, if he would go to the Charge. He told me he did not value the Expence, but he had no Faith in Charms. I convinc'd him at laſt, went to work, and accompliſh'd my Affair. The Quantity I made would ſerve a hundred Years, and I had a Bottle in my Trunk when I was trepann'd aboard, which if you had had the good Fortune to have taken, would have ſav'd you Time, and Money.

When I had brought my old Gentleman a Bottle of my Stuff, he ſeem'd even then to have little Faith in it; but I bad him have Patience till the Tryal. All he had to do was to convey about forty Drops in a Glaſs of White-Wine faſting. That, ſaid he to me, will be a difficult thing, for I know ſhe hates me, neither will ſhe ſtay in the Company where I am. However I told him I would do my Endeavour to find an Opportunity: So I order'd him to keep a ſmall Bottle in his Breeches Pocket, (for it muſt be warm'd naturally with the Heat of the Perſon's Body that is to give it.) And in two or three Days I prevail'd upon a Relation of mine to invite the Lady to drink Tea with her: I acquainted my old Lover that he ſhould come in as by Accident, and bring a Pint of White-Wine as a Taſte of a Parcel he was to diſpoſe of. Every Thing happen'd as deſired; the old Gentleman came in, and got an Opportunity of conveying ſome of the Drops into a Glaſs of Wine, and I had the Satisfaction of ſeeing her drink it. This paſs'd off, and we parted: But the poor Woman in leſs than ten Days was diſtractedly in Love with the old Gentleman, who took his Opportunity, enjoy'd her, and after despis'd her.

Now the Nature of this Elixir is, that if the Dose is not renew'd every time the Moon is in the full, the Object belov'd will sink into dull Indifference again.

My Captain told me he thought I might have made my Fortune by such a Secret. I reply'd I had forgot to tell him that my Uncle made that one of his Articles, that I should never sell a Drop of it, and I assur'd him I would always keep my Promise.

Our Story brought us to Town, and I was very much pleas'd, for I was both tir'd in inventing Lies to amuse him, and riding after the *Moorish* manner, with one's Knees almost to one's Mouth; and there's no altering the Stirrups.

We alighted at the Captain's House; he sent about the Town, and in an Hour bought a compleat *Still*. He went with me to the Jew's that dispos'd of Drugs, and by good Fortune, and a good Memory, I remembred the Names of a great many Sorts. I laid out some Money then, and told him I should want a great many other Sorts, and larger Quantities. Of this Jew I borrow'd a Crucible (thro' the Captain's Interest) to melt the Gold, as I told him. The things were order'd immediately to the Country House, the Captain desir'd I would make no Delay, so I return'd, and got home just by Sun-set. I immediately ran to my Green-house to see if the Piece of Paper was there, but I found it was gone; this pleas'd me.

I went to Bed and rose early in the Morning, and seem'd to be very busie about the Garden. I sent for my Eunuch out of the House, and told him what I had undertaken for the Captain; but I farther added, if he did not now and then
give

give me his Company, attended with a Bottle of the Juice of the Grape, I could not possibly go through with my Undertaking. He answer'd me, smiling, that he had Orders from his Master not to disobey me in any thing. But, added I, I have a harder Task than all this, for I am compell'd to have some Discourse with the Woman I am to work upon, to find out her Temper; for according to her Disposition I am to add or diminish several of my Ingredients. Nothing could have prevail'd upon me, continu'd I, to have undertaken this hateful Task, but the Hopes I have of Liberty; for that is the Agreement between the Captain and me, if I succeed in my Design, which I am in no doubt of. I should be glad, return'd the Eunuch, you might meet with what you desire, yet I should be sorry to lose your good Company. I shall with some Regret, answer'd I, part with you; but Desire of Liberty, and indeed of revenging my self on my unkind Uncle, which is natural to us Mortals, will make me as expeditious as I can in my Work. I order'd him to let me have a Couple of Servants, to go with me into the Fields that Night, to carry the Herbs I should gather; and he told me they should attend me.

I now began to think of acquainting the Lady with some Part of my Design, and therefore wrote her a Note to this Effect.

Madam,

I Hope to have the Honour of conversing with you without Fear, and even with the Consent of your Tyrant. I have laid a Scheme for our Liberty, that with the Blessing of God I hope will succeed. You'll smile when I tell you I am to understand natural Magic:

Magic: But I shall think nothing difficult, if in the End I can serve one who may ever command

Yours.

In less than an Hour I saw the Ladies coming down the Walk: I ran immediately up to my Peep-hole, and observed the Mistress of my Heart sauntring the same Way she us'd to go. Assoon as I had discover'd her in the Walks, again, I ran down, and found a Note in the room of mine; (at first I was uneasie, imagining she had not taken mine away) which contain'd to this purpose.

I *Am something reviv'd at your short Sentence I found upon the Ground Yesterday. I learnt your going to Town with the Captain by a Discourse between* Achmat *and* Mirza; *for I understand the* Morisco *Tongue enough to pick out the Sense of what they say: Yet I had not ventur'd to write, for fear my Note should have miscarry'd, if I had not seen you talking to* Mirza *out of my Window. Only consider my Time is very short, and if there is no other way to avoid the Captain, I must fly to Death as my only Refuge. Think of it, and Farewell. Let me have an Answer the soonest, for Doubt and Expectation are but lingring Torments.*

I wrote her the following Answer.

Madam,

I'*LL write to you no more, and beg the Favour you wou'd desist from giving your self any farther Trouble. I will have the Pleasure of talking to you openly to-morrow, and let you into the whole Scheme I have laid for our Liberty. But let me beg you to be chearful, tho' reserv'd in your Countenance when we meet, for fear we should be observ'd.*

She

She came to the old Place in an Hour after she had brought the last, with another Note (as she told me afterwards,) but reading mine, she did not leave it behind her.

After my Eunuch and I had din'd, I went into the neighbouring Wood with two of the Captain's Slaves that were Blacks: I loaded them with Herbs of several Sorts, any thing I could lay my Hands on, and order'd them to carry 'em into the Garden. I had taken Care to tie every particular Herb with a String, so that there was no Danger of mixing: These I hung in Bundles upon the Branches of several Trees in the Garden, and out we went again. In short, I gather'd a good Horse-load of different Sorts, and some I laid upon the Banks, and others I cover'd with Earth, that it look'd as if I was about Business. I could hardly forbear smiling sometimes when alone, notwithstanding my Anxiety for the Success of my Design, to think how soon I drew in the credulous Captain. Then I began to be in a thousand Fears of his discovering my Intention to some of the *Moorish* Physicians, for tho' generally ignorant, yet they would soon have found I was but an Impostor.

While I was amidst my Fears the Captain arriv'd, whose sight gave me some Trouble. He came up to me, looking about him at what I had done; Why this looks like Work, said he. Yes Sir, said I, I am willing to begin, that I may make an End the sooner: But Sir, I must intreat one Favour, that you would not impart the Secret to any one of your Family but *Mirza*, nor to no one else upon any Account whatsoever: If they seem inquisitive, tell 'em I am only distilling some simple Waters for your Closet. I like your Advice, answer'd the Captain, and will be sure to follow it: The Reason of my coming

coming down now was to take my Leave of you, for I design to set Sail to-morrow Morning early, for I am inform'd of a rich Vessel that will be in our Latitude in ten Days, from a Prisoner that's lately taken belonging to *Spain*: I can't tell how long I shall be out, but I hope by that time I come back, I shall find every thing in readiness. Sir, I return'd, I don't fear but to accomplish my Design before you come back. Well, said he, do you think you shall want any Thing else? I told him, nothing but now and then a Gallon of Sea Water. Well, said he, I shall leave *Mustapha* behind me in Town, who shall obey you in whatever you shall command. Well, said he, Farewell (and shook me by the Hand) I'll just go in and give 'em a fresh Charge concerning you, and then to Town again. I was very glad to hear him say so; and he was as good as his Word, for in half an hour he took Horse: He shook his Hand at me as he went by me, and I heartily wish'd it might be the last Time we might see one another; not as I could complain of my Treatment, for he had us'd me very handsomely; and if it had not been in regard to the Business of my Love, I should not have wish'd him ill.

Mirza came to me, and told me his Master had given 'em so strict a Charge to observe my Directions, that if I had a mind to dispose of his Estate, 'twas his own Fault, for we must not disobey you. Yes, answer'd I, if ever you find me requiring any thing foreign to this Affair, I'll give you leave to deny me; but there's one thing I must command you since I have the Power, and that is to come and sup with me, and bring some of the Nectar along with you, for I am really fatigu'd with stooping and walking in the Sun when I gather'd those Herbs. Well,

Well, return'd *Mirza*, I believe I shall not find much Difficulty in obeying your Commands; and I have one Favour to beg of you, which is, that you will lay your Injunctions on *Achmat*, that he may partake. Said I, not to-day *Mirza*, another time with all my Heart. Nay, reply'd *Mirza*, it is not out of Love to *Achmat* that I desire it, but that he may be as deep in Sin as my self; for if he should ever discover me, I can't tell the Consequence. Well, return'd I, we'll find an Opportunity. The Hour of Supper being come, *Mirza* arriv'd with a couple of Flasks. We eat and drank so heartily, that *Mirza* was incapable of helping himself; but was so inebriated with Wine, that I began to repent of my plying him so fast. I was forc'd to drag him, and lay him on my Bed. But how to conceal it from *Achmat* was my greatest Care; for I did not doubt but he would be wanted; and accordingly it so fell out. For about twelve a-clock at Night he came, and knock'd at my Door. I was up, and thinking of my Design. I open'd the Door, and understood by his Signs, that he wanted *Mirza*. I let him know by Signs, that I had sent him to gather me some Herbs by Moon-light. He was satisfy'd, and went back again. Now *Mirza* kept the Key of the Gate, so that my Story was feazable enough.

About four a-clock in the Morning *Mirza* wak'd, but frighted out of his Wits to find it Morning; tho' I soon compos'd him, by letting him understand how I had manag'd *Achmat*. He return'd me a thousand Thanks, and told me, he should never be able to make me amends. I ask'd him, how I shou'd order it to see this Woman, for I could not go to Work till I had convers'd with her: And yet by Heaven and
Paradise

Paradife (faid I) I fhall be more concern'd at the Interview, than at any thing which ever happen'd to me; (and that was but Truth, for my Mind was perplex'd between Hope and Fear, Joy and Anxiety.) I pity you indeed, faid *Mirza*, and I wifh I cou'd any way eafe you of the Trouble. Well, faid I, then let her come alone into the Garden, as I am fprinkling my Herbs by and by; for I think one Woman is enough to plague a Man. Oh (faid *Mirza*) all Men are not of your Mind. But I'll leave you, and hope to find you in better Humour, when I fee you again.

I had order'd a Slave to bring me fome Water, and a large Quantity of Salt, to mix with it, only to amufe 'em. With this I fprinkled the Herbs I had gather'd, and I was very bufy about nothing.

I faw prefently after the Idol of my Soul, and *Mirza* running before her. When he was near enough to me to be heard, he faid, I muft beg you to excufe my waiting on you for a little while; for my not being in the Houfe laft Night, as ufual, has let my Bufinefs fo encreafe upon my Hands, that I muft make ufe of all Opportunities to regain loft Time. I told him, I would not be his Hindrance, but was very forry I could not have his Prefence upon this Occafion; for I fhould be in a very great Dilemma. He made me no Anfwer (being the Lady was within hearing) but return'd into the Houfe.

Affoon as the Coaft was clear, I accofted her with a great deal of Timerity. Madam, faid I, the happy Time is come, that I may tell you, without Fear or Danger, how much you may command me. Sir, (return'd fhe) I am convinc'd of your fincere Defire to ferve me; and as I have wrote to you, in one of my Notes, if

Heaven

Heaven profpers our Wifhes, and we arrive fafely in *England*, I hope it will be in my Power to reward you. Madam, (faid I) the Succefs will amply reward me for all my Trouble; and as one Climate gave us Birth, it is my Duty to do all I can to ferve you, if I had no other Motive. But if you pleafe, let us confult, now we have Time by the Forelock, how we fhall order our Affairs. Sir, reply'd the Lady, I am convinc'd your Underftanding wants not to be inftructed; and if you pleafe, I'll be rull'd by you in every thing. Madam, (faid I) have you any Objection to be difguis'd in the Habit of a Man? for (added I) we may fo accomplifh our Liberty with more eafe. I have no Objection to it, anfwer'd the Lady; but how will you procure it? Pleafe to leave that to me (I return'd) and in lefs than ten Days I hope we fhall be out of Danger. I then inform'd her of the Scheme I had laid, which fhe mightily approv'd; and told me fhe thought my Underftanding outwent my Years. I told her fome Accidents in Life new edg'd our Thoughts, and if we fucceeded, the Infpiration came from her. I obferv'd fhe blufh'd at my Difcourfe, yet did not look as if fhe took ill what I had faid. But I was much concern'd to fee her change the Difcourfe. I did not think it proper to declare my felf any further, hoping when I had affected her Liberty, Gratitude would befriend me in her Heart. I obferv'd, by her Converfation, fhe had a large fhare of Underftanding, and a happy turn of Wit. In fhort, this Interview had fix'd my Heart intirely hers. I had feveral times thought of inquiring into her Fortune, and how fhe was brought into her unhappy Slavery, but defifted, till we had more Leifure. She told me, fhe fear'd we fhould make our Converfation too long; not faid fhe (with a

Look

Look that shot through my Heart) as I am oppress'd with your Company, but for fear we may be observ'd. I told her, I believ'd we should not have many more Opportunities; therefore I begg'd her to be ready in a few Days, to leave this hateful Place. She answered me, that she would wait with some Impatience my Commands, and any Hour should find her in Readiness. She farther added, that she wish'd she might be as ready, and as willing, at her last Call. I begg'd her to cast off all melancholy Thoughts, and trust to Providence. Upon which we parted; with this her Answer, that she was ever resign'd to the Will of Heaven; and whatever should happen, she would do her Endeavour to make her self easy, even if it was the Miscarriage of our Design.

When she was gone, I soon found the Sight of her encreas'd my Passion (if it was possible for Love like mine to suffer Augmentation.) But it was Love alone that work'd Miracles of old; it was Love that rous'd me from supine Slavery; for I must own once more, if it had not been for this fated Passion, I should never have attempted any thing to regain my Liberty. But even my Love slumber'd now and then, that industrious Diligence might wake, and I was resolv'd to put the Design in Execution with all the Expedition imaginable, for fear of Accidents. I went on amusing the House, with Variety of Works for my Preparation; and I was continually ordering the Slaves to Town, for one thing or other, to strengthen their Opinion.

Mirza came to me soon after. At his Approach, I did my endeavour to put on a Countenance with little satisfaction of Mind, but I am apt to believe I did it but aukwardly. For as the Face is the Index

Index of the Mind, I am of Opinion, a Person of nice Judgment and Observation may discover a false Passion, with as much ease, as a Jeweller would distinguish the different Species of Stones (if we may call them so.) Well, said *Mirza*, your fiery Tryal is over; but I perceive by your Countenance, your Chagrine would willingly wear off, if you'd but suffer it. Why truly, said I, I have two different Passions strugling in my Mind, that is, Joy and Grief. I am pleas'd to think I shall succeed in the Affair I have undertaken; and yet griev'd that I must be compell'd to suffer the Torment I endure to help the Operation. Consider the Reward (reply'd *Mirza*) that is to follow. I chang'd the Discourse, that I might not be put to the Trouble to speak against my Conscience any longer. I told him I should be obliged to go to Town for Salt-water out of the Sea, and other Necessaries, that I should stay for. Why, reply'd *Mirza*, you may send for Salt-water, without being at the Trouble of going your self. I told him I was obliged to go in Person, because I was to take it out of the Sea, when the Sun was in a particular Altitude. Nay, return'd *Mirza*, I am only concern'd upon my own Account, for I have engag'd *Achmat* to dine with you to-day, with a great deal of Trouble. Well, return'd I, I will not disappoint you. I'll stay one Day longer to oblige you. He return'd me many Thanks for my Condescension, and went into the House to prepare Things accordingly.

All the while he was absent, I was contriving my Scheme. When Dinner was ready, *Mirza* brought it in, accompany'd with *Achmat*. He had taken Care at several Times to bring Wine, and had plac'd it in a Vault in the Green-house. *Achmat* made his *Moorish* Honours, and we all

sat

fat down. *Mirza* beg'd I would call the Wine a Cordial, that the Captain had given me. But I might have call'd it what Name I would, for *Achmat* did not underſtand me; for *Mirza* was my Interpreter, and with much Perſuaſion we prevail'd upon him to taſte it. But when he had drank one Glaſs, he ſeem'd to like it mightily, and ſoon aſk'd for another; and in ſhort, ply'd his Hand to his Head ſo often, that he was oblig'd to get up, and play'd ſuch Pranks, danc'd and ſung, and roll'd about, that it put us in a Fright, for fear ſome one ſhould hear the Noiſe he made. Which to remedy, I made him drink more, till at laſt he dropt down, and fell aſleep. We laid him upon my Bed, and did not intend to diſturb him.

I told *Mirza*, now we had accompliſh'd this great Affair, I had a mind to go to Town even then, for the Sun ſhone, and perhaps it might not the next Day, and I was willing to take the firſt favourable Opportunity. He told me, what I pleas'd now the Jobb was done. Accordingly Horſes and Slaves were provided me, and away I went for *Sallee*. When I came to Town I found *Muſtapha* at home, who congratulated me with the Favour I had receiv'd from his Maſter, and farther added, that he had given him full Charge to obey me in whatever I ſhould command. I told him I ſhould want his Aſſiſtance immediately with a ſmall Boat, only he and I, and I begg'd him to take his Quadrant with him, for I ſhould want his Art a little. We took the Boat he had provided me, and row'd out of the Bay till we came to a ſmall Promontory, where I deſir'd him to take the Elevation of the Pole. When he had ſo done, we lav'd Water into a Veſſel we brought for that purpoſe, and went home again. From thence I went to the Jew's,

Captain Robert Boyle.

Jew's, and begg'd he would furnish me with a *Moorish* Habit for my present Wear; for the People of the Country do so stare at me, said I, being in a different Dress from them, that it makes me asham'd. He provided me with a very handsome one, which I had pack'd up carefully, that no one should observe what it was. I bought several Trifles of him that I had no occasion for, and at several Times other rich Habits; but one thing particularly that I hop'd I should want, which was a Pint of liquid *Laudanum*.

I went to *Mustapha*, and order'd my things to be got ready: While that was doing, I endeavour'd to sound him to know whether he had any Thoughts about his Liberty, for I remembred at our first Meeting he declar'd himself, as I thought, very frankly: But in all his Discourse now, I found him of a wavering uncertain Temper, and therefore I thought it the wisest way to keep my Design to my self, and go another way to work. I took my leave of him, and went home. I unloaded my Horses, and took particular Care of my Bundle of Things. My Salt Water I put into shallow Pans in the Sun, which in a Day's time produc'd small Quantities of Salt. I did not want to try Experiments, yet I was pleas'd to see the Operations.

I began to set my *Still* on Work the next Day, but was soon interrupted in my Progress by the hasty Arrival of *Mirza*. Said he, we have brought a fine House upon our Heads; yonder's *Achmat* won't be contented without more of the *Francks* Cordial [the *Moors* call all *Europeans* *Francks*.] I ask'd him how he order'd him when he wak'd, after I had left 'em; he told me, he was so greedy after the precious Liquor, that he drain'd the empty Bottles; and he believ'd if

Mahomet

Mahomet himself had made him a Visit, and *Achmat* had got a Bottle to his Nose, he would not have bid him welcome till he had seen the Bottom. Well, said I, you know the Liquor is not mine, but I'll stand by you in the Consumption of it. Well, if you please then, said *Mirza*, we'll trouble you with our Company to-night. With all my Heart, said I; so we agreed to sup together. *Mirza* farther added, that the Ladies had a mind to see my *Still* at work. I told him they might do as they thought fit, but I would get out of the Way; and accordingly he went to fetch them. The *Moorish* Women came down the Walk in a hasty manner to observe it, but the *English* Lady came alone as usual. I had got on the other Side of the Lawrel Trees, and took Care to appear in her Sight. Assoon as she saw me, she cautiously approach'd me, and told me softly she wanted to have a little Talk with me. I answer'd her, we had an Opportunity very favourable; and then let her know how the other Women were employ'd, (beside we had the Lawrel Walk between us, and I was out of Sight from every Body else.) She told me she had something particular to mention to me; said she, we shall certainly want Money to accommodate us with many Necessaries in our dangerous Voyage. I told her what Money I had sav'd for our Design, but that we should certainly have Occasion for more, if we were oblig'd to go for *Spain*. That was one of the Reasons, said she, why I wanted to confer with you: It is in my Power to procure a considerable Sum, and tho' it is not so much as I have lost by the Captain, yet I have even a Scruple to take clandestinely from him what I may say is my own justly. I soon remov'd her Scruples, and then she farther told me, what was in her Power to take

was

was chiefly in Jewels, which would be better for Concealment and Carriage than Money. By this time she obferv'd the other Ladies coming towards her, which she inform'd me of; upon that I took my leave, and abfconded. When they were gone off the Walks, *Mirza* came to me to releafe me, as he call'd it, and told me the Ladies were mighty well pleas'd with the View of my Work and Materials. I told him, I hop'd they would not give me that Trouble often: He anfwer'd, he would take Care for the future.

Now the Crifis of my Project was very near. I went to Town the next Day, and took *Muftapha* for more Water; and farther added, I fhould want him a Night or two hence to procure Water by Moon-light. He wonder'd at my Proceeding, but his Mafter had told him that I was fomething very extraordinary, and fufpected me of Magick; but he alfo inform'd him that I was ufing my Art for his Benefit. I told him I had feveral Materials to wafh in the Sea Water in the Full of the Moon (which was at that time) and then I fhould give him no farther Trouble. From thence I went to my Jew's again, and privately procur'd feveral forts of dry'd Provifions, as Neats Tongues, Biskets, dry'd Fifh, Wine, and a fmall Puncheon of Water, and feveral other Neceffaries, all to be ready at a Moment's Warning.

When I had provided every thing, I went home again, and got an Opportunity the fame Day to fpeak with my Miftrefs. I defir'd fhe would be ready about twelve a-clock at Night, with every thing fhe had a mind to take with her. She told me fhe could not tell how to efcape the Vigilance of the Eunuchs, for, faid fhe, they lock me up every Night when they go to Bed; nay, every Day, when they are not with me. I defir'd her to leave that to me. I invited *Mirza* and *Achmat* to fup with me that Night, for I told 'em I was oblig'd to fit up to watch my Work, being it was coming to a Head, and that I was to go to Town before Day. They comply'd with my Requeft with a great deal of Joy; and the Hour drawing near, they lock'd up the Doors of the Houfe, and came with a great deal of Contentment in their Looks. We fat down, and I ply'd them with Wine till they thought they had enough. For the finifhing Stroke I defir'd 'em to drink one Cup of a Liquor of my own diftilling, which they foon comply'd with. I went and fetch'd a Bottle of Brandy that I had procur'd on purpofe, in which I had convey'd a large Quantity of *Laudanum*, to be ready for this Occafion. I gave 'em each a good large Cup, which they fwallow'd, but did not very well like the Tafte. I told them I had diftill'd that Liquor on purpofe to keep the Fumes of the Wine (or *Cordial*, as *Achmat* would have it) out of the Head. They were very well pleas'd if it would have that Effect, yet defir'd another Glafs of Wine to put the Tafte out of their Mouths, which I comply'd with. The Liquor foon had its defir'd Effect, and a profound Sleep lock'd up all their Senfes. I with fome Fear took the Keys out of *Achmat*'s Pocket, and went directly to the Houfe, and at laft found the right Key that open'd the Place where my Treafure was repos'd. Tho' fhe found her felf at Liberty, yet fhe fhook with timerous Apprehenfions. I encourag'd her all I could, and brought her the Difguife which I had provided for her. While fhe was getting ready, I retir'd out of Decency, and got out my Horfes, and an *Italian* Slave, whom I had two or three times

taken

taken to Town with me: He underſtood a little *French*, and I had obſerv'd ſomething in his Countenance that ſpoke him worthy of a better Fate. I had not once mention'd to him any thing of my Project, for fear of any Accident, but I had order'd him to be ready to go with me that Night. When I came back, I found my Miſtreſs ready, and ſomething impatient. I inform'd her ſhe muſt ſubmit to another Diſguiſe. She ask'd me what that was: I took out a Paper of *Ombre*, and told her ſhe muſt permit me to rub it over her Face and Hands; which I did: But the Pleaſure of touching her Fleſh in that gentle manner perfectly put me in an Ecſtaſy, which ſhe obſerv'd, for I could not help ſoftly ſqueezing her Hand. She did not ſeem diſpleas'd at my Tranſport, but yet I thought the Occaſion ſhe had to make Uſe of me made her bear with me. Aſſoon as we were ready we went out, but I firſt lock'd the Doors and left 'em as I found 'em. My Mind was confus'd between Hope, Fear, Joy, and Terror, and I did not doubt but the Lady was in a worſe Condition; but all my Task was to comfort her. When I had help'd her up on Horſeback, I call'd for the *Italian* Slave, and we both mounted, for I would not let him walk on Foot as uſual.

When we were got ſafe from the Houſe, I began to ask the *Italian* Slave ſeveral Queſtions, as where he was born, how long he had been a Slave, and ſo forth. I found by his Anſwers that he had no Hopes of Liberty, for he had ſent ſeveral Letters to his Friends in *Italy*, and never could receive any Anſwer. Then I began to come nearer the matter, and gave him ſome Hint of our Deſign, but with this Addition, even Death ſhould not deter me from the Execution.

He had hardly Patience to hear me out, but begg'd he might share the same Fate with me, and if he got his Liberty through my Means, he should never forget the Obligation, but I might be Master of that Life I should be the Means of saving; for, added he, to live in Slavery is but to be always dying the worst of Deaths. I soon found by his manner of expressing himself that he was sincere in what he said. At last I told him all my Design; which he mightily approv'd of, and said every thing was so well concerted, that with the Blessing of God it could not miscarry.

When we arriv'd at the Captain's Town House, we found *Mustapha* waiting for me. I had consider'd we could not do without him, yet I would not venture to mention our Escape, till we had him safe upon the Sea. I order'd every thing into the Boat, and to hide my disguis'd Lady, I told *Mustapha* that it was a young Gentleman that had been bit by a mad Dog, and I had brought him to dip him in the Sea, by the Desire of his Friends that liv'd in the Neighbourhood in the Country, which was allow'd to be the only Cure.

When we had gain'd the main Sea, I began to open my Design to *Mustapha*, but was something surpriz'd to hear him call out for Help. I immediately drew a Pistol out of my Pocket (for I had procur'd several Pair) held it to his Breast, and threaten'd him with Death that Moment, if he offer'd to open his Mouth: I added, that we had gone too far to stop now; and I believe, if he had made any Resistance, I should certainly have dispatch'd him. When he found Resistance would signify nothing, he sat him down and wept bitterly. I was really sorry to see him so much afflicted, and comforted him

him all I could; and, to encourage him, I told him, assoon as we arriv'd at *Magazan*, (a strong Port belonging to the *Portuguese* upon the *Afric* Coast) where I had design'd to steer our Course, he should not only have his Liberty, but I would reward him with fifty Pistoles for the Pains he should be at. I further added, I would not have given him this Trouble, if I could have found a possibility of doing without him. He seem'd to be satisfied, and promis'd us all the Help he could. I told him we would make the best of our way to *Magazan*, not being above twenty Leagues South of *Sallee*: He seem'd very much pleas'd our Voyage was to be so short, for the Wind was fair, and we hop'd to arrive at *Magazan* in two Days at the farthest. I had provided every thing that was necessary for a much longer Voyage, and when we had directed our Course, and were settled in our Way, I desir'd the Lady to take some Refreshment, and compose her unsettled Thoughts, for we were now out of all manner of Danger. I said this only to comfort her, for I was even in fear of the Captain's Ship, or some other *Moorish* Vessel, meeting us by Chance; and the *Italian* put into my Head another Fear, that as I had declar'd I was never at *Magazan*, nor did not know where it was situated, he was not assur'd but *Mustapha* might steer his Course to some Place that was possess'd by the *Moors*. I gave *Mustapha* a Hint of it, with a Promise of a quick Dispatch if he betray'd us: But he assur'd me there was never another Port between that and *Magazan*. After we had refresh'd our selves, I intreated the Lady to acquaint us how she came into the Power of the Captain. Now we are something at Ease, said she obligingly, I shall inform you with Pleasure.

THE
HISTORY
OF
Mrs. *VILLARS.*

Y Father's Name was *Villars*, an eminent Merchant of the City of *Bristol*. My Mother dy'd when I was very young, so that I could never know the Loss of her. The Care of my Father atton'd for the Want of my Mother: He gave me all the Education that was proper to our Sex; but before I was Sixteen my Father dy'd. The Grief and Sorrow I felt for his Death, was not recompens'd by an Estate of two thousand Pounds a Year, which he left intirely at my own Disposal; besides several valuable Jewels of my Mother's. My Fortune, I suppose, brought me many Admirers; but as I was a Stranger to Love, I had no Inclination to marry: Yet being pester'd so much with their Company and Courtship, I retir'd to a Country House near the Sea Side; and as I did not care to see any of my Suitors, so whenever they came I always left Word I was gone abroad, or out of Order; and in a little time I got clear of their Impertinence.

I had the Misfortune to be a Woman of Business, tho' young; for my Father had several

Veſſels at Sea. The Captain of one of the Ships that traded to *Turky* brought me a Bill of Lading, and I happen'd to pleaſe him, (tho' more than I knew till afterwards.) In ſhort, he fell deſperately in Love with me, but hearing my Averſion to Matrimony, never declar'd his Paſſion to me; yet by Bribes and Preſents gain'd over to his Intereſt a Maid that liv'd with me, who for a hundred Pound had plac'd him in a Cloſet in my Bed-chamber. I came and undreſs'd my ſelf as Uſual, and went to Reſt: But I had not been long laid ere I found a Perſon pulling down the Cloaths, and attempting to come to Bed to me. I was prodigiouſly ſurpriz'd and frighten'd, as any one would imagine: I call'd for Help, but no one came to my Aſſiſtance; for the Maid had taken Care of that. I got out of Bed with much ado, and attempted to open the Door, but found I was lock'd in. I us'd Intreaties to the Wretch (who was diſguis'd in ſuch a manner that I could not know him, for he had got a Mask on) but all to no purpoſe: He ſeiz'd me, and I was ſo faint with Struggling, that he was very near accompliſhing his barbarous Deſign, when my other Cloſet Door flew open, (for I had one at each End of the Room) and there came out another Man diſguis'd. My Fear could not be well increas'd; but I was in ſuch a Terror that I did not well know whether I was really alive.

The Perſon who came out laſt ſeiz'd immediately on the other, who let me go to defend himſelf. I ran to the Door, and Fear adding to my Strength, I burſt it open; but how, or which way, I cannot remember. I ran to the Maid's Chamber, and the Noiſe and Confuſion we were in alarm'd the Men Servants. I had ſlipt on a Gown; and when I had got all the Men together,

ther, I told 'em the Reason of this Alarm. They immediately arm'd themselves, and ran up to my Chamber, but the Persons were both gone. In searching the Room we found a Piece of a Mask on the Ground, and a Handkerchief mark'd *L. K.* with Stains of Blood in several Parts of the Room. We could not imagine who they were; and I was so very much confus'd and frighten'd, that I did not examine the Bottom of it that Night, but went to Bed in another Room very ill with the Fright; though not before I had given Order to two of my Men Servants to watch at my Chamber Door.

I search'd the Closets of that other Room, and under the Bed, before I wou'd venture. And it being a Room where my Father us'd to lye, it had a Bar on the Inside, so I and my Maid went to Bed. Notwithstanding my Fatigue, Frights and Fears, I fell asleep, and when I woke in the Morning, found my self very well. I began then to think reasonably of my last Night's Adventure, and easily judg'd, that one or both of my Maids must be in the Confederacy, for my Door never us'd to be lock'd on the Outside before. I sent for all my Servants up, Men and Maids, and related to 'em the Night's Adventure. But they brought me Word, that Mrs. *Susan* was not to be found. I sent to examine her Room, but I was inform'd all her things were gone. We all concluded, that she was the Occasion of the last Night's Plot. I did not think fit to send after her, rejoycing I had escap'd such a base Conspiracy; till going up into my own Chamber, I found a Diamond Necklace, a Ring, my Gold Watch, and about sixty Guineas in Money taken away; my Escritore broke open, and a Bill of five hundred Pounds that

was

was due, taken away. I immediately sent to *Bristol* to stop Payment, but was told, that my Maid had come, as from me, for the Money, and had receiv'd it several Hours before. We made the strictest Search we could for her, but all to no Purpose. So I gave it all for lost. Six Weeks pass'd on, and no News concerning my Maid. One Morning as I was walking in my Garden, a Sailor brought me a Letter, which was to this Purpose.

Madam,

I Heartily repent of my Infidelity to you. When I committed that base Action, I took Shelter on Board of a Ship that belongs to my Brother, and now lies about six Miles off; where the Bearer will conduct your Ladyship, if you will be so good to come away immediately. The Reason of my Repentance, and Sorrow (tho' a sincere one) is at the Approach of Death, by the Accident of a Fall down the Hold of the Ship, where I broke my left Leg, and fractur'd my Scull, so that I have been senseless for two Days. But God granting me my Senses again (tho' with the Information that I can't live four and twenty Hours) has, through his Mercy, convinc'd me, that to expect Pardon from him, is to restore what is yours, with a sincere Confession of the fatal Night's Adventure, that corrupted my Honesty, and will be the Cause of my Death. And farther, if Heaven will grant me the Blessing of seeing you, I may put you in a Way to prevent something of Ill that may happen to you.

Your Repenting Servant,
Susan Prichard.

P.S. *I beg you to keep it Private; and to amuse your Servants that you bring with you, you may tell 'em, you are going on Board the* Turky *Ship, to see the Present the* Turky *Merchants are sending*

sending to the Emperor of Constantinople. *The Bearer will conduct you.*

Now I had heard of one of the *Turky* Fleet, that was obliged to put into the Road by a violent Storm: And that it had a Sedan, made with Looking-glass, of a very curious Workmanship, design'd for a Present to the *Turkish* Emperor. I ask'd the Sailor several Questions concerning the Letter, and he answer'd me bluntly, he could not tell any thing about it; but that there was a young Woman, who had fell down their Hold, and had almost kill'd her self; and that they did not expect she could ever recover. I resolv'd to go along with him, but to take two Men Servants and a Maid with me. I walk'd to the Water-side, which was about a quarter of a Mile from my House, and there I found a Ship's Boat with eight Oars, and very handsome. I stept into it, with my Servants, without any Hesitation, and put off. In about an Hour and a half we came along side of the Vessel, they mann'd Side for me, and I was handed up, and led into the Cabin, where I found my Maid upon a Pallat-Bed in one Corner of it. Assoon as she saw me, she attempted to rise, but seem'd not to have Strength enough, and fell down again. I desir'd she would not put her self to any Pain, but compose her Thoughts, that she might be the better able to inform me of what she had promis'd me in her Letter. O! Madam, she cry'd (with Hesitations, Sighs, and ready to faint every Moment) you do not know what I feel at the Sight of you. You bring into my Remembrance the Transaction of that fearful Night, but I hope your Goodness will forgive me. I shall put into your Hands what I have wickedly robb'd robb'd you of; and since I am going out of this World, I am assur'd your Good-nature will prevail for my Pardon. I told her I forgave her freely, and I hop'd Heav'n would do so too. She thank'd me, but said, she found her self so Ill, that she intreated leave to rest from speaking a Minute or two, to gather a little Breath.

I waited with some Impatience, but she remain'd so long silent, that I really thought she was expir'd. Upon that Supposition, I call'd to her, and she answer'd me but faintly. Well, Madam said she, as I find you impatient to know what I have promis'd you, I will tell you, as well as I am able.

Captain *Bourn* had for many Months a great Passion for you, but finding you averse to Matrimony, he tamper'd with me, and offer'd me such large Sums of Money, that beat down all my guard of Honesty, and overcame it quite. He gave me a hundred Pounds, besides other valuable Presents, to admit him into your Closet, before you went to-bed, which accordingly (dazled with the lustre of the Gold) I did. You know what follow'd, and if he had not been prevented by the sudden Appearance of another Person out of the other Closet, would have compass'd his Design. Said I (eagerly) pray do you know who the other Person was? Yes Madam, return'd the Wench, it was Mr. *Lawrence Kendrick*, your former Suitor and Guardian, convey'd there for the same base Intent by your Ladyship's Woman. How! cry'd I amaz'd, are you assur'd of that? Madam (pursu'd she) when you got out of the Door, Mr. *Kendrick* seiz'd upon Mr. *Bourn*, and they struggled together some time; but Mr. *Kendrik*'s Mask falling off, Captain *Bourn* knowing him, cry'd, Is it you! In short, they soon came to an Ecclaircisement, and went down Stairs unperceiv'd

by

by any of us in the Hurry. Where he declar'd to the Captain, that he had prevail'd upon Mrs. *Ellis* (your Woman) for a good Sum of Money, to convey him into the Closet, which she did unperceiv'd of any. Thus, (said I) may ill Intentions be ever frustrated.

When she had finish'd, she begg'd me to have a little more Patience, while she got a little more Strength, and she would restore me my Money and Jewels. I was unwilling to wait long, yet thought fifteen hundred Pounds too much to lose; for my Necklace, Ring, and Watch, were valued by my Father at a thousand Pounds. I believe I had been full three Hours on Board, and wanted to be at Home again; and after she had kept silent some time, I made bold to disturb her once more. I call'd to her, and told her, I had a great Way to go, and I was afraid of catching cold. She begg'd I would ring a Bell that hung by my Hand, which I did, and the Sailor came in that brought me the Letter. Pray, said the Maid, is my Brother ready to come in? Yes, answer'd he, and has been on Board this half Hour. It's very well, said she. Upon that she rais'd her Hand, and unpinn'd a Shutter, that fell down, and let Light enough into the Cabin, which was dark before; but I thought her Illness was the Reason of that. But to my eternal Amazement I saw her rise from the Pallate, as well as ever I saw her in my Life. Before I had Power to speak, Captain *Bearn* enter'd. I could not presently dive into this Mystery. I hope Captain (said I, at last) that you repent of your rash and bold Attempt. Yes Madam, (answer'd he) that I did not succeed in't, but I hope I have it now in my Power to finish my Design. I askt him what he meant. He told me I should soon be inform'd,

and

and if I would not confent to his Embraces, he would certainly ravifh me that very Night. Upon this Treatment, I began to call for my Servants; but the faithlefs *Sufan* told me they were taken care of, and fafe a-fhore. Yes Madam, return'd the Captain, they are twelve Miles behind us by this Time; and defir'd I would look out of the Cabin Window, which they had juft before open'd. I caft my Eyes behind me; and too foon perceiv'd that we were a confiderable Diftance from the Land. I did not look long, for the Sight took away my Senfes, and I fell down in a Swoon, and when I came to my felf it was far in Night; but I was fo faint and ill, that my feeble Limbs would not fupport my Body. Grief attack'd me fo violently, that it was thought by every body it would foon overcome me. By next Morning a ftrong Feaver feiz'd me, and all that I remember'd for fix Weeks was, that I was put to Bed, with the Wretch that betray'd me to attend me. But the Condition I was in really wrought upon her, and produc'd a true Converfion. She lamented more than I; and curs'd her felf a thoufand times.

When I had recover'd my Senfes, I was wore away to a Skeleton. And fure never any one in my Condition found any Relief but Death. But it pleas'd the Divine Being to work another Miracle, and infenfibly reftore me to my former health of Body, but a Mind involv'd in the moft cruel Torture paft Imagination.

When I found the Maid's Repentance real, I freely forgave her. The Captain in all this Time had never come near me, but only to enquire after my Health, as *Sufan* inform'd me. But when he perceiv'd I had regain'd my former Health and Beauty, (as he call'd it) I was tormented with his beaftly Addreffes. He told me,

if

if I would consent to marry him, and forgive the Crime he was guilty of, he would immediately steer for *England*, which he could reach in a few Days. I consider'd I was in a Wretch's Power, who, by what he had done already, would stick at nothing to gain his Ends; I therefore resolv'd to flatter him, by the Advice of my Maid; who, notwithstanding she had brought me into these Distresses, I had taken into my former Favour. In one of his troublesome Visits, I told him, if he would immediately restore me to my Liberty, I would upon the Instant make him my Husband, when we could procure a proper Person to tye the Knot. He answer'd me, that the only way to secure me to him, was to have Possession of my Body before-hand; and, continu'd he, if you think the Action criminal, I'll soon cure your Conscience, by the Licence of the Church. For, said he, if you intend what you propose, you will easily comply; and nothing else will convince me of your Sincerity. I'll give you one Day to consider on't; but, (continu'd the Wretch) if you refuse to submit by fair Means, I to-morrow by Force will enjoy you. So I leave you to consider on't; and saying this, left us in the Cabin. I had desir'd *Susan* to conceal our Reconcilement from the Captain, which she artfully had done; and in his Discourse, would often throw in a Word or two in his behalf.

When we were alone, I gave my self over to my Sorrows, and thought of nothing for several Hours but my unhappy Circumstances. We both continu'd silent, a considerable time. Nor indeed had I Power to speak, tho' Heav'n had indu'd me with that Fortitude, that I had resolv'd sooner to die, than to submit to his curs'd Proposals. I told *Susan*, that I had determin'd termin'd to put an end to all my Sorrows by Death; and when that fatal Hour arriv'd of his limitted Time, I would plung a Knife, I had conceal'd for that Design, into my Bosom. This Resolution once more renew'd our Griefs, and we mingled Tears together. We wept so much, that the Fountains of our Eyes were dry, and we again remain'd silent. At last *Susan* broke it, with a Speech to this Purpose.

Madam, in the Confusion of my Thoughts, I have chose out one that has some Probability of Success; but it will at least convince you of my Repentance, and the Desire I have to restore you that Peace I have barbarously broke. The Captain yet thinks me in his Interest, and if we can contrive it, I'll submit to his loath'd Embraces in your Room, which shall be manag'd in this Manner. (You shall treat with him upon't to-morrow Morning) The Articles shall be these; First, that he come in the Dark, and stay no longer than one Hour with you; and last, that he shall not repeat your Familiarity, till you are join'd by the Priest.

I must confess, this Proposal gave me a dawn of Hope; and if we could but succeed in't, I should not fear his farther Passion, when we were landed. For I knew it was easy to find Protection, when once on Shore in *England*, and I thought the Contrivance feazible enough; for we were much of the same Age, and no perceiv'd Difference in our Make, at least in the Dark.

She left it to me to manage: And I resolv'd to put on a more compos'd Countenance at the Captain's next Visit, which was soon after, tho' he had given me longer Time to consider. When he came in, he begg'd my Pardon for interrupting me, but he came to make me a Present,

sent, he said, and put a little Box in my Hand, desiring I would open it, which I did, where I found my Jewels and Money. I restore you that, Madam, (continu'd he) and would not willingly be oblig'd to you for any thing but your Person; and even all your Fortune shall be at your own Disposal, and the Moment you consent to my Desires, I'll deliver you a Paper that shall oblige me to sign whatever Terms you shall think fit to make me. I paus'd a short time, but indeed it was to think what my Tongue should utter so foreign to my Heart.

Captain, said I, you take the only Way to gain your Point; and I must confess, this Shew of Generosity (tho' it's in your Power to force 'em from me again) seems a little to lessen the ill Opinion I have Reason to bear against you: If you'll please to allow me one half Hour to think a little, I'll give you my final Answer to-night. He seem'd very much overjoy'd at my Discourse, and shew'd it in an extravagant unpolite manner, thank'd me, and went out.

I did not want that time to prepare what I had to say, but I thought it was better than to come into it on a sudden. The time expir'd, the Captain came in with an expecting Face. I bad him sit down, which I found by his Countenance he took as a good Prologue. Sir, said I, I have fully considered every thing, and if you will comply with a few Articles, you shall have Possession of what you desire to-night. Articles, Madam! I'll sign to a Blank (reply'd the Brute) if you please. I told him they were only verbal ones: First, said I, I'll have no Light in the Room; secondly, you shall stay with me but an Hour; and lastly, never to expect any more Favours till we are lawfully marry'd. Madam, return'd the Captain, you so overjoy me that I don't know
where

where I am: I'll comply with all your Articles, and you have made me the happiest of Mankind. He said a great deal more fulsome Stuff, that was as nauseous to my Ears as a Plague-sore to the Sight. He left us, with a Hope I would not long defer his Happiness. It was well I was in a dark Corner of the Cabin; for had I been in the Light, he would have perceiv'd the Confusion in my Countenance.

The hated Hour drew near, and *Susan* with a sincere Grief, and Tears running down her Cheeks, laid her self in the Captain's loathed Bed. I was really griev'd at the Sacrifice she was going to make me, for I was convinc'd she had no loose Desires about her. The Captain enter'd in the Dark, and was as happy as a false Imagination could make him. I must confess, I was in a thousand Frights and Fears left the Girl should have been discovered; but every thing succeeded too well, and the Captain rose within his limited time, and went out.

Assoon as he was gone, the poor Creature got up from her guilty Scene. Well, Madam, (said she, all drown'd in Tears,) I hope I have convinc'd you (tho' to my eternal Cost) of my Repentance and Sincerity; but I hope Heaven will pardon me, and not lay the Crime to me or you, when fatal Necessity was the only Cause. I gave her all the Comfort I was capable of, and told her I did not think it impossible to oblige him to marry her, when we had him in our Power on Shore, and that Formality would obliterate all melancholy Thoughts. How! (reply'd *Susan*) No Madam! tho' I have done all this, yet it was only to serve you; and before I would be his Wife, (or indeed any Man's Wife) I would submit to the most servile Offices of Life to support it: And if the Captain knew how we had deceiv'd him, and would offer to marry me to attone for his Fault, I could not confent, for I loath the very Thoughts of him. Well then, *Sufan*, faid I, when we have overcome all Difficulties, and worn off the Remembrance of our Sufferings, I will fettle a Competency for Life, that fhall put thee above all Fear of Want. Madam, reply'd *Sufan*, that's all I fhall defire; and then I'll go to fome Corner of the World, live retir'd, and repent of all my paft Crimes and Follies. I told her fhe needed not do that, fhe might, notwithftanding what was paft, live with me. No, Madam, that can never be, return'd *Sufan*; for you muft of neceffity, to clear your own Reputation, divulge the Secret, and then with what Confidence fhall I be able to look upon any one? I told her, it would be efteem'd as an Action wholly virtuous, without one Spot or Blemifh. All I was capable of faying could not alter her Refolution; but fhe perfifted in retiring from the World, and living recluse, and I defifted from fpeaking any more upon the Subject.

It had been much happier for us both, if we had never enter'd upon the Argument; for we had not remain'd filent a Moment, before the Captain enter'd, with a Light in his Hand, and the utmoft Fury in his Countenance. Thou Devil! faid he to *Sufan*, and haft thou betray'd me, Wretch! after what I have done for thee? but I fhall ftudy fome way to have ample Vengeance on thee: And for you, Madam, I fhall give you ftill the fame Terms and Time I firft propos'd; but that paft, expect not the leaft Hope, for I will enjoy you, tho' the Moment after Death fhould feize me. When he had done fpeaking, he went out: But it was a confiderable time ere we came out of our Surprize.

We

We were convinc'd that he had liften'd and overheard all our Difcourfe, though we fpoke but foftly; and we fear'd to utter our Thoughts to one another, as imagining he would overhear us ftill. But *Sufan* at laft broke out in thefe Words; Good Heav'n! I hope the Punifhments I am bound to fuffer will atone for all my Offences! If it will make my Peace with Thee, I'll undergo all the Torments in the World in that bleft Hope! I had not Words to comfort her, for the thoughts of my own Condition ty'd up my Tongue; but the Pain of Thinking, nothing could exceed. I pray'd to God to bring me out of this Misfortune, or give me Force of Reafon to fuffer with Patience a Diffolution from this World. When *Sufan* heard me, fhe told me, fhe could fee no Path to lead us thro' this Labyrinth of Misfortunes, but through the Gate of Death; and, added fhe, fince we muft die once, the fooner we leave this troublefome World, the fooner we fhall find Reft.

Death ftill bore to me a frofty Sound, however I foon refolv'd upon't; but the manner of it was what moft confounded me: At laft we both thought of Drowning, and had refolv'd, whenever the Captain came to accomplifh his wicked Intent, to throw our felves out of the Cabin Window. Will you fo? faid the Captain, (who had overheard us again, for Grief had taken all Caution from us) but I'll foon prevent that. He immediately took Hammer and Nails, and nail'd the Shutters fo clofe that it was not in our weak Strength to undo them. After he was gone, we fpent the Night in Prayer; and juft before the Morning dawn'd, we underftood by the rocking of the Ship, the Noife of the Sailors, and the Loudnefs of the Wind, that we were in a prodigious Storm. This gave us Hopes that the Ship would be caſt away, and that God had heard our Prayers, and would not let us lay violent Hands upon our ſelves. Nay, deceiving Hope was ready to enter our Thoughts, that we might be caſt away upon ſome Shore, and receive Aſſiſtance when we leaſt expected it. The Storm laſted the whole Day and part of the next Night; but as it ſenſibly abated, ſo our Fears increaſ'd. The Captain gave us another Viſit: Well, ſaid he, Madam, I hope you have had ſufficient time to conſider of my Propoſals, and I am now come for my final Anſwer. Said I, Heav'n has given you an Anſwer by raiſing the Storm; and if you have the leaſt Notion of a Divinity, you'll find 'twas his Voice that ſpok to you in that Tempeſt, to deſiſt from ſuch a baſe Attempt. Nay, Madam, if you imagine you can preach me from my Deſign, preach on a God's Name. Wretch that thou art! ſaid I, how canſt thou mention that ſacred Name, and yet have ſuch Thoughts as He abhors? I fancy, Madam, return'd the Brute, your Ladyſhip feels the Influence of the Moon, and for fear I ſhould catch the Infection, I'll leave you for a while; but with a Word by the by, If you don't conſent the next time I come, by Hell! (ſince you will not let me mention Heaven) I'll not only raviſh you, but every Sailor in the Ship ſhall do ſo too, if they think fit; and I believe they are ſharp enough ſett to fall too upon worſe Food than I ſhall ſet before them.

He ſaid a great many more groſs things, that would only become his Mouth to utter: And to convince you, Madam, that I will do what I ſay, ſaid he, I ſhall begin with Mrs. *Suſan*: Come Miſtreſs, ſaid he to her, now I have had the firſt Cut of you, I'll let my Sailors go to Dinner.

Dinner. With this he forc'd us both on the Quarter Deck, and call'd all the Seamen about him: Here my Lads, said he, I have but two dainty Bits, and I'll give you one among you, that you mayn't think I am over greedy. The Sailors star'd upon one another, and did not well know what he meant, till he told them in Terms plain enough, with Promises of Reward to him that would prove the greatest Rogue. *Susan* fell upon her Knees, and intreated them not to take Pattern from their barbarous Captain, but to pity a poor unfortunate Woman, reduc'd to the fatal Necessity of living no longer. Some of the Sailors made Sport with her Misery, while others began to pity her. One blunt Fellow cry'd, Damn it! I love a Woman well enough, but don't care to have her forc'd upon me: It's like eating against one's Stomach. Beside, said another, I suppose there's some Reason of the Captain's Liberality, or he would not part with her. I observ'd one of them that stood at some Distance, taking Notice of what was done, without seeming pleas'd. I thought I knew his Face too, and he appear'd above a common Sailor by his Looks and Cleanliness. I had not till now appear'd publickly. I was determin'd to speak to him, and to crave his Assistance. Assoon as he saw me, he seem'd amaz'd, and cry'd, Bless me, Madam! how came you here? I told him I was betray'd by the Captain. I was inform'd, said he, that he had two Ladies, Passengers for *Zant*, but I little thought you were one of them, for I was not on Board till an Hour after you arriv'd. I begg'd he would take me under his Protection; which he swore with a great Oath he would, or the Captain should cut his Throat. Madam, added he, I am Mate of this Vessel, put in by your

G 3   honour-

honourable Father; and had been Captain, if it had not been for the Tricks of that Rascal; (pointing to the Captain.)

The Sailors were so divided between themselves, that they had not proceeded to any Violence with *Susan*; and she remain'd leaning upon the Side of the Ship, all drown'd in Tears. The Captain had all this time been laughing at the Disputes of the Sailors; but perceiving the Mate in Conference with me, came up to him, and with a saucy Tone, ask'd him what Business he had with me. I have no other Business, answer'd the Mate, but to protect her from your ill Usage. You impertinent Coxcomb, cry'd the Captain, I'll teach you to intermeddle with my Affairs; and upon saying this, he lifted up his Hand and struck him: But the Mate soon return'd his Blow with Interest, and knock'd him down upon the Deck. The Sailors came and parted 'em; but the Captain swore that Blow should cost him his Life. He upon the Instant ran into the Cabin for some Instrument to dispatch him, as was suppos'd; but the Mate follow'd him close, and, knowing his violent Temper, barr'd the Door of the Cabin, so that the Captain remain'd a Prisoner.

The Mate took from his own Cabin, which was near the Captain's, a Cutlass, and put himself against the Door, and swore he would be the Death of him that first attempted to release him; and bad none of them offer to stir, till they had heard what he had to say.

The Sailors had cast off all Thoughts from *Susan*, to hear what the Mate could say; who declar'd who I was, and by what Means I was betray'd on Board. When the Sailors found I was their Mistress, and Owner of the Ship, they soon began to repent of what they were going

Captain Robert Boyle.

going about, and declar'd they would ferve me with their Lives. When I found I had gain'd moſt of 'em on my Side, I told 'em my Story at length, only concealing *Suſan*'s Affair with the Captain; and they ſeem'd all prodigiouſly amaz'd, and ſtood gaping upon me like ſo many Statues.

The Captain in the Cabin was all this time ſwearing, curſing, and making a Noiſe at his Reſtraint. I told the Mate, if he thought fit, we would releaſe him. Yes Madam, if you pleaſe, ſaid he, out of the Great Cabin, but we muſt confine him ſomewhere elſe; well knowing his turbulent Spirit would never be eaſy. I told him I would be guided by him, and if he pleaſed to accept of the Command of the Veſſel (if it was in my Power to give it him) it was at his Service. He return'd me a great many Thanks, and told me he would be very faithful in his Commiſſion. We releas'd the Captain out of the Cabin, but as ſoon as he came upon the Deck, he was ſeiz'd, with a great deal of Difficulty, Iron'd, and confin'd to another Cabin. He rag'd like a Madman at this Treatment, but all to no Purpoſe. I told him he ſhould want nothing but his Liberty, neither would I proſecute him, as his Crimes deſerv'd, when we arriv'd in *England*.

I deſir'd the Mate to make for *Briſtol* with all the Expedition imaginable; with a Promiſe that I would recompenſe every common Sailor with double the Wages they expected for their Voyage. They all huzza'd at the News, and one and all promis'd to ſerve me with their Lives. The Mate told me the Wind was againſt us in our Courſe, but that he would ply it to Windward (as they call it) in Expectation of its Changing. I ask'd him whereabouts we were,

and

and he told me, very near the Streights of *Gi-braltar*, and should have been at *Zant* by that time, but that they were hindred by contrary Winds, and drove back by the late Storm. I told him how the Captain had deceiv'd me, in telling me we were not six Days from the *English* Coast.

Susan's Joy cannot be express'd at our happy Deliverance; and you may be assur'd I was as well pleas'd as she was, though it did not appear outwardly so much: Besides I considered the Mutabilty of the things of this World; and we were soon taught, by Experience, the Uncertainty of humane Affairs; for before the Evening we were chac'd by a Rover, who soon came up with us, and took us after an obstinate Resistance; tho' we did not lose one Man, but the barbarous Captain, who was kill'd in the Place of his Confinement, without being in the Action.

The Captain of the Rover was the same we have now made our Escape from. He never would tell me what became of *Susan* and the Crew. Madam, said *Mustapha*, I can inform you: They and all the Crew were ransom'd for a thousand Pound, and their Ship given them again. They did their Endeavour to ransom you, but to no Purpose, for they could never learn what was become of you.

Mrs. *Villars* thus ended her Relation; only added, that the Captain fell desperately in Love with her, and would never hear of her Ransom; tho' he treated her with Decency, allowing her every thing but Liberty; with the conveniency of a Study of Books, which the Captain had procur'd by his Piracy; and ever left in her Closet, her Jewels, and other things of Value, that he had taken out of the Ship.

WHEN

WHEN Mrs. *Villars* had finish'd her Story, I return'd her Thanks for the Trouble I had given her. Sir, return'd she, Thanks will not recompense me for the Pains I have taken. I shall demand the same Satisfaction from you. I told her I should readily obey her Commands; but I begg'd leave to give her the Relation in *French*, that our *Italian* might partake; for I design, with your leave, to insist of the same from him. Sir, reply'd the Lady, I would have related my unhappy Story in that Language, if you had given me the least Hint. But however, I'll go once more over again, if you please, in *French*; at least the chief Circumstances, that we may more ingage the Person to declare, how he has shar'd the same Fate with us. I begg'd she wou'd give me leave to take that Trouble, if it were only to let her see, I had imprinted in my Memory what concern'd her so strongly, that I could repeat every Circumstance. She gave me leave to proceed, on which I told her Story over again in *French*, to the *Italian*. When I had finish'd, she gave me Thanks, for the Pains I had taken. Tho' I had not been so long in the Relation, yet I made up the Time in descanting upon her Danger, and hard Fate. That a Lady of her Birth, Beauty, and Estate, should be so far forsaken by Fortune, as to be reduc'd to wretched Slavery.

I then began my own Story, from my Birth, to our present State. Tho' in what related to my Passion for the Lady, I did not directly explain; yet I gave her Hints enough to understand, she was the Idol of my Soul, and (tho' Love like Hope does oft deceive us) I thought my obscure Declaration did not displease her.

We then desir'd the *Italian* to proceed in his Relation. He sighing, told us, he was too much oblig'd to me, to refuse me any thing, tho' it would call to his Remembrance Transactions, that would bring Tears into his Eyes. After some Pause he began to this Effect.

THE STORY OF THE *ITALIAN* SLAVE.

I Was born at the City of *Rome*, renown'd for its Grandeur and Antiquity, and I may say without boasting, of a noble Family; but had the Misfortune to come last into the World, and the youngest, of five Sons and two Daughters. My Father had a plentiful Fortune, but before his Death he had much weaken'd it, in giving Dowries to my two Sisters, who were both marry'd far above their Fortunes, tho' not equal to their Birth. But Riches now ballance every Thing, and weigh down Birth and humble Virtue, and he that has most Gold, is the greatest Man.

We

Captain Robert Boyle.

We loft our Mother in our early Days; and my Father follow'd, before I was ten Years old, having settled all his Estate on his eldest Son to keep up the Grandeur of the Name, and left three Brothers of us to depend on him.

My Father in his Life-time gave us an Education suitable to our Birth and Family; and my Brother, to give him his Due, compleated us. Two of my Brothers he procur'd Posts in the Army for, who both lost their Lives in one glorious Campaign. The other dyed young.

It was imagin'd by every body that had the Privilege to think for me, that their Deaths would be of no small Advantage to me; and it had for some Years the Appearance of it. My Brother had attain'd to his thirtieth Year, without once ever thinking of Marriage. But an advantageous Match being propos'd, it was thought convenient for him to pursue it. The Lady that was design'd for him he had never seen; but he was inform'd she was young, rich, and beautiful. He was brought to the Sight of her, and fell violently in Love with her at the first Visit, and his Passion encreas'd every Moment. The Day was fixt for their Nuptials by the Father of the Lady, which was to be the *Easter* following. I had attain'd to my eighteenth Year, and no Provision made for me; and it was thought that this Match would not bring me the least Advantage.

One Day my Brother told me, he had procur'd me the Post of Captain of the Pope's Guards; and tho' it was far beneath my Birth, yet I was pleas'd with it, that I might have the Means to subsist, without being subject to the Caprice of Fortune, and the Dependance of a Brother of an uncertain Temper. My Brother having some urgent Affairs, that call'd him hastily

haſtily out of Town, he gave me a Letter to deliver to his Miſtreſs, which was to excuſe his ſudden Departure.

Aſſoon as he was gone, I went to execute his Commiſſion; and being known to be the Brother of the intended Huſband, had the Liberty of preſenting the Letter to the Lady's own Hands. But what Misfortunes did that Interview coſt me! I no ſooner ſaw her, but I loſt my Heart, and the Regard I ow'd my Brother was of no Force againſt her Charms. I obſerv'd ſhe perus'd the Letter with Indifferency, which did not diſpleaſe me. Yet I ſo far overcame my growing Paſſion, as to add ſomething to the Excuſe my Brother had wrote. I obſerv'd, in our Converſation, that the propos'd Alliance was not very pleaſing to her; and ſhe at laſt frankly told me, Duty, more than Inclination, would make her comply with it. I told her, were my Brother's Condition mine, and I had been acquainted with her Sentiments, I ſhould not have the Fortitude to ſupport my ill Fortune; yet ſhould have ſo much Regard to her, whatever were my Troubles, not to be oblig'd to Duty, but Inclination.

She told me, with a riſing Bluſh, thoſe Eſpouſals never proſper'd, where the Hand could not beſtow the Heart. I agreed with her Sentiments; but added, I fear'd her Heart was already given, where ſhe could not beſtow her Hand.

Sir, ſaid ſhe, I have ever been a Friend to Plain-dealing, and Truth appears ſo amiable to me, that I neither will, nor can deny it to you. O happy Man, cry'd I, who-e'er thou art! Fortune has ſhed her happieſt Influence on thee, and it is not in her Power to make thee miſerable, when bleſt with ſo much conſenting Beauty.

Sir,

Sir, return'd the Lady, the Person you esteem so happy, is ignorant of my Inclinations for him, and Fear will make me conceal the Secret. And the chief Reason why I disclose it to you, is, that you would inform your Brother; for (added she, with Tears) if I am forc'd to wed him, I shall be for ever miserable. Her Grief touch'd me to the Heart, and she observ'd the Sorrow in my Face. I perceive, said she, the Love you bear your Brother affects your Breast. Madam, said I, since you have made me this frank Declaration, I also will be free, and utter all my Heart. The Grief you see rising in my Face, is owing to the Torments of my Soul. The very Moment I beheld your Charms, Love shot me with his sharpest pointed Dart, and all the Hope I have is cold Despair. She observ'd my Declaration with a great deal of Satisfaction, and remain'd silent some time, viewing me stedfastly: Upon which I cast my Eyes upon the Ground. Sir, said she (with an unconfirm'd Voice) I hope you are sincere in what you say, for the Supposition of it will draw another Secret from me, which is this; The Reason why I cannot love your Brother is, that I have long since given my Heart to—you: The first time I saw your Face, it left its peaceful mansion of Repose, and fled for Shelter to a Stranger's Breast. The Joy I felt at this free Declaration so transported me, that I knew not whether I dreamt or no; but being convinc'd of the Reality, I threw my self at her Feet, and uttered all my Tongue could express, flowing from a sincere Heart. She told me she had resolv'd on Death, before she would consent to wed my Brother: And inform'd me also, that her Passion had been increasing upwards of two Years. The first time she saw me, was taking my leave of my Brothers, when
they

they were going to that Campaign, from which they never return'd. In short, we were as much in Love, as ever any two were.

We agreed to meet the next Day, at the same Place, where I had the Liberty of coming, as her Brother-in-Law that was to be.

I was Impatient for the next Day, imagining Time to have no Wings. But the happy Moment came at last. We talk'd of nothing for several Hours, but our mutual Love; at last we fell on the ungrateful Subject of the approaching Nuptials, and how we should prevent 'em. I propos'd to her, running away, and tying our selves fast by the sacred Bond of Wedlock. Though, said she, I will never be any one's but yours, yet we must consider of Futurity: I know your Fortune is but small, and mine, tho' a large one, depends upon my Father: I'll find some Means to defer the Marriage; you may do your Endeavour to disswade your Brother, for I fancy Fortune more than Beauty has gain'd his Heart. I assur'd her to the contrary, and that he was very much in Love with her. We both wish'd it had been otherways, but resolv'd to love on. We parted, tho' we had not resolv'd on any thing, and appointed to meet the next Day, in a private Corner of the Town, at an Acquaintance of mine, that I could confide in; tho' I would not trust him with the Secret, well knowing a Matter of Importance inslaves the Person that discloses it. I told him I had an Intrigue with a Person of Quality, that I must be obliged to carry on at his House; which he consented to very willingly. We met according to our Appointment, but an Hour before the time prefixt, not willing one should be before the other. She came alone too, for she would not trust any of her Servants. We met

met there every Day; and one time above the reſt, Love being pregnant in both our Eyes, I took the happy Opportunity, and was bleſs'd in the Poſſeſſion of all I wiſh'd on Earth: But Enjoyment was ſo far from palling my Deſires, that it rather encreas'd 'em. We liv'd in all the Delight of Love for a Month, but then came the Bitter to all our Sweets. My Brother arriv'd, and the fatal Day appointed for the Marriage aproach'd. We had given our ſelves up ſo intirely to Love, that we did not think of what was to come; or if the intruding Thought did creep in, we would immediately lull it to Reſt like a froward Child.

When we parted, it was with ſuch a Regret and Sorrow, that foreboded our ill Fortune. The Father of my Miſtreſs had order'd every thing for the Nuptial Solemnity, with the greateſt Magnificence; but two Days before it was to be ſolemniz'd, it was reported all over *Rome* that *Don Antonio Grimaldi*'s only Daughter (who was my Miſtreſs) was taken dangerouſly ill. I was not diſpleas'd at the Rumour, as gueſſing her Deſign. My Brother was never from her, and I was pretty well aſſur'd the Sight of him gave her a great deal of Pain. One Day finding my Brother very melancholy, I ask'd him if it was the Indiſpoſition of *Grimaldi*'s Daughter that occaſion'd the Gloom I obſerved in his Countenance. He reply'd ſhe was the Cauſe of what he felt: He farther added, that he thought her Sickneſs counterfeit, only to avoid him; and that he had many Reaſons to believe ſhe had given her Heart to another. I us'd many Arguments with him to leave her, and that ſhe was not worth his farther Thought. But he aſſur'd me it was not in his Power to hate her. I began to reflect with Reaſon on the Conduct

of

of my Love, and found I had involv'd my self in a very dangerous and troublesome Affair: But notwithstanding all my Reasonings, I found my self more and more in Love; and Absence, which cures a light Passion, added Strength to mine; for I had not seen her in fifteen Days. I was resolved at last to visit her, and took the Opportunity when my Brother was with the *Pope* in his Closet. I found it no Difficulty to gain Admittance, knowing who I was: But notwithstanding all my Endeavours, could not get an Opportunity of speaking to her, there being a great many Visitants. I took an Occasion of feeling her Pulse, and we had the Happiness of moulding our Hands for a Moment. I durst not stay long, for fear my Brother should come while I was there; and yet I had resolv'd to inform him of my Visit, which I did the first time of our Meeting; but added, that it was Curiosity, and to oblige him, that I gave my self that Trouble. He thank'd me, and ask'd me what I thought of her Indisposition. I told him I could not answer for the State of her Heart, but I was assur'd that her Body was in a violent Fever. This I said, a little to undeceive him; for since he could not be persuaded to abandon her, I thought it would be more to our Advantage to make him believe it was a real Indisposition. He went to make her a Visit that Evening, and at his Return told me I had given him true Information, for the Physicians had order'd her to be let Blood, and that she was in a dangerous Fever, and her Father design'd to send her into the Country the next Day. I was mightily pleas'd that he was deceiv'd as well as the Father, and I did not doubt but she had persuaded the Physicians to favour the Deceit.

Accordingly

Accordingly the next Day she was convey'd in a Litter, to a Country House of her Father's, two Leagues from *Rome* upon the River *Tyber*. I flatter'd my self, that her being in the Country would give me a fairer Opportunity of conversing with her: But though I try'd all the Methods imaginable, I could not find the least Glimpse of Hope in above six Weeks time. I was perfectly like a mad Creature, and all my Friends (particularly my Brother) took Notice of my Uneasiness. But I kept the Cause of it intirely to my self.

Any one that's a Judge of Love, and has ever been in my Circumstances, may guess at what I felt. All I cou'd learn of my Mistress was, that she continu'd very ill. My Mind was tortur'd with a thousand Imaginations: Sometimes I thought her false, and that it was her own Desire which kept me from seeing her; at other times I fancy'd she was really indispos'd.

A Month more slip'd away, and I was as unlikely to see her then as at first. One Morning my Brother came into my Chamber, before I was drest. He seem'd over-complaisant to me, and express'd a Concern for the Alteration of my Temper. I fancy (said he) Brother, that Love has forc'd himself into your Breast; and that the Object of your Passion has no Regard to the Torments you endure. I excus'd my self to him, that Love had no concern in my Humour, but rather an inward Indisposition of Body. He said many kind things upon that Occasion, promis'd to assist me all he could, and left me.

Assoon as he was gone, I dress'd my self, and got on Horseback, in order once more to try my Fortune; and I had taken a Resolution to see my Mistress, whatever Hazard I should run.

H When

When I came upon the skirt of a Wood, within half a League of the Place where I was going, I was surrounded by a dozen Men on Horseback, who (notwithstanding the Resistance I made) got me down, bound me, and carry'd me into the Wood. I imagin'd 'em to be Thieves, by their Proceeding; but they never once attempted to take any thing from me, which alter'd my Opinion, and I began to think they had a Design upon my Life.

The State and Uncertainty of my Love made Death look like a Friend.

They kept me in the Wood till the Dusk of the Evening, then clapt me into a Litter, and travell'd hard all Night. The next Morning I was put into a Boat, and hurry'd on board a Vessel that lay a League off at Sea. Assoon as they had receiv'd me, they weighed and set Sail; and the Person that seem'd to have Command in the Boat, prov'd to be the Captain of the Vessel.

They carry'd me bound into his Cabin. When we were alone, he gave me a Paper, which I soon knew to be my Brother's Hand-writing; and in it an open Letter, whose Hand I could not tell by the Direction. Upon this the *Italian* took 'em both out of his Bosom. See, said he, the fatal Scroll, which has robb'd me of all Joy in this Life, and which I have kept during my Captivity.

The first Letter he read was to this Effect.

I *Will not call thee by the Name of Brother; That thou hast basely forfeited. But know, the Hand of Heav'n hangs over thee, to punish thy unfaithful dealing with one, who thinks it the greatest Curse on Earth, that our Parents should be the same. The enclos'd Letter came into my Hands, by the Honesty of her that was commiſſion'd to bring it to thee; who abhorring thy guilty Commerce with her ungrateful Miſtreſs, has diſcover'd thy Scene of Villany. Know, after thou haſt read this, prepare to ſuffer for thy Ingratitude. An Hour's Space is the Length of thy Life, and I think Death too ſmall a Revenge, for the Wrongs thou haſt committed againſt*

Hernando Alvares.

The other was as follows.

To Antonio Alvares.

LIFE of my Life! I have reſolv'd to hazard every thing to let you know the State of my Body and Mind. Though Body, Life, and Heart are entirely thine, yet I fear Death will rob thee of 'em. My counterfeit Illneſs, that Day you ſaw me, (without having the Happineſs of ſpeaking to each other) brought a real Diſtemper upon me, and my Fever took away my Underſtanding. I hope I have not in my Ravings declar'd the Secret of my Soul. The Sight of your Brother retards my Health, and the Hopes I have of my Recovery, is once more to ſee thee, thou Darling of my Heart. I have prevail'd upon one of my Women, with Preſents and Promiſes (whom I hope is honeſt) to deliver this to thee. Our private Meetings, I fear, will prove fatal to me; for I find our Commerce, if I ſurvive, will make me a Mother; but for fear it may touch me more in what thou art to ſuffer, if known to be the Father, Death ſhall releaſe thee from that Danger.

Upon the reading of theſe two Letters, different Paſſions ſwell'd in my Soul. My Heart was torn with Agonies for her I lov'd, and my Breaſt was fir'd with Revenge againſt my unnatural Brother: For as he had ſhook off all Brotherly

therly Love, I thought it was but Justice I should do so too.

I sat a considerable time in the utmost Agony, not for fear of Death; for I must confess, I had not the least Thought about it. The Captain of the Vessel seeing me in that Condition, spoke to me after this manner. Sir, tho' I am well paid by your Brother, to end your Life, yet I have so much Compassion for your Sufferings, (knowing your Crime to be only Love) to mitigate your Sentence, I'll put you into a Boat, with two Men to conduct you, and every thing that shall be necessary: Upon this Condition, that you will give me your Word and Honour, not to appear at *Rome* in forty Days.

I thank'd him for his Kindness, gave him my Word, and told him it was not in fear of Death, but only to disappoint my barbarous Brother. Immediately a Boat was hoisted out, and every thing that was needful for a Month's Voyage. My two Men were paid for the Voyage before-hand, and we left the Ship. I order'd 'em to steer for *Leghorn*, because there I could be furnish'd with every thing that I wanted, from my Sister, who had resided there two Years with her Husband, a Nobleman of *Florence*. But the Wind not proving favourable, we were drove out of our intended Course, and had it not been for a *French* Vessel, bound for *Malta*, who took us up, we had certainly perish'd. And happy for me, had it been my Fate to have had a Wave for my Winding-sheet; for two Days after we were received on Board, a Corsair of *Barbary* met with us, and took us all Prisoners.

I made no extraordinary Appearance, being I was always disguis'd when I went to the House where my Mistress lay indispos'd. *Hamet* (the

Captain Robert Boyle.

(the Name of our *Irish* Renagado) valu'd my Ranſom but at two hundred Pounds. I wrote to both my Siſters ſeveral times, and laid before 'em my unhappy Condition, but never could hear from 'em. So that I either fear'd my Letters had miſcarry'd, or they were willing to forget an unhappy Wretch like my Self. Tho', to ſay Truth, I never receiv'd any hard Uſage from *Hamet*; therefore if the Divine Being will favour us in our Eſcape, I'll faithfully ſend him my Ranſom.

When he had ended his Story, we condol'd with one another, for our Misfortues had a Reſemblance. By this time the Day began to dawn, and *Muſtapha* told us we ſhould reach *Magazan* before Night. We were all mightily overjoy'd, becauſe we expected to be a Day longer in our Voyage. I begg'd the Favour of Mrs. *Villars*, to let me cleanſe her Face from the Ombre; which ſhe conſented to. I was fill'd with Contemplation of her Beauty, but was rous'd from thoſe pleaſing Thoughts, by the Appearance of ſeveral lowring Clouds that ſeem'd to threaten us with a Hurrican, frequent in thoſe Parts; and tho' they ſeldom laſt long, yet they might prove dangerous to our ſmall Veſſel.

Muſtapha advis'd to make to Shore, but I could by no Perſuaſion agree to that, but ordered him to hold on his Courſe for *Magazan*. But the Tempeſt roſe ſo ſuddenly, and ſo violent, that we were oblig'd to leave our ſelves to the Mercy of the Waves; and we did not know which way we drove, for the dark Clouds had almoſt form'd another Night.

Our Boat was a new ſtout Boat, and bore the Weather very well, but it frighten'd Mrs. *Villars* very much; and I had no other Regard but for her. The Tempeſt continu'd for near half the Day, and when it grew Calm, and clear'd up, we were not in Sight of Land. By good Fortune I had provided a Compaſs; and I order'd *Muſtapha* to ſteer due South, the ſame Courſe we kept before the Storm began, which was before the Wind. But tho' we had ſail'd ſeveral Hours South, we could not diſcover any Land. *Muſtapha* adviſ'd us to put to Windward back, for he did not douht but we had over-ſhot *Magazan* in the Storm.

We were preparing to tack about, when we diſcover'd a Sail, within half a League of us; for it was hazy Weather, notwithſtanding the Storm was over, or we ſhould have perceiv'd her time enough to have avoided her. We kept upon a Wind, and it freſhning upon us, our Sail ſplit, and we found it was impoſſible to avoid the Ship, who gain'd upon us every Moment. We thought it our wiſeſt Courſe to lye by, and wait for her. Now all the Hope we had was, that the Veſſel would prove a Ship of *Europe*. I deſir'd Mrs. *Villars* to conceal her Sex, and begg'd the Favour of the *Italian* and *Muſtapha* to keep the Secret. The Ship was near us, and to our ſurprizing Joy, hoiſted *French* Colours. We immediately put on Board, becauſe they lay by on purpoſe.

We were ſoon inform'd Monſieur *Pidau de St. Olon* was on Board, the Ambaſſador from the King of *France* to the Emperor of *Morocco*, to treat of Peace between the two Crowns. I immediately begg'd to be brought to the Ambaſſador's Preſence, who receiv'd us very kindly. I told him all our Stories, but conceal'd that of Mrs. *Villars*, for fear of any Accident. He us'd us very civilly, and promis'd us his Protection. He ſaid his Affair would not detain him long, and he would be ſure to gain ſafe Conduct for us into our own Country. I

I return'd him Thanks for his generous Proffer, and begg'd he would command my Life, to see how readily I would obey him. He told me, since I was willing to oblige him, he would soon put it in my Power to serve him.

I have, said he, lost three of my Retinue in the Voyage, two by Sickness, and one drown'd by Accident. You'll just make up that Number, and you need not take any Care for Habits; I will provide for you. The fourth Person in your Company I believe you'll be satisfy'd should be taken Care of on Board our Ship, for his Landing on the *African* Coast may prove prejudicial to your Affairs. I was mightily pleas'd with his Proposals, and communicated it to Mrs. *Villars* and our *Italian* Gentleman. Mrs. *Villars* told me, she was intirely under my Conduct, and the *Italian* thought he should have a better Opportunity of getting into his own Country from *Mequinez*, than *France*. I would not suffer Monsieur *St. Olon* to cloath us as he propos'd; for I had procur'd of the *Jew* four rich Suits of *European* Cloaths, for a Trifle, which I design'd for Mrs. *Villars*, and my self; for we intended she should put off her *Moorish* Dress, the first Opportunity.

The Ambassador provided a Cabin for Mrs. *Villars* and me; and he seem'd mightily taken with her Youth and Beauty, (as a Boy;) and he would often say, Nature had mistaken her, designing her for the fairest of the softest Sex. These Encomiums made me very uneasy, fearing he should find out the Truth. But I understood afterwards, he had not the least Mistrust.

He treated us very splendidly at Supper, considering we were at Sea. When the Ambassador went to Rest, Mrs. *Villars* and I retir'd to the Cabin allotted us. What a sensible Pleasure did I feel, el, to have the Happiness of her Company alone, without the Fears and Terrors of offending any one! She perceiv'd a Satisfaction in my Countenance, that spoke the Joy of my Heart; and by her Discourse that ensu'd, she was in some Fear, lest a guilty Thought had work'd that Change.

Mr. *Boyle*, (said she) I hope you know what Regard to pay my Sex, and do not wrong the good Opinion I have conceiv'd of you. I own the greatest Obligation to you, and I am not displeas'd I am in your Power, while you use that Power with Moderation. I had hardly the Patience to hear her out. Madam, return'd I, be assur'd, your own Soul shall not be more pure than my Thoughts. But yet, I will take the Freedom to declare, no Person in the World has that Command over me as you have. I must own you have it in your Power to punish me, by slighting a Heart full of the most tender Regard for you; and all I ask, is only leave to hope; if I am deny'd that, the utmost of my Resentments to you, shall only be in hating Life, which will be a Burden not able for me long to bear. It would be base in me, (return'd Mrs. *Villars*) to give Tormens where I am oblig'd; I think to disguise our Thoughts, is an Art better lost, than learnt: And to deal frankly with you, I cannot find in my Heart any Aversion for you; which is a Declaration, if you knew my Temper, ought to satisfie you. I said all the tender things I was capable of, in return for this great Blessing, and our Conversation lasted several Hours. I told her at last, I was well assur'd she wanted Rest; and whatever Pleasure I took in her Company, I would deprive my self of it, and leave her to her Repose.

She seem'd very much concern'd, that I was oblig'd to leave her alone; well knowing I
should

should not get the Convenience of a Place to rest my self.

I told her there was not any Fatigue I would not undergo for her with Pleasure. I left her, and Night soon slipt away in pleasing Imaginations. I was surpriz'd to see her, who was ever in my Thoughts, come out of the Cabin dress'd. Madam, said I to her, I hope you have had nothing to disturb your Sleep. She obligingly answer'd me, Nothing but the Thoughts of your waking; and therefore she desir'd I would go and repose my self in the Cabin, and I think, said she, 'tis my Duty to watch now. I excus'd my self, and told her it was but for one Night more, for in all Probability we should land the next Day, and provide our selves with better Accommodation.

We went into the Cabin together, and our Conversation chiefly center'd on Love. She told me at last, she would leave her Acknowledgments to me, till she was more at Liberty, and in her own Country, for fear I should imagine the Need she had of my Service should make her declare her self in my Favour. When I found so fair a Beginning, I was resolv'd to push my Fortune; till with many Intreaties, Vows, and Oaths of my Fidelity, she own'd to me she had a tender Regard for me when she saw me first, for she was convinc'd of my Love at our first Conversation; not, continu'd she, that I had any Understanding in the Art of Love, but I knew the Hazard you had put your self in to serve me, could have no other Motive but that Passion; and the more I thought of it, the more I found my Heart inclining to believe you.

Those Persons that have felt the soft Passion, may make a Judgment of the Transports I was in at this Declaration. I kiss'd her Hand a thousand

sand times, and press'd it to my Heart. She begg'd me to curb my Transport, for fear of being overheard or observed; for, continu'd she, you may remember, in my Relation of my Misfortunes, how near we were suffering by such an Oversight. This kind Caution bridled my Tongue, but could not command my Eyes; they spoke the Language of my Soul.

Our silent Conversation was disturb'd by the Joy of the Sailors in discovering Land; and we thought it prudent to wait on the Ambassador, and congratulate him upon it. He receiv'd us very kindly, and told us he was pleas'd upon our Accounts, that we might recover on Shore the Fatigue of the Sea and our Captivity. The Captain told us we should come to an Anchor before Dinner in the Port of *Mammora*. I was mightily surpriz'd to find we were got to the South of *Sallee*, and found that the Tempest had drove us back beyond *Sallee* several Leagues. This we still esteem'd a greater Happiness, and if *Mustapha* had not been guided by me, we had miss'd the good Fortune of meeting with the *French* Vessel, and of course made the Port of *Sallee* whether we would or no. Upon this Thought, I began to imagine that *Mustapha*, as understanding the Mathematicks, knew where we were, and consequently had design'd to betray us. I communicated my Thoughts to Monsieur St. *Olon*, and he came into my Sentiments. He immediately call'd the Captain of the Ship, and order'd *Mustapha* to be strictly guarded in his Absence; and if any *Moors* came on Board, to prevent his seeing of them; but desir'd that he might want nothing but his Liberty. When we came to an Anchor, the Captain was sent on Shore to acquaint the *Moors* with the Arrival of an Ambassador from *France*; and presently

sently the Fort saluted him with one and twenty Guns, which was return'd from the Ship Gun for Gun. The Governour of *Mammora* in an Hour's time came on Board attended, who saluted our Ambassador, and begg'd he would have Patience to stay in the Ship, till he had acquainted the Emperor his Master with his Arrival. The Ambassador invited him to an Entertainment; and tho' I observ'd he refus'd Wine, yet he and his Retinue swallow'd the Punch so fast that their Heads prov'd as light as their Heels. When they went on Shore again, the Cannon of the Ship gave 'em a Salvo, which was return'd by the Fort assoon as ever they were landed. The next Day an Order came from the Emperor that we should immediately repair to *Mequinez*, the Place where the Emperor resided.

The next Day the Ambassador set forward with his whole Retinue, among which were Mrs. *Villars*, the *Italian*, and my self, drest richly after the *European* Fashion. We were provided with *Dromedaries* to carry us, all but the Ambassador, who was presented with an *Arabian* Courser. Within a Mile or two of *Mequinez* we perceiv'd the King at the Head of his Army in a great Plain. At first I thought it a Mark of Respect to the Ambassador of *France*; but found it was purely Accident, for our Guide led us out of the Way to avoid 'em.

When we arriv'd at *Mequinez*, we were led to a House belonging to the *French* Consul, or rather a House he had hir'd for that Occasion. Before we were well enter'd the House, a Guard of *Moors* was fixt upon us, and strict Orders given not a Soul should stir out, not even the Ambassador nor Consul. I thought this an odd Proceeding, and sometimes imagin'd it was upon
our

our Account, (as Fear is an expeditious Painter.) But my Timerity vanish'd, when Monsieur St. *Olon* inform'd me, it was the *Moorish* Custom not to let a Foreign Ambassador give or receive Visits till after his first Audience.

Mrs. *Villars* and I had one Apartment alotted us, with but one Bed in it, after the *Moorish* Manner. She told me, she could not bear the Thoughts of my watching every Night, and begg'd I would go to Rest with the *Italian*; but we found he was provided of a Companion, one of the Retinue, and there was no help for it. I always retir'd when my Mistress undress'd herself, and gave her time to go into Bed: I then with a Quilt laid my self down on the Floor, but was far from taking any Repose. The Thoughts of the Woman I lov'd being so near me, naked in Bed, kindled such a Desire in my Breast; and the Pain I took to smother it, perfectly burnt me up. I would have my Readers excuse me, if they are disoblig'd at any Part of my Story, because I am only relating Matters of Fact.

The next Day, when I rose from my boarded Bed, I retir'd to give the Loadstone of my Desires time to dress her self: When I enter'd the Room again, she observ'd my Countenance very attentively, and told me she was griev'd to find in my Features something that spoke a disorder'd Body; which I am sure, said she, is for want of Rest: But, added she, I beg it as a Favour, you will immediately undress your self, and go into Bed, and try to repose your self, and I'll make your Excuse to the Ambassador. I refus'd it a great while, but in short she forc'd me to comply with her Commands. I went to Bed, but new Thoughts again attack'd me, and drove Sleep away. Mrs. *Villars*
had

had retir'd, and ſtaid about an Hour. When ſhe came in again, ſhe ſtole ſoftly for fear of diſturbing me. My Mind was ſo violently agitated, that I really began to be out of Order, and feaveriſh, which ſhe obſerv'd, and came to the Bed-ſide, and with a tender Inquietude ask'd me how I did. I took hold of her Hand, preſs'd it to my Lips, and thank'd her for her kind Care of me. Alas! ſhe cry'd, you are very much indiſpos'd, and I am the Cauſe of it. Upon this the Tears ran down her Cheeks, like Morning Dew on Roſes. Her Tenderneſs gave me all the Joy imaginable; and as ſhe lean'd her Head over me, weeping, I preſs'd her ſoft Lips cloſe to mine, which plung'd my Soul in Ecſtaſies of Joy. She bluſh'd at my Freedom, yet ſtill begg'd I would try to ſleep. I told her it was impoſſible, while ſhe was there; upon this ſhe was going to retire in haſte, but I caught her by the ſoft Hand, and told her if ſhe went out it would be a greater Impoſſibility for me to reſt. She conjur'd me by that Love I profeſs'd, (if it was not a Falſhood) to declare to her the Torments of my Mind. She inſiſted ſo much upon't, that I told her the Secret of my Heart. She fell upon her Knees, and begg'd I would not mention it any more, for ſhe own'd her ſelf ſo much oblig'd to me, there was not any thing in her Power ſhe could refuſe me, but that. I begg'd her Pardon, and had reſolv'd to ſuffer Death ſooner than to have diſcloſ'd my Malady; but I would be ever ſilent upon that Theme, till ſhe commanded me to ſpeak. My dear *Boyle*, ſaid ſhe, (I am not aſham'd to call you ſo) ſtay till we arrive in *England*, and I here vow to make you mine, whenever you ſhall command me. Upon ſaying this ſhe join'd her Lips to mine, not
conſidering

considering that in endeavouring to suppress my Flame, she pour'd Oyl upon it, and made it burn the fiercer. I told her, true Love was above nice Formality, and that Marriages were made in Heaven. Said she, I hope they are, but beg by both our Loves to drop this Theme. I told her I would, tho' Death should follow. I remain'd silent for some time, while Tears stopt her Speech. We were interrupted by a Messenger from the Ambassador, who came to invite us to Dinner, (for he always did us the Favour of dining at his Table.) I begg'd to be excus'd, for I found my self a little indispos'd. The Messenger had not been gone a Moment before the Ambassador came in to enquire after my Health, and brought his Physician with him, who feeling my Pulse, told him I was in a Fever, but Bleeding he did not doubt would give me Ease. I told him I should be better in the Morning, if not, I would take his Advice. The Ambassador would have Mr. *Villars*, (as we had nam'd her) to Dinner with him, who had endeavour'd to compose her self while they had been in the Room. As she was going from me, she squeez'd my Hand, and said, Endeavour to compose your self to Rest, and you'll soon be better.

They retir'd and left me to my own Thoughts, which were various and disjointed. Mrs. *Villars* did not stay long; she came in softly as before, expecting that I might have been asleep. When she found I was in the same Disorder, she burst into Tears, and cry'd, Will nothing satisfy you but my Undoing? No Madam, said I, I will fight with my Desires, and am resolv'd to conquer or die. She staid with me till Supper, and our whole Discourse was upon the Passion of Love. When she came back from Supper,

Supper, I had got up and had dreſt my ſelf; but the Combat in my Mind had really diſorder'd my Body, which ſhe ſoon ſaw: She begg'd I would go to Bed again, and ſhe would watch me. I told her, the World ſhould not prevail upon me to break her Reſt; nor even ſhe her ſelf, who was more to me than the World. I had ſat me down upon the Bed, and Mrs. *Villars* came and ſat down by me. We remain'd ſilent a conſiderable time: at laſt ſhe took my Hands in hers, and preſs'd me by the Fingers.

Mr. *Boyle*, ſaid ſhe, I have overcome my ſelf: I cannot ſee you in this Torture of Body and Mind, and not contribute to your Eaſe. Here ſolemnly ſwear to be my Husband, and do with me what you pleaſe: I hope you are a Man of Honour, and that's what I rely upon. Nothing in this World could have tranſported me ſo much as thoſe few Words did: I fell upon my Knees, kiſs'd her Hands, and did I know not what! Madam, ſaid I, you have made me the happieſt Man the World contains; and if I thought my Heart and Tongue did not agree in what I am going to ſay, I would pull 'em both out this Moment. When I had ſaid this, I fell on my Knees, and made this ſhort Vow. *Thou God that know'ſt the Heart of Man; I do beſeech Thee puniſh me with Eternity of Torments, if ever I prove falſe to this Darling of my Soul, who before Thee I take (as the greateſt Bleſſing) to be my lawful Wife.* And here I ſwear (ſaid ſhe, kneeling) *to take no other to my Bed and Heart; and with this Kiſs*, ſaid ſhe, *I ſeal the ſacred Union*. I told her nothing could be more binding, and the Prieſt could but confirm what we had done already.

Now the tender Moment was approaching to crown my Joys with all I wiſh'd on Earth,

Kings on their Thrones to me seem'd poor and base, and I'd not have chang'd to be the Monarch of the Universe. I begg'd my dear Bride I might be her Bride-maid as well as Husband, and that she would give me leave to undress her. Said she, My Love, my Life, my Husband, I am to obey you in every thing that's in my Power, and when I fail in my Obedience, may I be miserable in the Loss of you. I was too eager to say any thing in Return, but I undress'd her, put her to Bed, and you may be sure I did not stay long behind. The Veil of Night was drawn round us, and I plung'd into a Sea of Pleasures, too delicate for Words to express.

The next Day, the Ambassador saw Contentment in both our Faces, and congratulated me for the Recovery of my Health. Never was there so tender a Wife; and the longer I had the Happiness of Enjoyment, the more my Love was rais'd. The next Day, the Ambassador was to have his first Audience, and we were all to be in Readiness by Seven in the Morning. I got up early, and dress'd my dear Wife in a new Suit of Clothes, on purpose for this Occasion. The Governour of *Alcassar*, *Hamet addo Riffy*, was to be our Master of the Ceremonies, who attended us with several *Moors* of Quality, and a Troop of the King's Blacks, as Guards. We set forward about eight a-clock, in this Order. 1. Twelve of the *Moor* Guards. 2. Several of the Nobility, two by two. 3. The Ambassador, with *Hamet addo Riffy* on his Right Hand, preceded by two Trumpets and Kettle-Drums, (the Post of Honour is on the Left among *Moors*, because you have the Command of their Sword.) 4. Twenty-four Gentlemen of the Ambassador's Train, two

two by two. 5. Twelve *French* Slaves that carry'd the Presents. 6. Twelve more of the Guards: And the Order was clos'd by a *Moorish* Mob, that abus'd us with their Tongues all they could; nay some of them attempted to throw Stones, but were bastinado'd by the Guards. We were all on Foot, though the King's Palace was a Mile from the Place where we set out.

I was mightily concern'd at the Fatigue my dear Wife underwent, for it was violent hot; tho' we had the best on't, for going next the Ambassador (who order'd we should do so) we had some Shelter from the Umbrella that was carried over his Head.

We enter'd the Palace through the Marble Gate, (so call'd from two Marble Pillars that adorn it) and from thence, immur'd with white Walls and black Guards on each Side, we arriv'd at a stately Pavilion; where a Halt was commanded 'till the King was acquainted with our Arrival. We waited some Time, but at last saw him coming, mounted on a white Horse, through one of the Avenues that led to the Pavilion. His Guards (who had lin'd that Passage on each Side) bow'd down to the Ground as he pass'd along. He made but a very indifferent Appearance. Assoon as he came to the Portico, he gave a Launce that he bore to one of his Guard, got from his Horse, and squatted down upon the Floor without any thing under him. He had nothing in his Dress to be distinguish'd from the rest of his Subjects, but was muffled up to the Eyes with a Chocolate-colour Handkerchief, that did not seem over clean. His Legs and Arms were bare: As to his Age, he seem'd to be about Fifty; of a very tawny Complexion, and very lean; his Hair black, inclining to grey; of a middle Stature,

I with

with hollow Cheeks, and Eyes black, a small hook'd Nose, and thick Lips. Some of his Courtiers sat down on each Side of him, bare-legg'd and bare-headed; and behind him stood a Black with a great Fan in his Hand, not only to cool him, but to keep off the Muskito's, a small Fly, very troublesome in most Parts of *A-frica*.

Mahumet ben Addo Otar, his chief Minister and Favourite, was the only Person that stood.

Assoon as the Emperor had squatted down on the Floor, he repeated these Words in *Arabic* three times, *Tay buon*, which is as much as to say, *You are welcome*; a common Expression when they are address'd to by a Foreigner. Then our Ambassador made a long Speech in *French*, prepar'd for that Purpose; which was only a Panegyric upon both Kings, fulsome enough; but the *French* deal much in wordy Compliments. The Interpreter, when the Ambassador had done, read the same in *Arabic* to the Emperor. The Speech was very long in *French* and *Arabic*, but the Emperor heard it out patiently, which was reckon'd a good Omen; he also excus'd himself that he did not admit him sooner to his Audience, it being their *Ramadan*, or *Easter*. When the Compliments were over, the Ambassador presented all his Retinue to the Emperor, but I observ'd he took a particular Notice of my Wife, and ey'd her several times, which gave me a great deal of Uneasiness; for it is as dangerous to be a handsome Man as a handsome Woman in *Morocco*, if the Brute of an Emperor should have a Fancy for 'em.

I long'd to have an end of our Audience.

After we were presented, the Ambassador order'd his Presents to be open'd and spread before the

the Emperor; which confisted of fine Arms made at *Paris*, feveral *Englifh* Watches and Cloth, two *Perfian* Carpets, and two Pieces of Gold and Silver Brocade. The Emperor, in return, gave the Ambaffador four young Slaves, three of 'em *French*, (tho' he took 'em all for the fame Nation) but the other was an *Englifhman*, and the fame Perfon I mentioned in the Beginning of this Relation, who went in the fame Boat on Board of the *Succefs*. I was very much confounded at feeing him, well knowing he was on Board when I fell out of the Ship. I long'd for an Opportunity to confer with him, tho' I could not perceive by his Looks that he knew me; but that might be from my Change of Habit, and the Sun's tarnifhing my Complexion.

The Emperor rofe, (when he had given the Slaves) mounted, and rode off; and we went home in the fame Order as we came there; only the chief Minifter, *Mahumet ben Addo Otar*, accompany'd the Ambaffador as far as the Marble Gate. I inform'd my dear Wife, when we came to our Lodging, the Anxiety I was in when the Emperor ey'd her: She told me fhe had made the fame Obfervation with much Uneafinefs; for, faid fhe, I had not the Prefence of Mind, upon the Inftant, to imagine my felf a Man. However, we both wifh'd our felves on Board, and the Embaffy well over, and then we might make ourfelves merry with our Fears.

The next Day our Fears were much encreas'd; for hearing a Noife in the Street, we went to look out to know the Reafon, and difcover'd *Hamet*, our *Irifh* Renegado, with feveral Prifoners manacled. We foon retir'd again, but learnt by other People, that they were going to the Emperor, that he might make his Choice. The Sight

Sight of him renew'd our Fears, as I said, and we resolv'd immediately to get Leave to go on Board, for fear of some unlucky Turn of Fortune.

I upon the Instant went to wait on the Ambassador, and declar'd to him what I had seen, begging Leave at the same time we might be suffer'd to go on Board. He told me he would comply with my Request for Mr. *Villars* and the *Italian*, but begg'd it as a Favour that I would stay with him, for he should have great need of my Assistance; and if any thing should fall out, he would engage for my Liberty. Though the Request cut me to the Heart, yet it was neither Prudence nor good Manners to refuse him. I gave him my Promise to obey his Commands, but begg'd he would not insist upon my going abroad but as seldom as possible. I went to my Wife, (my Readers, perhaps, may smile at my calling her *Wife*, but I will assure 'em we thought our selves as much marry'd, as if the Parson had executed his holy Function; nevertheless we did not intend to neglect that Ceremony the very first Opportunity) and told her the Ambassador's Request, and my Promise. She agreed with me in the Reasonableness of it, but yet could not forbear shedding Floods of Tears at our (we hop'd) short Separation. The next Day was design'd for their Journey; but the ensuing Night was spent with Sighs, Tears, and a Lowness of Spirit that look'd ominous. Yet we parted; and for several Hours I could not bring my Mind to any peaceable Form to wait on the Ambassador: But he sent for me at last, and told me the Reason of his desiring me to continue with him was this:———

The King his Master had commanded him to make some Observation of the Customs and Manners

Captain Robert Boyle.

Manners of this Part of *Africa*; and, added he, I have observed in you a Capacity fit to assist me in the Design. I told him he might command me in any thing that lay in my Power, and that I took it for an Honour he would think me worth his Employment.

We had Notice the next Day from the Person that attended my Wife with the Camels, that he saw them safe on board, which gave me some Comfort. I begg'd the Ambassador to give me Leave to speak a Word or two with one of the Slaves that the Emperor gave him. He order'd him to come before him, where I desir'd he would tell 'me how he came into the Hands of the *Moors*. He was prodigiously surpriz'd to see me there, and could hardly believe his Eyes; for it was thought by every Body that I had either been kill'd or drown'd; as indeed it was very improbable to think otherwise. He inform'd us, that three Days after the *Success* parted with the *Spanish* Man of War, another *Algerine* Rover met with them, and took 'em after an obstinate Fight; the Captain and several others being slain in the Battle. It was his good Fortune to be bought for the Emperor's Use; I call it good Fortune, said he, because I was presented to the *French* Ambassador, and am now in Hopes of my Freedom.

I told the Ambassador in *French* what he said; and he was pleas'd to say, that to oblige me he would take him into his Protection. I remember'd *Mahumet ben Addo Otar* was Ambassador in *England*; He came to visit the Ambassador often, and understanding *English*, I gather'd several good Hints for his Design; for he was courteous enough, though an Enemy in his Heart to the *English*.

I 3   I

I think it will not be much amiss here to give the Reader a succinct Account of the Customs and Manners of the *Moors* of *Fez* and *Morocco*; and we will first begin from their last Revolution.

Muley Ismael, the present Emperor of *Morocco*, pretends to derive his Birth from *Mahomet* himself. He was Son to *Muley Xerif*, King of *Taphilet*, but was succeeded by *Muley Archyd*, who dy'd with a Debauch he made among his Courtiers.

His unexpected Death in 1672 gave room for many of his Family to raise Rebellion in their several Provinces: But *Muley Ismael* being the greatest Favourite of the People, and of an enterprising Temper, proclaim'd himself King of *Taphilet*, and seiz'd his Brother's Treasures, which are the Sinews of War. His Nephew, *Muley Hamet*, gave him the most Trouble; for he had gain'd a Party, and declar'd himself King of *Sus* and *Morocco*, had several Battels, but at last was overcome as well as the rest, and *Ismael* was settled the peaceful King of *Taphilet*, *Morocco*, and *Fez*. I have given a Description of his Person already. His Empire spreads from North to South four hundred Leagues, from East to West upwards of a hundred and fifty.

There are three strong Places possess'd by the *Europeans* on the Coast of *Afric*. First *Magazan* on the Ocean, by the *Portuguese*; and on the *Mediterranean*, *Melissa* and *Ceuta* by the *Spaniards*. They had two more strong Holds, *Larache*, and *Mammora*; but the present Emperor drove them out shamefully. And *Tangier* once belong'd to the *English*, who abandon'd it a few Years ago, first demolishing the Fortifications.

The

The Emperor has but nine Sea-Ports in his whole Dominions, viz. *Sancta Cruz, Safy, Sallee, Mammora, Larache, Arzilla,* and *Tangier,* on the *Afric* Ocean; *Zaffarina* and *Tetuan* on the *Mediterranean*; though *Tetuan* is two Leagues within Land. To begin in Order as they are nam'd; *Sancta Cruz* (or the *Holy Cross*) is the first Port to the Southward. The Town is about a Mile in Length, and a Quarter broad. The chief Merchants are *Jews,* who trade with *England* and *Holland.* Their Vent is Hides, Dates, Copper, and Bees-wax.

Safy, or *Sophia,* appears next, a Town situated on a Hill; but drives a larger Trade than *Sancta Cruz.*

Sallee, situated 35 Leagues S. W. of *Cape Spartel.* It is divided into two Towns, the old and the new; (it is called by the Natives *Arbat.*) There's a very good Harbour, and a strong Castle well stor'd with Guns, if the *Moors* knew how to make use of them. The Town is large, and well inhabited, but the Walls are all demolish'd. I observ'd the Ruins of a Church, the Steeple yet standing, a noble fine *Gothic* Building. The chief Trade of this Town consists in the Prizes that are brought in by their Gallies.

About seven Leagues more to the North stands *Mammora,* once possessed by the *Spaniards.* It stands in a Bottom surrounded with Mountains, which renders the Air very unwholsome, by reason of the excessive Heat; but the Bay is fine, large, and secure from all Winds. This Town is generally the high Road to *Mequinez,* the present Capital of *Morocco.*

The next Port Northward is *Larache,* a Town of a pleasant Situation, and strongly fortified; but, to the eternal Infamy of the *Spaniards,* deliver'd liver'd up to *Ismael* after a Siege of five Moons; two thousand Soldiers and a hundred Officers taken Prisoners: a sufficient Force to have defended it against the whole Powers of *Muley Ismael*, for they neither wanted Provisions nor Ammunition. But we shall leave them and their Cowardice, and go on to

Arzilla, or *Azilath*, about twelve Leagues more North. A Place only fam'd for Tobacco, which they seldom trade abroad for, having sufficient Vent for it among the Natives of *Morocco*; and as we have but little Business with it, we'll come to

Tangier as fast as we can, a fine, large, well-fortified City, when in the Hands of the *English*; but since they have left it, and raz'd the Fortifications, the *Moors* have not thought fit to repair it.

The next, *Zaffarina*, is a Place of very little Note, and therefore we shall make no Observation concerning it.

The last is *Tetuan*, a Town six Miles within Land, without any Fortification. The Inhabitants came originally from the Province of *Andalusia* in *Spain*, as indeed did most of the *Moors* on the Sea-Coasts of *Africa*. They are white Men, pretty well civiliz'd, very kind to Strangers and Christians, and pay but little Regard to the Emperor of *Morocco*.

As to the Nature of the Inhabitants, they are most of a tawny Complexion, of a lazy, idle Disposition, and curs'd with all the Vices of Mankind; mistrustful to the last Degree, false, jealous, and the very Picture of Ignorance. They style themselves *Mussulmen*, or true Believers, yet their Word is not to be rely'd upon on any Occasion. The *Moors* are generally but indifferent Soldiers, and but seldom brave. They are often fam'd in the *Spanish* Histories for Men of Gallantry, but I could never find them inclin'd that way. They manage a Horse, it must be confest, with a great deal of Dexterity. They abominate the Christians, for the very Word signifies in their Language, *Dog*; and are continually seeking Means to destroy them. *Mahomet* has taught 'em in his *Alcoran*, that all of his Faith who dye fighting against the Christians, immediately enter into Paradise in Triumph; nay, even their Horses, if they die in Battle, are immediately translated into Heaven; for they hope to have the Pleasure of Riding there, as well as on Earth.

Though Poligamy is allow'd, yet they must marry but four Wives, and must settle a Dowry upon them; and if they ever put 'em away, they must return their Dowry along with 'em: But they may keep as many Concubines as they think fit; tho' they have this Privilege, when they can please 'em no longer, they sell 'em to the best Bidder; so that the Women of *Morocco*, in my Opinion, have but a sad Time on't: yet the Husband is oblig'd to keep all their Children. They esteem Ideots and Naturals to be Saints, if they are Men; for they believe the Women have no Souls, and are only form'd for Propagation. They will not allow 'em to enter their Mosques, because they esteem 'em uncapable of being receiv'd into Heaven: Yet they say their Prayers at home, and on *Fridays* resort to the Places of Burial, to weep over the Graves of their deceas'd Friends, cloath'd in Blue, which is their Mourning. They hire profess'd Mourners to grieve and cry at the Graves of Relations, and howl over them, as I have heard the *Irish*; asking them why they would die when they were provided with every thing that was

necessary

necessary in this World. Their Time is spent in Eating, Drinking, Sleeping, Dallying with their Women, Horses, and Prayers (for they never learn to read, and are forbid Gaming) and even their Prayers are hurried over so slothfully, as if they were asleep.

They have usually a String of Beads in their Hands, like the *Roman Catholicks*; and to every Bead they have a short Prayer, which as they repeat, they drop through their Fingers. The Prayer consists only in the different Attributes of God, as, *God is great, God is good, God is infinite, God is merciful*. The Emperor of these Wretches only differs from his Subjects in a larger Propensity to their ill Qualities, with the Addition of a degree of Cruelty and Avarice. I was told, that during his twenty Years Reign he had murder'd with his own Hands twenty three thousand Men: Nay I am apt to believe the Truth of it, for he put forty seven to Death in the one and twenty Days we were at his Court.

Every Nation is amaz'd to find his Subjects so submissive and patient under so excessive and cruel a Tyranny: But they should understand (bating their Want of Power) that they are taught to believe, if they fall by the Hand of a King who is a *Xerif*, (which signifies *Mahomet*'s Successor) they immediately go up to Heaven; and if there is any that would not willingly be sent to Heaven before their Time, they are sure to fly him when he is cloath'd in Yellow, which is his Colour of Murder; and he generally dyes it of a Blood-colour before he goes to Sleep.

As I was viewing some new Buildings one Day, near the King's Palace, I perceiv'd him giving Directions to some of the Workmen. There were several Carts drove by his Slaves with

with Materials for his Building; and as they pafs'd him, he baftinado'd fome for going too faft, while others, thinking to mend that Fault, were drubb'd by him for going too flow; one poor Creature, trembling for fear of what would follow, went bowing before his Cart; but the Emperor wounding the Horfe in the Flank, he gave a Spring, tumbled the Wretch down, and drove over him. Another following him, ran to affift his Fellow, but the Emperor threw his Dart, and ftruck him in the Shoulder. The Slave drew it out, and upon his Knees prefented it to him again, which the Emperor (when the Man had got fome Diftance from him) darted into his Chine. The Fool drew it out once more, and, cover'd with Blood, gave it to him back again; but as he was ftooping, he fell down with lofs of Blood at the Barbarian's Feet, who did him the Favour to pin him to the Earth through his Back.

I was fo fhock'd at the Sight, that I could not recover my felf for a good while afterwards. I thought the poor Fellow was a Fool; for if it had been my own Cafe, I would have return'd it through his Body the firft Time, for he was fure of Dying, and I think it would have been fome Satisfaction to have fent the Author of my Death the fame Journey.

This King us'd to murder his Slaves upon the leaft Complaint from the *Moors,* which they would make out of hatred to Chriftians. But the Wretch finding his Slaves decreafe too much, took another Method; and when the next Complaint was made, he killed the Slave, the Perfon complain'd againft, but order'd the Complainant immediately to pay him double the Price he coft him, or find him two more Slaves in his Room that Inftant, which he was oblig'd to do; but

this

this Proceeding ſtopt their Mouths for the future.

They ſay he has a great deal of Wit and Courage, is very active, and expert in riding, and hurling the Dart. He drinks no Wine, becauſe his Religion forbids it: but when he takes Opium, or drinks a certain Mixture that he makes himſelf, compounded with Brandy, Cinamon, Cloves, Anniſeed, and Nutmegs, woe be to him that comes in his Way. He's much addicted to Women, having no leſs than four hundred Concubines. He has one hundred and eighteen Male Children alive, and about two hundred Females. One of the Males whom he deſigns for his Succeſſor, (and which he had by a Black, who adviſes him in every thing, and is reckon'd a politic Woman) he has named *Muley Zeyden*. His Revenue conſiſts in Preſents from the Governors of his Provinces, and the *Arabians* who live in Huts about his Dominions. When he has a mind to ſqueeze, he ſends for a Governor from his Province, who knows well enough what he is ſent to for, and therefore provides accordingly; ſo that the Emperor fleeces the Governors, and they fleece the People. So that there is no one rich but himſelf, and yet he does not know what Uſe to put his Treaſure to, but hides it in ſecret Places; and the Perſon that aſſiſts him in the Concealment is ſure to loſe his Life for his Aſſiſtance.

Mequinez, the Capital, and the Place of his Reſidence, was formerly but a ſmall Village, but now it contains ſix hundred thouſand Inhabitants, and the Streets are ſo crowded, there's hardly any paſſing along. It is but a mean City, very ill built; and, if there falls any Rain, the dirtieſt Place I ever ſet my Foot in; for there is no Pavement in the Streets; and when it is dry the Duſt is ready to choak one. The King's Palace

Palace is indeed a very large Place, almoſt four Miles round, including his Gardens; but it is very ill contriv'd. Here you ſhall ſee a fine Pillar added to ſupport an old ruinated Place, and yet he employs moſt of his Time in Building. In ſhort, it looks like gold Lace upon a Hop-ſack.

His Stables are the moſt regular Building in all his Palace. But that's no wonder, for the *Moors* even reverence Horſes; and one that has been a Pilgrimage to *Mecca*, has as much Veneration as the Pilgrim himſelf. The King had one of theſe Horſes, which I have ſeen always finely caparifon'd, and a Slave to attend, who carry'd a Pot and a Cloth to keep him Clean. All the Horſes that are thus ſanctify'd are uſually freed from all manner of Service, and if the Owner cannot afford to keep it, which often happens, there is a Penſion ſettled upon 'em by the *Mufty*.

The *Jews* drive a great Trade here, but they pay ſufficiently for that Privilege; for they are oblig'd to wear black Caps, that they may be diſtinguiſh'd; and notwithſtanding their great Trade, they are but ſcurvily us'd, for if a Child inſults 'em, it is as much as their Lives are worth to reſiſt.

The Women of *Morocco*, I mean all that I had the Fortune to ſee, were very handſome, fine large full Eyes, round Faces, and every Feature exact. They are very amorous, and dexterous in contriving Methods to ſatisfie their Deſires.

A Gentleman of our Retinue told me, he had got an Intrigue with one of the *Mooriſh* Women, Daughter to a Governor of a Province; and his manner of going to the Appointment was in Diſguiſe. She ſent him by a *French* Slave of hers a complete Woman's Dreſs, which are

generally

generally all alike; and their Faces are all muffled up to their Eyes, so that they are often met by their own Husbands in the Street, without being known; by this Dress he got Admittance as a Lady coming to pay a Visit, and then they are very secure. For it is the Custom, whenever a Man, even the Husband, finds a pair of Women's Sandals, at the Door of his Wife's Chamber, he must retire; for it is the greatest Affront they can put on a Woman, to enter her Apartment when they have that Warning to the contrary. He told me she was a delicious Creature, and Mistress of the whole Art of Love. It is no wonder if they give themselves up to Love, when perhaps there are twenty, or more, (according to the Capacity of the Person that keeps 'em) Sharers in one single Man; and they must be contented to stay for due Benevolence, till their Tyrant pleases to send for 'em.

The Habit of the Men is generally White, (which is a Colour they extreamly delight in) with a red Cap on their Heads; that is the married Men; for all the Youth, from the Prince to the Beggar, before Wedlock, go uncover'd. They are close shav'd under their Caps, excepting one Lock upon the Crown of their Heads, which they never cut off; being they are taught, by that Lock, *Mahomet* is to draw 'em up to their imaginary Paradise. They only shave under their Chins, but suffer their Beards and Mustachoes to grow, which they take a particular Pride in the Length or Largeness of; and he that's well bearded, *must* be a wise Man.

Their Shirts are made like Shifts, only the Sleeves are so long that they hang down over their Hands. Under the Shirt they were linen Drawers, that reach down to their Knees, for their Legs are always bare; their Shoes are made
without

without Heels, like *Irish* Brogues. Over the Shirt is a Vest without Sleeves, which they surround with a silk Scarf, of what Colour they please (except Green, which is a Colour sacred to *Mahomet*, their Emperor, and the Clergy;) in this they thrust short Daggers, or Knives. Over all, is a Garment, which they call a *Hayick*, about five Ells long, and four broad, which they wrap round 'em, as we do our Cloaks. Some of the meaner Sort, especially in the Country, wear Straw-hats of their own Make. Their Dresses are all a-like, only some add a gold or silver Fringe round the Border.

As for Religion, they rise early and late to Prayers; but only like Children, do it because they are order'd. Their *Mufti*, or Head of their Religion, is reckon'd the first in the Empire, and disowns the Emperor's Authority; but yet he finds means to fleece him, as well as the rest of his Subjects, who obey him out of Fear; for if there was one Person found to love him, it would be as strange a Sight as one of their Monsters.

I could not forbear smiling to see the Providence of the *Moors*. Walking one Day about a Mile from *Mequinez*, it began to rain prodigiously; I got under a Tree to shelter my self from the Tempest. But I observ'd several of the Natives undress themselves with a great deal of Precipitation, make up their Cloaths in a Bundle, and sit on 'em stark naked; and all their Care was to keep 'em from the Wet, leaving their naked Bodies expos'd to the Fury of the Storm. When it ceas'd, they walk'd a little Way till their Bodies were dry, and then dress'd themselves. If a Man were to do so in *England*, he would be counted a Madman, or a Fool, yet I must own I thought 'em in the right; for be the Storm ever so violent,

lent, yet when it's over, they purfue their Journey with dry Cloaths on their Backs. But they have one Conveniency, they are dreft and undreft in half a Minute. Nay, I am inform'd, thofe that travel on Camels, or on Horfeback, have a Conveniency cover'd with an oyl'd Cloth, in which they thruft their Cloaths on the like Occafion, and ride naked. I fancy, to meet an Army in a Storm would create a terrible Fright, and do as much Execution to an Ignorant Body, as their offenfive Arms, and force 'em to feek for Safety in their Heels.

The Emperor is able to raife an hundred thoufand Horfe, and fifty thoufand Foot. When they are to make War among themfelves, they go very unwillingly into the Field; but when they oppofe the Chriftians, they do it with a great deal of Chearfulnefs; becaufe they expect Indulgences for the Expiation of their Sins. When they are ready to give Battle, they range their Armies after this Manner. They divide their Horfe into two Bodies, and place one at each Wing, the Foot is in the Middle, fo that the whole forms a Crefcent or half Moon. Before they begin the Battle, they give a great Shout, then make a fhort Prayer, and fall on without much Order very furioufly; fo that they foon overcome, or are as foon put to flight. Break but their foremoft Ranks, and you put their whole Body into Confufion.

I have faid before, that no Perfon is rich but the Emperor; neither do they take the Methods to be fo; or if they are, their greateft Wifdom will be to conceal it; for if once known, they are fure to lofe all their Wealth.

No Foreign Coin is currant in *Morocco*, except *Spanifh* Pieces of Eight, which are only receiv'd by Weight. But the *Jews* will fecretly take

take any Coin, and I suppose dispose of it again with the same Circumspection they receive it. They have but three sorts of Coin currant among 'em. The first a *Ducat*, of *Barbary* Gold. Second a *Blanquile*, of *Silver*. And last a *Felowze*, of Copper. The Image of the Emperor is not allow'd to be put on their Money, being expresly forbid by *Mahomet*, in his *Alcoran*; but they stamp 'em with *Arabian* Characters. Their way of reckoning is by the Ounce.

These are the Heads of what I observ'd in my small Stay among 'em. The Ambassador inform'd me, he was in some fear that his Embassy would not succeed; for he said, he found little else but Delays, Excuses, and nothing of Sincerity among 'em. We were inform'd, that the Emperor design'd to go speedily upon an Expedition against the *Moors* of the Province of *Oran*, who had newly revolted, and put to Death their Governor for his Avarice; he having extorted from 'em vast Sums of Money; and the Inhabitants after his Death, chose one of their own Province to command 'em. This hasten'd our Ambassador in his Legation, to get an Answer one way or other. But we were inform'd, the King design'd to set out the next Day upon his Expedition, and yet the Ambassador had not his Audience of Leave. This made him, and us, very uneasy; for we could not stir from *Mequinez*, without the Emperor's express Leave. But about seven in the Evening, the Ambassador had Orders to come and take his last Audience, which was the ninth of *June* 1693: We went in the same Manner, as we did at first. But we were inform'd by our Interpreter, that the King was in a very ill Humour, and that he had but an Hour before kill'd two of his chief Blacks,

K by

by stabbing 'em with a Dagger he continually wore at his Girdle.

We enter'd the Palace further than the first Time, where we waited a full half Hour. At last the Emperor approach'd richly drest, and finely mounted upon a white *Barbary*; the Saddle and other Accoutrements wrought with Gold and precious Stones in several Places. He was this Day in his Yellow, or Fatal Vest, and sprinkled in many Places with the Blood of those he had slain; and I thought his Countenance had something more of Horror in't, than at our first Audience. He had a Spear in his Hand, set round with Pearls on the Top, and a Cap with Estriches Feathers waving in the Wind. All his Attendants had fled his Presence, at the Notice of his having on his yellow Vest; and he had only about a dozen of his Guards waiting upon him trembling, but the *Alcaydes* and other great Men crept about us during our Audience.

The Emperor begun with his old Compliment of *You're wellcome*, but his Looks and his Words I thought did but ill agree. The Ambassador us'd many Arguments with him to bring his Embassy to a happy Issue, but to no Purpose. The Ambassador told me, the King was a Person that had not the least Regard to his Word, and even disown'd a Letter he had written to his Master the King of *France*. Therefore, said he, we'll take our leave of this Country of Monsters in two Days: for the King had sign'd his Departure, with all his Retinue.

I was very well pleas'd with this his Resolution; for now I should once more see that Treasure of my Soul, whose Absence had robb'd me of all Joy. I even thought these two Days the longest

longest of my Life; but at last they were past, and we set out very merrily; at least I did, and all the rest of the Retinue. Tho' I must own I could not answer for the Ambassador, for I believe the ill Success of his Embassy had a little chagrin'd him. I did my utmost Endeavour to divert his Melancholy upon the Road, which he took very kindly. We lay in Tents the first Night, which the Ambassador had taken care to provide us, and Provision likewise; for there is never an Inn between *Mequinez* and *Mammora*.

We rose the next Day very early, that we might avoid the Heat of the Sun. When we came within a League of the Town, we saw coming towards us our *Italian*, and by the Melancholy in his Looks, I began to tremble with Apprehension of some Accident. Assoon as he approach'd us, after paying his Obedience to the Ambassador, he address'd himself to me. Said he, in *French*,

I wish some one else would have taken my Commission upon 'em, for what I have to tell you will cut you to the Heart. The various Troubles in my Breast lock'd up my Tongue, so that I had not Power to ask him any Questions. In short, said he, your Mistress is forc'd away from us, through the Treachery of *Mustapha*. At hearing this fatal News, I drop'd senseless from my *Camel*, nor came to my self till we arriv'd at *Mammora*. I was a thousand times going to destroy my self; and I believe I had done it in the height of my Despair, if I had not been withheld. In short, the Ambassador was no longer ignorant of my cruel Loss: For in my Ravings, I had call'd her my dear Wife. He seem'd amaz'd at the Discovery, and reproach'd me in a handsome Manner, for not trusting him with the Secret. I was not in a

Condition to beg his Pardon, neither was there any one could give me Comfort. I was carry'd on Board, where I enquir'd in what manner she was taken away.

The Captain inform'd us, that *Muſtapha* had made his Eſcape out of the Cabin Window, by ſwimming. I did not tell any one of it, ſaid the Captain, becauſe I thought it would be to no Purpoſe; for I imagin'd there could be no other ill Conſequence to attend his Eſcape, but meerly the Loſs of him. He had been gone three Days, when on the fourth there came on board us the Governor of *Mammora*, the Fugitive *Muſtapha*, and one hundred Soldiers, who immediately ſeiz'd on the young Gentleman, whom they ſaid was a Woman, and Wife to a Renegado of *Sallee*. It was in vain to oppoſe 'em, eſpecially when I found by her Breaſts, that ſhe was really a Woman. They took her on Shore, notwithſtanding all her Cries, Shrieks and Lamentations, which pierc'd our very Hearts. They put her on board a *Saick*, and ſet Sail immediately, ſteering South, as we ſuppoſe for the Port of *Sallee*. This Gentleman, (meaning the *Italian*) took it upon him to acquaint you with the unhappy Accident; but, added he, I believe it is not poſſible to regain her. The Ambaſſador was ſo good as to offer his Aſſiſtance, in what lay in his Power. I begg'd he would be pleas'd to lend me a Boat, with ſome Hands to work her. He very willingly granted my Requeſt; and told me, he would lend me the Ship, but he fear'd it might occaſion a more publick Quarrel.

He lent me ten Hands, four Patareros, and ſufficient ſmall Arms, with every thing that was neceſſary. My kind *Italian* would accompany me, and the reſt of the Company went Voluntary. We ſpent but little time in fitting out;
and

and the Wind proving favourable, we set Sail, and made very good Way. The *Saick* had not pursu'd her Voyage above five Hours before us, so that we had hopes of getting up with 'em. I encourag'd my Companions, who labour'd incessantly. We sail'd and row'd all Night, and when the Morning dawn'd, we gain'd Sight of a Vessel, which we did not doubt was that we sought for. We labour'd hard to come up with her, and gain'd upon her every Moment. Before eight a-clock we came a long side of her, and I soon discover'd *Mustapha* giving Orders about the Engagement. I drew out a pair of Pistols, and shot him dead. The rest fir'd upon us, but notwithstanding all their Opposition, I jump'd into their Vessel, follow'd by the *Italian* and five more of the Men: And tho' they were superior in Number, yet we soon made 'em ask for Quarter. I upon the Instant enquir'd for her that was always in my Thoughts; but, to my great Grief, was inform'd by an *English* Slave at the Oar, that she was taken on board of a Galley by Captain *Hamet*, our *Irish* Renegado; and they assured me, it was impossible for 'em to be overtaken. Unspeakable was the Sorrow I felt, at this Relation; and all the Satisfaction I felt was, that I had rewarded *Mustapha* for his Treachery. We steer'd our Course back, but I was more dead than alive in the Voyage.

When we came on Board, the Ambassador condol'd with me for my Misfortune, and entreated me to take Comfort. I told him Death was now my only Comfort, and I hop'd he was not far off.

Our *Italian* had agreed for his Passage on board a Vessel in the Bay, bound for *Rome*: He begg'd that I would accompany him into *Italy*; and when he had settled his Affairs, he would (if it lay in his Power) come back to

Sallee, and do his Endeavour to find what was become of Mrs. *Villars*. I thank'd him for his Offer, and told him I would accept of it. I had Effects enough, having all the Money and Jewels we brought from *Hamet*'s Country-House. We took leave of the Ambassador, and gave him abundance of Thanks for his Civilities, and went on board the Vessel that waited for us; we set Sail immediately, and in two Months safely arriv'd at *Rome*; where our *Italian* did not care to go publickly on Shore, but stay'd till the Darkness of the Night favour'd our Landing.

We had all our Goods disembark'd, and took a Private Lodging in an obscure Part of the City, where we were sure of being conceal'd. We ask'd our Landlord, (who was a *Frenchman*) about the News of the Place. He told us a great deal of idle stuff, which signify'd nothing to us; at last, by the Advice of the *Italian*, I enquir'd of him, if *Hernando Alvares* were in Town, or no? He answer'd me, that he had been dead above two Months, and had left a noble Estate behind him. I ask'd him if he had not left a Wife to possess it. No, said he.

About three Years ago (continu'd our Landlord) he was to have been marry'd to a beautiful young Lady, an Heiress to a vast Fortune; but his Brother stept in between, and gain'd her Affection. Some say they were marry'd, and others not; but she was deliver'd of a fine Boy. Don *Hernando* took a barbarous Revenge of his Brother, as it is reported: He brib'd a Captain of a Vessel to put a Weight about his Neck, and drown him in the Sea. But to make amends for this inhuman Act, he has left his vast Estate to the Son his Brother had by the Lady, and has chosen his Holiness the *Pope* for his Guardian. Pray, said I, what's become of the young Lady? He answer'd me he

could

could not tell; but it is suppos'd she was gone into a Nunnery.

The *Italian*, while our Discourse lasted, had turn'd his Face to the Window, that we might not perceive the Disorder of his Countenance. Assoon as our Landlord was gone, he turn'd to me, and embrac'd me; said he, My dear Friend, let what will happen to me, I shall have it in my Power to serve you with my Fortune; and so much I think my self obliged to you, that if half will buy your Mistress's Liberty, you shall command it. I return'd him the Acknowledgments his kind Proffer deserv'd, but told him, I could not expect to be so happy. He bid me not despair. I begg'd he would not mention any thing of my Affairs, till his own came to a lucky Issue.

The next Day, we procur'd our selves Habits after the Mode of *Rome*, and resolv'd to go to *Grimaldi*'s Country-House, to hear, if it were possible, some Tidings of *Isabella*.

Antonio had drest himself in a mean Habit, and appear'd as my Servant. It being but six pleasant Miles, we had resolv'd to walk it. We enter'd a Village within half a Mile of the Place, and resolv'd to dine at a poor Inn, there to gain some Intelligence. I went for a *French* Merchant, and Don *Antonio* pass'd (as I said) for my Servant, and Interpreter, and inform'd me of the Discourse that past between 'em. That Gentleman, (meaning me) says he to our Host, has some Business to communicate to Don *Antonio Grimaldi*, (for we knew of his being there). Our Innkeeper told us, it would be a difficult Matter to talk to him about Business now, for he was that very Evening going to set out with his Daughter, in order to put her into a Nunnery at *Naples*; for all his Persuasions (added he) cannot prevail upon her, but she is fixt unalterably in her Resolution: This News, you may be sure, hasten'd our Departure; but we did not well know how to disclose the Secret we had to unfold.

Don *Antonio*, as not doubting *Isabella*'s Affection to him, was fearful lest an abrupt Discovery should have some strange Effect upon her: We therefore resolv'd, that I should first appear and break the Matter by degrees; for he had inform'd me that she spoke *French* very well. When we approach'd the House, *Antonio* stood at some Distance, while I went up to the Door alone. The Porter and I not understanding one another, I had like to have return'd as wise as I came. But at last a Servant in the Family happening to understand *French*, came and ended our sputt'ring at one another. I inform'd him I had a Secret of the greatest Importance to declare to *Donna Isabella*. He told me he would acquaint his Lord with it. The Servant went in, and immediately return'd with a grave old Gentleman, that seem'd to have been weeping. He ask'd me in *French* what I had to say to his Daughter, for she did not care to speak to any one. I begg'd that I might be brought to her Presence, and did not doubt but that I had something to say to her which would not displease her. Don *Antonio Grimaldi* gravely smill'd, and shook his Head; No, no, Sir, said he; you have nothing to give either her or me Comfort, unless you could revive the Dead. I answered him, he did not know what I could do. But I told him, the longer he delay'd my seeing her, the longer he deferr'd their own Happiness. Well, said he, I have no Hopes; but you shall see my Daughter, to convince you that nothing in this World can make us Happy.

He

He led me through several stately Apartments all hung with Black. And though it was high Noon, yet the Sun's Light was excluded, and dim twinkling Lamps usurp'd his Room. At last we enter'd a Chamber, where sat the fair Forlorn. I stop'd a Moment to behold her, and notwithstanding a fixt Melancholy on her Countenance, Beauty triumph'd there. She was caressing an Infant she had in her Arms. The Father enter'd first, and told her in *French*, that a Gentleman of *France* had a Secret to communicate to her, that would banish her Melancholy. The Gentleman (return'd the Lady) may promise Impossibilities, but rather than expose him, I would beg him not to open his Mouth upon that Subject. Madam, said I, I own my self a Physician, but I pretend to cure the Mind as well as the Body; and to acquaint you with what you know already, you mourn the Loss of a Gentleman, that you imagine was drown'd at Sea: But I can assure you he escap'd that Danger, and is now a Captive in *Barbary*, pining under the severest Want; and all the Hope he has of Freedom, is through your Means.

The Lady upon this look'd wishfully upon her Father, and said, Dear Father, don't endeavour to deceive me any longer; you know I have your Promise, and my Time's expir'd. My dear Child, I am amaz'd as much as you can be, return'd the Father; for by all that's Holy, I never saw this Gentleman in my Life before, and am so far from believing him, that (begging his Pardon) I fancy there must be some very great Mistake in't. Upon this I related to them all his Story, from the beginning, to our meeting in *Barbary*.

I found my Relation had stagger'd her Faith a little, for a pleasing Hope, rectify'd by powerful Fear, rose in her beautiful Face; and she threw her self at my Feet, notwithstanding all my Endeavours to the contrary. Dear Sir, said she, do not show me this light of Comfort, to put it out, and plunge me into eternal Darkness. Madam, said I, by Heaven, and heavenly Powers, I have seen him within these two Months, and what I have related to you, his own Mouth inform'd me; and having gain'd my Liberty, I made him a Promise to see his Friends in *Italy*, and inform them of his Condition. The Transports and Ecstasies that took Possession of both their Souls cannot be express'd by Words; they embrac'd me, kiss'd me, call'd me their Preserver. Unlook'd-for Happiness! (said *Isabella*) Heaven, thou hast heard my Prayers! and does my dear *Antonio* live! I'll immediately imbark for *Barbary*, and fetch him thence my self: Even all that I am worth, my precious Boy shall sell his Fortune too, to redeem his Father. O my young *Antonio*, Heaven has restor'd thy Father from the Dead, (said she to her Child) and I hope we shall see him again. The pretty Innocent mingled his Tears of Joy with theirs. After their first Transports were over, they again embrac'd me, and begg'd I would put 'em in a way to pay me the Obligations they ow'd me. Then they proceeded to enquire which way they must go about to accomplish his Liberty. I told 'em, I had a Servant waiting without, that I intended should accompany the Persons they would send to manage the Affair. They seem'd to reproach me for letting him wait without, and were immediately sending for him in. I begg'd they would give me leave to go for him my self, being he was a Foreigner, and they would find it a hard matter to make him understand them. Upon this I ran out, and call'd to *Antonio*, and told

told him in few Words how things stood. He follow'd me close at the Heels: I went into the Room first, and as *Antonio Grimaldi* was giving him his Hand to lead him in, he fell upon his Knees before him. *Isabella* casting her Eyes upon him, gave a Shriek, and cry'd out, 'Tis he! 'tis he himself! my dear *Antonio!* Joy took away her Speech, and she fell down in a Trance. He ran and caught her in his Arms, kiss'd and embrac'd her, and at last brought her to herself. Imagination must make up the Discourse between 'em. He told her at last, when Words of Sense took Place, that he was obliged to me for his Liberty; for he had sent several Letters to his Sisters, but never could get any Answer. They inform'd him, that both his Sisters were gone to reside at *Venice* with their Husbands, and that was the Reason his Letters never came to their Hands. Now, said *Antonio*, if my Friend (meaning me) was but happy, it would compleat my Joy. But to find a Wife, a Son, and Father kind, when I had many Reasons to think the contrary, must have some Alloy, or it would not be possible for me to bear it.

Antonio upon this related my unhappy Story, and they all lamented my hard Fortune. He afterwards enquir'd of his dear *Isabella* concerning her own Sufferings. Which she readily began.

Said she, that Day you left me, the Troubles of my Mind wrought so much upon my Body, that the Physicians declar'd I was in a violent Fever, and advis'd my Father to send me into the Country, which he accordingly did the next Day. The Thoughts of being so far from my dear *Antonio* encreas'd my Malady, and my Father had little Hopes of my Life. My Fever, after having brought me to the brink of the Grave, left me: And my Father imagining it was

the

the approaching Marriage had wrought this sudden Illness, told me one Day, that if it was that which lay so heavy upon my Spirits, he would remove it, by giving me the Power of refusing to be the Wife of *Hernando Alvarez*. I thank'd him, and told him he had taken the only way to restore my Health; and that if I was forc'd to wed him, I should be for ever miserable. He was the tenderest of Fathers, and inform'd me he would never force my Inclinations. The Kindness my Father shew'd me work'd so much upon me, that I began to recover.

Your Brother us'd often to visit me in my Illness, which retarded my Health. My Father seeing it would never be in my Power to like him, very frankly told him so, and begg'd that he would discontinue his Visits; for he was resolv'd his Daughter should never give her Hand, where it was not in her Power to give her Heart. They parted with many Words between them, but my Father persisted in his Resolution.

I began to discover that I was with Child, and a new Sort of an Illness seiz'd me. I knew this was an Accident that could not long be conceal'd, therefore I resolv'd to let you know my Condition; and I gain'd my Woman, by several Promises of a Reward, to deliver a Letter to you: But she betray'd me to your Brother, which I suspected from her not appearing. I therefore declar'd the Truth to my indulgent Father. He was very much enrag'd at the Discovery; but paternal Love prevailing over his Passion, he forgave me, and promis'd to make me happy with my dear *Antonio*. These Promises made my Sickness vanish, and I had no other Disease but what attends breeding Women. My Father went to *Rome* to enquire for *Don Antonio*, but could not get the least Information

of

of him. This gave me a new Shock. But what bitter Agonies did I feel, when I receiv'd a Letter from your Brother, with a Copy of that I had written to you enclos'd; which was as follows.

UNgrateful *Woman!* *Yet I will no more upbraid thee, but let thy Crime be thy Punishment. He that betray'd me I will not call by the Name of Brother: He has paid for his Ingratitude with his Life. I only give thee this Notice, that thou may'st feel some of those Pangs thou hast thrust into the Breast of*
Hernando Alvarès.

The Reading of this Letter sunk me down, and I call'd for Death, as my last and only Hope. I resolv'd to refuse all Food, and had starv'd my self to Death, if a good Priest had not convinc'd me by his Arguments my Soul was in Danger, and I should be guilty of a double Murder, my self, and Infant. I lingred on in a restless State of Unhappiness, till the Time of my Delivery came, which I pray'd to Heaven to end with my Life: But it pleas'd the Almighty Power to spare me to be happy.

The Sight of my precious Infant call'd to Mind the Loss of his Father; but I resolv'd to banish all Thoughts of Death, that I might take Care of his tender Years. But I begg'd my Father to give me leave to go into a Nunnery. With much Importunity he granted my Request, on this Condition, that if I continued in that Mind at the End of two Years, I might do as I thought fit. Tho' I thought the Time an Age, yet I unwillingly consented.

My Father us'd Means with the *Pope,* to have your Brother call'd to an Account for
your

your Death; and it had gone hard with him, if we could have procur'd any Witnesses; but for Want of that he was acquitted. In a little time a heavy and deep Melancholy seiz'd him; and he 'profess'd so sincere a Repentance, that even I almost forgave him. He begg'd he might see the Child; which my Father made me comply with. He shed such abundance of Tears over it, that my Father wept for Company; and spoke so tenderly of the Loss of his Brother, that wip'd off all Suspicions of his Repentance. Since thou hast lost a Father, said he, through my Barbarity, it is but just that I should prove a Father to thee. He frequently came to see him, though I could never be prevail'd upon to accept of a Visit. At last his Grief seiz'd him so violently, that he was given over by his Physicians. When he was upon his Death-Bed, he made his Will, and bequeath'd my little *Antonio* his whole Estate; leaving the Pope his Guardian. He dy'd full of Repentance for his Crime, and no doubt his Soul took her Flight to Heaven.

The generous *Antonio* could not refuse some Tears to the Memory of his repentant Brother; but Joy succeeded Sorrow. The *Pope* was acquainted with the Story, who sent to congratulate their happy Meeting. Nothing but Mirth and Pleasure ran through the *Villa*; which increas'd my Sorrow.

Don *Antonio* told me one Day, that he did not think he had a Right to rejoice without me; and now, said he, I have nothing to afflict me but what you feel, therefore will bend my Thoughts if it be possible to relieve your Grief. I can procure a Fryar of my Acquaintance to go to *Sallee*, one that knows the Nature of the Business we shall send him about, being he has

often

often gone to redeem Captives: We'll send for him, and you may give him what Instructions you think fit. I thank'd him, and was very sorry for the Trouble I should give him, but was resolv'd to accompany him my self. He told me he would not have me go by any means, for I could be of no manner of Use in the Affair, but rather a Hindrance; and if I should be once discover'd, might fall into the same State we both lately escap'd from; and perhaps meet with much worse Usage than I had before. His Advice was so reasonable, that I resolv'd to take it, whatever Violence I did my self. The Fryar was sent for, had his Commission and Instructions given him, and withal to spare no Cost. *Antonio* told him whatever he gave should not be thought unreasonable.

He was to have a thousand Crowns for his Expences, and two thousand more if he succeeded.

The Fryar undertook his Voyage with a great deal of Alacrity, and gave us great Hopes of his Success by his Willingness; and he embark'd the next Day for *Genoa*, that Port being the properest Place to get a Vessel for *Barbary*. We wish'd him a good Voyage, and recommended him to Fortune.

Don *Antonio* did all he could to divert my Melancholy: We often went a hunting, shooting, fishing, and visiting the Ladies. In short, he made me partake in all the Diversions *Italy* could afford. But though I seem'd often to be diverted, yet I had always my Condition too much at Heart to be merry. We view'd all the Rarities and Antiquities of ancient and modern *Rome*. I must confess, these Amusements lull'd my Sorrows often, but when I had Time for Reflection they rush'd upon me with the greater Force.

I shall not trouble my Reader in describing Places treated on by Pens far above my weak Capacity; but only give a short Description of *Naples*, whither *Don Antonio* would have me go. I was not much averse to the Journey, though a pretty long one; and we set out with a very handsom Equipage. *Donna Isabella*, with her little Son, accompany'd us; but *Don Antonio Grimaldi* was oblig'd to attend the *Pope*, to settle the Affairs of his Son-in-law's Estate. I was oblig'd to appear chearful, if it was but in Complaisance to *Don Antonio*.

We arriv'd at *Naples* in three Days, without meeting any thing extraordinary upon the Road. Certainly, never any City in the World can boast a finer Situation: Add to that, their Buildings are sumptuous, every private House seems a Palace, and every Palace looks like the Court of a King: The Streets spacious; a mild Air and free from Tempests; strong, both by Art and Nature. In short, if I was obliged to live out of my native Country, (which every Man is fond of) *Naples* should be the only Place. It has a Wall kept in very good Repair, with three Castles almost impregnable. The chief is seated on Mount *Erasmus*, so call'd from a Chappel dedicated to him: But if it is *Erasmus Roterdamus*, I can't imagine how the *Roman Catholicks* came to have such a particular Regard for him, when it is very well known he was no great Friend to them; at least he was a Scourge to their Absurdities in his Writings.

This is not only a Safeguard to the City and adjacent Country, but might prove its Scourge. In 1587 it was blown up by Lightning, penetrating to the Powder Room, which mightily damag'd the whole City. The second is *Castello nuevo*, or the new Castle, built by *Charles*, King of *Naples*. This Castle commands the Haven, and is generally the Viceroy's Dwelling. The third stands on the South-east Corner of the City, built upon a little Rock, join'd to the Continent by *Lucullus* the *Roman*, and is sometimes call'd by his Name, but oftner *Castello del Ovo*, or the Castle of the Egg, from its Form. They have also a fine Arsenal for their Gallies, very well kept, and furnish'd with great Store of Ammunition. But I think the Mole the most extraordinary Piece of Work, being it defends the Haven from the stormy South; lin'd of each Side, and pav'd on the Top with noble square Stones, and in the middle a fine large Fountain of Marble; the whole Extent is five hundred Paces, and ten in Breadth. The Inhabitants often boast of the Antiquity of their City, founded twenty years after *Troy*'s Destruction, and call'd by the antient Poets *Parthenope*, which *Virgil* does sufficiently testify in his *Georgics*,

Ille Virgilium me Tempore dulcis alebat
Parthenope, *studiis florentem ignobilis oti.*

This City has suffer'd many Revolutions, but none more extraordinary than that in 1640, when a poor Fisherman, without Shoes to his Feet, in five Days time commanded the whole Power of *Naples*; and might have liv'd in that Grandeur, if his Mind had chang'd with his exalted State; but he was still a Fisherman. His short-liv'd Fire blaz'd too fierce to last, and he fell a Victim to the Rage he himself began.

Their Churches are noble Structures, and beautify'd with Paintings by the best Hands. Their Women are most of 'em beautiful, but my Heart had no Room to think of them.

The City is govern'd by very wholesom Laws, but one particular Article adds much to the Quiet of it; none are suffer'd to wear Swords but those of the Garrisons; so if there's any Rencounter in the Streets, a Bout at Fifty-Cuffs generally ends the Dispute: Tho' Bravo's are to be hir'd to do a Murder here as cheap as at *Rome*, and Men of Honour too; for we heard of a Quarrel between two *Neapolitan* Gentlemen, where one, according to Custom, hir'd a Bravo to murder the other, and gave him his Reward beforehand. But it so fell out, that some Friends to both Parties reconcil'd the two Gentlemen. The Person that had bargain'd with the Bravo for the Job, sent to him, and told him of their Reconcilement, but that he might keep the Money. The other told him it was not in his Power to return it him, but he was above receiving Money without doing his Work, and therefore the Gentleman must of necessity suffer Death. He intreated him, and us'd many Arguments, but all to no purpose. When he found nothing would prevail, he told him he would immediately acquaint the Gentleman with his Design, which he did accordingly. Notwithstanding, the Bravo the same Evening found his Opportunity, and left the other Gentleman for dead upon the *Mole*; tho' he recover'd after a lingring Illness. But the Bravo had the Impudence to go to the other (when he found the Gentleman was in a fair way of Recovery) and told him he begg'd his Pardon that he had not been as good as his Word, but he would take Care and mend his Hand very quickly. In short, he was found so resolute in the Matter, that the Gentleman was oblig'd to hire another of the same Trade to give him

him a Cast of his Office, and dispatch the Bravo before he could execute what was design'd; and the next Day he was found dead at the very Door of the Gentleman's House he had intended to assassinate; waiting, as it was suppos'd, for an Opportunity to do his Business.

After we had view'd every thing within the City, we went to see the much fam'd-*Vesuvius*, or the burning Mountain, a League and a half East of the City. The *Neapolitans* call it the Bed-chamber of the Sun, because he appears to them first from the Top of that Mountain. Round the Bottom of it is the richest Spot of Ground in the Universe, I'll not except even the Mines of *Potosi*; for the yearly Vintage produces twelve hundred thousand Ducats. The Middle of the Hill is very pleasantly shaded with Chesnut, and several other Fruit Trees. The Mountain has a double Top; that to the North terminates in a Plain finely cultivated: The other towards the South, which is the *Volcano*, rises much higher.

When we had gain'd the Summit, we descended gradually into its Bowels, by large Steps cut on purpose. It has, in Times past, done much Damage to the Country round it, by its sudden Eruptions; but now it forebodes nothing but Rain, when the Top is envelop'd with Clouds.

When we had sufficiently satisfy'd our Curiosities at *Naples*, we took a Tour to *Putzol*, or *Pofuolo*, through a Hollow of a Rock, a Mile in Length, and no other Light but what came in at both Ends, and one in the Middle from the Top of the Rock. This subterraneous Passage is pav'd with Stone all through, and the narrowest Part of it is ten Yards over. About the Middle is a small Chappel dedicated to the Virgin

gin *Mary*. We visited all the Rarities of the Place, particularly *Virgil*'s Tomb, which is almost cover'd with Ivy. They told me of a Laurel Tree that sprouted naturally out of it, but (not to take from that incomparable Man, whose Works are ever-living Laurels) I could not see any such thing. We also view'd the Lake *Agnano*, so call'd from the multitude of Serpents or Snakes that fall into it from the pendent Mountains. The Water is of two different Qualities; that tasted upon the Surface is sweet or fresh, but that taken deeper is of a brackish Taste, suppos'd from some Minerals that inviron it.

On the South Side of the Lake stands a natural Stove, which is call'd St. *German's Stove*; but we had not Curiosity enough to enter it, nor Faith enough to believe a ridiculous Fable that is told concerning it, (tho' it is reported a Saint declar'd it for a Truth) which I shall put down here, and leave my Reader to judge of it himself. St. *German* was advis'd to repair to this Stove, to cure him of a dangerous Malady: When he came there, he found the Soul of a very pious Man that he knew, tormented with the Heat of the Place. St. *German*, as understanding the Language of Souls, ask'd him how so good a Man as he was in his Life-time, came to be condemn'd to such a severe Punishment. The Soul very civilly answer'd him, that it was for siding with *Laurentius*, who oppos'd *Symacus* in the Popedom; but he was convinc'd that his Prayers would fetch him out of that Hot-house. St. *German* pray'd heartily, you may be sure, and got the Soul of the Man from out thence; but where it went after, no one could tell. But the Place was call'd ever after St. *German's Stove*.

To the East of the bordering Mountain is a Place they call the Cave of Death; for whatever Thing of Life ventures to the farther End, they say immediately drops down dead: Tho' a Person that liv'd in a neighbouring Village ventur'd in often for a Reward. When he came out again he was all of a Sweat, and hardly able to stand for five or six Minutes. When he had recover'd himself, he took a Dog out of a Bag he had brought with him, and by the means of a wooden Instrument made for that Purpose, thrust him in to the very End, and drew him out dead to all Appearance. When he had remain'd some time for us to view him, he took him up by the fore Legs, and threw him into the Lake *Agnano*; where he recover'd immediately, swam out, and ran away from us. Don *Antonio* told me it was a hard matter to get a Dog there; for assoon as ever they saw a Stranger, they would run away into the Woods, and sneak home again when they were gone; which was the Reason the Person that went in, always secures one for the Occasion.

A Mile farther we went to the Court of *Vulcan*; a Place unpleasant enough, continually smoaking, and such hot Vapours arise from the Pores of the Earth that it almost overcame me. In some Places Water bubbles out of the Cavities; and if we threw a Stone into it, it rebounded back as if you had struck it against a Pavement. But the Place is reckon'd to cure a great many Distempers; especially to make Women pregnant, and to cure Diseases of the Head and Eyes. *Donna Isabella* was carry'd over it in a Sedan; but I believe she did not want it upon the score of Barrenness, as you may understand in her Story.

We spent six Weeks in this not unpleasing Entertainment, and *Don Antonio* being pretty well satiated as well as my self, we went back again to *Rome*.

And now my Melancholy gain'd such Ground upon me, that it was not in the Power of Dissimulation to hide it. *Don Antonio* and all the Family express'd a great deal of Trouble for my Sorrow; and I am well assur'd there was not any thing in their Power they would have refus'd, to have given me Quiet: But the Mind's Disease baffles the Physician's Art. At last a Letter arriv'd from the Fryar, which gave us no other Account, but that he was safe return'd to *Genoa*, and intended to embark for *Rome* in a few Days. This lame Account quite dishearten'd me, for now we had not the least Hope, being we all agreed if he had succeeded he would have been forward enough to have acquainted us with it. The Knowledge of this cast me quite down, and my Body was forc'd to submit to the Troubles of my Mind. A strong Fever seiz'd me, and brought me to the Brink of the Grave: And tho' I wish'd for Death, yet, like common Friends, he fled from me in my Necessity.

Don Antonio and his Lady seldom went from my Bed-side, and had I been a Brother to 'em they could not have regarded me more. But Nature, in spight of my Misfortunes, prevail'd, and I gather'd Strength even against my Will. They had inform'd me in my Illness (by my Importunity) of the Fryar's Arrival, and that he had not succeeded in his Negotiation: But yet they had not told me all the Particulars. I desir'd the Fryar might be sent for, and conceal nothing from me of what had past. Accordingly he came, and gave me the following Relation.

lation. Sir, said he in *French*, assoon as I arriv'd at *Sallee*, I met with *Hamet* the *Irish* Renegado. He receiv'd me at first after a bruitish manner, but when I declar'd I came to pay him his Demand for one of his Slaves that had made his Escape, he began to be less sour in his Treatment. He said a great many handsom things concerning *Don Antonio*; but when I began to mention you, he fell into a violent Rage, and vented bitter Reproaches against you; saying you were a vile Impostor, had basely deceiv'd and robb'd him doubly, of his Mistress and his Money. I told him I came to ransom the Lady, and pay for whatever Damages you had done. As for the Lady, said he, she's Food for Fishes long ago; for rather than she would submit to me, she threw her self overboard, (before we had gain'd the Port, when I had taken her out of a *Saick* one of my Slaves had brought her in from *Mammora*) and, in spight of our Endeavours to the contrary, sunk for ever to the Bottom. And is she gone! said I: O Proof of virtuous Love! Happy had I been to have embrac'd the same Fate!

The Relation of this killing Disaster took away my Senses for some time; but when I had recover'd, he went on. I had some Hope at first that this was only a Fiction of his own; but I found in the Town that it was no Secret, and every body declar'd that it was Truth. A Jew confirm'd me in't, whom you had bought several Things of for your Voyage. He told me that *Hamet* arriv'd without any Woman with him; for he saw him land in a very ill Humour, and had complain'd of him for assisting you, to his Superiour at *Mequinez*, and he receiv'd a sufficient Check from him. I was too well convinc'd of the Truth, and therefore hasten'd hasten'd my Departure, and am very sorry I could not succeed; but it was not in Fate, and I hope you will calmly submit to the Will of Heaven, who sends these Afflictions for Tryals.

The good Friar gave me a great many wholsome Admonitions: But I was not in a State much to observe 'em. I now began to be carelefs of the World, because there was nothing in't (since the Death of my dear Wife) worth my Notice. I had no Thoughts of returning to *England*, tho' I had Opportunities enough; but took a Resolution of going to some remote Part of the World; imagining, the farther I was from my native Country, I should be the further remov'd from my Anxiety. But alas! Sorrow is too constant a Companion, and there's no parting with it, but by Death.

I begg'd Don *Antonio*, if he heard of any Ship bound for a long Voyage, he would acquaint me with it, which he promis'd me to do, (after finding Persuasion had no Effect on me.) Two Months pass'd away, and no news of a Ship; when I began to be very uneasy, and told *Antonio*, I would e'en make a Voyage to *Genoa*, where I could not well fail of a Vessel. When he found nothing could stay me, he ask'd me to what Part of the World I would chuse to go? I told him I did not much care where. Why then, said he, if you please, my Father, and I will fit you out a Ship of what Burden you think fit, either for War or Traffick. I thank'd him, and told him I would have it for both, if he pleas'd, and I would be their *Supra-Cargo*, if they thought fit to give me so great a Trust. In short, a Ship of two hundred and fifty Ton was bought of an *English* Merchant at *Naples*; a stout new Vessel, that mounted six and twenty Brass Guns, and we mann'd her with a hundred Hands, most
English;

Captain Robert Boyle.

English; who understanding I intended for the South Sea, were glad of the Opportunity. Don *Antonio* took care to provide every thing necessary for Traffick; and I was made Captain, and *Supra-Cargo*. I told him, I hop'd I should in a few Years bring him a good Account of his Lading. He obligingly answer'd me, that he hop'd I would come Home reconcil'd to my self, and he should think himself very happy. The worst of it was, we had no Commission, neither would I suffer *Antonio* to procure me one: For we resolv'd, like *Englishmen*, to fight only with the Enemies of our Country.

I christen'd my Ship the *Isabella*, out of Respect to *Antonio*'s Lady, and hoisted *English* Colours on Board. When the Day came I was to go on Board, there were Tears shed on both Sides. I could not, without some Regret, part with so good a Friend as *Antonio* had prov'd to me; and I am very well convinc'd that they were as sincere in their Sorrow,

We set Sail from *Ostia*, (where our Ship lay ever since she came from *Naples*) the second of *March* 1692, with Intention to steer our nearest Course for *America*. Our Ship prov'd an excellent Sailor; and we made the *Streights* Mouth in twelve Days from our first Departure. When I beheld the Coast of *Africa*, it brought fresh to my Memory past Transactions; and I long'd for an Opportunity to be reveng'd on the *Moors*. The next Day our Men discover'd two Sail bearing down the Wind upon us. We thought our selves too well provided to run away; tho' we kept on our Course; and perceiving but one of 'em that follow'd us, I ask'd my Men if they were willing to speak with that Vessel, and they cry'd one and all, they would with all their Hearts. We prepar'd for an Engagement with

all

all the Expedition imaginable, for fear she might prove of *Barbary*. We hoisted our *English* Colours, and they did the same. When we found that, we lay by, that we might be inform'd of the News in *England*. But assoon as ever they came a-long Side of us, they pluck'd down their *English* Colours, and hoisted those of *Morocco* in their Room; calling to us to surrender that Instant, or it should be worse for us. We were a little surpriz'd at first in being disappointed; but notwithstanding this, my Men desir'd I would begin the Fight. We had not open'd our Ports yet, and I order'd my Men not to do it till I gave 'em the Word. I sent a Man to busy himself about the Halliards of our Ancient, that the *Rover* might imagine we were going to strike. We were well provided with small Arms, and all manner of warlike Stores. I order'd every Man to their Posts, but not to appear till they heard a Whistle; upon which they should open their Ports, and fire both great Guns and small Arms. The *Rover* thought us long in striking our Colours; he therefore call'd out to us again, and told us if we did not strike that Instant, they would pour a Broad-side into us. Just upon that, I blew my Whistle; my Men obey'd my Orders punctually, they burst open our Ports, thrust out their Guns, and gave 'em a Broadside, with a Discharge of their small Arms. This put 'em in much Confusion, as not expecting any Opposition, and I am certain we kill'd a great many of their Men; for imagining we should be their Prize without fighting, they had crouded upon Deck all their Hands.

I had tack'd about, and given her another Salute, before they return'd us the Favour. But they were not long backward, but pour'd in upon us very fast. My Men did their Business very

very well, and the Fight continu'd half an Hour with the utmost Fury. I began to fancy we should have but dry Meat (as the Sailors say) and looking upon their Quarter-Deck, I soon spy'd the Renegado *Hamet* giving Directions. At the Sight of him I was both surpriz'd, and pleas'd; but my Soul was fill'd with an unusual Fury. We were so near, that I could hear every Word he said, tho' I could not understand him, because he spoke in the *Moorish* Tongue. As we were tacking about, and charging again, I shew'd my self to him: I told him he was the only Man in the World that I hated; and that very Day he should be in my Power, or I in his, or Death should put an End to both our Lives. He seem'd surpriz'd, but gave me a great deal of abusive Language. I encourag'd my Men, and desir'd 'em to fight bravely; for if we fell into their Hands, we should have no Mercy. I had fir'd my Piece at Random before, that is, at the first Person I saw; but now I levell'd all at *Hamet*, and he the same at me. At last I had the good Fortune to fetch him down. At this Sight I could not forbear giving a Shout of Joy, which so affected those that were near me, and understood the Business, that they fought like so many Furies; and after an obstinate Fight of two Hours, they struck to us. We gave God Thanks for our Victory; and I immediately went on Board 'em, where we had made a terrible Slaughter, they having lost by their own Account ninety seven Men.

I ask'd some of the Men, what Ship that was which stood aloof from the Engagement; and they inform'd me it was a Prize they had taken a few Days before, laden with Wine and other Commodities. I then thought of a Stratagem to get her into my Power. I order'd our Ship to
strike

strike her Colours, and then we hoisted those of the *Moors*, and took our Ship in Tow. When the Prize saw us in that Posture, she imagin'd the *Moor* had conquer'd, and made all the Sail she could to come up with us; so that we soon came near enough to send our Long-Boat arm'd on Board her.

There were but twelve *Moors* on Board, besides Prisoners that were put under Hatches. When our Men had taken care of 'em, I went to 'em, and order'd the Prisoners to be releas'd, desiring the Person that was the Master to come upon Deck. The *Moors* had not taken any of the Lading out of her: She was a Ship of ninety Tons bound for *Leverpool*, laden, as I said before, with Port-Wines, and several Jars of Oyl. I told the Master, he was at Liberty to pursue his Voyage when he thought fit. The poor Man was some time before he could believe what I said to be real: But when he was convinc'd, he return'd me the Thanks suitable to the Present I had made him. Yet he would make me a Present of a couple of Hogsheads of Wine, two Jars of Oyl, and two of Raisons; besides six of each to the Ship's Crew. I had lost seventeen of my Men in the Engagement, and eleven wounded; which I supply'd, by taking as many of the Slaves they had on board of *Hamet*'s Ship, all by their own Choice; and the rest that did not care for so long a Voyage, I recommended to the Master of the Prize, who promis'd me to land 'em all in *England*.

We pillag'd the *Corsair*, and found very good Booty. We had out of her to the Value of two thousand Pounds in Goods, which I enter'd in the Ship's Books for the Use of the Company. We did not know well how to dispose of her Crew; and tho' they deserv'd Death, yet in cool Blood

Captain Robert Boyle.   157

Blood I thought it was inhumane; and I considered they never had injur'd me. So I releas'd 'em by the Consent of the whole Company, with this Agreement; that they should make a Present from me to *Mirza* the Eunuch of fifty Pound in their *Moorish* Money, which he that had Command over the rest swore by *Mahomet* to perform. When we had taken every thing that was needful for our Voyage out of her, we let her go, and pursu'd our Course.

We touch'd at the *Canaries* (or Fortunate Islands) to take in Fresh Water, and turn'd the Lading we had taken out of the *Corsair* into Money: And I shar'd it among the Sailors, reserving a fourth Part for my self and Owners, as I call'd 'em. I gave the Men by Lotts leave to go a-shore, where they soon dispos'd of their Money for things they wanted; but the chief of their Commerce was for Wine and Brandy, knowing we had a long Voyage to make.

We were obliged to leave the Place sooner than we design'd, by reason our Pilot had unfortunately kill'd a *Portugueze*, and the Governor threaten'd to have our Ship stopp'd if we did not surrender him up. I understood that the Deceas'd had been in the Wrong, and therefore rather than run the hazard of losing him, we set Sail from thence the tenth of *April*. The Castle fir'd several Guns with Shot to stay us, but we did not regard it, but kept on our Voyage.

We met with nothing worth Notice till we made the Island of St. *Vincent*, one of the *Cape Verde*, and came to an Anchor in ten Fathom Water, in a fine gravelly Bottom.

These Islands are the *Hesperides* of the Ancients. The Natives are Blacks, a poor miserable People. They brought us a few Tortoise, which we exchang'd any Trash for, and they
were

were contented. The Rivulet of fresh Water would hardly supply us, it being almost dry'd up. But we had Wood enough. The whole Island is not above two Leagues and a half in Length, and half a one in Breadth; very barren of Fruit, Grass, or Roots, and even Animals. I saw only a few wild Asses, and some Goats, which were too nimble for us, or so far off that they were not worth our wasting Powder and Shot.

The Island of St. *Anthony*, about two Leagues to the North, is a well-inhabited Island, belonging to the Crown of *Portugal*. We resolv'd to go and Anchor there; but the Wind proving fair, we pursu'd our Voyage, pass'd by the Island *del Fogo* in the Night, and we could perceive the *Volcano* burning like the Flame of a Glass-house. Twenty Days afterwards we pass'd the Æquinoctial Line, with the usual Ceremony of ducking all those Persons that had never been there before. But I bought off the best Part of the Delinquents for an Anchor of Brandy.

The next Day we bury'd two of our Men, who dy'd of the Wounds they had receiv'd in the Fight; but all the rest happily recover'd. We gave 'em three Guns, and committed 'em to the Waves.

In the Latitude of twenty two, we saw a great Number of Fowls, and therefore judg'd we could not be many Leagues from Land, which we discover'd soon after to be *The Island of Ascension*, about two Leagues to the North; but we pass'd by it, and in two Days more anchor'd in six Fathom Water at the Island of St. *Catharines*, about half a Mile from the main Land of *Brasil*.

This Island lies in twenty seven Degrees thirty Minutes of South Latitude. It is almost a continu'd Grove of Trees, and but thinly inhabited by *Portugueze*, and a few Blacks. They are in want

want almost of all the Necessaries of Life, besides Provision, which is plentiful enough, such as it is. The Inhabitants are courteous enough, and would not take Money for any thing we had of 'em, but Linnen and Woollen. And after I had got every thing that was necessary for the Ship, I sold 'em Goods to the Value of four hundred Pounds, which I receiv'd in pure Gold. They never have Peace with the *Indians* of the Continent; and being so very near, they have often formerly made Inroads, and carry'd off the Inhabitants. But they have prevented such Attempts for the future, by building several Redoubts, where they keep constant Guard.

They pay no other Taxes but the Church-Tythes, (which they'll be sure not to lose;) and for Religion, they had but one Friar when I was there; and all his Business was, as I was inform'd, only to receive his Tenths.

A *Frenchman* told me a pleasant Story of one of the Inhabitants, an industrious Fellow that had ten Children; but, notwithstanding his Industry, found it a hard Matter to bring both Ends together at the Year's End: Tho' the worst of his Grievances was the Priest's Tythes, and his Money. He often endeavour'd to persuade the Father to forget him a Year or two, but all to no Purpose. One Day the Father paid him a Visit, in order to receive his Dues. The poor Man told him ingenuously he had it not in his Power to give it him. But he still insisted. At last he told him he had but one Way to procure it, and that he fear'd the Church would not allow of. The Friar told him he was the best Judge of that, if he would tell him what it was. Why, said the Man, a Person that lives on the Continent has several fat Pigs, of a very fine Breed. Now, said he, I could bring one over with me unperceiv'd ceiv'd of any one, as I come from my daily Labour; and such a one (naming a Neighbour) will give me a good Price for it. The Friar paus'd some time, but at last gave him this Answer. It is certainly a Sin to steal, but yet it is a greater Sin to rob the Church of its Due, and therefore I will absolve you. But bring the Pig to me, for if it's worth so much to your Neighbour, it is worth as much to me. The Man told him he would be sure to bring it him that Night, and the Friar said if he was not at Home, he would leave Word with his Servant to take Care of it. Now the Friar had no constant Dwelling here; for they are sent from *Lagoa*, a Town upon the Continent, about ten Leagues to S. S. W. and their Tythes were usually sent there in a small Bark kept for that Purpose. The Priest took care to be out of the way (that he might swear he knew nothing of the Matter, if it was found out) at the Time when the Man was to come with his Pig; but gave his Servant a strict Order, whatever was brought should be immediately carry'd on Board, and taken a great deal of Care of.

When the Time came, the Man was as good as his Word, and brought to the Priest's House his Promise in a Hand-basket. The Servant obey'd his Master's Orders, and went to carry it on Board; but before he could get to the Harbour, what he had in his Basket began to cry out. The poor Fellow was very much frighted to find he had got a Child in the Basket; but fearing, by the Charge his Master gave of it, he was deeply concern'd in the Affair, made all the haste he could on Board: And the Vessel setting Sail that Night, he went with his Charge to *Lagoa*, where he very secretly delivered it to the Brotherhood.

The

The Prieſt at St. *Catharines* thought his Man had robb'd him, and made his Eſcape, being he was miſſing ſo long; for he had carry'd a great many other things on Board before the Child. The Imagination of this made the Father very uneaſy; and the Wind continuing fair, he imbark'd on board a Veſſel, and arriv'd at *Lagoa* the Day after his Man. But what was his Surprize, when he found he had got a ſucking Child, inſtead of a ſucking Pig! He told the reſt of his Brethren the Affront that had been put upon him; and they reſolv'd to ſend the Bantling back again: but either for want of due Care, or through the Fatigue of the Sea, the Child dy'd. When the Friar came back to St. *Catharines*, he ran open-mouth'd to the poor Man, and ſwore he ſhould be excommunicated for playing Tricks with the Church. The Man told him, he was forward enough to have his Tythes; ſo having ten Children, and finding nine too many to keep, he was reſolv'd he ſhould have his Due, and have the Tenth. And farther added, if he offer'd to make any more Stir about it, he would acquaint every body with his encouraging him to ſteal from his Neighbours.

The Father finding the Man had too much Underſtanding to be Prieſt-ridden, thought it his beſt way to hold his Tongue. But the Secret was diſcloſ'd, and the poor Prieſt led a ſad ſort of Life: For whenever he came for his Tythes, many would merrily ask him if he would have his Tithe Pig. In ſhort, the Friar was ſham'd out of the Iſland, and the Fraternity were obliged to ſend another Man in his Room, who very often hears the Story of the Child, tho' much againſt his Will.

We anchor'd at first within a Bow-shot of the *Island of Parrots*, in seven Fathom Water: But we were inform'd the best Place to water our Ship, was two Leagues beyond the Island of St. *Catharine*. We had our present Wants supply'd from the Continent, tho' not enough to water the Ship; so we resolv'd to steer for the watering Place, in the Bay of *Arazatiba*.

We steer'd between the Island and the Continent, and all the way on each side we discover'd a beautiful Prospect of Houses, inviron'd with natural Woods and Groves, which gave the Eye a vast Delight. When we approach'd the Bay of *Arazatiba*, we perceiv'd a Ship, with *English* Colours, with her Anchor a-peak, in order to discover who we were. I immediately hoisted *English* Colours, but prepar'd for an Engagement, as imagining her to be *French*, (or some *English* Pirate;) for there was War between the two Nations: But I found it was a Privateer, commanded by Captain *Dampier*, who made me a Visit, after having hail'd us. When he was on Board, he us'd many Persuasions to engage me to consort with him, and follow the Business of Privateering; but I told him, I had other Affairs to manage. After I had treated him handsomely with what the Ship afforded, he took his Leave, and invited me to dine on board his Vessel the next Day. I gave him my Promise to wait on him, and I accordingly went, where I was very handsomely treated; and there we agreed two Days after to make an Entertainment jointly for the Officers of both Ships on Shore; and the Day after that, for the rest of the Crew.

In order to this I commanded a large Tent to be pitch'd, capable of holding fifty Persons; and we strove who should send the most Materials on shore for our Feast. We had the

Musick

Musick of both Vessels; but mine proving to be the best, as being *Italians*, gave the most Delight: not but they join'd in Consort, and agreed very well.

After Dinner, Captain *Dampier* told me, tho' he could not oblige me with *Italian* Musick, yet he had an *English* Eunuch that sang admirably; he added, he could not answer for his Judgment, but he was very well convinc'd he never heard a finer Voice in his Life. The Person was brought in; but my Readers may guess at my Surprize, when, in the Person of the Singer, I discover'd my Mistress's Lawyer, whom my Master and his Friend had equipt for a fine Singer. I knew him assoon as ever I saw him, but I perceiv'd by his Behaviour he had no Knowledge of me; neither was it very possible he could have known me, because he had never seen me but once, and then he had too much Concern to make any Observations: But the Occasion had imprinted in my Mind a lively Idea of him.

He sung admirably well, and with good Judgment. I ask'd the Captain how he came to be an Eunuch; he told me he could not inform me, neither could he ever prevail upon him to let him know it. We were very merry for several Hours; and I may safely declare that during that Time I had bury'd my inward Malady.

I told the Singer, I believ'd I could let Captain *Dampier* into the Secret of his Castration, if he would not be offended at it. He seem'd very much concern'd, and blush'd; but imagining I knew nothing of the Matter, he gave me his Consent to say what I thought fit; yet with the utmost Chagrine in his Face, as believing he was only going to be the Jest of the Company.

But when I began to name my Master, and enter'd into some Part of the Story, I found him in the utmost Confusion, insomuch that I pity'd him, and told him I would not proceed any farther, without his Consent. He told me in bad *French*, (for he had observ'd that the Captain and I sometimes talk'd to one another in that Language) that I was very welcome to tell his unfortunate Story, but not to so many Auditors; for, added he, I perceive you know it very well. I gave him my Word only to tell the Captain, for which he thank'd me; but I told him, in return, that he must let me into the rest of his Story; which he promis'd to do. The Captain and I, with my quondam Lawyer, took an Opportunity of leaving the Company, and walking a little way up the River Side, where I inform'd him that I came to the Knowledge of his Story, by the Porter that dogg'd him, (for I did not think it convenient to let him know that I was a Person concern'd) and that seeing him go into the Coach in *Lombard-street*, I remember'd his Face again. He gave us his Story in the following manner.

I was bred up to the Law by my Father, an Attorney of *Lincolns-Inn*; who dying, left me a small Estate, which I soon spent in none of the best Company. I had no Thoughts of Business, 'till drove to it through the utmost Necessity. But finding Want approaching began to open my Eyes, I took Chambers in *Cliffords-Inn*, and resolv'd to stick to Business. I soon found Clients enow through the Credit of my Father; and understanding the rough as well as the smooth Part of the Law, I got Mony enough to supply even any Extravagance. I had ever been a very great Admirer of the Female Sex, and had the good Fortune,

tune, or rather the Ill, to succeed in most of my Amours.

The first time I ever saw the fatal Cause of my Misfortune, was at St. *Dunstan*'s Church; (which, to my Shame I must own, I too often frequented without Devotion) Our Eyes often told us the Language of the Heart. I got the Opportunity of sitting in the next Pew to her, but had never once disclos'd my Passion.

One *Sunday*, as the Clerk had set the Psalm, she begg'd I would lend her my Book; saying she had left hers at Home. When she had done, she return'd it me, and thank'd me. I had resolv'd with my self to have waited on her out of the Church, but was prevented by the Person that was afterwards her Husband. When I came home, I pull'd my Prayer-Book out of my Pocket, but perceiv'd it would not shut as usual, which put me on examining it. I found a Note pinn'd to the last Leaf, which I had not observ'd before: The Contents were to invite me to an Assignation that Evening at Six.

I was very punctual, and found her there before me. I begg'd her Pardon for making her wait, which she easily granted with a gentle Reproach; and we soon came to a right Understanding: for that very Night, before we parted, I had what I wish'd; the Sweet which was follow'd by the worst of Bitters.

She told me she had long had a Passion for me; which, tho' she resisted all she could, got the better of her Modesty, and forc'd her to declare it. She inform'd me too, that she was speedily to be married to the Man that led her out of Church, tho' it was much against her Inclination; but she was oblig'd to comply with her Mother's Commands.

M 3   We

We had many Meetings: sometimes at my Chambers, till I was taken too much Notice of by some of my Neighbours: And when she was married we often met at different Places, and she as often made me handsome Presents. He then related how he was discover'd at my Master's House by one of the Prentices, (meaning me; but as he conceal'd his Face by turning it to the Window, he could not remember him.) He also related all that I have declar'd in the former Sheets; and added, that when the Operation was over, his Mistress, as knowing him of no farther Use to her, left him without speaking a Word.—When I had recover'd Strength, said he, to write, I sent for some of my intimate Friends, and among the rest a Surgeon. I told him my Misfortune, and was examin'd by him; but I was obliged to stay at the Inn several Days. At last (tho' almost a Miracle) I was perfectly cur'd, and return'd to my Business; but my Story getting Air, I was made the Scoff of every Body that saw me; till in short my Life became a Burthen to me, and I took a Resolution to go to some Part of the World where no one should know me; and getting acquainted with Captain *Dampier*, he favour'd me so far as to enter me Steward. I had learnt to sing when I was young; and my Voice, growing clear by my Loss, is much improv'd. I had kept my Misfortune a Secret to all the Crew, if I had not receiv'd a Wound in my Thigh by an *Indian* Arrow on the Coast of *Florida*, a Year ago; for the Surgeon coming to dress me, when the extream Anguish had taken away my Senses, perceiv'd my Condition and disclos'd it to the Company: But I have the good Fortune not to be flouted at.

When

Captain Robert Boyle.

When the Story was finish'd, we join'd our Company again, and ended the Day in Mirth and Jollity. The next Day my Crew went on Shore to regale themselves; for Captain *Dampier* and I had alter'd our Resolution of sending both Companies together, for fear of Quarrels and Disorder. And his Crew went on Shore the following Day.

About Noon, as I was reading in my Cabin, I heard the Report of several Pieces; upon which I ran out, and went my self to the Topmast Head, where I perceiv'd my Men, who were filling our Casks at the River of *Parrots*, surrounded by a multitude of *Indians*. I upon the Instant let slip our Cables, and having a strong Sea Breeze, steer'd full into the River's Mouth at all hazards, ordering every Man to his Arms, and to load all our great Guns with Musket Ball. By good Fortune the Tide was almost at the highest, so that we came on broadside the Rivulet where our Men were defending themselves. They had made a Rampart with the empty Casks, and had kept off the *Indians* with their Pieces; but just as we came, they had spent all their Ammunition, and had resolv'd to submit to the *Indians*. But assoon as they perceiv'd us, they took to their Heels, and ran towards our Ship, and the *Indians* after them; but we soon stopp'd their Career, by firing our double and round, which kill'd 'em above fifty Men, and put the rest to Flight. We took our Men on Board, and intended to fall out of the River, but found the Tide turn'd; and before we could get out our Ship ran a-ground, so that we were oblig'd to wait till the next Tide. I was very uneasie at this Accident, and order'd my Lieutenant to take the Boat, and acquaint Captain *Dampier* with it.

In the mean time, not to be idle, I arm'd twenty Men, and order'd them to guard the rest while they fill'd our Casks; which was accordingly done, and with the Long-Boat brought on Board. I would not let them be hoisted into the Ship, for fear of hurting her now she lay aground; tho' it prov'd to be a clayie Bottom.

An Hour before Night we perceived an *Indian* running very swiftly to us, who call'd to us in *Portugueze* to fetch him aboard. Assoon as he was in the Ship, he told a Man that understood *Portugueze*, that the *Indians*, to the Number of a Thousand, design'd in the middle of the Night to attack our Ship, and that they would come down in Canoes; for they very well knew we could not get out till Tide of Flood.

This Man, whom we took for an *Indian*, was a *Portugueze* the *Indians* had taken Prisoner a Year before, and understanding their Language learnt their Resolution; and while they were calling their Number together, he took his Opportunity to make his Escape. I order'd him to be told he should be rewarded for his Intelligence. I immediately call'd all the Officers together to consult about the Danger, and we agreed to send to Captain *Dampier* for Help, who came with fifty Men well arm'd: And by his Advice, assoon as it was dark, we landed six of our Cannon, and rais'd a small Battery without any Noise or Bustle; these were pointed up the River flaunting. Two of our Guns were loaded with double and round, in the Stern of our Ship. The rest of our Men were order'd in close Coverts on each Side the River, with Directions to let the *Indian* Canoes pass 'em, and not to fire till they were all gone by.

Every thing was concerted and settled, and every man order'd to his Post, to expect the Charge;

Charge; and we had contriv'd it so well, that none of our Fires could hurt one another.

About one a-clock in the Morning we could hear their Paddles in the Water, and soon after perceive 'em silently falling down the River, to the Number of two hundred Canoes. We let them come within fifty Yards of our Ship, before we fir'd; but when we began, we made such a terrible Slaughter of 'em, that I pity'd 'em. We took one Canoe with twelve *Indians*, and their Chief among them. When the Morning dawn'd, we were amaz'd to see what Havock Death had made; the very Shores were stain'd with Blood, and we had not lost one Man of either of our Crews. The *Portugueze*, who gave us Notice, I rewarded with a hundred Pound, and two new Suits of Cloaths, both Linnen and Woollen; and we made Use of him for our Interpreter. He told us we had one of their *Caciques* among the Prisoners, and a Man of great Power among the *Indians*. I order'd him to ask him the Reason of his Enmity to us, since we had never offended them. He told him that he took us for *Spaniards*, or *Portugueze*, Nations they hated from the barbarous Usage they had met with from them: But he was sorry he had molested us, being he was convinc'd we were *Englishmen*, and Enemies to the *Spaniards* as well as themselves: But however, he would pay sufficiently for his Ransom, if we would spare his Life; and accordingly we agreed for a hundred Weight of Gold Dust, and twenty in Ingots, and he order'd one of his Retinue to fetch it. In the mean time, we took the Advantage of the Tide, and fell down to our old Station.

The next Day at Noon two Canoes arriv'd, one with the Gold, and several Persons of Quality

lity that came to wait on their King; and the other laden with Fruits and Provisions, which I had equally parted between both Ships Companies. I took the Ingots for my Sharers, and the Dust was divided among us according to our Allowance. Captain *Dampier* and his Crew were mightily pleas'd with their Dividend, and once more press'd me to accompany them: but I gave 'em a flat Denial for the present, with this Hope, that when I had visited several Places in the *South-Sea*, I would return to St. *Salvador*, and wait two Months for them there.

We put the *Indians* on Shore, and the next Day weigh'd Anchor again, saluting Captain *Dampier* with 11 Guns, who return'd the like Number, and we steer'd our Course with a fresh Gale, for the Streights of *Magellan*, I intending to pass thro' those Streights into the *South-Sea*; for I was of Opinion it would shorten our Voyage; and then my Curiosity strengthen'd that Opinion: But I was advis'd by my Lieutenant to venture up to *Buenos Ayres*, a Town belonging to the *Spaniards*, where he assur'd me we might drive a very good Trade underhand with the Merchants. I communicated the Matter to the whole Company, who unanimously agreed it was the best Course we could steer. So we kept in with the Shore, and steer'd for the *Rio de la Plata*, or the *River of Plate*, which we reach'd in twenty Days without any Accident. As we had War with *France* and *Spain*, I had hoisted *French* Colours, that we might have the Liberty to trade with more Safety.

Buenos Ayres is situated above fifty Leagues up the *River of Plate*, which above the Town receives the Name of *Paraguay*; and takes its Rise many Leagues up the Country; which is possess'd by a numerous Nation of *Indians*, who
sometimes

sometimes trade with the *Spaniards*, but oftner murder 'em when they can meet 'em conveniently; for the Spirit of Revenge is suck'd in with their Milk, and handed down from Father to Son; so that they imagine it to be a very meritorious Deed to dispatch one of them; and they are generally rewarded by their *Cacique* for it.

The Town of *Buenos Ayres* takes its Name from the excellent Temperature of the Climate, and its pleasant Situation. They have Commerce with the Ships of *Europe* not above once a Year, which bring 'em the Necessaries they want, and in Return ease 'em of their Gold; that being a Metal less esteem'd than Iron, which proves more useful to them. When we were within two Leagues of the Port, we came to an Anchor in a little Creek in eight Fathom Water, a sandy Bottom. We did not care to go nearer the Town, for fear the Governour should have taken it in his Head to have hinder'd our going out again.

Though we were not in Sight of it, yet we had Canoes on board of us in an hour after our anchoring; and some of Note came *incognito*, to be inform'd what we dealt in. One of them told me, he believ'd it would be no difficult thing to dispose of my Cargo, if I thought fit to make the Governour a small Present. Accordingly I took his Advice, and sent my Steward in my Name, with a Piece of Holland, and half a dozen Pieces of *Italian* Silks; which he receiv'd as a very valuable Present, and sent me Word he would not in the least molest me, provided I did not deal too barefac'd. I understood him, and therefore was very cautious, selling but to one at a time, nor would I suffer another to enter my Ship, till the former was dispatch'd. In

In two Days I got rid of all the Cargo that I intended to part with, to a very great Advantage; and then I allow'd my Men Liberty to do what they thought fit with what they had, which gave them a general Satisfaction. The next Day I invited the Governour on Board, with some of the principal Merchants, and entertain'd them in my Cabin; and in return, I was to dine on Shore at the Castle. But I left a strict Order with my Lieutenant how to behave himself if I should be stopp'd; for I knew the *Spaniards* to be unfaithful People.

When we landed, I observed the Town made but a mean Appearance, consisting only of two Streets built in the Form of a Cross, and surrounded with a Mud Wall. The Castle it self made but an indifferent Figure: but however I was very elegantly entertain'd. The Governor seem'd to have less of the Formality of the *Spaniard*, than ever I met with in any of them. When I took my Leave of him, he made me a Present of two *Indian* Slaves, and a Bar of Gold that weigh'd three Pound two Ounces. When I came on Board, I call'd a Council, to know what Course we should steer next; for as to Traffick, I had no Pretence to go to the *South-Sea*, being all my Cargo was already dispos'd of. We debated for some time, and at last we all agreed to go for the *South-Sea* upon the score of Privateering. We communicated our Intentions to the Company, and they all seem'd very much rejoic'd at the Resolution I had taken.

Now I began to repent I had not join'd with Captain *Dampier*; for I wanted Men for any notable Exploit, but I did not despair of meeting with him in the *South-Sea*. We weigh'd Anchor, and steer'd for the Streights of *Magellan*

Captain Robert Boyle.

lan with a fair Wind. One Morning my Servant wak'd me, and told me that a Sail bore down upon us, and the Lieutenant defir'd to know how to behave himfelf. I rofe upon the Inftant, and, by the help of my Perfpective, faw it was a Veffel with *English* Colours; but I imagining they were put up only for a Shew, I caus'd *French* Colours to be hoifted, which foon was anfwer'd by the fame in the Ship that purfu'd us. I order'd every thing to be prepar'd for an Engagement without any Hurry, commanded my Men not to appear upon Deck, and kept on my Courfe with crouded Sail, that our Purfuers might imagine I was willing to get from them; yet I order'd it fo by falfe Steering, that they gain'd upon us. About Three in the Afternoon they were within half a League of us, firing every Quarter of an Hour a Gun to Leeward, to let us know we were to take them for Friends.

I order'd our Men to tack about, hoift up *English* Colours, and bear upon 'em. We foon perceiv'd we had much furpris'd 'em, but notwithftanding they kept up their *French* Colours, and feem'd to prepare for the Engagement, tho' they were much inferior to us. When we came along Side I hal'd 'em, and (after owning they were *French*) commanded them to furrender; but was anfwer'd with a Broadfide, which we return'd fo faft, that they foon ftruck, and call'd for Quarter. I order'd the Captain to come on Board, who inform'd me that his Veffel was call'd the *Felicity*, belonging to Monfieur *de Gennes*, and had been feparated from the Fleet three Days before. I us'd the Captain very handfomly, for the Sake of Monfieur *St. Olon* the *French* Ambaffador. I gave him a Letter and a fmall Prefent for that Gentleman, and

and difmifs'd him without taking any thing from them. I found this Action did not pleafe fome of my Men; and not caring to have them uneafie, I fummon'd them upon the Deck, and told 'em the Obligations I had to the *French* Ambaffador; acquainting them, as this was a Ship of War, there was not much to be expected from 'em, therefore I told 'em I would fhare five hundred Pound among 'em to make 'em Amends for their Difappointment. But not one of them would accept a Penny; and in return I told them, I did not intend to make any more fuch Compliments to the *French*, if ever they came into my Power again. They were very well pleas'd with my Declaration, and fome of them prais'd my Generofity; for tho' moft Sailors are rough and blunt in Speech, yet they can in their way admire a generous Action as well as other Men.

Our Officers were under fome Apprehenfions of meeting with the Squadron of Monfieur *de Gennes*, which being a Fleet of five Sail would certainly be too hard for us; and we were inform'd by the Captain of the *Felicity* that they were fail'd for the Streights of *Magellan*. I found their Fears very reafonable, and it would be a fool-hardy Action to encounter a Force fo much fuperior: For though Life was burthenfome enough to me, yet Humanity oblig'd me not to hazard the Lives of fo many Men that were not out of Love with this World. So I refolv'd to wave my Curiofity, and make for *Le Maire*'s Streights; which in five Days time we difcover'd, known to Sailors by three Rocks, call'd the *Three Brothers* from their Likenefs to one another.

We found a ftrong Current fetting Northward, and an unufual Toffing of the Ship;
but

but we got through the Streights in two Days with Safety, and made for the *South-Sea*.

The next Day we difcover'd the *Magellan Clouds*, fo well known to Sailors, which convinc'd us that we were over-againft thofe Streights that run into the *South-Sea*. Thefe Clouds are always feen in the fame Degree, and the fame orbicular Form. We kept on our Courfe, not intending to come within Sight of the Continent for fear of a Difcovery; and the Weather favour'd us, it continuing very hazy.

About an Hour within Night we heard the Sound of a Trumpet, which we conjectur'd muft be on oard of fome Veffel, becaufe we were well affur'd we were not near enough the Land; upon which I immediately gave Orders to put out all our Lights, and fteer our Courfe that Way we heard the Sound; which Sounding often gave us true Notice of their Courfe; and in half an Hour, tho' pretty dark, we gain'd Sight of 'em: But their Mirth was foon chang'd when we got up with 'em, thruft out our Guns, and hail'd 'em. We underftood they were *Spanifh*, and I order'd 'em to be told if they did not upon the Inftant lye by, and fend their Commander on Board, I would immediately fire upon 'em. They very readily comply'd with my Orders, hoifted out their Boat, and the Captain came on Board me, whofe Name was *Don Juan Villegro*, and his Ship the *Wild-fire*. He was employ'd by the Viceroy of *Peru*, to carry condemn'd Perfons to *Baldivia*, which is the Refidence of moft of the Rogues of *America*. But we were alfo inform'd they had the *Real Situado* on Board, which is a Sum of Money fo call'd, that is fent from the Viceroy of *Peru* to pay and cloath the Garrifon, as

well

well as to repair the Fortifications of *Baldivia*. This Sum usually amounted to four hundred thousand Crowns, but we could find no more than two hundred and fifty thousand; but then, to make Amends for the Deficiency, we met with a great many valuable *East-India* Goods, brought from thence by their *Manilla* Ship; for the Merchants always put their Supply for *Baldivia* in the Ship that carries the Money to pay the Garrison, that being the only Time to dispose of their Goods.

This Prize made my Men mad with Joy, and I fear'd it would make 'em think they should have enough, and consequently desire to return home. But I soon found it had the contrary Effect, and they all expected, from this Earnest of good Fortune, Riches enough in the Voyage we propos'd, to make 'em for ever.

I treated the Prisoners handsomely, which were forty-six, including fifteen Felons, who were well pleas'd to have chang'd their Masters; expecting better Usage from us than from the *Spaniards* of *Baldivia*, where they were design'd. There was one *Roberts*, an *Englishman*, among them, who, I have been inform'd, has been executed since for Piracy; him, two *Frenchmen*, four *Spaniards* and the Trumpeter, I enter'd in my Books to reinforce my Crew; understanding their Crime was only Suspicion of Piracy, therefore I was convinc'd they were good Sailors. But I did not know how to dispose of the Ship and the rest of the Crew. If I should give 'em their Liberty, they would of course alarm the Country; and if I kept them with me, Provisions would fall short; for they were victual'd but for a Month's Voyage.

The *Spanish* Captain being inform'd of my Fears, told me by an Interpreter, that he had receiv'd receiv'd such handsome Usage from me, that he would upon his Honour steer to what Port I thought fit, and report if I pleas'd that I was sail'd back again for the North Sea. I told him, though I could rely upon his Honour, he could not answer for all the rest. At last I thought of a Stratagem to deceive the *Spanish* Captain as well as the other Prisoners, as follows. In the first Watch of the Night (the Prisoners being all under Hatches) I came to our Sailors upon Deck, and told 'em the ill Consequence of keeping or letting go the Prisoners; and therefore concerted with 'em that they should pretend a Mutiny the next Day, and all declare for going back through the Streights into the North Sea. When the first Watch was reliev'd, I acquainted the other Moiety of the Company, and then retir'd to Rest. But my Slumbers were broken with Visions of my dear Mrs. *Villars*: I dreamt I saw her in the Arms of the Renegado *Hamet*, struggling and calling out on me for Help, and before I could come to her Assistance, Death had freed her from the barbarous Wretch. This Dream had brought to my Mind all my Afflictions, and I can't tell how long I should have continu'd feeding upon my Sighs, if I had not been alarm'd with Shouts and Noises upon Deck. I ran out to see what was the Matter, and found my Men, as was design'd, in their feign'd Mutiny. I had forgot at first, and was much alarm'd; but recollecting, I carry'd on the Cheat. And Grief had so seated herself on my Countenance, with Thoughts of my Dream, that one of the Quarter-Masters told me afterwards, my Looks were enough to deceive all the World.

The *Spaniards* had leave to be upon Deck all the Day, and Care was taken to let them into the Secret. At Dinner I told the *Spanish* Captain (for he and the Merchants always eat with me) that I thought his Speeches yesterday were prophetic, for I was compell'd to comply with my obstinate Crew, and sail for the North Sea again. He reply'd, he wish'd me happy where-ever I went: And to carry on the Deceit, we steer'd our Course back again.

In the Afternoon *Roberts* came to me, and told me that one of the *Spaniards*, who was willing to stay with us, would undertake to bring me ten thousand Pieces of Eight in ten Days, if I would let him have the Prize. Upon what *Roberts* said, I sent for the Man, and had him examin'd by *Roberts*, who understood *Spanish* very well. The *Spaniard* told me, he would not have me enquire into the Matter till it was done; and for the better Security I might send who I thought fit with him, provided he had one of his Companions that was to help in the Design. Accordingly I order'd twenty Hands, and to obey the *Spaniard* in this Expedition as if he were their Captain.

We agreed to wait for them the limited Time, in the same Degree we parted from 'em. I inform'd the *Spanish* Captain, by an Interpreter, that his Countryman was gone upon some secret Expedition, and assoon as he return'd we would pursue our Course. He answer'd, whatever he had undertaken he was of the Opinion he would succeed in it, for he had certainly as much Cunning as any Person in the World; he had been condemn'd to *Baldivia* once before, and had made his Escape from thence; and he did not doubt but he would get from them again, if he had been carry'd there the

second

second time; and farther gave me some Hints that he might deceive me in this Undertaking.

I began to be in some fear of having a Knavish Trick play'd me, and would have recall'd the Vessel if it had not been too late; but hoping for the best, I resolv'd to cruise till the Time appointed was expir'd.

I had cloath'd my two *Indians*, that were presented me by the Governour of *Buenos Ayres*, in *European* Habits very handsome; and instructed them in the *English* Tongue: They very readily learnt; and I gave them all the tender Usage imaginable, which they were obligingly sensible of; and I believe they would have sacrific'd their Lives to have serv'd me. I found them very handy, and docible, and very good-natur'd; which convinces me, if mild Methods were us'd with them, they might be very easily wrought to be Friends to the *Europeans*, especially the *English*. And I think 'tis great Pity such a vast Body of People should be ignorant of the Divine Being that form'd the Universe. Though the *Spaniards* (it's true) send *Missionaries* among them to inculcate Christianity, yet they generally neglect their holy Functions, and strive all they can to inrich themselves, by laying exorbitant Taxes upon the poor *Indians*: And I have been inform'd, that in some Parts of *America* all the Wealth they get is deliver'd to the *Mission*, reserving to themselves only what is needful, and that but from Day to Day. I had my two *Indians* made Christians; one by by the Name of *Robert*, and the other *Joseph*; being mine and my Father's Names. And I hope, in the Sight of God, Lay-Baptism will suffice; especially when we had not the Happiness of the other Form. And it is not impossible,

impossible, if they lead good Lives, they may find the Road to Heaven as well as if they had been christen'd in a Church, by an orthodox Clergyman.

Three Days before the Time I expected my *Spaniard* back, we discovered two Sail making up to us, which made us prepare for an Engagement; but we soon perceiv'd it was our Prize, with another Vessel. The *Spaniard* came on Board, and inform'd me that he had been something better than his Word, for he believ'd that in Money and in Goods he had brought to the Value of 80000 Dollars. He gave us the following Account, by *Roberts*. Last time I was Prisoner at *Baldivia*, I was compell'd to work for one *Don Sancho Ramirez*, a sordid, covetous, jealous, malicious Wretch, one that us'd to deal in Merchandize. It was his usual Method to wait at a Country House near the Sea, for the Arrival of the *Real Situado* Ship, (which was the same I had taken) and then go privately on Board to deal with the Merchants. The Knowledge of this made me undertake this Expedition, as well to get Money, as to be reveng'd on the old Villain, for the Stripes he has often given me without any Provocation. When we arriv'd within half a League of the Place, we perceiv'd a Bark riding at Anchor. I began to demur, as fearing we might be discover'd; but at last resolv'd to proceed, let what would happen. The Bark weigh'd and made towards us, which occasion'd another Surprize; but my Fears were soon over, when I perceiv'd *Don Sancho* upon Deck. He hail'd us, and desir'd we would slacken Sail, that he might come on Board. Accordingly we ran into a small Creek, and came to an Anchor. I did not appear at first, but let the other *Spaniard*

Spaniard that went with us perſonate the Captain, and inſtructed him accordingly. Aſſoon as he came on Board, he enquir'd for *Don Juan Villegro*, (for that Gentleman us'd to command the *Real Situado*) and was anſwer'd that he was very ill, and could not ſail this Voyage. Then he enquir'd for the Merchants, telling him that the Governor had diſcover'd his uſual Practice of Dealing firſt with them; therefore he had contriv'd to meet us in one of his own Veſſels, that was ready laden for *Buenos Ayres*, and only ſtaid for our Arrival to ſet Sail. I was glad to hear of that, becauſe I intended to make Prize of it. The *Spaniard* invited him into the Cabin, while I went on board his Bark with ten Men arm'd, and ſecur'd it, there being but five Men and a Boy in it. The reſt of the Crew were on Shore.

I cut her Cable, and our own, and made out to Sea again. When we were under Sail, I came on Board, and ſhew'd my ſelf to the old *Don*, and in a few Words made him underſtand his Condition. I thought at firſt we ſhould have been obliged to have bury'd him, for he look'd for a great while like one that was dead. But I recover'd him a little, by ſhewing him the Box that contain'd his Heart and Soul, (I mean his Money). He did his Endeavour to fly at me to be reveng'd on me, but he was held; but to give him a little more Comfort, I read over to him his Bill of Lading, and told him plainly, I would not deal with him, if his Goods did not anſwer his Bill. When he found he could do no good by Paſſion, he told me he would give me half his Money, if I would reſtore him his Ship and Cargo. I was very well as I was, I told him; and ſince I had got it all in my Poſſeſſion, I would have no more Dealings with him, only the

the odd ten thousand Pieces of Eight more for his Ransom. He was so thunder-struck at this, that he did not so much as offer to open his Mouth to speak; but kept so long silent, that I fancying he would never speak again, took him upon Deck, that he might behold the lovely Prospect of the Water; for by this time we were out of Sight of Land. His Heart then began to melt, and he fell down upon his Knees, and begg'd he might have his Liberty, notwithstanding we had robb'd him. I was in a very great Passion, and order'd him to mollify the Word, and call it Over-reaching; which with much Chastisement he did. But I told him he was obliged to make your Honour one Visit, and accordingly I have brought him to wait on you.

I must confess, I could not help admiring the *Spaniard*'s Ingenuity, and yet I did not greatly relish the Action; for tho' it was lawful Prize to us, yet I thought it was downright Robbery in him. However, I gave him the Thanks our Interest requir'd; and further told him (by *Roberts* our Interpreter) that he should be very well rewarded for his Undertaking.

The old *Spaniard* was brought on Board us, more dead than alive; and understanding we were *English*, he spoke to me in that Language, and begg'd he might be set at Liberty. I told him he need not apprehend any thing, for he should have his Liberty, and civil Usage. He thank'd me as well as his Grief would give him leave, and I invited him to dine with me, which he did accordingly the same Day.

I order'd the Cargo out of the Bark, which was very considerable, and most of the Provision, because I fear'd it would be what we should want. The other Vessel, as belonging to the King of *Spain*, and one who could pretty well bear

bear that Loss, I intended to keep for our selves. The Bark I restor'd to *Don Ramirez*, with several Bales of Goods that would prove of small Use to us, tho' of Value to him; nay I would very willingly have given him all his Goods and Money too, if it had not been for wronging my Crew; for, as I said, I look'd upon it as gain'd by Fraud. However, I ventur'd to give him back twenty thousand Ryals, which did not amount to mine and my Owners Share. He return'd me his Acknowledgments, by giving me a very handsome Ring, that they had not taken from him, and told me, he ever thought the *English* generous Enemies.

I caus'd all the Prisoners to be put on Board the Bark, and took my leave of 'em. They return'd me abundance of Thanks for my kind Usage; and vow'd, if ever Fortune should send any of our Countrymen among 'em, they should fare the better for my Sake. I must own, I was not displeas'd with their Acknowledgments. A Man feels a secret Pleasure within himself, when he has done a humane Action; when on the contrary, if a Person has been guilty of Baseness, Horror and Remorse gnaw his Inwards.

The Day after I had parted with the Prisoners, I summon'd all my Men upon Deck, and told 'em what the *Spaniard* had done for 'em, and advis'd with 'em what Recompence I should make him. We soon agreed he should have five thousand Pieces of Eight, his Companion five hundred, and the rest of 'em enter'd to a Share of the Booty we had before taken. Accordingly I sent for 'em, and told 'em what I intended. The *Spaniard* return'd me suitable Thanks in *French*, for he had been inform'd I understood that Language. I found in his Discourse a ready turn of Wit and Humour, and of a Person that had read Mankind. He did not seem to be above thirty Years of Age, of a free and open Nature, having nothing of the stiff Formality of the *Spaniard*, tho' born at *Sevil* in *Old Spain*. I told him, I expected a short Account of his Life; he readily answer'd, he should be proud to comply with my Desires, but he begg'd I would defer it for some Time, till he might be a little more us'd to my Conversation; for, said he smiling, mine has been a very merry and odd sort of a Life, and therefore till I have more Freedom, I shall desist, because I shall lose the Spirit in telling it.

We steer'd our Course towards *Panama*, depending that our Prisoners would spread the Report of our going back again for the North Sea. In thirty six Degrees, and forty five Minutes, we discover'd a Vessel steering the same Course; I order'd the Prize to chase her, and before Night she took her. It was a Bark laden with Tallow and Hides, bound for *La Conception*. I repented the taking of her, for we soon found she was but a heavy Sailor, and therefore could not keep Company with us, and it was not proper for us to let 'em depart.

Don *Pedro Aquillio*, which was the Name of of our Intelligent *Spaniard*, told me, he would undertake to dispose of the Cargo and Bark to a good Advantage, if I could tell how to dispose of the Men, which were but four, that is three *Indians* and a *Spaniard*. The *Indians* were very well pleas'd to be receiv'd as Servants on Board; yet we allow'd 'em a half Share in our future Purchases. The *Spaniard* we intended to detain on Board till we had made our cruising Voyage, and then release him. So depending on Don *Pedro*'s Ingenuity, I let him go off with the

the Bark, with three *Spaniards* to affift him, having his Promife to return the next Day. We were then within five Leagues of *La Conception*, and therefore refolv'd to remain in that Station till his Arrival, keeping *Mamelles de Biobio*, or the Dugs of *Biobio* (two Rocks fo call'd) in View.

The next Day we perceiv'd him coming with a Pirogue, a fmall *Spanifh* Boat with one Sail. He brought me a handfome Prefent of Fruit, and enough befides for the whole Crew. Well, faid he, I have made but an indifferent Bargain; I have brought you but twenty thoufand Pieces of Eight: The old Rogue of a Governor would not give any more. He told me that the Governor of *La Conception* ingroffed all the Tallow and Hides, and forc'd the Retailers to give him his own Price; fo he went boldly to him, and fold him Bark and Cargo.

Don Pedro advis'd us to cruife for the *Manilla* Ship, which was daily expected. His Advice was approv'd on all Hands, therefore Orders were given to Wood and Water the Ships for the Voyage; and accordingly we made for *Juan Fernando*, and arriv'd there the fifth of *September* 1695. It being a remarkable Day with me, it lives in my Memory; for the lofs of my Journal by an odd Accident, hinders my keeping a regular Account. We fpent but two Days in wooding and watering, and killing Goats, which are there in great Plenty.

There are three Iflands that bear the Name of *Juan Fernando*, the firft Difcoverer, tho' there are no other Inhabitants on them than Goats. There's a noble Bay on the North Side of the Ifland, capable of containing five hundred Sail, where you anchor at fixteen Fathom Water, a fandy Bottom. We left it with a favourable Wind for our Defign, and made farther up the

oaft

Coast *January* the first; and it was fear'd we had miss'd our Booty, for the *Manilla* Ship generally arrives at *Acapulco* about *Christmas*; however we resolv'd to coast about for twenty Days longer, and if we fail'd of her, to return into the North Sea, with a Design to cruize down the Coast.

We kept out of Sight of Land, for fear of being discover'd.

On the sixth we perceiv'd two Sail, and accordingly gave 'em Chace. Don *Philip* assur'd me it was the *Manilla* Ship, and a Guard-Ship along with her. We call'd a Council immediately; where it was resolv'd the Bark should attack the *Manilla* Ship, while ours was to engage the Man of War: And this was the Reason Don *Pedro* gave for it; that the *Manilla* Ship was so very unweildy, the Bark could play round her, and being so small, she was out of the reach of their Cannon, for they could make no Use but of those upon their upper Deck. The Man of War seeing we gave 'em Chace, slacken'd her Sail to stay for us, imagining we should both attack him, but he found himself mistaken. Our *Pink* past him, without firing a Gun; but assoon as ever we came a-long Side, we gave him a Broadside, with a loud Huzza. He soon return'd it; but we ply'd him so close, that he began to make off; but we follow'd him close at the Heels, and coming under his Starboard Quarter, gave him another Broad-side, which brought his Main-Mast by the Board; upon which he immediately struck.

The Sea being very smooth, tho' a handsome Breeze of Wind, we mann'd our Long-boat, and I went on Board with forty Hands, well arm'd. When I came upon Deck, I order'd the *Spaniards* to be taken on Board, and secur'd

Captain Robert Boyle.

secur'd under Hatches; but I was much surpriz'd to find but sixteen Men in the Ship, besides eight that were kill'd, and not one that appear'd like an Officer among 'em. But we were soon inform'd, the Captain had order'd one hundred and fifty of his Men on Board the *Manilla* Ship, assoon as they had discover'd us in the Morning, because her Crew were most of 'em sickly.

We imagin'd our small Vessel must have warm work on't, being not above thirty five Hands in all. So we resolv'd immediately to cut off the Rudder of the Man of War; and leave her; for having lost her Main-Mast, she could not follow us to do us any Damage; and six of her Men we took on Board us, who finding we were *English*, seem'd very willing to serve us; and I promis'd 'em their Share in the Booty, if we succeeded. These six Men were old *Christians*, as they call themselves, and they value themselves very much upon it, despising the *Creolians*. We made all the Sail we could after the *Manilla* Ship, and soon overtook her; for our small Vessel had kept her very well in Play, tho' she had warm Work on't, and her Rigging was very much shatter'd, tho' they had not lost a single Man, but she was obliged to fall a-stern to mend her Tackle. I order'd 'em to send me twenty Men on Board, which I was oblig'd to lye by for. I had brought all my Guns to bear on one Side, and did not fire one till I came under her Stern; and then I pour'd 'em into her, and tack'd about to charge again. I observ'd a Boat busy about her Stern, but could not imagine what they were doing. However I resolv'd they that were in it should find a difficult Matter to get on Board again. But I was much surpriz'd to find it my own Boat with *Don Pedro* in it, who had

had taken the occaſion in the Smoak of our firſt Broad-ſide to nail up the Rudder, ſo that the Ship could not tack about. He made what haſte he could on Board the Bark, which had now mended all her Rigging, and got under her Stern; and as faſt as the *Manilla* Ship ſent Men to clear her Rudder, he prevented 'em with his Small-ſhot. In the mean time we ventur'd to come a-long Side of her, notwithſtanding her monſtrous Bulk, and gave her ſuch Entertainment, that they call'd out at laſt for Quarter, and ſtruck their Colours. I order'd all the Officers to come on Board, which they did. I receiv'd 'em all very civilly, and immediately after went on Board the Prize. I was amaz'd at her vaſt Bulk. She had ſeven Decks, and built ſo ſtrong, that not one of our Shot had gone through; yet they had above ſixty Men kill'd, through their Ports, and other Vacancies; and what was very ſurprizing, we had not one, and but two wounded.

They had above one hundred Men ſick on Board 'em, ſo that the Ship look'd like an Hoſpital. It was very richly laden, and valu'd at 1800000 Dollars, and upwards. We found but little Money on Board, beſides the Plate belonging to the Governor of *Luconia*, one of the *Philippine* Iſlands, who was coming home to his own Country, being a Native of *Mexico*.

Tho' this was the richeſt Prize that ever was taken, yet we did not know well what to do with it. It would be an Impoſſibility to work her into the North Sea, or back again to the *Eaſt Indies*, without farther help; for we had more Priſoners by two to one, than we had Sailors on Board. So we once more advis'd with *Don Pedro*, who counſell'd us to ſend to *Acapulco*, and have the Ship and Men ranſom'd.

We

We all thought it would be both difficult and dangerous. *Don Pedro* told us there should be neither, and he would undertake to do it. But however, as it was a thing of very great Consequence, we desir'd he would tell us in what manner it should be done; Why as thus, (said he) I'll take the Bark, with the Captain of the *Spanish* Man of War, the Quondam Governor, and one or two more of the best Quality, who shall make the Case known to the City of *Acapulco*, and no other way but by Letter; for I will suffer but one of them to go on Shore, and I'll take care to order it well enough to give you Notice, if they should send any Force against us, tho' there is no Danger they should. For, added he, they have no Man of War within two hundred Leagues of 'em, that which was taken being all they had to guard their Coast. We were well satisfied with his Reasons, and gave him leave to proceed as he thought fit; and accordingly the next Day he set Sail with those Persons mention'd along with him. And by the Advice of all, we follow'd him, being very well convinc'd by the *Spaniards* themselves, there was nothing of Force to be apprehended. I had fitted up the *Spanish* Man of War again, and resolv'd to keep her, and dispose of the Bark. Therefore, assoon as we came within Sight of Land, I order'd every thing to be taken out of her, and put on Board the *Spaniard*, who we found was a very good Sailor.

The Day following *Don Pedro* came on Board, with several Merchants and Persons of Quality, to treat about the Ransom of the Prize; and we agreed for 1200000 Dollars, after we had taken several Bales of rich Goods out of her. The Money was to be paid in six Days, and we were to stay where we rode; for I did not much care to trust 'em too far.

In the mean time we sent all their sick and wounded on Shore. The Bark we dispos'd of for Provision, and other Necessaries, and took the Opportunity of waiting for the Money to Water our Ships. At the Time appointed, the Money came, and we surrender'd the Ship to the *Spaniards*. Now we agreed by joint Consent to go home, for we were all rich enough, and every one of the Crew thought so: Yet we resolv'd to touch at St. *Salvador* on the Coast of *Brasil* (and make our Way through the *Magellan* Straits) as well to take in some Refreshments, as to dispose of the rest of our Goods, and careen our Vessels.

Accordingly we put our Design in Execution, and made the best of our Way for the Straits of *Magellan*, and discover'd those noted Clouds, which are a sure Guide to Sailors, the third of *May*. We found the Weather extreamly cold, and the Mountains cover'd with Snow; but we were well provided with good Liquors, and all convenient Cloathing. We anchor'd in *Port Famine*; formerly call'd *Knight's Bay*, by the *Dutch* in a Voyage 1598, with a Fleet of five Sail; where meeting with many Troubles, and to eternize the Memory of the Voyage, (it being the first the *Dutch* made to those Straits) the Admiral knighted six of the Officers, by the Title of Knights of the furious Lion. The Oaths they receiv'd at the Ceremony were, never to do, or consent to do, any thing against their Honours, or to prejudice their present Voyage, to expose their Lives for the Service of their Commonwealth, and to do their utmost in driving the *Spaniards* from their

golden

golden World. They were install'd on Shore, with a Sea-green Garter, and a Table built, with their Names engrav'd on it.

We saw several of the Inhabitants, who were easily prevail'd upon to come on Board us. But I could find nothing extraordinary in their Height, as is fabulously reported. The tallest I could see among them did not exceed six Foot. They are certainly a poor miserable People, but very harmless; and I am apt to believe all former Stories of their monstrous Height and Cruelty to be Fables.

We got through the Straits once more into the North Sea, and by degrees came into a warmer Climate. But a terrible Storm overtook us, just as we were in Sight of *Pepy*'s Island, which drove us within Sight of Port *Desire*, upon the Continent; and therefore we thought it the safest way to run into the Bay, which accordingly we did, and came to an Anchor in seventeen Fathom Water.

At the South Side of the Port, lies *Penguin* Island, so call'd from a multiplicity of those Birds resorting there. Our Men went on shore, and in three Hours time brought on board five hundred of the Fowls, and several thousands of their Eggs, which prov'd delicious Food. They are call'd *Penguin*, not from their Fatness, as some Authors affirm, but from their Whiteness mix'd with black. They are about the bigness of a Goose, weighing between nine and fourteen Pound; and tho' their chief Diet is Fish, yet they have no fishy Taste. Their Skin is very thick, their Bill is like that of a Raven, tho' not altogether so crooked; their Neck is short and thick, and the rest of their Body resembles a Goose, excepting the Wings, which are only two Stumps cover'd with Feathers, which they make

Use

Use of in Swimming. Their Feet are black, like those of a Swan. They breed in Holes of the Rocks, which are so numerous, there is no walking hardly for fear of falling into them. When they walk on Shore 'tis upright, with their Wings hanging down, so that they appear in that Posture like small Pigmies. We staid but two Days here, and then steer'd our Course for *Rio Janeiro*, or the River of *January*, intending to touch at St. *Sebastian*'s first, and if we did not succeed there, to sail for St. *Salvador*. When we arriv'd there, the *Portugueze* would not admit us to enter the Bay, but fir'd several Guns from the Forts laden with Shot, to deter us from anchoring; we could not imagine the meaning of it, but however we left 'em in that Humour, and steer'd for St. *Salvador*, and in one and twenty Days we discover'd *Praya de Zumba*, a Place very easily known from a Number of white Spots, which appear like Linnen hung out to whiten, or dry.

We past Fort St. *Anthony*, and saluted it with eleven Guns, which return'd us an equal Number, without the charge of Shot, and came to an Anchor within half a League of the City; which we also saluted with eleven Guns, and receiv'd but seven in Return.

By Advice of the Officers, we shar'd among the Sailors a thousand Pieces of eight a Man, which pleas'd 'em exceedingly. The next Day, I went to wait on the Governor, who receiv'd me very civilly, and desir'd I would dine with him. We were very magnificently serv'd, and a Band of *Italian* Music play'd all the while. After Dinner I made my Presents, which he accepted of very kindly, but when I came to treat about our Commerce, he flatly deny'd me, telling me it was against the King of *Portugal*'s express exprefs Orders, to fuffer any Trading with Foreigners. I begg'd his Pardon, if it was not to be comply'd with. He would have return'd my Prefent, but I prefs'd him to accept it in fo obliging a manner, that he did; and told me in *French*, that fince he faw my Generofity, he would comply with me. He immediately fent for feveral Merchants, and took 'em into his Clofet, where they ftay'd fome time. When they came out again, the Governor told me thofe Gentlemen would go on Board, and view our Commodities, and if we could agree, he would be anfwerable for the Money. One of the Perfons feem'd to be of a more free and open Difpofition than the *Portugueze* generally are. (Tho' moft of the Inhabitants of St. *Salvador* affect the Manners of the *French*.) We foon made an End of our Bargain, and my merry Merchant would oblige me to go a-fhore and fup with him that Night. He prefs'd me fo heartily, that I could not refufe him; and accordingly I went with only my two *Indian* Servants, who began to be underftood in *Englifh*.

When we arriv'd at the Merchant's Houfe, I was furpriz'd to find it fo magnificent. He led us into a handfome Summer-houfe in the Garden, where he told me we were to fup; and, faid he, to convince you that you are welcome, I'll bring my Wife and Daughter to keep us Company, which is reckon'd as a thing extraordinary among us. But, added he, I have been in *England* and *France*, and I find the Women are not the lefs Honeft, for having their Liberty. I told him, I thought Conftraint did but whet their Inventions to gain their Defires. Said he, I am of your Mind, therefore give 'em all the Liberty they defire, and I can't find I have had any reafon to repent it.

In a little time he ufher'd in the two Ladies, his Wife and Daughter, both very beautiful, and, notwithstanding the Heat of the Climate, very fair. The Wife seem'd about five and thirty, the Daughter about sixteen, and they both spoke very good *French*. Our Conversation was kept up with all the Spirit I was capable of: I soon discover'd a great deal of Wit in them both, and made 'em my Compliment in finding Ladies so extraordinary in so remote a Part of the World.

When we had supp'd, the Merchant (whose Name was *Don Jaques*) told me it was his Custom to provide Beds for his Guests, as well as Supper: And after we had walk'd a Turn or two round the Garden, we all retir'd to our several Apartments.

The next Morning we drank Chocolate together, and I invited *Don Jaques*, with his Wife and Daughter, to dine with me on Board the next Day, which he confented to. I now begg'd Leave to be gone; but it being very hot, he had provided me a Silk *Palanquin*; which is a Thing like a Hammock, with a Canopy over it, carry'd by two Blacks, with each a Rest to hang it on while they take Breath. This is all the Vehicle in Use at St. *Salvador*, by reason of the Unevenness and Steepness of the Situation.

I prepar'd for them with all the Magnificence I could the next Day. And when they saw the Variety of Dishes, dress'd after the *English* Manner, they were mightily pleas'd; and, to add to their Satisfaction, the Musick I had on Board play'd several elegant Pieces, accompany'd with the Trumpet I had got from on Board the *Spanish* Prize, (for notwithstanding his being Trumpeter to the Garrison of *Baldivia,*

via, yet he was better pleas'd to be where he was.) We drank the King of *England*, and the King of *Portugal*'s Health several times, with the Discharge of our Cannon: And when the Time for their going on Shore came, I fasten'd a small Present of several sorts of Silk upon the Wife and Daughter. *Don Jaques* perceiv'd what I was about, and merrily said, That is not fair; we did not pay you for your Company Yesterday, and yet I believe it was as valuable as that you receiv'd to-day, at least in my Opinion; I sha'n't answer for the Ladies, said he, they are both capable of speaking for themselves. I receiv'd many Compliments on all Hands; but not dealing much in them, I am very willing to forget 'em.

In a Day or two after *Don Jaques* came on Board, and told me the Money for the Goods was ready, but I should not have it, unless I came my self to receive it. I accordingly went with him, and he made me continue there all Night, where we had the Conversation of the Ladies as before.

When I was going away the next Day, he told me he should soon find if any thing else besides Money had the Power to bring me to see him. I told him, to convince him of that, I would come and dine with him the next Day; which accordingly I did. After Dinner I express'd a Desire of seeing the most remarkable Places in the City, which he comply'd with, and order'd two *Palanquins* to carry us.

The City of St. *Salvador*, the Capital of *Brasil*, is situated in the Bay of *All-Saints*, in 12 Degrees 45 Minutes Southern Latitude. It is divided into two Towns, the upper and the lower. The Streets are strait, and pretty broad, but most of them very steep; and all the Goods are hoifted in and out of the Veffels by Machines for that purpofe. It was formerly under the Dominion of the *Spaniards,* but taken from them by the *Dutch* in 1624, and pretty well fortify'd by them; yet notwithftanding that, the *Spaniards* retook it the next Year. I could not learn how long the *Portugueze* have poffefs'd it, but they all agree upwards of fifty Years. They have made it a regular fortify'd Place, and very ftrong; having five Forts befides the Caftle, well ftor'd with Cannon, and other Ammunition, and fmall Arms for ten thoufand Men. This is the ufual Seat of the Viceroy of *Brafil;* but when I was there it was without one, tho' he was expected every Day,

The Cathedral is a magnificent Pile of Building, finely adorn'd, and painted after the modern Manner. The *Jefuits* Church is a noble Structure, all of *European* Marble ; with a fine Organ, the Pipes gilt. There are many more fine Churches, twenty in all, befides feveral Convents and Monafteries.

This Place is alfo the Refidence of a Bifhop, who has a handfome Palace; and for the Reverend the Clergy, I never faw fuch a Number for the bignefs of the Place any where, as *Benedictines, Francifcans, Carmelites, Auguftins, Capuchins, Dominicans,* and *Barefoot Fryars;* (tho' I think moft of the People I faw there wore no Stockings.) There are three Nunneries, well ftor'd with Nuns, but not to be feen; nor hardly any Women in the Town, but common Whores, or black Slaves ; for the *Portugueze* lock up their Wives and Daughters as carefully as they do their Money, and would have none look upon them but themfelves ; except my Friend *Don Jaques;* which is fomething the more extraordinary.

It

It is a Place of great Trade to *Guinea*, and other Parts, and is accounted one of the richest Cities in the King of *Portugal*'s Dominions. By moderate Account there may be about 20000 Whites, (or I should say *Portugueze*, for they are none of the whitest,) and about treble that Number of Slaves.

Don Jaques would make me take five Days up in viewing the several Parts of the City, and oblig'd me to be at his House without going on Board during that Time. Some Part of the Day we play'd at *Ombre*, a Game mightily in Vogue among the *Spaniards* and *Portugueze*, and a very entertaining Game for three, invented by the jealous *Spaniards* for that Number, to prevent any clandestine Doings between two. But alas! I believe there are more Opportunities gain'd than lost by it.

We had provided every thing we wanted now, and began to prepare for our Departure.

Don Jaques was very sorry to lose me, he told me; and indeed it was with some Regret I left him; for his Civility had drawn from me a Friendship insensibly. I went to take Leave of the Governour, who made me a Present of *American* Sweetmeats, and begg'd I would dine with him, which I could not in good Manners deny. When Dinner was over, *Don Jaques* was so obligingly pressing for me to sup with him the last Time, that I could not refuse; but I begg'd he would excuse my staying all Night, and he gave me his Word he would not press me. I sent one of my *Indians* to order the Boat to fetch me at Ten that Evening.

When the time of my Stay was expir'd, I took my Leave of *Don Jaques* and the Family, after having forc'd him to accept of a

Gold

Gold Watch, and the Ladies a Prefent of each a Diamond Ring, that I receiv'd from the Governour of *Luconia*, for my Civility in returning him his Plate and Jewels, when we took the *Acapulco* Ship in the *South-Sea*.

Well, faid *Don Jaques*, I fee you will pay for your Board in fpight of my Teeth. I had taken Leave of the Wife and Daughter before, who had left us in Tears. I muft own I thought my felf very much oblig'd for their Tendernefs; and it drew fuch a deep Melancholy upon my Face, with Thoughts of my dear Wife, that *Don Jaques* imagin'd it was Grief for parting with him and his Family. I did not take any Pains to undeceive him. Well, faid he, I fee a Friendfhip may be contracted in a few Days, as well as Love, efpecially where there is a Harmony of Souls.

We had agreed to correfpond together, and I had undertaken to fend him fome *European* Goods, if it pleas'd God to guard me fafe to *Europe*. I had continu'd longer with *Don Jaques* than I had intended to do, therefore, whatever Violence I did my felf, I took my Leave. *Don Jaques* tenderly embrac'd me, and was fo much overwhelm'd with Grief, that I could not forbear fympathizing with him: But I order'd his Servants, (whom I had liberally rewarded for the Trouble I gave) to fhut the Door, to prevent their Mafter's going any farther.

I walk'd towards the Port very melancholy, though with fome Precipitation; but was rouz'd out of it by one of my *Indians* crying, Mafter, take a Care, take a Care! I turn'd about, and faw four *Portugueze* purfuing us. I made a Stand, and drew my Sword, took my Cloak from my *Indian*, and put it acrofs my Arm to
defend

defend my felf the better. They all four attack'd me at once; but my *Indians*, whom I had order'd to wear Swords on Shore, fell upon 'em furioufly, and difpatch'd two of 'em immediately; and I had made a fhift to drop a third, though not without receiving feveral Wounds. The fourth ran for it; but my *Indians* being as nimble-footed as Does, foon overtook him, and dragg'd him down the Hill by the Hair of his Head; while he cry'd out all the while, *Mifericordia! Mifericordia!* The Noife we made had brought up my Boat's Crew, who were all arm'd with Piftols and Cutlaffes; and the Guard coming in the mean time, and feeing my *Indians* dragging the Fugitive, fell upon us: But my Crew and *Indians* charg'd 'em fo furioufly, that they foon put 'em to Flight, though treble our Number: Though this avail'd us but little, for the whole Garrifon was coming down upon us. I then order'd my Crew to refift no more, but fubmit to 'em; for as we were innocent, I did not much fear to come off clear.

The Buftle had rouz'd *Don Jaques*, and his Servants, who were foon inform'd of the Condition I was in, and he came in good time to interpofe his Authority; for the *Portugueze* began to be outragious. But the Governour had fent a Gentleman to bring us before him: And accordingly I went, accompanied by *Don Jaques*. But the Wounds I had received bled fo much, that they were oblig'd to carry me to *Don Jaques*'s, and fend for a Surgeon. My Hurts were not dangerous, but I was very faint with Lofs of Blood.

Don Jaques waited on the Governour, and inform'd him of the Condition I was in: But the Governour not underftanding who was the Aggreffor, order'd a Guard of Soldiers at the Door

Door of the House where I was. My Boat's Crew soon got on Board, and alarm'd both the Ships, who immediately weigh'd and came close to Shore, where they had prepar'd to fire upon the Town, if I was not releas'd instantly. I understanding the Matter, sent one to inform them, that the Guard was set upon me to secure me from the Insults of the *Portugueze*, till the Truth of the Matter was discovered. This would not serve their Turn, but a hundred of 'em, with the Officers and *Don Pedro*, landed, all well arm'd, and vow'd to wait the Event on Shore. The Governour did me the Honour of a Visit, and enquir'd into the Cause; and I inform'd him, as well as my Weakness would permit me. When they had examin'd the dead *Portugueze*, they found one of them was Nephew to the deceas'd Viceroy. Upon the Discovery of which, the *Portugueze* began to be very much exasperated, and were hardly restrain'd from rushing into the House, and tearing me to Pieces; for though they did not regard the Nephew, yet they had a great Veneration for his deceas'd Uncle, who behav'd himself with a great deal of Candour in his Post, and the Inhabitants mightily regretted his Loss. The Governour appeas'd their Fury, by telling 'em I should have no Favour shewn me if I were guilty, let the Consequence be what it would. And immediately a Court was summon'd to try me, tho' it was Midnight, and I was carry'd there in a *Palanquin*, weak as I was. But I was oblig'd to send for my Lieutenant, and tell him that there was no Danger; and also order'd him to send the Crew on Board again. When we came to the Place of Justice, the Governour order'd me a Seat: But the Business was soon ended; for the *Portugueze*

tugueze we had secur'd, own'd that his Master had design'd to murder me, because he was inform'd I was his Rival in the beautiful *Donna Bianca*, (which was the Daughter of *Don Jaques*.) I was very much surpris'd (as well as *Don Jaques*) at this Report, and we both declar'd it was only a jealous Suggestion of the Gentleman; which every one came into: And the Grounds he had for it, was my often frequenting *Don Jaques*'s House, upon the score of Friendship only, and lodging there.

The Governor handsomely dismist me, and told me he was very sorry I had been detain'd from my Affairs. I return'd, that I was as sorry to be the Cause of so unhappy an Accident, in a Country where I had receiv'd so much Civility.

Don Jaques begg'd I would go back to his House, and stay till my Wounds were well; but the Governour took us aside, and said to us in *French*, I know, *Don Jaques*, 'tis your Friendship for the Captain that makes you desire his Company; but, if I might advise you, I would have him go on Board upon the Instant; for though he is very innocent as to the Matter, yet I doubt some of the Deceased's Friends or Relations, which are numerous, not having Regard to Justice, will contrive some Method to dispatch him out of the Way: for most of the *Portugueze* are jealous, malicious, and revengeful, and very seldom look into the Merits of the Cause.

I thank'd the Governour for his kind Caution; and *Don Jaques*, notwithstanding his Friendship, could not but come into what he had said. I therefore order'd my self to be carried on Board that Moment. It being broad Day, the Governour and his Guard would accompany me to the Water-side, but *Don Jaques* would

would go on Board with me. In the Boat he told me he had some Thoughts of coming to reside in *England*, for, said he, I have enough, and therefore I will, in two or three Years more, leave off Traffick and live quiet in the World. But he begg'd I would write to him assoon as I arriv'd in *Europe*, and let him know the Place I had chose to live in; for, added he, let it be where it will, if it is ever my Fortune to arrive safe in *Europe*, I'll take another Voyage only for the Hopes of seeing you. I return'd him the Acknowledgment due to so much Friendship, and we parted with Tears on both sides.

Assoon as I had got on Board, the Wind being fair, we weigh'd and stood out of the Bay. When we were out at Sea, a Letter was brought me written in *French*, the Translation of which is as follows.

SIR,

I Was resolv'd to make Tryal of you before I suffer'd my Heart to chuse you for a Friend; and I am so well convinc'd of the Sincerity of your Soul, that I will confide in you a Secret dear to my Repose. I had an Amour with a beautiful Lady before I was marry'd, that produc'd the Bearer of this Letter. I have kept him conceal'd from my Family hitherto; but the Person I trusted with his Education and this Secret, being dead, I fear'd I should find some Difficulty to conceal him any longer here: Therefore, depending upon your good Nature and Friendship, I have ventur'd to send him to you, with Sufficient to bear his Expences in his Education, which I would have suitable to the Estate I have in my Power to give him. I shall *ever own this Obligation, and always think it my greatest Happiness to subscribe my self*

Your sincere Friend and Servant,

Jaques de Ramires.

I must own I was very much surpriz'd at this Epistle, and could not imagine his Reasons for concealing it from me. I order'd the Person that brought the Letter to be conducted in, and immediately enter'd my Cabin one of the beautifullest Boys I had ever set my Eyes on. He seem'd about Fifteen, his Hair fair and long, curling down his Shoulders: In short, every Feature so exact and uniform, and so innocent withal, that I was amaz'd. At last I took him by the Hand and embrac'd him, and told him for his Father's sake he should be as dear to me as my own Son. But finding he did not answer me, for I spoke to him in *English*, I repeated the same in *French*. He return'd me Thanks, and said he did not doubt but he should find it so.

After some time, he deliver'd me a Casket, in which were Jewels to the Value of five thousand Pistoles, and a little Box which contain'd a thousand Moidores. I told him I would take as much Care of them as if they were my own.

These, Sir, said the Youth, are design'd to bear my Charges. Then ordering another Box in, had it open'd, and told me what it contain'd was a Present from his Father to me. When I examin'd it, I found six Silver Dishes, and three dozen of Plates of the same Metal; a dozen of Knives, Forks, and Spoons in Gold, and half a dozen of Gold Sweet-meat Plates.

In a larger Box was variety of all manner of Conserves and Cordials; and I was informed he had made small Presents to every Officer in the Ship, and to the common Sailors a Week's fresh Provision, with Liquor in proportion. I was amaz'd at his Bounty, for his Present to me was what a Prince might have receiv'd. I thought it was my Duty to shew all the Kindness I was capable of to the Son of so generous a Father; therefore I order'd him a Field-Bed in my own Cabin; and his Behaviour was so engaging, that I felt as much Tenderness for him as if he had really been my own Child; and having Skill in Surgery, I trusted him with the Management of my Wounds; though I had a very good Ship-Surgeon, who supply'd him with what he wanted. My Hurts, which were not dangerous, soon heal'd, and I recover'd my Strength again. I could not prevail upon young *Don Ferdinand*, (*Don Jaques*'s Son) to go often upon Deck. He said he would rather chuse to stay in the Cabin, where he had *French* Books of his own, and some of mine to entertain him; for I had taken my Opportunity to procure several at St. *Salvador*, and among the rest a *French* and *English* Grammar and Dictionary, which mightily pleas'd *Don Ferdinand*, for he had a great Desire to learn *English*: I gave him all the Helps I could; and he in return, instructed me in the *Portugueze* Language; so that in a short time we could discourse in either.

We had resolv'd to steer our Course for the Island of *Tercera*, the Capital of the *Azores*; and after fifty Days Sail, we discover'd the Peak of one of the Islands of *Azores*, which is called *Pico*, from the Mountain. It is in the Resemblance of a Pyramid, and may be discovered as many Leagues off as the *Pike of Teneriff*; for we we were then by Obfervation thirty Leagues off from it, and yet could fee it diftinctly.

In two Days more we difcover'd the Ifland of St. *Michael*. We were all pleas'd that we had enter'd that Part of the World we call *Europe*, the Birth-place of moft of us; and what pleas'd us more was, that we had made all our Fortunes.

Auguft the 19th, 1696, we anchor'd in the Bay of *Angra*, the Capital of the *Azores*, in the Ifland *Tercera*. I can't give any great Commendation to the Port, being I think it a very indifferent one. We did not defign to ftay long, only to get fome Water, and fome frefh Provifions; for we were inform'd there was no riding out a Storm there. We got in what we wanted with all Expedition we could, while the Weather was favourable.

The City is feated at the Bottom of the Bay, under the Brow of a Hill call'd *Monto de Brafil*, or the *Brafil* Mountain; but for what reafon fo call'd, I could not be inform'd. It is very well fortify'd, having two ftrong Caftles, and eight Batteries befides, with Guns of thirty Pounds Shot. But it is very indifferently garrifon'd, having no more than two hundred Men in Pay, and moft wretchedly fupply'd, having no cloathing for three Years.

The Town is very agreeable, having a Stream of Water running quite through it, which drives feveral Miles for the Ufe of the Publick; and almoft in every Quarter are publick Fountains of excellent tafted Water. From this Place are brought the fineft Canary-Birds, tho' lefs than thofe of the *Canaries*, yet they exceed 'em far in the Excellency of their Pipes.

Money is very fcarce here, and confequently every thing cheap. I bought two Months Bifcuit for the Ships, much cheaper than in any

Port of *Europe*. Corn is their chief Commodity, which they send to *Portugal*; but for any other Trade, I believe the King of *Portugal* gets but little Advantage.

I was grown such a Proficient in the *Portugueze* Tongue, that I could make a shift to be understood; and by understanding that Language, soon found a Gate to the *Spanish* Tongue, by the help of *Don Pedro*, who had learnt to speak *English* very fluently. We got acquainted with one of the Fathers of the *Cordeliers*, who shew'd us the Churches, and other things of Note in the City. The Cathedral is a very handsome Building, and well painted, which goes by the Name of St. *Salvador*; and there is no danger of missing that Title, and St. *Anthony*, every where among the *Portugueze*. There's no less than twenty, besides the Cathedral; with four Monasteries, and four Convents, that have each their Chapel beautifully adorn'd. When we had got what Refreshments were wanting, we set sail for the *Straits*, intending to touch no where, before we were got into the *Mediterranean*; and because we met with nothing extraordinary in our Voyage to *Gibralter*; I will, to divert the Reader, give him, (instead of Bearing of Coasts, Changes of Wind, and unexpected Storms,) the Life of my Companion *Don Pedro Aquilio*; which he related to us duriug the Voyage, in the following Manner.

THE
LIFE
OF
Don *PEDRO AQUILIO*.

MY Father residing in *France*, when the Commotions were ingendring between the King and the Parliament, was made fast to the Interest of Cardinal *de Retz*, by marrying one of his Neices of a very great Fortune: He had a Hand in most of the secret Transactions of those Times; and wading too deep in those Seas of Trouble, was obliged to retire to his native Country. He foreseeing what would happen, took care of his Affairs accordingly; sold his Estate in *France*, and sent my Mother to *Sevil*, the Place of his Birth, whither he soon follow'd. The King of *Spain*, having a very great Regard for him, gave him several Offices of Honour and Profit; and when I was born, I was Son to the first Man in the City. My Father, by living so long in *France*, had contracted the Manners of the *French*; and the Formality of the *Spaniard* seem'd as strange to him, as if he had been born in another Climate. He had several Children,

tho'

tho' none surviv'd but my self. When I had Years enough over my Head to fear the Prejudice of Education, he took a Resolution of sending me to the College of the four Nations in *Paris*, to compleat my Studies. And the first thing I learnt, was to shake off all the Customs of *Spain*, which was soon done; for they had taken but small Impression in my Mind, because I found my Father was averse to 'em. I contracted a Friendship with several young *French* Noblemen of my own Age; for Parity of Years is the first Step to Friendship.

When I had reach'd my fifteenth Year, I began to think of a Mistress, to compleat my Studies. And as I found it was a Method among my Companions, to supplant each other in their Females without any Animosity, I set my self so willingly about it, that out of half a dozen *Madonas*, I made my self Master of six of 'em. This occasion'd many Plots and Contrivances to regain the flying Fair Ones: Tho' I perceiv'd most Money laid out in Presents had a prevailing Force with 'em. We had our Allowance paid quarterly, and getting all my Companions into gaming, I had the good Fortune to strip 'em all. They seem'd to be a little uneasy, in losing their Mistresses and Money too; and my telling 'em, as I had got the Females, I should have the most occasion for the Money, signify'd nothing, but they all begg'd it as a great Favour, that I would lend 'em half what I had won, to be repaid the next Quarter; which to oblige 'em, I comply'd with, and to play we fell again; but Fortune chang'd her amiable Looks from me, and I soon lost all I had won, with my own Share too. The fickle Dame favour'd one of the Company, that would not lend any of us a Penny. This chagrin'd the rest very much. But to prevent

vent any more Importunity, he went away to his own Chamber, leaving room in all our Pockets for the Devil to dance a Saraband, for we had not one Cross to keep him out; and what was our greatest Mortification, the Holydays were approaching, that us'd to give us the Opportunity of rambling into the Country. The Person that won our Money, happen'd to be the last that was added to our Society; and tho' he had not been long among us, we began to be tir'd of him, as much from his odd Humours, as his Effeminacy. I at last thought of a Project to be reveng'd on him, and it was very much approv'd by the rest of my Companions. The Holydays being come, we design'd for our Country Rendezvous; but he that bore the Purse would not go with us, without we could produce every one so much Money. This put us to our Shifts again: But my Man, who was an arch Wag, begg'd that I would accept of what he had; for I had been so lucky as to have paid him his Wages, before my Loss. I accepted of his Offer, and took from him ten *Lewis d'Ors:* We contriv'd it so well, that they were shown to old Sir Snip, from every Person of our Society. Well, said he, sixty *Lewis d'Ors* will do our Business; but who should be Purse-bearer was what he cavil'd at; and not caring to trust any of us, (and we resolv'd not to trust him) he pitch'd upon my Man to be Cash-keeper for us all. And accordingly he put down in his Pocket-book, so much Money in Bank, receiv'd of such and such Persons, when in reality he had but twenty *Lewis d'Ors*.

When we had contriv'd every thing, we took Horse, and rode six Leagues that Evening, to the Place where we design'd to put in Execution our Project. We had agreed to pay every
P   Night

Night the Expences of the Day, and have it set down in my Man's Book. But when he was call'd for (as we had concerted) no Man was to be found. There was strange Enquiry made to no purpose; and we all agreed he had taken the Opportunity to rob us, and run away with our Money. All that we had to do, was to beg of Snip to discharge the House. But he declar'd he had not half a Pistole in his Pocket: which we knew very well, for he had sew'd all the rest into his Wastecoat. Since it falls out so unluckily, said I, don't let us make known our Wants to the House, but go to rest, and consult to-morrow. I lay with Snip, for fear he should take it into his Head to sneak off. In the Night, when I found he was fast a-sleep, I bundled up all his Cloaths, and threw them out of the Window to my Man that waited for them.

When Morning came, I desir'd him to rise, that we might get all together to consult; but no Cloaths were to be found. He began to storm, and swear, but all to no purpose; for not one of his Oaths would bring back a Rag of his Cloaths. He told us in his Ravings, that he had lost so much Money, sew'd up in his Wastecoat. We upbraided him for his Covetousness, in not letting us share with him; but it did not signifie any thing. He threaten'd to go to the *Provost*, and have the Landlord secur'd; and would have don't, if he had not been naked.

After raving to no Purpose, he was oblig'd to go to Bed again to avoid catching cold. He ask'd us what he should do in his Condition, but all the Advice we gave him brought him no Consolation.

He

He was very tall, and large made, and we us'd to call him in Ridicule the *Infant*. He propos'd to sell his Horse to cloath him; but being so much out of Size, there was not any thing to be had ready made that would fit him: This was still worse and worse; and tho' the Horse was sold for twenty *Pistoles*, we contriv'd it so, that my Landlord seiz'd the Money for his Reckoning. This put him almost beside himself, and he was ready to expire with Vexation.

I pretended to be much concern'd at this Usage, while the rest of our Company laugh'd at his Misfortune. I seem'd to be very angry with them; and told 'em I would do my Endeavour to remedy every thing. I made 'em acquainted, that I had just call'd to mind a Person, a Friend of mine, that liv'd in the Town, much of the Infant's Size, and I would go to borrow a Suit of Cloaths for him. He seem'd very much rejoyc'd at this; for he resolv'd, assoon as ever he was dress'd, to take up the *Landlord*, and swear the Robbery against him.

I went as he suppos'd about his Cloaths; and after staying some time below, I went up with a Bundle, and seem'd very much concern'd that I could not succeed. I told the *Infant*, the Gentleman was gone to *Lyons* about Business of Concern, and had carry'd all his Cloaths with him. But I had brought him a Masquerade Habit that he had left behind him.

He express'd some Satisfaction at the Sight of it, that he should not be confin'd to lie in Bed. But, said he, if it were not only for the Name of Cloaths, a Man might as well go naked, for there's no stirring abroad in this Dress.

It was the Habit of a Satyr, that we had made on purpose for the Occasion, before we left *Paris*. When we had equip'd him, it was as much as I could

could do to keep my Countenance at the Figure he made; and he feem'd very much diffatisfy'd with it, but however he wore it for the Conveniency of not lying in Bed.

When we were at Dinner, we had many Contrivances to get away, but none feazable.

I told 'em at laft, I had thought of a Defign would certainly do our Bufinefs, and make up our Loffes, if the *Infant* would confent to it. He readily reply'd, he would ftick at nothing to do that. Why then, faid I, if you'll fuffer your felf to be fhown in that Habit, as a Monfter newly arriv'd, I'll anfwer for the Succefs of it.

After much talk, he agreed to do it, on this Provifo, that his Face fhould be difguis'd. I told him, I would ftep to my Friend's Houfe, for the Mask that was made to the Habit. I return'd and gave it to him, and he was foon fatisfy'd with the Project.

Notwithftanding the Buftle we made, none of the Houfe (but the Landlord) knew any thing of the Matter, and the next Day it was given out about the Town, that a Monfter was to be fhown in the Afternoon. We had procur'd a Chain, and other Materials, to carry on the Joke; and when the time came to fhow away, we had fuch a Concourfe of People to fee our Monfter (it being in the Holydays) that our Profit gave us fome Satisfaction. For when the time of fhowing was over, our Money amounted to three and twenty *Piftoles*; and the Monfter behav'd himfelf fo well with our Inftructions, that he gave a general Content.

We had taken care he fhould appear fo fierce, that none fhould approach near enough to difcover the Deceit. We had a great deal of Diverfion at the ignorant People's Suggeftions. One Country Fellow afk'd how old he was? I told him

him four Years, three Months, and five Days. Lord bless me! (cry'd he out) why, by that time he comes to be twenty, no House will be able to hold him.

In fine, we show'd him so long, that our Money mounted to upwards of one hundred Pounds, which pleas'd our *Infant* so well, that he desir'd to continue a Monster all the time of the Holydays. But we resolv'd to carry the Joke no further, tho' we did not tell him so.

We left the *Infant* chain'd to the Post of the Window, as usual, went down to my Landlord, and gave him Instructions how to behave himself. We took care to satisfy him very well for the Trouble he had been at.

We all rid away to the next Village, and putting up our Horses, return'd on Foot, one by one, back again to the Inn; and stole up Stairs unperceiv'd by any one but the Landlord. The *Infant*, finding we staid longer than ordinary, began to make a great Noise: which my Landlord hearing, sent up one of his Servants, that knew nothing of the Secret; when the *Infant* saw him come in, he made several Signs to him; but as the Fellow knew nothing of the Jest, he did not much like the Action of the *Infant*, but ran down to his Master frighted out of his Wits.

We had made Peep-holes in the bordering Room, where we could perceive every Action of the *Infant*'s; but he was so very much enrag'd, that he sat down biting his Nails for Vexation; for he began to perceive the Trick we had put upon him. After sitting Melancholy some time, he rose up, and endeavour'd to undo the Chains; but as they were ty'd close behind, and made fast to a Staple in the Wall, all his Efforts prov'd vain. All our care was to contain from laughing,

ing, which was a very hard Task. When he found he could not free himself, Rage entirely possess'd him; and the Noise he made with stamping, and rattling his Chains, brought up several of the Servants arm'd, who open'd the Door cautiously; but notwithstanding their Valour, ran away assoon as they perceiv'd his menacing Action; and tumbling over one another, took the shortest way down Stairs.

When we thought he had Mortification enough, we sent my Landlord into him with a good Horsewhip, and a Letter in his Hand. Assoon as he had got within the Door, he spoke after this manner, in a Landlord-like Tone. I was pretty well assur'd at the beginning that thou wert a rank Cheat; but now I am convinc'd of it, I will chastise thee first, and reason with thee afterwards, like other criminal Judges, punish first, and enquire into the Demerits of the Cause afterwards, that Justice may not wait for any body.

These Words were follow'd with some smart Strokes, and the Dialogue soon began to be in much Confusion; for between the roaring of the Infant, the bawling of my Landlord, and the smacking of the Whip, it was a continual jargon of Noise: And we were obliged all of us to own, our Host executed his Commission to a Hair.

When he had a little recover'd himself, he began to reason with his Patient; who, that he might the better hear him, laid himself down on his Pallate to condole his afflicted Body. But their Questions being very long, and the Answers but short, consisting of two Monosyllables, Ay, or No, I will not trouble you with the Relation.

After

Captain Robert Boyle.

After their Dialogue was over, he gave him the Letter, which difcovered our Defign upon him. He was thunder-ftruck at our Combination; and utter'd fuch Imprecations of Revenge, that my Landlord was oblig'd to anfwer him with his Whip, which foon reduc'd him to Reafon.

We began to be tir'd with our *Infant*, and fo put an end to our Diverfion, and his Torture, by fending him his Cloaths; tho' fome of our Company would have had him gone to *Paris* in that Trim.

In a few Days after the Frolick was over, he commenc'd a Suit of Law againft us all, for a Robbery; but the Judges finding it only a Trick of Mirth, fined every one of the Defendants fix Livres a-piece, and every one to pay his own Cofts. This but enrag'd the *Infant* the more, and he began to meditate a more pernicious Revenge; for now he appear'd the Ridicule of the whole City, and he could never ftir without a Train of Boys at his Heels.

The firft Inftance of it was as follows: My Servant having fome Intrigue on his Hands, had made bold with my Cloaths to carry it on; and coming home pretty late, was fhot thro' the Back with a Piftol Ball, juft as he was entring the College Gates. Though it was well meant, the poor Fellow efcap'd with Life, yet he lay dangeroufly ill for feveral Days. He could give no Account of the Affair at all, not having feen the Perfon that wounded him. But the Accident made me very uneafie, for I was convinc'd the Favour was meant to me. This made me cautious how I ventur'd out of the College; for it was eafie to imagine it was a Proof of the *Infant*'s Refentment, who had left the College upon the lofs of his Tryal.

I began now to repent our Confederacy against him, and wrote him a Note to assure him of my Contrition, with my Share of the Money we had taken from him. He receiv'd the Cash, and sent me Word he heartily forgave me. Imagining him sincere, I ventur'd into the City, and soon frequented my old Rendezvous; but I had so much Regard for my self as to get to College betimes.

One Night as I was going home, four Men in Vizor Masks rush'd out from behind a Wall of a House that was building; They all fir'd upon me, and ran away assoon as they had discharg'd their Pieces. I must confess, at first Fear made me imagine my self no Man of this World: But by degrees getting over my Apprehension, I found I had not got any Hurt. This Accident to me seem'd prodigious; for they were all four so near me, that several Grains of the Powder stuck in my Face. But I was brought out of my Labyrinth of Thought, when I receiv'd the following Letter the next Morning.

SIR,

I *Must own my self one of those unfortunate Men, that, for want of better Employment, receive Money as the Price of Blood. Though this I can say with a clear Conscience, I never have yet put my Trade in Practice. Yesterday Morning I was sent for to the House of Monsieur* Gomberville, *commonly call'd the* Infant, *who employed me to take away your Life; and, that he would be sure of the Execution, made one of the four that fir'd upon you last Night; but as I had the ordering of our Arms, I took care nothing should be put in 'em that was hurtful. The Acquaintance I had with your noble Father, made me the more cau-*

tions

Captain Robert Boyle. 217

tious concerning his Son. I beg in Justice to me you would keep your Chamber, and cause it to be reported that you are dangerously wounded. I need not caution you to be careful of your self, for the Infant's Malice seems to me implacable. We never have any Words made of these Things, because we know how to revenge our selves; therefore let no one else know the Contents of this, and be thankful for your Life from
Jaques Marriot.

When I had read the Letter, I order'd my Servant to bring the Bearer before me; where I soon found, by his manner of Talking, that a little Money would be very acceptable to the Sender; and therefore I sent him ten Pistoles, with my humble Service, giving him to know that I would exactly comply with the Contents.

I began now seriously to think on the Danger I had inconsiderately drawn upon my self, for an innocent Frolick; and that it would be but ill trusting to the *Infant*'s Resentment. I gave out that I was dangerously wounded; and the better to carry it on, I got a Surgeon (a Friend of mine) to visit me frequently.

When I had kept my Chamber long enough for the time of my Cure, I ventur'd abroad, but never without four or five of my Friends for a Guard, and came home in very good Time.

During my Confinement, I receiv'd Letters of Condolement from several of my Mistresses; and when they heard of my Recovery, as many of Reproach for not coming to visit them as usual. One in particular, and my favourite Fair, was very pressing for a Meeting; and her chief Reason was to pay her with my Presence for the Affronts she had sustain'd from the *Infant*
upon

upon my Account. I sent her Word I would not fail waiting on her the *Sunday* following, after Dusk. Accordingly when the time came, I stole out without any of the College Marks on, and arriv'd safe at my *Madona*'s.

After Supper, and two or three Bottles of *Hermitage*, we went to Bed; and when we had made our selves as merry as we could in the dark, I address'd my self to Sleep: But notwithstanding my willingness to receive the gentle God, he still flew from me, and several Hours pass'd without closing my Eyes.

About Midnight, I thought I heard Whispers in the next Room, which very much alarm'd me: But my Fears were trebly increas'd, when, looking through a Chink of the Door, I discover'd the *Infant*, and four other Fellows with Masks in their Hands, spreading Saw-dust on the Floor, and on the Table lay several Sacks.

I soon imagin'd what their Preparations meant, therefore consulted my Safety as well as I could in the Confusion of my Thoughts.

I went always well arm'd since the last Rencounter, having two Brace of Pistols in my Pockets, a good cutting Sword, and a Stilletto. But I was confounded, when searching for my Cloaths where I had laid them, none could be found. I now began to think of Death seriously, and beg Pardon sincerely of God for all my Sins; for I knew it would be Madness to think of escaping, naked as I was, without any Thing for my Defnce. In the Chaos of my Thoughts I remembred a Closet which had a Window that look'd into the *Seine*; and tho' it was three Stories from the River, yet, as I could swim, I thought it better to trust Providence by leaping into the Water, than those Cut-throats. I stole softly to the Window,

but

but to my great Confternation found it too faft for me to open; but by good Fortune in groping about, I found my Cloaths. I put 'em on with a great deal of Precipitation, and having prepar'd my Arms, refolv'd not to die alone.

I waited fome Time before the Chamber Door open'd. When it was open, I could perceive 'em coming in with Masks on, and the foremoft with a Dark-lanthorn. I did not think fit to wait till they fhould difcover I was not in the Bed, but rufh'd on the firft, and fhot him dead on the Spot; and in two feconds of a Minute, difpatch'd two more, one with my Sword, and the other with one of my Piftols; and had made as quick work with the other two, but they fell on their Knees, and begg'd for Mercy; which I granted, on Condition that one fhould tye the other, which was readily comply'd with; when that was done, I bound the other my felf, and coming to fecure my falfe Miftrefs, found her expiring in the Bed. She had Breath enough left to tell me, fhe had been caught in her own Trap; for defigning to poifon me in the Wine I drank, the Servant had miftaken the Bottle, and given it to her.

I ask'd her the Reafon of her Hatred to me, being, as I remember'd, guilty of no Fault. She told me, the *Infant* had inform'd her that I was falfe to her, which converted her Love to the moft implacable Hatred. I muft own, this Woman was Miftrefs of my Heart, and I had feveral Proofs of her Sincerity; but fhe was of a Temper compos'd of Fire and Fury. She further told me, that I had rais'd her Rage to that height, that fhe was refolv'd to put an end to my Life her felf; not caring to truft her Revenge to any Hands but her own.

She

She begg'd I would forgive her, and immediately expired. I examin'd my two intended Murderers, and found they were Servants to the *Infant*, and compell'd to what they did; therefore I resolv'd to pardon 'em.

I thought once of going to the Provost, and give him a particular Account of the Action; but one of the Fellows inform'd me, he was a near Relation of the *Infant*'s, and had a very great Love for him, which made me apprehend his Passion would overcome his Justice. Therefore I resolv'd the next Morning to set out for *Spain*, which I put in practice before Day, and gave my Man Orders to follow me.

I left *Paris* with this Reflection, that from the meanest triffling Accident, often dreadful Effects follow'd; and a Woman once provok'd was the most dangerous Enemy a Man could have.

I met with nothing extraordinary in my Voyage to *Cales*; but when I arriv'd at *Sevil*, I was inform'd, my Father, who was Governor of that City, was at his Country-house about six Leagues off.

Tho' I was very much fatigu'd with my Journey, I resolv'd to wait on him that Night. I hir'd a Mule (for I had my Servant's Cloaths on) and set out. But my Beast being none of the best, tir'd with me about a League before I came to the Villa where my Father resided.

I left him in the adjacent Village, and pursu'd my Journey on Foot. As I was willing to get to my Father's House, I made all the Speed I could. And tho' it was very dark, I knew the Way perfectly.

I overtook two Men in a narrow Lane, that call'd to me, asking why I had stay'd so long, and where was *Don Lewis*.

Captain Robert Boyle.

I fancy'd there was something of Villany going forward by the Name of Don *Lewis*, being he was an inveterate Enemy of my Father's. I did not answer 'em immediately, which brought 'em upon me; they soon found their Mistake. They ask'd me where I was going at that time of Night; I told 'em I was going to *Saragoza*, to my Friends, for I had serv'd a Gentleman in *Cadiz*, that had discharg'd me, for getting his Maid with Child; and I was obliged to walk all Night, being I had not any Money to pay for a Lodging. I answer'd a great many other Questions, with the same Truth and Simplicity. And after talking some time, two more came up to us, and ask'd the others who they had got with 'em. They went all together, and after a little talk, one that seem'd to be the Superior, came up to me, and told me, if I would make one of their Enterprize that Night, he would not only reward me well, but take me into his Service; but if I refus'd after he had disclos'd it to me, they would murder me upon the Instant.

I told him I would stick at nothing to get Bread. Why then, said Sir Gravity, my Name is Don *Lewis:* I have a mortal hatred to *Ferdinand Aquilio*, Governor of *Sevil*. I have waited many Years for my Revenge, but never could get an Opportunity to execute it till now. He has receiv'd one of my Servants into his House as a Domestic, who this Night will open the Door to us, where I shall quench my Hatred of him with his Blood; and further, to dispatch all fear of Resistance, I can assure you there are but two more Servants in the House, whom my Fellow has made drunk, which shall be order'd so, as if they had murder'd their Master.

It

It was well for me that Darkness cover'd the Hemisphere, or the old Devil could have discover'd the Confusion in my Countenance. But notwithstanding my Consternation, I told him I should be proud to serve him in this, or any other Adventure. Gramercy, said the old One, and here's something to encourage thee, (clapping a handful of Dollars into my Hand.)

I'll leave you to guess the Confusion of my Thoughts at this Declaration, and I was casting about in my Mind, how I should prevent this intended Villany.

When we arriv'd at my Father's, we found the Treacherous Villain wating for his Master. Assoon as ever he saw us, he cry'd softly to Don *Lewis*, I am glad your Honour is come; but Don *Ferdinand* is in his Closet, and does not intend to go to Bed to-night, because he is to be at *Sevil* early in the Morning, and he has shut his Closet-door. Why then, said Don *Lewis*, we'll break it open. But, return'd the Servant, he has Arms always ready in his Closet, and I fear the Enterprize will be a little Difficult, for he's a tough old Blade.

Upon this Account a small Pause ensu'd, which gave me Leisure to think, and to the Old one I utter'd my Thoughts.

Sir, said I, submit this Business to me, and I'll inform you how I design to execute it. Your Servant shall accompany me to the Door of his Closet, and knock, and assoon as ever he opens it, I'll give a good Account of the old Gentleman.

Thou counselleft well, reply'd the old Don, and I'll reward thee accordingly when the Work is done. And I shall deserve it, thought I to my self, if my Intention succeeds.

Upon

Captain Robert Boyle.

Upon this Resolve, we went into the House, and the Fellow conducted me up Stairs very softly. The Closet was at the end of a large Room, the Door of which I bolted on the Inside with one Hand, and plung'd my Ponyard to the Heart of the Fellow with the other, who drop'd dead at my Feet. At the Noise he made in falling, my Father cry'd out Who's there! and rush'd out of his Closet, with a Pistol in his Hand. I reply'd, 'Tis I, your Son.

You may imagine the Surprize my Father was in at this sudden Appearance, and to see one of his Servants weltring in Blood, and dead before me. Sir, said I, banish your Surprize, and go with me into your Closet, where I will inform you of this sudden, and unlook'd-for Appearance; and must farther add, that the Hand of Providence, by me, has sav'd you from Death.

My Father follow'd me into his Study, without speaking: Where I declar'd, in as few Words as the Time would permit, all that had befallen me that Night; and we soon came to a Resolution what to do.

We took each of us a Blunderbuss with a brace of Pistols, went down the back Stairs, and came in upon 'em, a way they little expected. I came first into the Hall, as we had concerted.

Assoon as the old Wretch saw me, he cry'd, Well my Lad, hast thou dispatch'd the Villain! Yes Sir, said I, and have drag'd him down that you may behold what I have done. When he heard that, he gave a Leap for Joy, and came running forward to view the pleasing Sight. But Words cannot express his Looks, when he saw my Father confronting him with a Bluderbuss in his Hand. He stood motionless, as if he had been turn'd to Stone.

The

The other three endeavour'd to make their Escape, but I discharg'd my Blunderbuss, and stopt two of them with my hasty Messengers. The Report of my Piece made *Don Lewis* fall down, as imagining himself slain; the third Person finding it impossible to escape, became desperate, and like a Stag at Bay defy'd us. He pull'd out a Stilletto, and ran upon me like an angry Lyon, and notwithstanding I shot him in the Breast with a Brace of Balls, wounded me in three several Places; I grappling with him, we came down together upon the Body of *Don Lewis*, who with our Weight began to cry out; and that Moment had been the last of my Life, if my Father had not ran to my Assistance, and with his Sword nail'd my Antagonist to the Pavement.

The Report of our Fire-Arms had waken'd the two drunken Servants of my Father, who came half frighten'd out of their Senses. By this time *Don Lewis* had recover'd himself, and seeing Death before him, fell down upon his Knees, and implor'd my Father's Mercy.

Thou base Man! reply'd my Father, how canst thou expect to live after thy barbarous Attempt upon his Life that never wrong'd thee? He told him he did not expect to be forgiven, only to be allow'd a Priest, and Confession, and he would die with a hearty Penitence for his Sins.

Wretch! cry'd my Father, thou may'st see how Heaven abhors thy Fact, by blasting thy Design. This Man thou seest before thee, whom thou didst employ in thy black Design, is my own Son, whose coming hither was like an Angel sent from Heaven to my Assistance. I see, return'd the *Don*, the Seal of Providence is upon you, and I heartily repent the Crime I
intended

intended to commit: And if you will forgive me, and forget what is paſt, I'll eſteem you as the Saver of my Life; and, to unite our Friendſhip, I'll match my Daughter with a noble Dowry to this your Son, and may they ever live happy.

My Father was too much a Gentleman to murder in cold Blood, though he had ſufficient Excuſe on his ſide if he had done it. On the other hand, his Daughter was a very great Fortune, even beyond his Hopes.

After ſome ſmall Pauſe, he made him this Reply. Sir, you know within your ſelf, that you have forfeited your Life by the Law, in ſo baſely attempting mine; but as I can forgive any Injury deſign'd me, if you perform your firſt Promiſe, I am reſolv'd to forgive all that's paſt. Sir, reply'd the other (tranſported with Joy) I am ſo much oblig'd to you for my Life, that I will not ſtir out of your Houſe till I have ſign'd Articles of Agreement; and I muſt farther add, that nothing ſets my Shame more before my Eyes than this your Goodneſs.

My Father begg'd he would take a particular Care how he gave way to Hatred; which, by the way, only commenc'd in my Father's getting the better of him in a Law-Suit, and was heighten'd by the King's conferring on him the Honour of the Government of *Sevil*, which *Don Lovis* had ſome Hopes of.

We took care the next Day to let the Country know, that theſe Fellows that were kill'd had attempted to rob our Houſe, but we having timely Notice had prevented 'em by their Deaths.

The old Gentleman was as good as his Word; for Articles of Agreement were drawn up between

tween 'em, and I had Leave to visit' the Lady when I thought fit.. But I was obliged to go back to *Sevil*, to put my self in an Equipage suitable to the Occasion, and *Don Lewis* follow'd after with his Daughter.

I must confess I was charm'd with her Person at the first Interview; and the Day was fix'd for our Nuptials, which rejoic'd the whole City of *Sevil*, that two of the noblest Houses were going to bury in Oblivion their long Enmity.

I took the Privilege of an intended Husband in my Visits to my design'd Bride, and in her Conversation found she had no Aversion for me, (at least I thought so,) and I promis'd my self the utmost Felicity in her Enjoyment.

One Morning, about a Week before the intended Wedding, I came early to wait on her, but was inform'd she was not come out of her Chamber: therefore I resolv'd to take a Walk in the great Piazza of the City, to give her time to dress her self; but as I was going out, I observ'd the Maid to my Mistress conferring with a Country Fellow; the Sight of me, I observ'd, gave the Woman some Confusion. My Heart told me I was concern'd in their Interview, therefore I went to the Corner of the Street, and waited till their Dialogue was over; which did not keep me long, for the Fellow soon parted with the Woman, and went out of the Gate that leads to *Cordova*.

I had my Man with me, whom I acquainted with my Fears, ordering him to dog the Fellow, and get out of him, by fair Means or foul, his Business at *Don Lewis*'s House, and I would follow after him on Horse-back.

Away ran my Man, and I soon got my Horse, and overtook 'em about a League and a half from

from *Sevil*. When my Man got Sight of me, I obſerv'd he took a little Basket from the Countryman, and ran away over the Fields with it. I fancy'd by that he had ſucceeded in his Commiſſion, ſo turn'd my Horſe and follow'd him.

When I had overtaken him, we went behind a Tuft of Trees a little out of the Road, where he told me he had made the Fellow believe he was ſent by *Tereſa* (the Name of the Maid he was conferring with) to give him Notice that he would be purſu'd by a Cavalier, and forc'd to deliver what he had receiv'd from her, and perhaps be in Danger of loſing his Life; and that he had Orders to conſult with him for his Safety.

The Countryman, being none of the wiſeſt, ſoon diſcovered the whole Affair to my Man, and at Sight of me deliver'd the Basket to him, and ran to a publick Houſe in the next Village, to wait till he could get clear of me, where my Man was to bring him his Basket again. In the Basket were four Melons, and in one of them we found a Letter very artificially put up, which I took out, and with Terror of Mind read the Contents, which were as follows.

Life of my Life, and Treaſure of my Soul! I receiv'd yours, which gave me all the Conſolation my diſconſolate Heart was capable of receiving. But the fatal Moment is approaching, when I muſt give up this Body to another Perſon, but without a Heart, which always dwells with you; and be aſſur'd, unleſs ill Uſage force it thence, ſhall ever dwell in the Manſion of your Breaſt. But, my Soul, grieve not; for maugre my Tyrant Huſband, I will find Time to ſee the Darling of my Eyes, and in the Pleaſure of thoſe dear Arms forget

forget the dull Embraces of a Husband. Let Ten be the latest this Evening, when you shall find at the usual Place; with long-expecting Love, your

Isabella.

I was Thunderstruck at the reading of this Letter, yet blest my providential Stars that guided me to this black Secret, before the Priest had join'd our Hands. And, tho' a *Spaniard*, my Resentment did not rise to Jealousy, but my Fancy ran upon the Enjoyment of this false Fair-one, without the Marriage Chain. And what prompted me the more to it, was, a Postscript to her Letter, wherein she bad him come in his usual Disguise, and in the dark. In order to the Accomplishment of my Design, I went into a neighbouring House, and wrote the following Letter, which was put in the Melon in the Room of the other.

My Love,

I *Have not Time to write my self, I am so guarded by my Father, and my Tyrant Husband that is to be, so that I am oblig'd to employ* Teresa. *Don't come to the usual Place till you hear from me, which shall certainly be To-morrow. Adieu, thou Life and Soul of*

Isabella.

Now all the Hopes I had were, that the Fellow knew what Disguise this amorous Spark wore, and where was the Place of Rendezvous.

I left it all to my Servant, who had Cunning enough to outwit twenty of the Countryman. After I had deliver'd him his Commission, I went back to *Sevil*, full of Hopes and Fears;

Fears; and in two Hours my Man arriv'd: He gave me a Description of his Converse with the Countryman, (which was diverting enough) and how happy they were in escaping my Hands.

He inform'd me, the amorous Gallant came disguis'd in the Habit of a Peasant, and was admitted through the back Garden of *Don Lewis*'s House by the Maid, who always attended the Hour, and convey'd him to her Apartment in the Dark; which was according to my Wish: and by Description of the Spark's Person, we were not unlike as to Proportion or Age, and Darkness would conceal the rest.

I soon provided my self of the Habit I was to wear, and impatiently expected the coming Hour, which came at last, though the intervening ones seem'd the longest of my Life.

I did not wait long before I was admitted by the too-faithful Confident. We went over the Garden to a small Room at the Entrance of the House, where I soon discover'd my false Fair-one, (tho' in the dark.) She was undress'd, and disincumber'd of every Lett to Enjoyment. I found, by her eager Kisses and Embraces, there was no Parlying requir'd; so I e'en fell to and fed very heartily; my Partner in Pleasure seem'd to like what was prepar'd for her; and, before we parted, gave me to understand I had done Wonders, and much beyond her Expectation.

When we had dally'd away about four Hours in our Feasting, the Maid came to tell me it was time to part, which we did, after snatching another Morsel.

I went immediately home, was soon in Bed, and had no want of any Provocative to Sleep.

When I arose in the Morning, I began to weigh maturely the last Night's Adventure; but could come to no Resolution as to the forming my Behaviour to my false Mistress: But I resolv'd to be determin'd by hers.

I went to visit her about Noon, and found her more than ordinary civil to me.

In short, I was so charm'd with the Sight of her, that I resolv'd to give her another Visit in my Disguise the same Night; and all I had to do was to be first at the Place.

When the Time came, my Conductress was as ready as before; but going softly in, she clapt to the Door a little too hastily, and fasten'd my Coat in't; and to give me the more Uneasiness, she the same Moment dropt the Key out of her Hand; and though I could see where it lay, yet I could not stoop for it, because my Coat was secur'd in the Door.

After groping about some time, she took it up, and open'd the Door to release her Prisoner: But on the very Instant my Rival appear'd, and, finding himself there before he came, rush'd in, and fasten'd upon me.

The Maid, at the Sight of two *Sofia's*, clapt to the Door in a Fright, and ran screaming away; so we had the Happiness to be lock'd in the Garden together. But however, to make the best of a bad Market, (as the Saying is,) I got my Rival down, and belabour'd him with my Fists; for, as good Fortune would have it, we had neither of us any offensive Weapons.

The Noise of the Maid, and our bustling, alarm'd an *English* Mastiff that was Watchman to the House, who, without saying *By your Leave*, had the Impudence to fasten upon my Rival by the Arm, and worry'd him very handsomely: But, notwithstanding my Reasons to the

contrary,

contrary, I took Pity of him, and by Force of Arms deftroy'd the Dog; that is, I held him fo faft about the Throat with my Hands, that his laft Breath flew away in a Huff.

My difguis'd Spark feeing himfelf fo unexpectedly reliev'd, gave me Thanks for his Safety; and, affoon as ever he fpoke, (for we had been fullen before, neither of us having open'd our Lips) I knew him by his Tongue to be one of my particular Acquaintance.

Why how now, *Don Juan!* faid I, how came you thus difguis'd? Nay, reply'd the *Don*, I ought to ask you the fame thing. With feveral Queftions and Anfwers we came to a right Underftanding. If I had known, faid he, your Pretenfions here, I fhould never have made any Attempts to your Prejudice. Come, come, faid I, it's very well as it is. So we turn'd that to Mirth and Ridicule, which perhaps others of our Nation would have turn'd to Blood. Our next thing was to make our Efcape, for the whole Houfe was alarm'd, and coming upon us with their domeftick Weapons, as Pokers, Spits, Fire-fhovels, &c. My Companion led me to a Place of the Garden, where the Wall was fomething lower than any where elfe; and juft as we had gain'd the Afcent, we perceiv'd a Man mounting from the other Side; but my Friend did him the Favour to tumble him down again; he quickly got up, and ran upon him moft furioufly with his Poniard, and gave him feveral Stabs; but my Friend clos'd with him, wrefted his Weapon from him, and ftabb'd him to the Heart.

Affoon as he was fped, we made off; but did not go far before my Companion dropt down dead of his Wounds. I was very much griev'd at the Accident, but made the beft of my way home, for fear I should come into Trouble about it, if I was caught near the dead Bodies.

I went to Bed, but very much perplex'd in Mind, and had no Rest all Night. But what was my Grief in the Morning, when my Servant brought me Word, my Father and *Don Juan* my Friend were found murder'd, in the Habits of Peasants, under *Don Lewis*'s Garden-Wall! The Relation depriv'd me of the Use of Speech for some time, and my Reason forsook me. I was more than once going to put an End to my Life, and had certainly done it if I had not been prevented by my faithful Servant. But when my Reason return'd again, I began to think of the Adventure with some Calmness; for though I had all the Grief imaginable for the Loss of so good a Father, yet I was of a Temper not to grieve long at any thing; and then the Fortune I thought my self Master of, appear'd so lovely to me, that it soon dry'd up my Tears.

The City imagin'd my Father came by his Death through *Don Lewis*'s Means, as remembring the antient Enmity of the two Houses; and being found so near his House, strengthen'd the Opinion of every Body; and I was the only Person satisfy'd to the contrary.

The Servants that brought in my Father's Body, gave me several Papers found in his Pockets; among which were two Letters that partly let me into the Truth of this unhappy Adventure. The first was to this Purpose;

SIR,

YOur Generosity has prevail'd, and I can no longer withstand your Offers, (on the Condition as you promise in your last, that you will break off the

Match

Match between your Son, and my Lady.) *You must provide your self of a Peasant's Habit, and to-morrow I will send you a Note to instruct you farther.*

Yours, &c.

Teresa.

The Second was as follows.

BE *at the West End of the Garden at one in the Morning, and ascend a Ladder of Rope you will find there, and bring it over with you; near the Corner you'll perceive an Arbour, go in there, and wait till I come to conduct you to your Wishes. I'll take care nothing shall be in your way to interrupt your Privacy; and be sure you be careful of your Tongue, for if you speak, we shall be both undone.*

My Thoughts were in the utmost Confusion about the unravelling of this fatal Affair; and running over in my Imagination my past Conversations with my Father, I remember'd in our last, he told me, he thought it a little of the soonest for me to marry; and that it would be more for my Interest, to delay our Nuptials; and perhaps, said he, I may give you sufficient Reasons for the contrary. Whatever his Reasons were, I little thought of the true one.

I sent a Letter to the Maid of my false Mistress; but she fearing she should be found out (as she really was) absconded.

Don Lewis sent to condole with me in my great Loss; but I could perceive it gave him some Satisfaction, that I was in actual Possession of that Estate, which I had only Hopes of in the Life of my Father. His Visit was but short, yet I thought it too long; for as I had no Design of marrying the Daughter, I was very willing to drop my Acquaintance with the Father. Tho' I gave him Hopes, when Decency would permit, I would not fail in my Addresses to his Daughter.

After the Interment of my Father, I began to examine his Affairs, and was not very well pleas'd to find the best Part of his Estate mortgag'd for twelve Years to several Persons; and instead of seeing my self worth twenty thousand Crowns a Year, soon found I was not worth the sixth Part.

It was agreed, that my Father was very profuse in his way of Living, always keeping open House; yet it was every body's Opinion he did not expend half his Income.

I sometimes imagin'd there was some underhand Dealing in the Affair, but it was past my finding out: I therefore took an odd Resolution, I determin'd with my self to undergo a voluntary Banishment, till the term of Years on the Mortgage was expir'd.

I made a Visit to *Don Lewis*, and told him of my Resolves, and my Reasons for it, which he could not chuse but applaud; for it was easy enough to perceive Interest was the Jack he aim'd at. He did not press me to see his Daughter, nor I him; but after Assurance of remembrancing on both sides, we parted.

I must own, my Soul long'd for another Taste of the delicious Banquet; and I hope you will excuse me when I own to you, my Passion could not be call'd Love; but as I found it impracticable, I made my self as easy as I could.

In a few Weeks I had finish'd my Affairs, and waited for the sailing of the *West-India* Fleet; resolving for the City of *Mexico*, where I had an Uncle very rich, who had often express'd press'd in his Letters to my Father, the great Desire he had to see me.

I had rais'd out of the Ruins of my Father's Fortune six thousand Crowns, without so much as touching any of his Plate, or Furniture; the care of those Things, with all my Writings, I trusted to a near Kinsman, Superior of a Monastery in the City.

One Day, going about two Leagues out of Town, my Horse's Girt broke, which obliged me to a light at a Sadler's to have it made good. The Man ask'd me if I would not take a walk in his Garden while he was doing his Work, which I accordingly did.

At the end of the Walk was a pretty Arbour, and in it sat a Woman reading; who at the Sight of me, gave a great Shriek, and was for running out; but I stopp'd her, and begging Pardon for disturbing her, told her I would retire, and leave her alone. But upon finding it was *Teresa*, Maid to my quondam Mistress, I resolv'd to stay with her, that I might know something of my Father's Affair.

She appear'd confounded at the Sight of me, as imagining I had come on purpose to apprehend her; but I soon undeceiv'd her, and with a little soothing Language, and a couple of Pistoles, she dispos'd her self to give me all the Information she could.

Sir, (said she) I hope you will pardon me; for what I did, was purely by the Influence of Gold.

Your Father declar'd to me, at first Sight of my Mistress his Heart and Reason forsook him; and often inform'd me, if he could not enjoy her, he should be obliged to put an end to his Misery by Death. I often lay'd before him the Injury he would do to you his Son, but he as often

often declar'd he would break off the Match between you; for he was well assur'd you had no very violent Inclination for her, and there were other Women in *Sevil*, of as great a Fortune as my Mistress, that would be proud of his Alliance.

The many rich Presents he made me, overcame my Honesty; and that unfortunate Night that brought him his Death, was to have compleated his Happiness. But, said she, (after some Pause) I am very much at a loss to find out one thing. What's that, Madam? said I. Why, Sir, return'd *Madona*, since I know how Matters stand between you and my Mistress, I shall give you to understand, that you were not the favour'd Lover; and that another Gentleman revell'd in those Delights, you perhaps thought to have the whole Possession of; and that was the Reason I was so willing to comply with your Father, for I had intended to introduce him in the Habit of the said Gentleman, unknown to my Mistress, and had provided a Story accordingly. For assoon as ever the Gentleman was gone, your Father should have taken his Place in the same Disguise; and I intended to impose on my Mistress, that her Lover was return'd to take another Farewel of her. And this Cheat was easy to be carry'd on, being they were obliged to Silence, old *Don Louis* lodging in the next Room. But what amazes me, (as I was saying) opening the Door to let my Mistress's Lover in, another in the same Disguise rush'd in upon me, which I am sure was not your Father. I soon clear'd up this Affair with her, and let her know how I had supplanted my Rival.

She seem'd very much surpriz'd at the unravelling of this Secret, but was very glad she had nothing to apprehend from my Resentments; being

ing that was the chief Cause of leaving her Mistress, as imagining I should find the Letters she had sent him. And upon this she resolv'd to go to her Mistress again, for she heard every Day from the Family, and knew how Matters stood; and that her Mistress wanted her, that they might condole together for the loss of *Don Juan*, her old Spark. But she declar'd, she was not very sorry for his Loss, for Mony came very hard from him; and you know Sir, said she, it is our Business to make Hay while the Sun shines.

Madam, said I, since I know what you love best, if you'll pursue my Intrigue, twenty Pistoles are at your Service. Indeed, Sir, return'd Madam, it must be something very extraordinary that I shall refuse for such a Sum. Why then I'll let you into my Plot, said I; you shall inform your Mistress *Don Juan* is not Dead, as was reported; but after a tedious and dangerous Illness, was recover'd to a Miracle, but conceal'd his Revival, being under some Apprehension of answering for the Life of my Father.

Sir, said she, I like your Plot so well that I'll answer for the Success on't, and I'll go about it instantly, for I long to be fingering the Gold. Why then, said I, you shall finger it before-hand, and when the Business is done, I'll double the Sum. She was mightily pleas'd with the Amendment to the Bargain; and the third Night after was concluded on for the Time, when I was to attend as before.

I took leave of *Teresa*, and pursu'd my Journey, made merry with my Friends, and return'd.

At length the happy Moment came, that I so long expected. My mercenary Confident was ready; I enter'd, and once more took Possession of all my Treasure; and as I thought it would be the
last

last time, was profuse enough. My Lady seem'd very well pleas'd with my Night's Work, and in plain Terms told me so.

I had prepar'd a Letter, in which I had disclos'd every thing. When our loving Affair was over, she ask'd me softly how I was engaged in that Adventure. I told her as softly as I could, that I knew she would be inquisitive, and talking being dangerous, I had brought the Account in Writing, which I put into her Hand, and with some regret took my Leave; for the next Day was intended for our Imbarkation. As I walk'd over the Garden, I ask'd *Teresa*, how long the Amour had been between *Don Juan* and her Lady; she told me about two Years, and this was the Commencement.

Don Juan, whose Country-house lay about two Leagues from my Master's, was set upon by Thieves, and dangerously wounded; and there had lost his Life, if *Don Lewis* had not very fortunately for him come that Way attended, and drove off the Thieves. *Don Juan* was so very much hurt, that it was not thought safe to carry him home; therefore my Master order'd him to his House, where his Wounds kept him a great while. When he had recover'd Strength enough to walk, he usually employ'd his time in the Garden, where my Lady often seeing him, fell desperately in Love with him. She made me the Confident of her infant Passion, and I being a very proper Person to be trusted with such Secrets, advis'd her to let the *Don* see her, which we contriv'd thus.

She was to go into an Arbour at the farther end of the Garden, (where I had observ'd *Don Juan* sat every Day) and pretend to be asleep. She took all the care that was necessary in her Dress, and did as I directed her. It succeeded to her Wish; for the *Don*, at Sight of her, imagining her an earthly Goddess, kneel'd and kiss'd her Hand. She seem'd to wake in a pretended Fright, but it was not long before they came to a right Understanding.

That Place was made the Rendezvous of the Lovers, when Opportunity would permit; but he recovering (tho' he pretended a Weakness for some time) was obliged to take leave of our House; tho' in the Father's Absence, they often found Opportunity to satisfy their Loves; and when they resided in Town, he continu'd his Visits in the Disguise of the Countryman he us'd to send to my Lady with Presents of Fruit, and by that means they received Letters from each other.

When she had finish'd her short Relation, I gave her the tewnty Pistoles I promis'd her, and took my Leave. She seem'd to be in some Confusion about managing it with her Mistress, for she would certainly find her out, she said, when she would be confirm'd of *Don Juan*'s Death; but she comforted her self with telling me, her Mistress durst not disclose it to any body, for fear of betraying herself. But poor *Teresa* little thought her Mistress would find it out so soon as the next Morning, when she had read my Letter, that I put into her Hand, when I left her. The next Day, I order'd my Equipage on board our Ship, which lay at *Cadiz*, and follow'd my self; but the Wind chopping about, hinder'd our setting Sail. I then repented the leaving my Letter with my Mistress, for by the help of my Money with *Teresa*, I might have made another Meal with her.

I did not think it Prudence to go on Shore, fearing her Resentments might form some Designs on my Life. I therefore contented my self on Board, till the Wind ſhould prove fair for ſailing. As I was reading in my Cabin one Day alone, my Servant brought me a Letter: The Contents were theſe.

Noble Sir,

UNderſtanding you are bound for Mexico, the Place of my Birth, I ſhall think it the greateſt Honour in the World, if you pleaſe to take me into your Protection. My Father was a rich Merchant of that City, who going to another World, has left me a conſiderable Eſtate in this. Thoſe Perſons who had the care of my Education here, ſeem to have Deſigns againſt my Fortune; therefore I have made my Eſcape from 'em, but muſt return to my Betrayers, if you have not the Goodneſs to be my Guardian to Mexico, where I ſhall return the Obligation you ſhall pleaſe to lay me under, in being my Protector.

I ask'd my Man who brought the Letter, and he told me a young Negro. I bid him bring him in. I ask'd him ſeveral Queſtions, and found him ready with his Anſwers. He inform'd me, that his Father, tho' a Negro, was a Man of Subſtance, and had ſent him in his Infancy to be educated at *Sevil*, and for the reſt the Letter inform'd me.

I was mightily pleas'd with the Perſon of the black Gentleman, and treated him civilly, with the Aſſurance of delivering him ſafe to his Friends at *Mexico*.

When we were alone, he told me he had a farther Secret to diſcover to me, if he was ſure of not being interrupted. Upon hearing this, I order'd my Servant on Shore for ſome Neceſſaries, and inform'd him, we need not fear any Interruption for ſome Hours.

After

After a long Pause, and casting his Eyes on the Ground, he began.

This Veil of Night would not hide my Blushes, if I were not convinc'd in your Knowledge of my Frailty. But if you'll consider my Youth, Climate, and Opportunity, you will allow few of my Sex could withstand the Temptation. Be not surpriz'd to find in this Disguise the Daughter of *Don Lewis*, who is so far subject to the caprice of Love, as to disclose to you the inmost Secret of her Heart.

The Letter you left with me produc'd a contrary Effect than I believe you imagin'd; and instead of Rage and Indignation taking Possession of my Breast, a softer Passion stole in, and I felt all the Tenderness imaginable for *Don Pedro*.

I expect nothing but ill Usage from you for my past Conduct; but if you can believe there is any Sincerity in Woman, after what I have been guilty of, I am assur'd you may depend on what I say, that no other Object shall share my Heart with you. I do not mean the tye of Wedlock, but if you will accept of me as I am, I'll be as subservient to your Commands, as your meanest Slave.

I was so confounded between Pleasure and Amazement, that I imagin'd all I heard and saw was a Dream; but being sweetly convinc'd of the Reality, I said all my Passion could suggest in return, not giving my self time to consider of the Oddness of the Accident: 'Twas sufficient I had in Possession all that was lovely in Woman, in my Imagination; and I had no other Thought, but how to keep her from the Knowledge of her Father on Shore, and the Sailors on Board, for we did not know when we should set Sail.

My Mistress told me, if she had not succeeded with me, she resolv'd for a Nunnery, but since we were reconciled, she had laid by all Thoughts of the Habit. She made her Escape from her Father's, without the Assistance, or Knowledge of any one but *Teresa*. But what favour'd her Escape was, the Absence of her Father for ten Days in the Country; yet she fear'd, when he came home again, he would fright *Teresa* into Confession, or by Promises get it out of her; for that she was mercenary enough to sell any thing she had to the best Bidder. To prevent which, we agreed to dress her in the Habit of a Man, and let her wear her own Complexion.

Accordingly we both went on Shore at *Cadiz*, and soon equipt our selves with what we wanted, and on Board I brought my Spark, as a Relation of mine, that had a Mind to run his Fortune with me. The next Day the Wind proving favourable, we set Sail, and left our Apprehensions behind us.

I was obliged to let our Servant into the Secret, that I might have it kept so; well knowing, if he had discover'd it himself, it had not been a Secret long, tho' the Fellow was very faithful to any Secret that was trusted to him.

We touch'd at the *Madera* Islands, pass'd the Pike of *Teneriff*, got over the Line, duck'd our Men as usual, and met with no extraordinary Accident; but in fifty three Days, arriv'd safe at the City of *Sancta Domingo*, (or St. *Dominick*) the capital City of the Island *Hispaniola*.

I was very well pleas'd to find so delightful a Place as this was, after the Fatigue of our Voyage. My Mistress and I took us a Lodging at a good-natur'd *Spaniard*'s, that treated us very well—for our Money.

Here

Here my Lady told me, she felt the Effects of our Familiarity. I endeavour'd to persuade her I had no Hand in't; but she insisted upon't, that the Deed was done by me, and gave me some Proofs to believe it.

I was very much concern'd to find Means to hide it from the House; for she began to have those Qualms which attend that natural Distemper; and by the Beauty of her Face, I fear'd her Sex might soon be distinguish'd.

I kept her from the Sight of our Ship's Crew in the Voyage, she always staying in the Cabin; and it was very dangerous to discover a fine Woman in this Part of the World, because there are few that are handsome.

I was upon Thorns till our Departure for *Mexico*; but the Fleet staying longer than I expected, I took a Ramble to the most noted Places in the Island; and since I understand by your Story you never were there, I'll give you a short Description of it.

Hispaniola is seated from seventeen Degrees, to nineteen Degrees Latitude, in Length about one hundred and twenty Leagues; and Breadth (about the middle Part) fifty. The Air much the same for Heat, as at *Sevil* in *Spain*; the Fruits delicious, and some peculiar to the Place.

The capital City, is St. *Domingo*, which gives a delightful Prospect from the Fields about it, being mix'd with pleasant Gardens and Rivers.

Here the Governor of the Island resides, and here are kept all their Offices, and Courts of Judicature, and it is likewise the Store-house to the whole Island.

There are two Cities more, St. *Jago*, and *Nuestra Sennora de alta Gracia*; the last of which is to the South, and is famous for the beft Chocolate in the World.

The Cathedral of St. *Domingo*, is a handfome Pile of Building, and the other Churches are anfwerable to the Grandeur of the Inhabitants, whofe very Artizans are wealthy.

The Fryers live as luxurious here, as in any other Part of the World, and follow the Steps of their Brethren, in chufing the nobleft Situations.

This Ifland was difcover'd by *Columbus* in the Year 1492, and kept in the Hands of the *Spaniards* ever fince that Time; while moft of their other Acquifitions are fell to the *Englifh*, *French*, and *Dutch*.

Tho' the *French* have fome Plantations in the Ifland at prefent, yet they were of their own acquiring, and not taken from the *Spaniards*; and being chiefly Hunters, and not very rich, the *Spaniards* make no Attempt upon 'em.

No Ifland can boaft of more convenient Ports than this, and every Port difembogues fine Rivers (ftor'd with palatable Fifh) into the Sea; but then to qualify that Bleffing, they are very much infefted with Aligators, and Crocodiles. I faw one lying on the Shore-fide like a Log of Wood, and as a Buffalo came there to drink, he fprung upon him, dragg'd him to the Bottom, and there devour'd him; tho' they are eafily to be avoided, from the aromatic Smell that comes from their Skin.

I was much furpriz'd to find in moft Houfes, Serpents inftead of Cats, that were greater Enemies to Rats and Mice; but what was more pleafing, they were not the leaft Offenfive, having no Venom in 'em. But then, they will often play the Fox with the Poultry, and deftroy many of them, unlefs narrowly watched.

The

The *Scolopendria* of the *Greeks* is found here, and very large Scorpions; but by the Divine Providence, neither of 'em hurtful.

I shall not trouble you with any farther Account of this Island, because there is not any thing to be found there, but what is upon the Continent, unless some particular Herbs; and as I am no Botanist, I shall not take any notice of 'em.

The time came at last for our embarking for *Vera Cruz*, in order to go to *Mexico*, and I left St. *Domingo* with some Regret; as imagining I should not meet with any other Place in *America* so pleasant.

During our Voyage, my Mistress was mightily disorder'd.

We embark'd for *Vera Cruz*, where we arriv'd without any Accident; and having no Business there, we set out by Land for *Mexico*, and got safe there. But enquiring for my Uncle, I was inform'd he was gone to reside at *Lima*, the capital City of *Peru*. My Concern was the more, in that I fear'd I should not meet with proper Accommodation at *Mexico*, for want of him, in the Affair of my Mistress; for her Condition would not bear the Fatigue of another Removal.

I was entertain'd in the House of a near Friend of my Uncle's, and one who kept a Correspondence with him; he was very civil to me, and of a freer Disposition than generally the *Spaniards* are; but he had the same Vanity as all the old Christians have, who Pride themselves very much upon't. I let him into the Secret of my Lady, and her Condition; and by the help of his Wife, we made her reassume her proper Dress. But we kept her private.

The time of her Delivery came, and the Product prov'd a lusty Boy, who staid among us three Weeks,

Weeks, and then left us. I had no Scruples about being the Father, for it was plain enough to be seen; it being my Picture in a little. My Mistress continu'd very weak longer than the usual Time; and I being alone with her one Day, she told me she was under some Apprehensions concerning our Landlord, Don *Manuel*, who had made her secretly many large Offers, and the Nurse was his Emissary. I told her I had the same Proposals from his Wife; and tho' the Woman was not disagreeable, nay might pass for a Beauty, where Women were so scarce, yet I could not find any Tenderness for her in my Heart.

After many Arguments between us, a Thought came into my Head, which I hop'd would produce some Mirth among us. I desir'd my Mistress to give Don *Manuel* some small Encouragement, and leave the rest to me.

My Landlord soon found an Opportunity, thro' my means, to see my Mistress. She follow'd my Advice, and transported the *Don* out of his Senses; his Joy was not to be contain'd, he forgot the Gravity of a *Spaniard*, and caper'd about like a *French* Dancing-master. When I learnt all their Discourse from my Mistress, I begg'd her to continue her good Humour to him, and promise him a meeting that Day Sevennight in the Summer-house of the Garden. She did as I directed.

In the mean time I took my Opportunity to confabulate with the Wife, and gave her Directions the Night appointed, to go to the same Summer-house, but to avoid Speech, being it was over the Water, and Men were continually passing to and fro. The good Woman was as much overjoy'd as her Husband; and the better to carry on my Design, I gave it out, that I was

to

Captain Robert Boyle.

to go with some Gentlemen a hunting the Buffalo for two or three Days. I desir'd my Landlord (a Title I had given him out of Mirth) to take care of my Wife in my Absence. I told my good Landlady, this was a Contrivance of mine, that we might not be suspected.

My Mistress had made just the same Agreement with the *Don*. The Time came, and the good Man and good Woman were left to worry one another, with their extraordinary Passion.

The next Day at Dinner, (for we generally eat together) Don *Manuel* cast many a Sheep's Eye at my Wife, and his good Lady at me.

The same Day, as I was reading in the Garden, *Madona* came to me, and in bitter terms of Reproach gave me much ill Language; and told me I had betray'd her to her Husband basely, by giving him the Ring she gave me the last Night. I soon found that she had made a Present to her Husband of a Ring, taking him for me, and she had observ'd it upon his Finger. She made so many Speeches about it, that at last I was compell'd to tell her the whole Truth, to get rid of her tiresome Passion, but I soon repented of my Declaration; for she flew upon me, and with her Nails play'd the Cat with my Face, and I had much ado to disengage my self from her. So furious does a disappointed Passion make a Woman.

Her confounded Temper made me resolve to leave *Mexico*. The Husband began to suspect something of the Affair; but his Imagination, that he had the Company of my Wife in the Summer-house, curb'd his Resentment.

The Woman's Rage was unsurmountable, and it was not in my Power to bring her to Temper: Therefore I chose to avoid her as much as possible.

sible. As I was at Supper with my Miſtreſs, ſome few Days after the Accident happen'd, ſhe told me, ſhe had receiv'd a Preſent of Cordial-water from Don *Manuel*'s Wife. Now I had not told her of *Madona*'s Reſentment, becauſe I imagin'd it might make her uneaſy: But aſſoon as I heard of the Preſent, ſomething ſtruck my Mind, there was ſomething uncommon in it; I therefore deſir'd my Miſtreſs not to drink any of it. Lord ſaid ſhe, my Dear, I have already, and deſire you would taſte it too, for 'tis the pleaſanteſt Liquor I ever drank in my Life.

I was mightily diſturb'd at it, and two Hours diſcover'd the fatal Effects.

My Miſtreſs began to be very much out of order; and notwithſtanding all the Aid of Phyſicians, ſhe expir'd in my Arms, and every body agreed ſhe had been poiſon'd. I had, in my Fury and Ravings, declar'd to Don *Manuel* the Author of this black Deed; and when he went to enquire after her, was inform'd ſhe went out before Night, and was ſuppos'd to have gone to the Town of St. *Jago*, on the Lake, to one of her Relations. Don *Manuel* ſent after her, but ſhe was not to be found. He grieved at the loſs of my Miſtreſs, as much as I did; and I dare avow, if he had found his Wife, he would have ſacrific'd her to the *Manes* of my dear Miſtreſs.

I was very much griev'd for the Loſs of my Miſtreſs, for I had reaſon to be convinc'd her Paſſion for me was unfeign'd. You may eaſily imagine, there was no ſtaying for me in the Houſe where this diſmal Accident happen'd; but as I was preparing to be gone, the *Corrigidore* ſent for me to appear before him, to give him the beſt Account I could of this Action. I related to him the whole Truth, as I have told it you;

you; only I declar'd it was my Wife I had loft. Don *Manuel* was feiz'd, and put in Prifon, notwithftanding I infifted upon his Innocency; but he proceeded in that manner, being it was fuppos'd he was acceffary to his Wife's Efcape. But a few Days after he was fecur'd, News was brought, that his Wife was found murder'd in the Woods, as it was fuppos'd by fome *Indians*, as fhe was endeavouring to make her Efcape from the Hands of Juftice.

Thus fhe met her Reward for her barbarous Murder of a Woman that never wrong'd her, tho' indeed the Favour was defign'd for me.

A few Days after this fatal Accident, I heard of fome Merchants that defign'd to crofs the Continent to the *South Sea* with a good Guard. I made Acquaintance with 'em, paid my Quota to the Charge, and fet out along with 'em, leaving behind me the hateful City of *Mexico*, where I had loft the only thing I efteem'd on Earth. And I muft own to you, notwithftanding my Philofophy, I never thought of her for fome time without the utmoft Heart-breaking. I have endeavour'd indeed, by forcing my Temper to Mirth, to bury the Remembrance; and Time, with good Company, has brought me fome Affiftance; yet neverthelefs, I do firmly believe, no Woman's Charms will ever for the future break my Reft; for I am fatisfy'd, my late Miftrefs made a Hole quite through my Heart.

But to purfue my Difcourfe.

We fet out, with a Guard of fifty *Spanifh* Soldiers, for fear of the *Indians*, who had made it their daily Practice to fet upon every body that went through the Country, if not too ftrong for 'em. I need not tell you, that *Mexico* is one of the fineft Cities in the World, or that it lies

upon

upon a Lake, and no other Paſſage to it but over three broad Cauſways from different Cities on the Land. But what is ſomething extraordinary, one part of the Lake is brackiſh, and noiſome, with no living Creature in't; and the other is freſh, wholſome, and ſtor'd with palatable Fiſh. But as there are many exact Accounts of the Continent of *America*, and its Conqueſt, by my noble Countryman *Hernando Cortes*, I ſhall ſay no more of it; but I will take the Liberty to add that *Cæſar* and *Alexander* were but Pigmy Conquerors to him; and every body will be of that Opinion, if they will give themſelves the Trouble of reading his Hiſtory.

We met with no *Indians* to oppoſe our Paſſage, and arriv'd at *Segovia*, an inland Town inviron'd with Rocks, and but meanly built. Some of our Company ſtaid there, and I was willing to ſtay along with 'em to refreſh my ſelf; for it's but indifferent travelling over rocky Mountains, and croſſing Rivers upon Hurdles, that is Pieces of Timber laſh'd together with Ropes; and it is ſometimes dangerous, tho' we got over ſafe with our whole Company.

I ſtaid fifteen Days at *Segovia*, with fifteen of my Companions. I was very much ſurpriz'd at the Relation of ſome of the Inhabitants of that Place, who told me, about two hundred of your Countrymen the Year before (Free-booters) in ſpight of all Oppoſition came from the *South Sea*, to the *North*, with a very great Booty, defeated the *Spaniards* when ten to one, and poſted to all the Advantage in the World, ſeveral times. The People of *Segovia* talk of 'em as ſo many Devils; and that they were aided by the black Gentleman, or it had been an Impoſſibility to have gone through what they did. But

it

Captain Robert Boyle.

it muſt be confeſs'd, your Countrymen deſpiſe Hazards, and laugh at the greateſt Dangers.

After we had ſufficiently refreſh'd our ſelves, we took our Leaves of *Segovia*, and purſu'd our Journey to the *South-Sea*, with a Guard of *Indians*, ſubſervient to the *Spaniards*. And I muſt own to you, there is not a People in the World more true to their Truſt, than thoſe confederate *Indians* that own the Dominion of *Spain*.

Our Journey to St. *Fee* was pleaſant enough, through a rich, level, pleaſant Country, and we rode upon Mules, a Beaſt of a ſure Foot; and our chief Diverſion was ſhooting of Monkies, that play'd us ſeveral comical Tricks, running up the Trees, and frequently did us the Favour to urine in our Faces, and ſometimes ſomething worſe.

When we arriv'd at St. *Fee*, a ſmall Town and Port in the *South-Sea*, we had the good Fortune of meeting with a Veſſel ready to ſet Sail for *Lima*. We went immediately on Board, and got clear of the Shore that Evening.

We arriv'd at *Lima* after a Voyage of twenty five Days; we landed at *Calao*, the Port that all the Ships of *Spain* anchor at, and one of the fineſt in the *South-Sea*.

The Town is built upon a Point of Land that runs into the Sea. It is very ſtrongly fortify'd, and well garriſon'd. I ſent my Servant to my Uncle at *Lima*, to acquaint him that I was coming to wait on him the next Day; but my Servant return'd in four Hours, with my Uncle's Coach, who inform'd me, that he was impatient till he ſaw me. My Uncle was Judge of the Civil Courts, and a Man in very great Power. He ſent his *Major Domo* to wait on me, with his Excuſe, that he had come himſelf, but that he was afflicted with the Gout. I only ſtaid
till

till I had put on other Cloaths, and immediately after went in the Coach with the *Major Domo*, and arriv'd at my Uncle's juſt within Night. He was very well pleas'd to ſee me, and careſs'd me in an extraordinary manner. But I was ſomething ſurpriz'd to find that he had reſolv'd for *Spain* within a Month, there to end his Days.

I told him the Story of my Father's unhappy Fate, only concealing his Love to *Donna Elvira*. He was very much ſhock'd at the News, owning to me his chief Reaſon of going to *Spain*, was to have the Happineſs of living together. I then told him, I ſuppos'd as that could not be, that he would alter his Reſolution, and think no more of his Voyage: But he anſwer'd, moſt of his Effects were gone for *Spain* two Months before, and that he muſt of neceſſity follow.

I gave him to underſtand, that it was not in my Power to wait upon him. He took a great deal of Pains to perſuade me to it, but when he found it was to no purpoſe, he told me ſince I was not to be prevail'd upon, he would leave me Maſter of a ſmall Fortune in *Lima*.

During his Stay, he introduc'd me to moſt of the beſt Families in the City, and the Viceroy was pleas'd to ſhow me good Countenance, and promis'd my Uncle to provide for me.

When the time came of his embarking for *Spain*, I waited on him on Board, where we took Leave, though not with dry Eyes; and I have repented many times that I did not accompany him. But we muſt ſubmit to Fate; and what is allotted us by Fortune will come.

He left me Maſter of a well-furniſh'd Houſe, and a Plantation whoſe Income would provide

every

every thing Necessity requir'd in the middle Station of Life, with a Promise that at his Death I should inherit the Remainder of his Estate; for he was a single Man, and had no nearer Relation than my self.

I took all the Pleasure the Place would afford; and to say Truth there was no want of any thing at *Lima,* except the Conversation of the Female Sex; though I must freely confess I did not always want that.

The Viceroy prov'd very kind to me, but Death taking him away suddenly, I mightily griev'd his Loss, as indeed I had Reason; for the Person that succeeded him prov'd the Reverse. He made a general Remove of all the Officers the Deceas'd had put in Posts, and among the rest I was one of the Sufferers; and farther, upon all Occasions he made it his Business to flight me; and often affronted me so grosly, that nothing but his Dignity shrouded him from my Resentment: and many other People in Power, (as the Injudicious generally copy the Frailties of their Superiors, and neglect their Virtues) treated me in the same Manner; but I was resolv'd not to bear it.

One Day as I was coming from my Plantation upon my Mule, attended only with my old Servant, I met a Nephew of the Viceroy's in his Chaise, in a narrow Road, and not being willing to give way to him, we were both at a Stand; which so enrag'd the cholerick Gentleman, that he flew out of his Vehicle, and ran his Spado into the Belly of my Mule, which dropt down dead.

I did not want so much Provocation to raise my Choler, therefore I drew upon him, and left him in the same Condition with my Beast, grov'ling upon the Sand. He had several People

ple that attended him, who rush'd upon me and my Man, overpower'd us, and dragg'd us immediately to the Viceroy's Palace; who, being glad of any Pretence to wreak his Ill-nature upon me, condemn'd me to *Baldivia* for Life, in spite of the Intercession of those few Friends I had.

It was in vain to complain of this damn'd Trick of Fortune; and the more to plague me, he left Orders that I should be dispos'd of to *Don Sancho Ramires*, a Relation of his; the Wretch that I have sufficiently reveng'd my self of, and, in part, of the inhumane Viceroy; for they were Partners in Trade.

Ramires us'd to put me upon the most slavish Business, but as I had Money I usually bought it off; for I receiv'd yearly my small Estate from *Lima*, I mean from my Plantation, for the Viceroy had seiz'd all the rest of my Moveables; and would have done this, but that the honest *Indian* who had the occupying of it, insisted on its being my Uncle's.

This old Hunks had a beautiful Daughter, that I found was in Love with a Colonel of the Garrison of *Baldivia*. This Colonel, notwithstanding my Condition, was not asham'd of my Acquaintance, and often told me the Torments he endur'd for the young Lady.

I ask'd him if the Lady knew of his Passion; he inform'd me that he flatter'd himself with the Return, though they had never spoke to each other, but he had receiv'd obliging Glances from her fair Eyes, from the Gallery which overlook'd the Court of Guard.

I agreed that if he would write a Letter, I'd pawn my Life she should have it, and an Answer into the Bargain; if she had any Inclination to send one. He embrac'd me, and thank'd me me for my kind Proffer, and wrote a paſſionate Letter to the Lady; which I accompanied with another, to let her know I was devoted to her Service upon the Colonel's Account.

In two Days I had an Anſwer convey'd into a hollow Tree in the Garden, as I had concerted in my Note to her, that waited upon the Colonel's.

Theſe Paper Meſſengers brought Matters to bear, and the kind Lady reſolv'd to venture her ſelf with the Colonel.

We contriv'd a Ladder of Ropes long enough to reach from her Window to the Terras on the Court of Guard; and I convey'd a ſmall Bundle of Packthread for her to throw down, which we faſten'd to the Ladder of Ropes, and the Lady with much Difficulty pull'd it up, and faſten'd to an Iron Cheſt which was in the Room: But as ſhe came trembling for Fear down the Ladder, it drew the Cheſt along the Floor above, which awaken'd that old Devil her Father. He immediately alarm'd all the Servants, as well as Slaves; but the Captain had got ſafe off with his Miſtreſs.

When old Huncks had ſummon'd us all together, he went into the Room to ſee what the Matter was; but when he found his Money ſafe, his Diſtraction began to abate. I muſt own, I wiſh'd heartily we could have clear'd his Money too, as well as his Daughter. It was ſome time ere he miſs'd her, as having no Notion of her Elopement; but when he found ſhe was gone, his Paſſion was unſurmountable; for the good Lady had made bold with Writings of an Eſtate, that it ſeems were left her by an old Aunt; and I was very well pleas'd ſhe did not go empty-handed to my Colonel; for I take Money to be the Sinews of Love as well as War. The

The inrag'd *Don* ran up and down like a Madman, with about a dozen of us at his Heels; and as we approach'd the Ditch of the Castle, which happen'd to be free from Water, being the Tide was out, but pretty well provided with Mud, some of his Servants imagin'd they saw something lie on the Mud. The old *Don* being very peery, was stooping down and gazing to be satisfy'd; and the Devil prompting me just at the same time, I clapt my Knee into his Bum, and down fell the poor *Don* into the Mud.

I was the first that cry'd out for Help, yet I did not make extraordinary Haste to assist him; but at last Ropes were brought, and after he had flounder'd about a Quarter of an Hour, we lugg'd him up in a sweet Pickle.

By good Luck, he did not mistrust that the Favour was design'd him, but purely accidental. I had an Opportunity the next Day to find out the Lady and the happy Colonel, who had brought a Commission from the Priest to go to Bed together. He was so well pleas'd with my Service, that he promis'd to ransom me from *Don Sancho*, and did not doubt but he should succeed, being the *Don* made Money his *Summum Bonum*. But we were surpriz'd at the Refusal, for he had such a strict Charge from the Viceroy of *Peru* to hold me fast, that it was more his Interest to keep me than part with me. Nay this Proposal open'd the old *Don*'s Eyes, for he saw plainly I was at Bottom of his Daughter's Affair. This so enrag'd him that he order'd a great wooden Clog to be lock'd fast to my Leg, which I was oblig'd to lug along with me.

This Proceeding drove me almost to Despair, and I lost all Hopes of ever procuring my Liberty.

Captain Robert Boyle.

The Colonel and his Lady (who had recover'd the Fortune from *Don Sancho*) were very much griev'd at my ill Usage, and try'd all manner of Means for my Liberty, but to no purpose. I past three Years in this uncomfortable Life, and had the Pleasure to hear that my implacable Enemy, the Viceroy of *Peru*, was summon'd to *Spain*, upon the Account of some Male-Administration. At the hearing of this News my Hope of Freedom began to revive, but it was soon clouded again; for the old Devil, *Don Sancho*, was resolv'd to keep me a Martyr to his own Revenge; and I weather'd out two Years more in my wretched Confinement: Though, Thanks to Heaven, nothing depress'd my Spirits quite.

The Colonel got an Opportunity to tell me that there was a Vessel in the Road bound for *Lima*: and the Captain being a very good Friend of his, he had prevailed with him to take me on Board him, if it was possible for me to get out of Hunks's Clutches.

I made all the Efforts imaginable, but to no purpose; and I was once more in my Imagination given up to eternal Slavery.

The same Night, as I was endeavouring to compose my troubled Thoughts, I heard a great Noise in the Castle-Yard, and was very much surpriz'd a while after, when I saw an Officer and a File of Soldiers come to seize me, as a Plotter against the State, and carry'd me to the Colonel's Lodging. But my Surprize was turn'd into Joy, when I found he had us'd this Stratagem to gain me my Freedom. I told him he had trebly repaid the Obligation he was pleas'd to say he lay under to me, and I was resolv'd not to accept of my Liberty till I found what Stir *Don Sancho* made about it: but the

S   Colonel

Colonel resolv'd me that he had the Means in his own Hands to pacify him.

I went on Board, and set Sail the same Evening. We had but an indifferent Voyage, being involv'd in many Storms; yet at last we arriv'd safe at *Calao*.

I shall, if you think fit, give you a short Description of *Baldivia*, because few Foreigners are permitted to enter their Port.

Baldivia, or *Valdivia*, takes its Name from the first Founder, a *Spaniard*. The old Town stood a little higher than the new one, till it was destroy'd by the *Indians*. For *Peter Baldivia*, and the rest of the *Spaniards*, were such Tyrants over the poor Natives, that they took Heart, laid an Ambush for 'em, and destroy'd 'em every one. But in the new Town they are sufficiently guarded from their Insults, or Danger of a foreign Enemy; which have often attempted 'em to no Purpose. This being reckon'd the richest Country for Gold Mines in all *America*, Nature has befriended 'em very much in the Strength of the Place; for there is so large a Sand-Bank in the Mouth of the Bay, that Vessels are obliged to come within five hundred Yards of the Shore (which is guarded by a strong Castle) to avoid it. It is a difficult Harbour to enter, but when you are once at Anchor, no Wind on the whole Compass can hurt you, tho' it blew a Storm; it is so well shelter'd by the Land on all Sides of it.

The Inhabitants are chiefly made up of banish'd Persons, who generally work in the Mines for so many Years; and the Time expir'd, they have so much Land of their own to cultivate; and most of them find the Means to be rich; but how honestly I'll give you leave to judge. The Country about it is very fruitful, and

produces

produces great Quantities of Apple Trees, from which they make very good Cyder. But the Juice of the Grape is very uncomatible there, and those that do procure it must pay extravagantly for it.

This City, for it's no less, is esteem'd the Key to the *South-Sea*.

The Governour and Officers are generally sent from *Lima*, but the Soldiers are compos'd of those Persons that are sent there for a Punishment. And tho' few Persons chuse to be sent there, yet as few desire to leave it when once they are settled.

Notwithstanding the People could make shift to live without Religion, yet there are seven Churches and three Monasteries; but they seem to be in a ruinated Condition: And I don't doubt but an Age or two hence, those that pass that Way may find them totally ruined.

As I said, we arriv'd safe at the Port of *Calao*. I was resolv'd to remain *incognito*, till I had enquir'd into the Affairs of the City.

I took an Occasion to send to my *Indian* Tenant, who came to me, and was very well pleas'd to find me at Liberty.

I sent him to several of my Friends, to acquaint them what Circumstance I lay under, who soon inform'd the Viceroy of my Misfortune, and he as readily comply'd with my Desire, allowing me the Liberty I had enjoy'd before I was sent to *Baldivia*.

I once more made my Appearance at *Lima*, renew'd my Acquaintance, and began to divert my self as before. By degrees I crept into the good Graces of the Viceroy, who gave me a Post in the Government, that brought me a considerable Income; and with the Esteem of most People I past on a whole Year.

S 2   The

The Viceroy not liking his Situation, found the Means to be recall'd to *Spain*: Yet recommending me to his Succeſſor, I remain'd in the ſame Station he before had given me; though I cannot brag of any more Favours beſtow'd on me by my new Superior; for he was a Man of an uncertain Temper, proud, and revengeful. He was newly marry'd to a very rich Widow of *Lima*, who had a very beautiful Daughter, by Report; for ſhe was not ſuffer'd to take the Liberties of the Place.

I often had a great Deſire to ſee her Face, for I had obſerv'd her veil'd many times at Church, which was all the Liberty ſhe had. I was inform'd ſhe was deſign'd a Wife for the *Supreme Judge*, though much againſt her Inclination, being there was a Diſparity of Years, which is certainly the greateſt Bitter to the Sweets of Matrimony; but nothing is conſulted now more than Wealth.

I receiv'd a Letter from my Uncle at *Sevil*, wherein he deſir'd I would leave *Lima*, and come to *Spain*: And, to induce me to it, he gave me the Promiſe to make me his Heir. I muſt own I began to be pretty well tir'd of this Climate; and the Time drawing on for the Expiration of my Mortgage, I ſet my ſelf to prepare things accordingly.

I diſpos'd of my Plantation to my faithful *Indian*, for an under Price, being I thought I was under many Obligations to him. I reſign'd up my Office in the Viceroy's Palace, indeed, becauſe I could not get Leave to diſpoſe of it.

I turn'd all my Effects into Gold-Duſt, and ſent it before me to my Uncle; and now I only waited for Company to go over Land to *Vera Cruz*, a Port in the North Sea, where I ſhould have Convenience of imbarking for *Spain*.

I

I began now to think of settling in the World; and indeed it was almost time, for I had past my twenty-eighth Year, and at that Age the Heat of Youth should be pretty well over; for if a Man cannot see his Follies on this side thirty, he is in Danger of being incorrigible all the Days of his Life. Beside, I had very good Encouragement to Stability, my own Fortune, and the Prospect of my Uncle's; who in all Probability had not many Years to live, being in his eighty-third Year.

Well then, as my Story is almost off the Stage, I'll throw you into the Bargain a short Account of one Place more, for my Catastrophe, and then to my Epilogue for detaining you so long, and that shall be the Description of *Lima*, as it is at present.

Lima, the Capital City of *Peru*, is seated about two Leagues from the Sea-Port of *Callao*, in 12 Degrees 6 Minutes of Southern Latitude, and 79 Degrees 45 Minutes of Western Longitude. It is built in a noble Plain, with Hills at a Distance.

Francis Pizarro was the Founder, in the Year 1535, tho' it has chang'd its Name since his Time, from *La Ciudad de los Reges*, or *City of Kings*, to *Lima*, which is only a Corruption of the *Indian* Word *Rimac*, which was the Name of an *Indian* Idol, formerly worship'd in that Place.

This is the finest City (next to *Mexico*) in all *America*. All the Streets are in a direct Line, exactly measur'd out, and much of the same Length and Breadth, being fifty Yards wide.

In the Heart of the City is the noblest Square my Eyes ever beheld, and in the midst a Fountain of Brass, adorn'd with eight Lions, continually spouting Water, supply'd by the River of *Lima*, that runs through the Skirts of the Town, cover'd with a handsome Stone Bridge that leads to the Suburbs. Within the Suburbs is a fine publick Walk, beautify'd with Orange Trees, and in the Evening is crowded with the best Company of the City. Although this City is so beautiful, it was mostly destroy'd by an Earthquake in the Year 1682. There are no less than fifty-seven Churches and Chappels (with those that are in the Monasteries) in this City, and twenty-four Monasteries for Men, and twelve for Women. The Cathedral is very magnificent, as are most of the other Churches, tho' chiefly built with Wood from the first Story, by reason of the Earthquakes.

The Viceroy of *Peru* has his Residence here, and is so powerful he hardly owns the King his Master to be his Superior. Here are likewise kept all the Courts of Justice, and from the High Court there is no Appeal. Among the rest, they have settled an *Inquisition*, which, on my Conscience, is worse than that of *Spain*. Heaven keep every Body from it; for in this Court the Informant is a Witness, and the Accuser is ever behind the Curtain, and to mend the Matter, the Witnesses are never brought Face to Face.

To compleat the Grandeur of the Place, there is an Archbishoprick, and an University of three well-fill'd Colleges; tho' the Students don't always follow Learning, for I have found some ignorant enough.

There are twelve Hospitals, and one of them for *Indians*.

This City is garrison'd with two thousand Horse, and six thousand Foot; but very indifferent Troops for Service against a foreign Foe, being chiefly compos'd of *Creolians* and *Indians*. These *Creolians* (who are so nam'd from owing their

their Birth to *America*) are moſt of 'em proud, lazy, and ignorant, and generally Tyrants whenever they have Power, tho' ſharp enough as to Trade, and will over-reach you if they can.

They are all inclin'd to Venery, and will ſacrifice every thing to gratify that Vice. The Women (who are really very handſome) generally ſit at home all Day croſs-leg'd, and as mute as Fiſhes; but at Night it is cuſtomary for 'em to haunt the Streets veil'd, and will as hardly be refus'd a Favour, as the Men with us on the like Occaſion.

As I was ſitting one Evening in my Lodging, diſpatching ſome Letters for *Spain*, I heard ſome body knock ſoftly at my Door. My Servant was gone abroad, and therefore I aroſe and open'd it my ſelf, but was ſurpriz'd to ſee a Lady veil'd, who, without making any Words, came in and ſat down on a Couch. After ſhe had repos'd her ſelf ſome time, ſhe unveil'd, and diſcover'd to me one of the ſweeteſt Faces I had ever ſeen. I was almoſt turn'd into Stone at the Sight of ſo much Beauty, and was ready to fall down to worſhip her as a Divinity. Said ſhe, I come not here to be gaz'd at; I like you, and if you can do the ſame by me, I believe you will not uſe me ill.

Madam, I return'd, I know no other way to convince you that I like you, but one. With that I took her into an Alcove, where we ſoon came to a right Underſtanding. Aſſoon as our ſmall Matter of Buſineſs was over, ſhe deſir'd to be diſmiſs'd, yet with a Promiſe to give me another Viſit the next Evening; but, ſaid ſhe, if you ſhould chance by any Accident to ſee me in any other Place, take your Eyes from the Object, for fear of Danger; for thoſe Meſſengers of the Soul often betray their Truſt.

I promis'd to obferve her Directions, and left her, but yet could not help my Curiofity; for when fhe was got down Stairs, I put on my Cloak, follow'd her, and obferv'd fhe went into the Viceroy's Palace. I was convinc'd, by the Drefs fhe wore, that fhe was none of the common Sort; and much diverted I was at the Accident.

The next Day fhe did me the Favour of another Vifit, when we pafs'd our time as pleafantly as we could; and my *Incognita* feem'd very much pleas'd with my Company.

After our Toying was over, fhe told me fhe was afraid of lofing me, for fhe had heard I defign'd for *Spain*. I inform'd her, nothing had Power to ftop me, but the Paffion I had for her.

She at laft difcover'd herfelf to me: She was Daughter-in-Law to the Viceroy: She told me that fhe had refpected me a great while, and had many Difputes with her Honour and Love; but the former was forc'd to give way to the latter. She likewife let me know of her approaching Marriage, and added that the Knowledge of my Perfon would make her Averfion to her Husband the ftronger. We had many Meetings, to the Content of us both; and fhe made me feveral Prefents of Jewels, which I intend to keep for her fake, having preferv'd them thro' all my Fortunes. Our Meetings now began to be lefs frequent, being the Wedding-Day was fix'd, which gave me a great deal of Uneafinefs. To divert my Melancholy, I ufually took a Walk in the Orange-Grove, where, in my mufing Fits, I often ftay'd longer than ufual.

As I was going home one Evening, I heard the Clafhing of Swords at a Diftance, and immediately after faw a Perfon running towards me, me, who cry'd, For the Virgin *Mary*'s fake, if you are a Gentleman, lend me your Sword, to defend my felf againft a Villain who has offer'd me the vileft indignity. I made him no Anfwer, but gave him my Sword (for he look'd like a Man of Quality) and follow'd him.

Juft as I turn'd the Corner I faw him engag'd, and his Antagonift drop down dead.

The Gentleman feeing that, took to his Heels.

The Street being alarm'd with the Buftle, as I came near the Body, I was feiz'd as the Murderer. What ftrengthen'd their Opinion, and I muft confefs had but an indifferent Look, was my Sword remaining in the Body of the Deceas'd. All my Affeverations of Innocence fignify'd nothing: I was carried before the *Corrigidore*; but having no Witneffes of my affaulting him, and one Fellow by good Fortune proving I was not the Perfon that engag'd him firft, I was only once more condemn'd to *Baldivia*. I curs'd my hard Stars a thoufand times, and the Grief of parting from my Miftrefs was like to rid me of Life; but Time began to wear it off.

I was fecured in the Caftle of the City till the Veffel was ready to fail.

While I was confin'd, in order to be tranfported to *Baldivia*, a Gentleman came into the Prifon, and begg'd half an Hour's Converfation with me. I had been fo liberal to the Keeper with my Money, and pretty jovial in my Humour, that I believe if I had ask'd him to let me go, he would not have deney'd me; fo that I begg'd the Favour to admit the Gentleman, and his Abfence, during our Confabulation. He obey'd me in both, and the Gentleman enter'd my Room; which, though but mean, was the beft in the Prifon.

Affoon

Assoon as the Gentleman had repos'd himself upon a Chair, (none of the best) he ask'd me if I would please to refresh my self with any thing the Place afforded: But I answering in the negative, he made half a dozen Humms and Haws, and open'd his Mouth to utter Sense.

Sir, said he, you see before you the unhappy Person that is the occasion of your Confinement. I should not be thus free with you, if I were not assur'd of your generous Good-nature. Once more I must tell you, you see before you the unhappy Man who is guilty of that Fact you are to suffer for. I am a Gentleman by Birth; and tho' I had not the good Fortune to owe my first Being to old *Spain,* yet I have this for my Consolation, that my Parents were born at *Cordova* there; but the Frowns of Fortune driving them to this part of the World, grew asham'd of her ill Looks, and greeted 'em with Smiles of Favour. In a few Years, *Plutus* the God of Wealth made 'em a Visit, and took his Leave of 'em with a Promise of his frequent Return; and he prov'd as good as his Word, for in a little time Fortune became a neuter Gender, that is, believing they did not want her Assistance, they were no more her Devotees.

Sir, said I, the sooner you will please to come to plain *Spanish,* the sooner I shall be in the ready Road to your Business.

Why then, said he, not to keep you in Suspence, I am the Person that was oblig'd to you for your Sword on such a Time, which prov'd the Instrument of my Revenge on a base Wretch, that deserv'd an Eternity of Torments after this Life, for wronging the best of Women. And since I find you love the shortest way, without the tedious outward Flourishes of Rhetorick, I
will

will inform you of my Story, with as much Brevity as I am capable of.

My Mother dy'd about seven Years since, and I may very justly say the rest of my Father's Life was a Delirium; but Death taking Pity of his Griefs, came to his Aid, and about two Years ago I was left Master of a plentiful Fortune.

As Death is the End of all things, and Age must pay its Tribute to him, I shook off my Grief for my Father's Loss; and in six Months after his decease, fell in Love with a young Lady of an incomparable Beauty, at least in my Eye. My Fortune gave me easy Access to the Father of my Fair, and when I had the Happiness of conversing with the Object of my Wishes, she did not seem averse to my Passion. Every thing concurring to my Desires, *Hymen* join'd those Hands whose Hearts were united before.

For several Days we revell'd in the Sweets of Love; and I may justly say, Possession had not the Power to pall Desire; each Moment of Enjoyment seem'd new, and my utmost Wish was center'd in her Breast: But the dire Fiend, tormenting Jealousy, at last crept in, and pall'd my Appetite to ardent Love; the fatal Bitter to our mutual Sweets.

I had a Person that I call'd my Friend, who shar'd the Affluence of Fortune with me: We had the same Desire to Love and Hate: I therefore thought I was but poorly blest till my Friend saw the Idol of my Soul. But oh! what Pangs that fatal Moment cost me! His Eyes receiv'd the Bane to all his Peace, and in one Moment render'd up his Heart. I gave him Leave (for what could I refuse to such a Friend?) to visit my Wife, when Business demanded my Absence.

Abfence. He often declared his Paffion to her, by plaintive Sighs and languifhing Looks. When my Wife perceiv'd he importun'd her too far with his Love, fhe threaten'd to tell me of it; but in the mean time he had acquainted me with what had pafs'd between him and my Wife. Said he, My Friend, I imagin'd your Wife was like other Women, prone to change, therefore in your Abfence I counterfeited a Paffion for her, to fee whether fhe had that Regard fhe ought to have for you, and I am pleas'd to find you have made fo worthy a Choice.

I muft own to you I was mightily pleas'd with this Tryal of my Friend, as believing it fprang from his Kindnefs to me; and I had much to do to reconcile my Wife to his Vifits. She would often fay, I wifh your Friend be fincere in his Profeffions to you; for my part, I greatly doubt it.

In a little time after this Accident, I perceiv'd my Friend began to look very melancholy; I endeavour'd to fift the Secret from him, but to no manner of Purpofe for fome time.

One Day, as we were riding out to take the Air together, he feem'd more deeply plung'd in Sorrow than ufual. I told him, I fhould not take him for my Friend any longer, if he did not let me into the Caufe of his Diforder. At laft, with much Reluctance, he told me that the good Opinion he had before conceiv'd of my Wife was falfe, for he was well affur'd fhe was not true to my Bed.

You muft imagine what a Thunder-clap this muft be to me, from a Friend who I was affur'd in my felf would not relate a Falfehood. It was fome Moments before I could open my Mouth; and all the time of my Silence, he feem'd fo much griev'd that he had declar'd the Secret to me, me, that I had no Doubt of the Truth of it.

When my Grief had given me Liberty of Speech, I begg'd he would give me the Foundation of his Sufpicion; but he defir'd to be excus'd till he had certain Proof of her Infidelity, which he did not doubt but he fhould foon have, tho' it was what he wifh'd to be deceiv'd in: And farther added, he would not have me take any Notice of it, but carry it fair to her, as if nothing had happen'd; for if you fhould, faid he, you'll never come to the truth of the Matter.

I promis'd to comply with him, and went home; but Heaven knows with what a Heart.

I follow'd my Friend's Advice punctually, but yet could not help fhowing the Difcontent of my Mind in my Countenance. My Wife was mightily concern'd for my Melancholy, and was very preffing to know the Caufe; and in a very tender manner feem'd to be difquieted, which I took all for Art, and the Cunning of her Sex.

I muft own to you, that fometimes I imagin'd my Friend had deceiv'd me; but whenever we had an Opportunity of converfing, he ftrengthen'd my Jealoufy to fuch a degree, that I began to wifh the Caufe of it no longer in this World. And if it had not been for my revenging my felf on the fuppos'd Partner of her Guilt, I had certainly taken Methods to difpatch her hence.

I had fome Affairs to tranfact at *Segovia* every Year; and the time drawing on for my Journey, my Friend told me, before my Return I fhould have Demonftration of her Infidelity; for, faid he, your Abfence will give her the Opportunity fhe wants, and fhe'll be fure to take hold of it.

It

It was a great while before I could be prevail'd upon by my Friend, to undertake really this Journey, but only to feign as if I had, that I might be convinc'd of her Perfidy, and punish it my self; but my Friend laid me down so many Reasons for it, that I at last very unwillingly agreed to go. But in the mean time, said he, you must order that I may have Admittance in your Absence, that I may take my Opportunity to observe all Passages. Why, said I, I never knew you debarr'd the Liberty of my House. But you know, said he, since my false Declaration of Love, to try your Wife's Virtue, she has look'd upon me more like an Enemy than Friend, as knowing I was not sincere in my Passion; for Women, be they ever so vicious, yet they abhor the Man that doubts their Virtue. Well then, said I, if you will, we'll sup together to-night; and then I'll take an Opportunity to leave Directions with my faithless Wife, to allow you the same Privileges in my Absence, as you now have. Why then, return'd my Friend, don't you be surpriz'd at what I shall say to her.

We parted, and went to prepare every thing for my intended Journey. When I was at Dinner with my Wife, I gave her some Hints concerning my Friend, and that I desir'd he should have Admittance in my Absence; I observ'd she chang'd Colour at my Discourse, and seem'd to be in the utmost Confusion, altho' I did not seem to see it.

After some Talk about indifferent Matters, she told me, if I thought fit, she intended to live private in my Absence, and admit of no Visitors. For Sir, said she, the World will be censorious, and receiving Visits from a Man, when you are from Home, is not consisting with our *Spanish* Customs. She found by my Discourse that I was

deter-

determin'd it should be so, wherefore she left off arguing upon that Subject: but I could perceive all the time we were together, my Resolves sat very uneasy upon her; and it was with much Difficulty she restrain'd her Tears. Her Sorrow struck me to the Heart, and it was the greatest struggle I ever went through to keep my Temper: For I imagin'd all her Grief was to have this Spy upon her Actions.

When Night approach'd, my Friend came according to Appointment, and during our Supper, I told my Wife, she was to look upon him as my only Friend, and give him the same Admittance, as if it was my self, in every thing he should desire; well knowing (I told her) he would ask nothing contrary to our strict Amity.

Sir, said my Friend, I am very sorry I can't comply with your Desires; for I have receiv'd Letters from a near Relation at *Panama,* and I am obliged to attend his Nuptials, being he can't make proper Marriage Settlements without I am upon the Spot, and I fear I shall hardly return this six Weeks. I was at first very much surpriz'd at this his sudden Resolution, and was going to say something upon't, till I observ'd he wink'd at me. I then began to remember what he said to me in the Morning, that I should not take Notice of what he said. But I observ'd, the Cloud upon my Wife's Face began to disappear by degrees, which seem'd to me the greatest Proof of her Infidelity. I was so provok'd with the imaginary Wrong, that I could not help shewing it in Words and Actions; but yet I had so much Reason in my Madness (for Passion is no less) that I conceal'd the real Cause.

My Wife seem'd confounded at my incoherent Anger, having never seen my Fury before; and when

when my Friend was gone, begg'd I would tell her the real cause of my Uneasiness, for she was well assur'd some secret Cause had ruffled my Temper; but I persisted in the Obstinacy of not discovering it to her, and the next Day pursu'd my Journey with a dismal Idea of what was to come.

Thought had so much impair'd my Strength, with its violent Workings, that I found it a difficult thing to sit my Horse; and when I came to my Inn at Night, I was carry'd to Bed in a violent Feaver, and all Night was in a Delirium. My Servants sent for a Physician, who gave me something to resist my Malady; and while he was with me, I utter'd some Words in my Ravings, that gave him to understand my Disease proceeded from the Mind. When I came to my self, I was something surpriz'd to hear him speak to me after this Manner.

Sir, I have so long dealt with Diseases of most kinds, that I have Knowledge enough to perceive when they proceed from an ill habit of Body, or those Maladies of the Mind that slight all Physic; and be not amaz'd when I tell you, I have often cur'd the Latter by wholsome Advice. You are a young Man, and perhaps may have taken a wrong Conception of Things; if you will be pleas'd to tell me your Case, I'll give you my Advice without a Fee; and don't think me impertinent to desire it, I have seen more Years than you. You may conceal your Name in your Relation, and if my Advice does not please you, you are but just where you were: I shall be as faithful in keeping your Secret, as your Confessor.

You may be assur'd I was very much surpriz'd at his Proceeding, and I easily perceiv'd a Sincerity in his Discourse, that gain'd him my Esteem; and I was resolv'd to let him
into

into my Story; which I did, as much as I have to you.

After a Paufe, he faid I had juft come up to his Imagination of my Cafe; and now Sir, (faid he) I will proceed to my Advice. Confider well what you are about; you have confefs'd, your Friend own'd to you he made pretended Love to your Wife to try her Virtue, and yet I don't find he advis'd with you about it before he had put his Device in Practice. To give you my Sentiments of this Matter, I believe your Friend to be falfe to you, and that he really is in Love with your Wife. The Diftrefs of your Spoufe, proceeded from her Indignation to him, and Love to you. His telling you, after his Attempt upon her, was no more than to be the firft in the Declaration, as imagining fhe would of courfe inform you with it! her keeping it a Secret from you, was, not to make you uneafy; and his declaring his Sufpicion of her Virtue afterwards, was either to be reveng'd on her for flighting his Paffion, or to give him an Opportunity in your Abfence to wrong your Wife.

This, in fhort, I fancy will prove the whole Truth. Neither is this Judgment hard to make, for I am apt to believe any difinterefted Perfon would make the fame Judgment; your Paffion has blinded yours; yet neverthelefs, if you can give your felf time to think calmly, I don't in the leaft doubt but you'll be of my Opinion. This I am affur'd of, Jealoufy is a certain fign of Love; and if you fhould in the heat of Paffion do a rafh Deed, every Moment of your Life will prove a Torment to you. Lovers Eyes are often falfe, and too quick in falfe Creations. Call Reafon to your Affiftance; that will prove your beft Friend. Take fome time to think of my Advice and Counfel; Friends may affoon prove falfe as

T   Wives,

Wives, and you had better lose the former than the latter.

All the while he was fpeaking, methought I was liftening to an Oracle; and at the end of his Difcourfe, I could not help blaming my felf for my rafh Belief. I call'd over in my Memory every Moment of my Wife's Behaviour, and could not find any one Action ftart up, to give me that hard Opinion I had rafhly conceiv'd againft her.

I return'd the Phyfician of my Mind, as well as Body, many Thanks for his cordial Advice; and would have paid him in another Coin, but I could not prevail upon him to take a fingle Dollar. No, faid he, in accepting of your Money, I fhall make it appear, that, like Lawyers, I pleaded for my Fee. No Sir, all the Recompence I fhall ask of you, is only to let me know the Truth of every thing, when the Cataftrophe is over, which I hope will not affect your Wife; And if I might throw in one Word of Advice more, if you prove the Friend you have fo much confided in to be falfe, fhew your Refentment by flighting him, and leave Revenge to Heaven. I promis'd to follow his judicious Advice in every Thing, and fo we parted with a very good Regard for each other.

I was refolved to proceed no farther on my Journey, but make the beft of my Way back again; and as I went along, confider of my Behaviour, and let Time alone for Proof. The Reafon I gave my Servants for returning, was, that I had not Strength to purfue my Journey; which in Reality was no Falfhood, for I was weak enough; and I am convinc'd, that Diforders of the Mind weaken the Body more than habitual Diftempers. In part of my Journey back, I could not come to any Refolution how to behave;

have; and therefore resolved to lye one more Night upon the Road, to see if my Pillow would advise me. When I arriv'd at my Inn, one of my Servants told me *Don Roderigo* was just alighted. Hearing him nam'd, my Blood ran a wild Course about my Body, and immediately it struck to my Mind something was not right.

I ask'd my Servant, if *Roderigo* had seen him; he told me no, and that he seem'd disguis'd, as if he did not desire to be known. This strengthen'd my Suspicion of some Ill intended, or done already, and that he was making his Escape. I order'd my Servants not to appear: But when Supper was ready, I sent for my Host to bear me Company; where, after some trivial Discourse, I ask'd him what Guests he had in the House. He made no Scruple in telling me; but when he came to *Don Roderigo*, he declar'd he did not much like him; for he seem'd very willing to be private with two of his Servants, and he had observ'd 'em often whispering. They design, said he, to be going very early in the Morning, but I don't know which Road they travel. I conceal'd my Disturbance of Mind from my Host, but resolv'd to be going as early as *Don Roderigo*; and to be sure of being early enough, I determin'd not to go to Bed, notwithstanding the Weakness of my Body requir'd Repose.

In the middle of the Night, I heard People whispering in the next Room, and I could easily distinguish *Roderigo*'s Voice: tho' I could gather little of their Discourse, yet I could hear mine and my Wife's Name often mention'd.

At break of Day, I found they were preparing to be gone; and tho' I was pretty expeditious, yet they were got out of the Inn, before

I could get on Horse-back with my Servants. I was much vex'd at it, yet pursu'd my Journey homeward. But I was very much amaz'd, when about two Leagues from *Lima*, I met my Wife in a Coach with her Maid, and two *Indian* Servants. The Servants, assoon as they saw me, were overjoy'd, and my Wife could not open her Mouth for some time. I then began to relapse into my former Jealousie, and imagin'd she was following *Don Roderigo*.

At last she open'd her Mouth with a great deal of Joy. Lord, my Dear (said she) is it you in Reality, or are my Senses deceiv'd? I ask'd her the Reason of her Journey, and her mighty Surprize. Sir, answer'd she, that Question confounds me; have I not a Letter from you, to come with all Speed imaginable? Here it is, continu'd she. I took the Letter from her, and read the Contents.

My Dear,

PUrsuing my *Journey*, I had the Misfortune to fall from my Horse, and break my Arm, which prevents my writing to you. The Accident is attended with a violent Feaver, which I am told is very dangerous. I have refrain'd writing to you till now, as expecting some Amendment; but finding my self worse, I beg you will come to me with all the Expedition imaginable, for fear you should never see me more alive.

Your Affectionate Husband.

There needed no Sphynx to unriddle this Enigma; and I observ'd, by my Wife's Countenance, we both knew the Author of the Letter. While we were confus'd, the Coachman that drove the Coach was stealing away; but my my Wife cry'd out to stop him, for that was the Messenger that brought the Letter to her; and farther told her, he was to conduct her to me, for the Coachman we had before was drown'd; and that Circumstance deceiv'd her more than any thing else: The Fellow also told her that I had prevail'd with a Gentleman in the Neighbourhood where I lay hurt, to send him to drive the Coach. I rid after the Fellow and brought him back, order'd him into the Coach-box, and forc'd him to drive out of the Road to a neighbouring Village, where liv'd a Gentleman of my Acquaintance. He very unwillingly comply'd with my Commands; and we kept very close to him, to prevent his making away. When we arriv'd at my Friend's House, we secur'd the Fellow in a strong Room, and I left two of my *Indian* Servants to guard him. I made my Friend acquainted with the Accident, and that this Visit was not intended, but by meer Chance. He gave me to know I was welcome, let what would bring me there.

When my Wife and I with my Friend were alone, I tenderly embrac'd her, and begg'd her Pardon for my unjust Suspicions of her Virtue, and related the whole Progress of my Jealousie, without omitting the least Circumstance. She gave thanks to Heav'n, for the Danger she was sav'd from, and related to me the manner of her being deceiv'd by the Fellow that brought the Letter, as follows.

The fifth Day after you had left me, as I was musing in the Garden, my Maid told me a Person had a Letter to deliver me from you. I began to tremble with timorous Apprehension, and my whole Frame felt violent Disorders. I order'd the Bearer to be brought to me; and when I had read the Letter, Grief lock'd up my Tongue,

Tongue, and I had not power to speak for some time. When I had recover'd Speech, I ask'd the Fellow where you were. Madam, said he, he is at Don *Florio*'s Country-house, (*naming a Friend of mine, that my Wife had heard me often mention*) and knowing you had never a Coachman, my Master sent me to conduct you to your Husband. I would not spend time in dressing my self, but just as I was, with my Maid, and the two *Indians*, pursu'd our Journey. I never once dream'd of any Treachery, tho' I always doubted your false Friend; but as he had never been to visit me in your Absence, it wip'd away all Suspicions of him. I observ'd the Coachman, by his Looks, did not like the Company of my Servants, but I was too much concern'd for you to think of it much.

We congratulated one another again at our happy Deliverance, and admir'd the workings of Divine Providence, and the second Cause, my friendly Physician.

My Wife express'd a great Desire to see him, to return him Acknowledgments for his inspir'd Advice, and in the Morning I promis'd her to go to him, if we could get any convenient Carriage: For we were not very fond of making Use of the Coachman that brought her out.

I defer'd his Examination till the next Day, being too much fatigu'd to do it then, tho' I order'd he should want nothing but his Liberty; for I consider'd him only as an Instrument to work his Master's Ends. When I was up in the Morning, I order'd him to be brought before me; but after some time, they brought me Word he had made his Escape, by creeping through the Cieling of the Room, and throwing down the Shingles; for it was a single Apartment near the Garden. I was a little uneasy

easy at his getting away, as well as my Wife, for fear his Master should make some Attempt upon us in the House where we were; it being a quarter of a Mile from the Village, and the Gentleman, my Friend, had but few Servants. Therefore it was thought the safest Course for us to go immediately to *Lima*. And assoon as we could procure Mules, we set out, and reach'd that City without Molestation.

I heard nothing of the faithless *Roderigo* for several Days, neither did I think it strange; for I imagin'd, if he had any Shame left, he would not dare to appear publickly at *Lima*; but if he did, I had resolv'd to take my friendly Physician's Advice, (which had prov'd so successful to me) to show my Resentment in slighting him.

One Night, as soft Repose had lock'd up our Senses, we were alarm'd from our downy Sleep, by a fearful cry of Fire! Fire! I rose, and ran into my Wife's Apartment, where she remain'd frighted almost to death; and as People generally in the alarm of Fire know not what they do, she ran to the Chamber where the Maids lay, and dress'd herself in her Servant's Cloaths; the Maid being equally frighted, when she found she had no Cloaths to put on, clap'd on her Mistress's which I had brought after her, and was running down Stairs to free herself from the Danger. As she was going through the Hall, I observ'd four Men in Masks seiz'd her, and carry'd her off. I follow'd with my Sword in my Hand, till one of the villanous Company came behind me, and run me through the Back. My Servants, who came after me, bore me in faint with loss of Blood; but by good Fortune the Wound did not prove dangerous, tho' well meant.

We could never come by the Truth how the House was set on Fire, tho' it was soon extinguish'd; but we were assur'd it must be by some one of the Domestics. It was easy to judge Don *Roderigo* was the Cause on't, by running away with the Maid, as mistaking her for my Wife, because she had in the Hurry put on her Mistress's Cloaths and Vail.

I was advis'd, by my best Friends, to summon him before the supream Judge, for it was dangerous to let him go on with Impunity. But he would not obey the Summons, therefore he was design'd to be out-law'd by due course of Law. But as that takes up several Months, I was oblig'd to keep a Guard in my House; for I received several menacing Letters frequently from him, either thrown over the Wall, or left so, that we could never secure any Person that brought 'em. While our Suit was going on, our new Vice-Roy arriv'd, who proving a Friend to Don *Roderigo*, a *nolle prosequi* was issued out, and I was obliged to stand at the whole Charge of the Law-suit. This violent and unjust Proceeding of the Vice-Roy's rais'd my Gaul to that degree, that I said many warm things against his Administration, which came to his Knowledge: for there are generally poor-spirited Wretches in all Governments, that have no other Merit than to improve Tales, and feed the Ears of their Superiors with nauseous Flattery and Lyes.

I was sent for to the Vice-Roy, and examin'd concerning these Reports; and I so far incens'd him with my Replies to his Questions, that if I had not met with some Friends that palliated the Matter, I don't know how far his Resentment would have carry'd him. I was dismiss'd with my Liberty, but a multitude of Menaces, if for the future I ever gave my Tongue another loose;

and

and I soon found the Effects of his Resentment, by losing a small Place in the Government; but as Providence had put me above wanting it, I was not much griev'd at the Loss.

My Wife begg'd me to remove from *Lima*, a Place where I had receiv'd so many Insults; and it was not improbable but I might receive more; which prov'd but too true.

In a few Days after I had appear'd before the Vice-Roy, the Maid that was forc'd away (by mistaking her for my Wife) came home, miserably ill us'd, and brought me a Letter from the ungrateful Don *Roderigo*, which you may read if you please: upon that he took the Letter out of his Pocket, and I found it as follows.

I Declare my self your inveterate Enemy, tho' I have no just Reason to be so; you may be sure my Enmity is rooted for ever in my Heart, and I shall have no Rest in this World, till thou art out of it. I should not perhaps be so free in declaring my Mind by Writing, if I was not very well assur'd, thy publishing it would do thee no good. I have so much Honour in me still, as to assure thee, I would venture my Life to hazard thine, and if I have ever the Opportunity, I shall put it to the Hazard; therefore be well guarded whenever thou appearest abroad. Minds like mine are never appeas'd. I always was a Villain, but had so much Cunning to hide it from the World till now this Affair has publish'd it. And be assur'd, I shall study every way to compass my Revenge, whilst I am

Roderigo.

The Insolence of this Letter was not to be born, and I was as impatient to meet him, as he could be to meet with me; and I must own to you, I thirsted for his Blood, for his Usage was beyond

yond the nature of Man to bear. I examin'd the poor Girl of what she knew of the Wretch, who inform'd me that they put her into a Coach, and carry'd her a League out of Town; but when they found their Mistake, the Usage she bore from 'em was insupportable, and the Brute *Rederigo* told his Servants, if they pleas'd to make use of her in the vilest Manner, they were welcome. The Wretches that serv'd such a Villain, must have very near the same Sentiments of Honour and Honesty, or they would seek another Master; they were too forward to neglect such a Cruelty, and four of 'em by turns ravish'd her. Strangers to the nature of the Wretches, who are Superiors in this Part of the World, would imagine such Deeds should find Punishment by Law: But alas! Justice is fled the Place, and we may expect more Mercy from the worst of Cannibals, than is to be found here.

The poor Creature in a little Time felt the farther Effects of their Cruelty; for they gave her a Distemper that ended her Life.

Before her Death she gave me Knowledge of the Place where they led her; for they had not any Caution in their villanous Proceeding, but assoon as they had gratify'd their Lust and Cruelty, turn'd her out of Doors.

I had no farther need of any thing to whet my Revenge; but I must own, the Death of this unfortunate poor Creature added Fuel to the Fire. My Wife was almost distracted at the unhappy Accident, and had no other Consolation, but that she had escap'd their cruel Hands.

I did not acquaint her with my Intention of seeking this Villain, but I made it my only Business; I went to the Place the poor Maid had directed me, where I had Information that he had left the Place, and now resided in *Lima*. I was

very

Captain Robert Boyle.

very forry he had chang'd his Habitation, becaufe I fhould find it a more difficult thing to execute my Refentment with Safety in *Lima*. But however, I fent him the following Letter.

THY Ufage to me is not to be born; therefore, if thou haft that Spirit, (which I much queftion from thy Villany, for Villains are always Cowards) meet me in St. Juftin's *Field to-morrow at fix in the Morning; as I imagine there is no Second in thy Villany, I fhall expect thee alone, and I hope thou wilt not fail to meet the injur'd*

Alonzo de Caftro.

I chofe St. *Juftin*'s Field, for the Conveniency of a fmall Publick-houfe which over-look'd it, where I went before Day, that I might difcover if he came alone; for I had but little reafon to expect fair Play from fuch a Villain. When the time came, I faw him go by the Houfe alone; I let him pafs by me, to fee if he was not follow'd by any of his curfed Crew; but finding none, I hafted after him, into the middle of the Field, and call'd to him; he turn'd about, and with the Image of Hell in his Face, he cry'd, I thought your Refentment would have brought you firft into the Field: But as I am here before you, it fpeaks me no Coward, tho' your vile Scrawl would intimate as much. Come, faid I, no Words, thy Breath is Poifon to me, it will infect the Air; Only this Sir, faid he, as you had not nam'd any particular Weapon, I have made bold to bring a pair of Piftols with me, and to let you fee I have fome Honour, you fhall take your Choice. I gave him no Anfwer, but took one, and we agreed to ftand at fuch a Diftance. As I was going to Fire, he cry'd out
Hold

Hold! I will tell you one Secret more before we engage, and that's this; Your Piſtol is only charg'd with Powder, but mine with Ball, which I put in ſince you made the Choice; and now prepare for Death, be aſſur'd this is the laſt Moment of thy Life. I did not give my ſelf time to anſwer, but fir'd my Piſtol, and then hurl'd it at him, and had the good Fortune to cut him in the Face with it; and in the Confuſion and Surprize his Piſtol went off without hurting me. Now, ſaid I, thou Wretch! we are once more on equal Terms, and Heav'n I hope will favour the juſteſt Cauſe. We drew, and in a few Paſſes I laid him for dead on the Ground; tho' in the Encounter I had receiv'd a dangerous Wound in the Breaſt. I went home, notwithſtanding my Hurt, and ſent ſecretly for a Surgeon of my Acquaintance, who dreſs'd me, and told me I was in no Danger.

My Wife was very much griev'd at the Accident, tho' ſhe could not but be pleas'd at *Roderigo*'s Death; yet her Fears increas'd, as imagining I ſhould ſuffer for it, by the violent Temper of the Vice-roy: But her Grief began to blow over, when in ſeveral Days after, no Enquiry was made, nor even any Notice taken of his Death.

I was very much ſurpriz'd at it, imagining I had really kill'd him.

Aſſoon as my Wound was well, I went to the little Houſe to enquire if they knew any thing of the Body; (for the Owner of the Houſe was formerly my Servant, and a Man of much Probity, who knew all my Story;) he inform'd me, that a little while after I paſt by his Houſe home again, five Perſons ran that way, and coming to the Body, ſeem'd to mourn over it, and went the Road that leads to St. *Dominick*; *a Village about half a Mile from the Place where we fought.*

I

I imagin'd they had bury'd him privately in that Village, and went home to acquaint my Wife, who fhar'd my Contentment.

I now went abroad as I was wont, and all the Difcourfe was of Don *Roderigo*'s fudden difappearing. Servants and all had left his Houfe, but no one fufpected any thing of his Death. Some of my Acquaintance told me, they imagin'd this to be fome Trick of his, and that he only lay dormant to meditate fome Mifchief to me.

I feem'd to come into their Fears, but in my Mind flighted their Advice, as imagining I had nothing to fear, I paft on a whole Month without any Danger at all; but as I was going one Day acrofs the Bridge to a Warehoufe I had in the Suburbs, a Fellow came up to me, and privately ask'd me if I would be his Chapman for fome *Eaft-India* Goods. He told me a long Story, that he was oblig'd to make up a Cargo and leave this Part of the World, for his Credit began to fail, and if he did not get away fpeedily, his Creditors would lay him up. We went to a neighbouring Tavern, where he read me his Bill of Parcels. He told me he had been encourag'd to offer his Goods to me, from the fairnefs of my Character; and was coming to wait on me when he had the good Fortune to meet me. The next Day was agreed on for me to go and view the Goods, for I was not to pay for 'em till they were enter'd my Warehoufe. Accordingly, as appointed, I went to the Houfe of the Perfon, in the *Benedictine* Street. I was fhown into a Room till the Goods were brought; but as I was looking on fome Paintings, five Men rufh'd out of a Clofet in the Room, and feiz'd me. They difarm'd me, took out every thing that was in my Pockets, went out, and lock'd me in.

You

You may imagine the Surprize I was in, which was very much increas'd when I saw my Enemy *Don Roderigo* enter the Room. I in my Confusion thought I had seen a Ghost, for he look'd very pale; but he soon convinc'd me of the contrary. And have I got you at last? said he: I now will revenge my self at leisure; but to compleat my Revenge, I have sent a Token for your Wife, that I may ravish her before thy Face; and then I'll devise Tortures to rack every Joint about thee. He gave me to know that he had sent my Watch for a Token, and that she would bring such a Sum of Money to pay for the Goods. The Torment of my Soul no Tongue can express; and I am assur'd, if they had not taken my Sword from me, I had put an End to my wretched Life.

The inhumane Villain insulted me so much, that I rush'd upon him, unarm'd as I was, and had certainly choak'd him, if his wicked Assistants had not dragg'd me from him.

It is well, said he, I have no other Passion but Lust reigning in my Breast at this Instant; but when I have sated my Desires on thy Wife, I'll then add another Pang for this Usage; but in the mean time I'll leave you to think of this Matter alone, for I fancy you don't much care for my Company.

Assoon as he had made an End of this Speech, he and his Gang went out, and fasten'd the Door on the other side. I'll give you Leave to imagine the Confusion of my Thoughts. I remain'd some time without moving; but accidentally casting my Eyes on the Door, I observ'd there was a Bar to shut it on the inside. I immediately barr'd it, and began to look about to see if I could find any thing for my Defence; but to my Grief could perceive nothing.

thing. I enter'd the Closet, and search'd there, but to no purpose. Looking upon the Floor of the Closet, I perceiv'd one of the Boards seem'd to be loose: I essay'd to pull it up, but wanted some Engine to effect it. I at last thought of the Bar of the Door, ran to it, and by main Force wrench'd it from the Staple; for I thought if it would not serve me to make my Escape, it would serve me to defend my self: but I easily forc'd up the Board, and with my Bar beat down the Ceiling under me. I was resolv'd to explore the hidden Place, whatever was the Consequence; for it could not be worse than to remain where I was. I therefore ventur'd down, though something of a difficult Descent; for the Joyces were so close together, I had much ado to force my Body through; but at last, with much Difficulty, I press'd through, and had a desperate Fall to the Ground.

I soon found I had got into a Cooper's Cellar, for there were several Pipe-staves, and Tools to work with. I seiz'd upon some of them, and by Force wrench'd open the Cellar-Door, which led me once more into the Street before *Don Roderigo*'s House. I did not give my self Time to consider, but ran towards the Bridge to get to my own House; and just as I enter'd the *Cordeliers* Street, I met my Wife with her Maid, and the Wretch that had decoy'd me to the House. I ran upon him, seiz'd him by the Throat, and flung him over the Bridge, where he met with the Reward of his Villany. I had not Power of Speech to inform my Wife of the Accident, but made Signs for her to go home. By this time it was dark; and the profligate Villain *Don Roderigo*, fancying his cursed Emissary staid too long, came out of his Door which fac'd the Bridge. As-
foon

foon as I difcover'd him, I ran towards him, and feiz'd him: Now Villain, faid I, I will not part with thee till thou haft render'd up thy Soul to Hell. We both ftruggled, and I kept him down; but the reft of his Company coming up to his Affiftance, I quitted him; and running to fee if I could meet with fome one arm'd, I had the good Fortune to light on you. Affoon as I receiv'd your Sword, I ran back, and juft met the Villain as he was entring his Door. I ran the Weapon into his very Heart; and I believe you were a better Witnefs of his Death than my felf, being you were found near the Body.

Affoon as I faw him fall I made the beft of my way home, not imagining you would meet with any farther Damage than the Lofs of your Sword.

The Darknefs of the Night, I fancy, conceal'd me from the Servants that came to the Affiftance of their Mafter, for I never once was fufpected; or perhaps if they did know me, Fear kept 'em from difcovering me.

When I heard of your Tryal, I came my felf into Court, and if you had been condemn'd, refolv'd to have difcover'd the Truth; but finding you were to be banifhed to *Baldivia*, I conceal'd the Fact, imagining I had it in my Power to gain your Freedom, by paying your Ranfom; which was the Reafon I came now to wait upon you, to offer you my Service in that, or any thing elfe that lies in my Power. I return'd him Thanks for his Offer; and confidering his Story, I told him I was glad I was in fome fort an Inftrument of his Revenge. He would force upon me a Ring, and two hundred Pieces of Gold, and begg'd he might be rank'd in the Number of my Friends. He made me many ny Visits, and once brought his Wife with him. She was a very handsome Woman, and seem'd to have a great deal of Wit. She made me several very handsome Compliments in behalf of her Husband, and begg'd I would accept of their Pictures set round with fine oriental Pearls.

He accompany'd me on Board when our Vessel was to set Sail, putting in the Captain's Hands fresh Provision, and several sorts of good Liquor to comfort me in my Voyage.

I had the Happiness to have Pirates for my Fellow-Sufferers; and the Viceroy had given out, to take off all Censure from him, that I encourag'd 'em in their Piracy.

We took our Leaves, with Protestations of a lasting Friendship; and I liv'd as merrily as I could, till the Day we had the good Fortune to meet with you, which has not given me any Reason to change my Humour.

WE were mightily diverted with the Relation of *Don Pedro*, and I found I was not deceiv'd when I took him for a Man that understood the World.

We had now gain'd the Streights of *Gibraltar*, and had enter'd the *Mediterranean* Sea: But I must confess I could not see the *African* Shore, without Numbers of Sighs for Misfortunes past; and I found my Griefs renew'd with the Remembrance: And all the Mitigation I had was the affectionate Concern from *Don Ferdinand*, to whom I had told my whole Story. We had not made a Day's Sail in the *Mediterranean*, ere we perceiv'd two Sail making towards us. I must own I had no Desire to engage, being so richly laden; and therefore, by the Advice of both the Ships Company, made all the Sail I could to avoid 'em. But our Vessels being foul with so long a Voyage, and never once clean'd during our whole

U   Course,

Courſe, they gain'd upon us, do what we could. When we found there was no getting from 'em without Fighting, we were as much determin'd on the other Hand to fight our Ships to the Bottom of the Sea rather than ſurrender. Having fix'd this Reſolution, we prepar'd for the Engagement; and when we had got all Things in Readineſs, we leſſen'd our Sails that they might come up to us. I order'd every Sailor to load as many ſmall Arms as they could, and not to fire a Gun till I gave 'em Orders; but aſſoon as ever they had fir'd the great Guns, to diſcharge their ſmall Arms upon 'em. I could not prevail upon *Don Ferdinand* to keep below, though I ſaw Fear liveiily painted in his Face. When they came within Piſtol-ſhot of our Ship they hail'd us, and commanded us to ſtrike immediately. We made no other Anſwer than with our Guns and ſmall Arms, which ſurpriz'd 'em, and did 'em a great deel of Damage in their Rigging; for cutting the Topſail Halliards with our Shot, the Topſail fell down upon the Cap, and hinder'd their Ship's Way very much; and I believe we might have made our Eſcape. But I perceiv'd the *Villars* was hard put to it, (our *Spaniſh* Man of War, whom I had nam'd the *Villars* in Remembrance of that dear One.) By this time we were prepar'd again, and I order'd every Man, aſſoon as they had diſcharg'd, to lye flat upon their Bellies till we had receiv'd the Fire of the Enemy; which accordingly we did. They fir'd in upon us, but kill'd us not one Man. Then our Hands roſe up all together, and fir'd in our ſmall Shot. We had ſo damag'd their Rigging with this Broadſide, that we fell aſtern till we were charg'd again; and then I gave our Men Orders to fire into the Body of the Ship, and point their Guns low on purpoſe;

pose; which we soon found had the desir'd Effect: For they had several Shots between Wind and Water, so that they were oblig'd to heel the Ship on the Starboard Side, to prevent the Water running in on the Larboard. I seeing there was not much to be fear'd from her, bore down to assist the *Villars*, because she was over-match'd. But when her Antagonist found my Design, and understood the Condition of the other Ship, she made all the Sail she could, and fled for it. We did not think fit to follow her, but sent a Boat on Board, to enquire how it stood with 'em in the *Villars*. They sent me Word they had lost eight Men, had three wounded, and were very much mawl'd in their Rigging, as well as their Hull, and had receiv'd a Shot between Wind and Water, and the Ship leak'd very much. I bad 'em search for it; but there was no coming at it; therefore I order'd them to get out as many of the Goods as they could, and bring them on Board me. The Weather proving very favourable, they went to Work as fast as they could.

Our Men brought me Word that the Ship we had engag'd was sinking. They fir'd several Guns for Assistance, and their Consort being almost out of Sight, I bore down to help them all I could; but before we could come to 'em she sunk to the Bottom. The Men had put out their Long-boat and Barge, and were got in them, and made towards us. Assoon as they came within hearing, they call'd out for *Quarter*, which I promis'd 'em they should have. There were 123 of 'em; and as their Number exceeded ours, we were oblig'd to confine 'em, for fear they should take it in their Heads to set upon us.

The Captain was kill'd in the Engagement, but the Lieutenant inform'd me they were two

Men

Men of War, of forty Guns each, set out from *Barcelona* to cruise upon the Coast; and mann'd each with two hundred Men: But the rest of their Crew were either kill'd, or being wounded sunk with the Ship. I did not think it proper to carry 'em to *Italy*, for fear it should prove prejudicial to *Don Antonio*; and understanding that in removing the Goods on Board the *Villars*, they had found out the Leak and stopp'd it, I intended to put 'em on board her, and give 'em the Ship with their Liberty; but first I order'd out the Guns and Ammunition, and her Goods, leaving 'em nothing but Provision and Water, which they return'd me many Thanks for, and so we parted.

The next Day there arose such a Storm as we had never felt before, and continu'd in the utmost Violence for fourteen Days, so that now we were in Danger of drowning; and I believe most would have parted with their Wealth to have been safe on Shore. At last we discover'd Land, but were very much surpriz'd to find it *Candia*, for now we began to be in fear of the *Turkish* Pirates. So we resolv'd to steer for *Zant* as fast as we could, and there make Dividend of our Prize-Money and Goods. And accordingly we arriv'd there safely, *Sept.* 3. 1696.

This Island of *Zant* belongs to the *Venetians*, therefore we were out of Danger from the *Turks*. The Town, which bears the same Name with the Island, is above a Mile in Length, seated upon a Beach of the Bay. It is built mostly of Stone, and has a noble Look from the Sea. To the West of the Town stands the Castle, built on a high and very steep Hill, where most of the Merchants dwell, and is very near as big as the City below. It is a Bishop's See, and the Governour is of the Nobility of *Venice*.

The

The chief Commodities they deal in are Wine, Oyl, and Currants, which are esteem'd of the best Growth. They grow on Vines like other Grapes, and are gather'd in *July*, and then pack'd in Hogsheads ready for the Merchants.

Our Men being well pleas'd they were out of Danger, and in a Place where Wine was to be bought cheap, traffick'd so much for that Commodity, that most of them fell into dangerous Diseases; therefore I resolv'd to leave *Zant*, and make for *Sapienza*, an Island with a good Harbour, not inhabited, where they would not be under the like Temptation; so we came to an Anchor there, *Sept.* 8. I order'd twelve Guns on Shore, and rais'd a Platform capable of defending us from the Insults of an Enemy. In a pleasant Green we put up a large Tent, and others smaller by it for the Officers and Sailors: But I having but one Bed put up on Shore, *Don Ferdinand* was forc'd to lie with me, tho' as I thought very unwillingly. Our sharing the ready Money took us up four Days. I reserv'd a fourth Part to my Owners, which amounted to upwards of sixty thousand Pound; and a twelfth Part for my self, which, with what Presents and other Things that I had, amounted to the value of fifty thousand Pound. Every Sailor from first to last shar'd above twelve hundred Pound a-piece; but when we came to divide the Goods, we knew not which way to go about it; so with one common Consent of the Sailors, I was oblig'd to accept of them, without paying one Penny for them.

We set Sail for *Ostia* the next Day, after we had finish'd our Dividend, and arriv'd there *Nov.* 1. after a Voyage of two Years and seven Months, and the richest Prize that ever came into any Port of *Italy*. I sent a Letter to *Don Antonio*, to give him Notice

Notice of my Arrival, and Advice to come and take Care of his Cargo. In two Days, he, *Donna Isabella*, and their little Son came on Board in a Pleasure-Boat. I found they were in Mourning, and I told 'em I was afraid to ask 'em who it was for; they inform'd me that *Isabella*'s Father had been dead above two Years, but they had resolv'd never to wear any other Colour, till they had seen me. Never was a more tender Meeting between Friends, than between us; and I must confess, for some time all my Cares lay hush'd.

When I came to inform *Don Antonio* of the Wealth I had brought him home, he stood a‑maz'd: For besides the Money which I told him of, the Goods I had on Board exceeded in value the Freight I went out with. I could hardly prevail upon him to accept of such a Sum of Money, till I inform'd him it was but bare‑ly his Due, and that I had very near as much to my own Share.

I presented *Don Ferdinand* to *Antonio* and his Lady, who seem'd very much pleas'd with him; and *Don Pedro*, out of his free merry Humour, told me he hop'd I would not forget him, be‑cause he was older, for he thought he had more Right to my Friendship than *Don Ferdinand*, being he was an older Acquaintance. I let 'em into some of his Life and Humour: they re‑ceiv'd him very friendly; and we all went to *Don Antonio*'s *Villa* together.

After staying a Week, I began to be tir'd with so much Pleasure, and therefore begg'd Leave of *Don Antonio* to visit *Rome*, only to shew *Don Ferdinand* that celebrated Place. *Don Antonio* sent before to his Palace to prepare for our Reception, and the next Day we follow'd. We visited all the Rarities, ancient and mo‑
dern,

dern, where we might fee the Grandeur of the antient *Romans* by thofe ftupendous Ruins ftill left. As *Rome* was formerly a Nurfery of War and Greatnefs, it is now a Nurfery of Arts, but chiefly Painting, Architecture, and Mufick. There have flourifh'd in one Century, *Lanfranio, Dominichino, Pietro du Cortona*, the *Poffine's, Camaffei, Guercin da Cento, Chivoli, Andrea Sacchi*, the immortal *Raphael, Hannibal Carache, Guido Reno, Mutiano*, and many more excellent in the Art of Painting. Then *Palladio, Vitruvius, Scamozzi, Pozza*, and many more, famous for Architecture. Then the divine *Corelli* for Mufick, whofe fweet Compofitions will be always new; and we may fay by him as a great *Englifh* Poet faid of our Countryman *Shakefpear*, that the former had pull'd up the Roots of Mufick, as the latter of Poetry, and tranfplanted 'em into their own Gardens, where all thofe that follow muft borrow a Branch from them.

I fhall not fay any thing more of *Rome*, nor of *Naples*, where we went once more, upon *Don Ferdinand*'s Account. I would have perfuaded him to have begun his Studies at *Rome*, (for I fuppos'd him a *Roman Catholick*) but he would not hear of it, and begg'd he might go with me into *England*, which I promis'd him he fhould.

Donna Ifabella had an Orphan Coufin, that liv'd with her, of a vaft Fortune, beautiful to a Miracle; who having feen Don *Ferdinand*, fell defperately in Love with him. But he did not feem to have the leaft Regard for her. *Don Antonio*, difcover'd to me the Secret, and pitying by Experience his Kinfwoman, defir'd I would foward the Match. But when *Don Ferdinand* underftood my Defires, he fell upon his Knees, and begg'd I would never mention it more;

more; for he had made a solemn Resolution never to marry any Woman breathing. I press'd him all I could, and laid the Folly of such a rash Resolve before him; but it was preaching to a Tempest; and all my Arguments had no Power upon him. On the other hand, the merry *Don Pedro* was as deep in Love with *Donna Felicia,* which was the Name of the Orphan Lady. But his manner of Courtship was so odd, and out of the way, that he caus'd more Diversion than we could have imagin'd. If she went to Bed, he would lay himself down at her Chamber Door, and sing Songs all Night; that if she had any Inclination to have rested, he was resolv'd she should not; and he would often say, he intended to plague her into a Complyance. If she went into the Garden, he was sure to follow her close; or even at Church, he would often tell her, it was in vain to pray for a Blessing from Heaven, when she was committing Murder with every Look. In short, he would often force a Smile from the afflicted Lady her self.

I was still endeavouring with *Don Ferdinand,* to forget his rash Vow: But he desir'd me, in such moving Terms, not to intreat him further, that I resolv'd never to trouble him any more on that Theme. Notwithstanding which, I begg'd of *Donna Isabella* to try what she could do with him, for I imagin'd Complaisance might work more upon him than Friendship. She sent for him into her Closet, and they remain'd together several Hours; and I was very much pleas'd the next Day to see him walking in the Garden, only with *Donna Felicia.* I did not think it proper to interrupt them; but when I had an Opportunity, I declar'd my Satisfaction, and told him I easily forgave his not complying with me, and yielding to the Perswasion of
Donna

Donna Iſabella. He ſeem'd in ſome Confuſion at what I ſaid to him, which I attributed to his denying me, and his Condeſcenſion to *Donna Iſabella*. But in a few Days after that, I was ſomething more ſurpriz'd to ſee *Don Pedro* eagerly addreſſing *Donna Felicia*, and ſhe regarding him more favourably than uſual. And my Surprize was encreas'd, when *Donna Iſabella* told me the nuptial Day was fix'd between *Don Pedro*, and *Donna Felicia*. I told her I was very well pleas'd, the Lady had ſo ſoon forgot her violent Paſſion; but I added, that the ſtronger the Flame, the ſhorter the Duration. If ſo, return'd *Donna Iſabella*, we may hope your Paſſion is bury'd long ſince. I told her, I did not Love like others, for I was reſolv'd to carry mine with me to the Grave. By what I have formerly heard (return'd *Donna Iſabella*) from you, as well as my Husband, you have not the leaſt glimpſe of Hopes. Madam, ſaid I, that is the Reaſon I muſt deſpair; for no other Fire ſhall ever warm my Breaſt, but what was kindled there by my firſt Flame. We had much Diſcourſe upon the ſame Subject, and *Donna Iſabella* told me at laſt, I was a Pattern for all faithful Lovers.

When we were at *Naples*, I had provided Goods and Conveniency of ſending to St. *Salvador*, according to my Promiſe given to *Don Jaques*; and the Veſſel being to touch at *Oſtia*, was to ſend to me for my Letters to *Don Jaques*. I deſir'd *Don Ferdinand* to write to his Father; but he begg'd to be excus'd, for fear it ſhould fall into the Hands of his Lady; and for the ſame Reaſon he begg'd I would be cautious how I mention'd him. I told him he ſhould ſee what I had wrote before I ſent it; which was as follows.

SIR,

SIR,

I Know not how to make you Acknowledgments sufficient for those Favours so generously conferr'd upon me; and the Manner of doing it stamps a double Value on the Obligation. If there is no way to repay the mighty Debt, yet I shall with the utmost Gratitude remember Don Jaques, and his kind Benefits. I have done my self the Honour to send you those Things you were desirous of, the last Time I had the Happiness of conversing with you; which I beg you will accept, only for this Reason, that you may see you shall ever live in the Remembrance of one, who shall think it the best good Fortune can fall upon him, to subscribe himself

Your sincere Friend and Servant,

Robert Boyle.

P. S. *I also beg you to give my humble Duty to your good* Lady *and virtuous* Daughter; *and be assur'd, whatever you have given me in Charge shall have the same Regard, as if an immortal Spirit had descended from above, and written in my Heart your Commission. Whatever Letters you are pleas'd to honour me with, direct for me at the Palace of* Antonio de Alvares *in* Rome, *who will take Care to send 'em to me where-ever I am; for as yet I am undetermin'd where to settle my self, but I have* England *in View.*

I wrote this Letter in the *Portugueze* Language, and shew'd it to *Don Ferdinand*, who approv'd of what I had written.

I had dispos'd of the rest of my Goods on Board, and the Money amounted to upwards of fifteen thousand Pound; but I could not prevail

vail upon *Don Antonio* to accept of one Penny.

No, my dear Friend, said he, you have already brought me the Fortune of a Nobleman; tho' it is not worldly Wealth I covet. I have all the Earth contains in the Possession of my adorable Wife: and even that, my greatest Happiness, is owing to you; and all the Allay of Joy I have, is, that I cannot see you as blest as I am. But, continu'd he, Time that wears out all things, will, I hope, cure this amorous Sickness of your Soul. I let him know my Grief was as fix'd as Destiny, and I had nothing else to do but to wing to the Place where the Joy of my Life did once reside; with this only Hope, that the lively Imagination of my Loss would put an end to all my Sorrows, by sinking me into the Arms of Death.

He was so very much concern'd for me that he could not avoid shedding Tears; and us'd all the Arguments he could to persuade me to reside in *Italy*. I told him I had more Reasons to go for my native Country than what I had given him, and that was the Education of young *Don Ferdinand*, who begg'd to cultivate his Studies in *England*.

I turn'd all my Money into Bills of Exchange, well knowing the Casualties that attend Travellers; and I intended to go by Land to *Flanders*, with *Don Ferdinand*, my two faithful *Indians*, and one Servant more.

All my *Spanish* Sailors that I had pick'd up by the Way, had by my Consent their Discharge, and were gone to their several Homes, in Circumstances beyond their Expectations; though they all declar'd, if I intended another Voyage, they would never forsake me. Some of my *English* Sailors had married *Italian* Women, and so design'd to settle in *Italy*.

When I desir'd *Don Antonio* to take Charge of the Ship, he told me he had nothing to do with it, declaring it was mine, and therefore desir'd I would make no more Words about it; for, said he, you don't know but you may meet with something to change your Mind, and we may have the Satisfaction of seeing you once more.

In a few Days after this, the Nuptials were celebrated between *Don Pedro* and *Donna Felicia*, who design'd for *Spain* (assoon as I left *Italy*) where he intended to take up the Mortgage of his Estate, the Time being almost expir'd. I must own, the Uncertainty of Women's Tempers gave me much Cogitation; and I thought this Marriage was a very odd Thing.

I now began to think of my Journey; but first I order'd a Goldsmith to make me every way the same Parcel of Plate as I received as a Present from *Don Jaques de Ramires*, which I presented to *Donna Isabella*, that she might remember me. She gave me many Thanks for it, but seem'd very unwilling to accept of it a great while. I told her, as merrily as I could, if she made any more Words about it, I would return her the Ship that bore her Name, and would be no longer under her Command. Well, said she, I'll accept 'em; but as you allow me to be your Owner, I'll give you Orders in Writing, that you must not break open till you come in such a Latitude, that is, a Fortnight after you are settled in *England*. I promis'd to obey her punctually. The next Day she gave me a seal'd Paper, which she told me were the Orders she mention'd.

I had given my Lieutenant Charge of the Ship, with Directions to make for *Bristol* with all the Expedition practicable.

The next Day, being *Feb.* 6. 1696, I took my Leave of all my Acquaintance; and notwithstanding I am not us'd to weep, could not forbear shedding some Tears at parting with such true Friends as *Don Antonio* and his Lady had prov'd. I rode the first Day overwhelm'd with Melancholy, and not one Thought of being possess'd of such a Fortune, from nothing, in so short a Time, ever enter'd my Breast. But seeing *Don Ferdinand* by his Countenance partake of my Sorrow, I was forc'd to appear less melancholy, to oblige him to be so too.

I would have shewn him the Rarities of *Italy* in our Travels, but he seem'd very little inclin'd to Curiosity: And we arriv'd at *Antwerp* without any Adventure. We staid some time there to recover the Fatigue of our Journey, but more upon *Don Ferdinand's* Account, being he was something indispos'd, having never travell'd on Horse-back so far before.

As we approach'd the Town, he and my *Indians* were surpriz'd to see the Manner of Begging. The Boys and Girls would run before you, and of a sudden stop short, stand upon their Heads, and clap their Hands, saying their Prayers all the while.

The City of *Antwerp* is finely seated upon the River *Scheld*; it is very well fortify'd, and upon the Walls are planted Trees that give an agreeable Shade, and make it pleasant Walking. The Castle, both strong and beautiful, was founded by the Duke of *Alva*. The City in Bigness may compare with *Bristol*; their Streets spacious, and Houses very magnificent. The Church of *Sancta Maria*, their Cathedral, is a superb Building;

ing; and of that Neatness, that the Emperor *Charles* the fifth, of *Germany*, would often say *it was only fit to be kept in a Case*. The Inside is as glorious and neat as the Out. The Paintings were perform'd by Sir *Peter Paul Rubens*, an Inhabitant of *Antwerp*, and are equal to any thing that ever he did. The Jesuits Church is also very beautiful, adorn'd with abundance of curious Marble Pillars, and all the Pannels painted by the same Hand as the other. There are several more beautiful Churches and Chappels; but as these mention'd are the chief, we shall take no farther Notice of 'em.

The third of *April*, (having pretty well recover'd our Fatigue by a Rest of ten Days) we set out for *Calais*, being the shortest Cut to *Dover*, and arriv'd there *April* 6; making short Stages.

From this Place we might behold the white Cliffs of *Dover*. I must own I had some secret Satisfaction in viewing my native Country: and the next Day, early in the Morning, we embark'd, and reach'd the Town by Noon, having a very favourable Passage. Here landing, I had like to have lost one of my *Indians*. Slinging his Horses into the Boat, he would get upon the Back of one of them, thinking he would go out quietly. But just upon the Instant, a Vessel riding by the *Peer* fired a Gun, and frighted the Horse to such a degree, that he plung'd into the Sea, and swam from the Shore; and the *Indian* being thrown off with the Start, had his Foot so entangled in the Stirrup, that (notwithstanding his Skill in Swimming) he must have inevitably perish'd, if the other *Indian*, seeing the Misfortune, had not plung'd in, and with a Knife cut the String. He then took the Horse by the Bridle with one Hand, and swim-

ming

ming with the other, brought him safe to Shore.

 Don Ferdinand not being over-pleas'd with riding on Horse-back, we took the Flying-Coach the next Day, and safely arriv'd at *London*. I order'd my *English* Servant and the two *Indians*, with our Baggage, to make two Days of it; and gave 'em Directions to wait at the Place where the Coach inn'd, till I sent for 'em.

 When we arriv'd at *London*, I did not care to go to any of my Acquaintance, but rather chose to lie at a *Bagnio* for a Day or two; but I sent privately for my Uncle's Clerk, that had endeavour'd to prevent my being kidnapp'd by putting a Letter in my Pocket, mention'd in the Beginning of this Relation. He came to me according to my Desire, but was overjoy'd and surpriz'd to see me, though he hardly knew me at first, for I had not sent him my Name.

 He inform'd me that my Uncle had been dead above a Year, and had left his Estate to his eldest Son, and his Business to his youngest and him: But they would often talk of me, not believing I was in the Land of the Living; yet they had increas'd my small Estate with their utmost Care, intending, if ever I came back again, to restore it to me. I let him into my whole History, and he was very much pleas'd to hear that I had gain'd such a plentiful Fortune. I got him to provide us convenient Lodgings, and private, for I did not intend to go abroad much; and also to go to the Inn to fetch my Servants.

 My two *Indians* spoke *English* very well, and I had learnt 'em to write and read; and being in modern Habits, they were not much gaz'd at.

The

The Time being expir'd that I was to look into my Commiſſion, (as *Donna Iſabella* call'd it) I reſolv'd to break it open, having ſome Curioſity. But it was gone, and notwithſtanding all my Search, I could not gain any Tydings of it. I could not imagine how I ſhould loſe that, and nothing elſe. I muſt own I was very uneaſie, fearing it might be ſomething of Importance I was to do for *Donna Iſabella*; therefore I diſpatch'd a Letter to *Italy*, to tell 'em of my ſafe Arrival, and my Loſs of the Packet, (and to ſend me a freſh one) with Directions where to write to me.

While I ſtaid in Town, I purchas'd an Eſtate of 2000*l.* a Year in *Somerſetſhire*, and yet had 25000*l.* left, which I employ'd in the publick Funds. And now I had ſettled my Eſtate, as well as that I had for *Don Ferdinand*, I was willing to forward him in his Studies, and propos'd to ſend him to *Oxford* with a Tutor. But he ſtill begg'd to ſtay a little longer with me.

I therefore took a Reſolution of going to *Briſtol*, only with *Don Ferdinand*, and one Servant, with no other Buſineſs than to ſee the Place where my loſt Treaſure once liv'd.

When we were arriv'd, I enquir'd which was the Houſe that Mr. *Villars*, late Merchant, formerly dwelt in. We ſoon found it out, but were inform'd one Capt. *Kendrick* dwelt there. I was inquiſitive to know if there was any Tydings of one *Suſan*, who was formerly Maid to Mrs. *Villars*, Daughter to the deceas'd Merchant; and at laſt got Information that ſhe liv'd at a Country Houſe near the Sea-ſide.

I went immediately away for the Place, tho' near thirty Mile off, and late in the Evening. Before we had rid far, the Skies became gloomy, my, and a violent Storm threaten'd us, which soon overtook us with such Fury, that we were forc'd to put into a little House out of the Road for Shelter. When we came within, we could not see any Body in't but a little Child, playing with some Toys it had before it; and all we could get out of it was, that *Mamma* would come by and by. It was as lovely a Child as ever I saw, and we were still admiring it, when a Man and Woman came in. They were much amaz'd to find us there; but I begg'd their Pardon, and told 'em the Storm drove us in to take Shelter.

The Man told us we were very welcome to such as his House afforded, but he fear'd we should find but poor Accommodation. In short, the Storm kept up in its full Force, and now it grew dark, and we were two Mile from any Inn; and to add to our Distress, we were Strangers to the Road. The Man seeing us so put to it, told us he had but two Beds, but we should be welcome to 'em, such as they were.

I told him I would gratifie him for his Trouble, and thereupon gave him a Guinea. He was very well pleas'd with my Present, and began to shew it in his Looks, as well as the Woman. I gave him another, to provide us something to eat, and to take care of the Horses. He said he had but bad Stable-room, but if I pleas'd he would take my Servant, and all the Horses, (with one of his own to bring him back again) and leave 'em at an Inn in the neighbouring Village. I agreed to it; and while he was gone I ask'd the good Woman many Questions about the Child which we saw there, and soon found it was none of their own, but a Gentlewoman's, a Stranger to them, and one they had never seen but once. Why, said I, how

how are you paid for the keeping of it? She seem'd amaz'd at my Question, and was some time before she answer'd me; but at last she said she was always very well paid.

I finding she did not much care for talking upon that Subject, chang'd the Discourse. Soon after the Man came in, and we went to Supper. I would have had *Don Ferdinand* to have lain with me; but the Man understanding we usually lay asunder, would give us both the Beds, and they would sit up. I ask'd them where the Child lay; and they told us in a Cradle. I began to be concerned for the Infant, though without giving any Reason. When we had supp'd, we went to Bed, and had but little Rest; and when we rose in the Morning, (it proving fair and pleasant) we resolved to walk to the Inn where our Horses were, with our Host for our Guide. When we arriv'd, I dismiss'd him with another Guinea; and would have got immediately on Horse-back, but *Don Ferdinand* was so very much disorder'd that he was not able to mount. I was very much concern'd for his Indisposition, and begg'd he would repose himself there, while I pursu'd my Journey; with a Promise to return the next Day, or send my Servant for him. He consented that it should be so, and I set forward.

Coming to a Place where several Roads met, I was confounded to know the right, and therefore was some time at a Stand, not knowing which to take: But hearing several Voices in an adjacent Barn, I made up to it on Foot, giving my Horse to my Man. The nearer I approach'd, the more Noise they made; but I could not understand 'em. This awaken'd my Curiosity, and I stole softly to the Barn, where I could observe through a Crevice (unseen) upwards

of

of twenty Gypsies, sitting in a Huddle, with a Child in the midst stark naked, which they were rubbing over with Walnut-Shells; and every time it cry'd they set up that confus'd Noise. But I was very much surpriz'd to find in that Child the Features of that I had seen the Night before at my Country Landlord's. I beckon'd my Servant to come near with my Horses; being arm'd, I made to the Barn Door, and forc'd it open. I ask'd 'em, in an imperious Manner, what they were doing with that Child; and further affirm'd they had stole it from such a Place, giving them to understand I had People coming to apprehend 'em. Upon hearing this, they all took to their Heels; and some (I found) that had come there with Crutches, ran very nimbly away without 'em; but the Child was left behind. I now began to consider with my self what I had done; and that I had gotten a Child, but did not know what to do with it. They had rubb'd the poor thing all over with the green Walnut-Shells, that made it look like one of their Fraternity. By good Fortune they had left his Cloaths behind 'em, as also some Rags, which I suppose were to be put on instead of the others.

My Man and I dress'd it as well as we could, and aukwardly enough; but when we had finish'd (notwithstanding my Haste) I resolv'd to go back again, and enquire into this Affair. When we came to the Inn, I gave the Infant to the Care of the Woman of the House till my Return; and understanding *Don Ferdinand* was gone to Rest, I proceeded to my Host's House without disturbing him. When we arriv'd there, I met the Woman at the Door. Pray, (said I to her) good Woman, where's the Child that I saw here last Night? Where's the Child? (return'd

turn'd the Woman fnappingly) why the Child's in his Cradle afleep. Let me fee it; faid I. No, faid fhe, I won't difturb it for you, nor no one elfe. I told her peremptorily I would fee it that Inftant, in fpight of her, for I fear'd fome foul Play. She feeing me refolute, and lighting from my Horfe; Well Sir, feeing you are fo defirous (faid fhe) I'll go and bring it to you. When fhe was gone, I began to imagine my felf miftaken, and that Children might be very like, without being the fame; but I knew a Guinea would foon reconcile her to my Rudenefs. I ftaid waiting a confiderable time, taken up with feveral Thoughts; and not obferving how long I had waited, till my Man told me the old Woman was long a coming. I began to call, and no body anfwering, I order'd him to go in, and fee for her. He came out again, and told me fhe was not in the Houfe, nor any one elfe; but that he believ'd fhe had flip'd out of the back Door, and got away through the Garden. I began to think there was fomething very extraordinary in the Adventure of the Child, and refolv'd to be ftrict in the Examination. I enter'd the Houfe my felf, and fearch'd, but to no Purpofe. I fent my Man in the mean time in purfuit of the Woman. But he return'd without her. There was never a Neighbouring-houfe to enquire, no nearer than the Village where I had left the Child. So I had juft got on Horfeback in order to go back, when I perceiv'd the Man coming towards his own Houfe. I fpur'd on to meet him, and he feem'd much concern'd; I feiz'd him by the Collar, and told him, I came to fecure him, for the Murder of the Child I faw at his Houfe laft Night. The Man was in fuch a terrible Fright at what I faid, that he was more dead than alive. Sure Sir, faid he, it can't be, it is not
muder'd.

murder'd. I bid him produce it, or he should be try'd for it. In short, I frighted the poor Fellow so much, that he told me, if I would have a little Patience, he would tell me all that he knew concerning it (still crying, I hope it is not murder'd.) I told him the Child was safe. We went back to his House, where after the Fellow had a little compos'd himself, he made me the following Relation.

About three Years ago, a Gentlewoman came to my Wife, and made a Bargain with her to keep this Infant, and by paying us handsomely, we imagin'd it belong'd to some Person of Distinction; for we receiv'd ten Pounds every Quarter, and that before it was due. The Lady would often take the Child for a Day or two, and return it again. My Wife, being a worldly Woman, laid several Plots how to know the truth of the Child, but to no Purpose; but by all Circumstances we believ'd the Parents did not care for owning it. One Day my Wife told me she had a Design in her Head, but she would not disclose it, till she could be sure of succeeding; and when the Lady came the next time to take the Child away for a Day as usual, my Wife was in Conference with her for some time. And when she was gone, she told me that she had prevail'd upon the Lady to pay her one hundred Pounds before hand, and that she brought her to it, by telling her we should make a Purchase of the House we live in. In short, my Wife (who wears the Breeches) made me consent to carry on the Deceit; and the next Day the Lady brought the Child, and the hundred Pound and gave it my Wife, without any thing under my Hand, and left us in a small time after. When she was gone, my Wife discours'd me after this manner.

Husband, we have now one hundred and fifty Pounds (for we had been very saving) besides our Goods, and Cattle, which will fetch us one hundred more. With this Money we may go into my Country (which was the *Isle of Man*) and live contentedly all our Lives, without any fears of bad Crops, and ill Markets. Well, but said I, what will become of the Child. I quickly found by her Expressions that she resolv'd to murder it. I was struck with Horror at her Proposition, and notwithstanding her violent Temper, oppos'd her in't; and told her, upon no Conditions would I consent to do so barbarous a Deed. I found her so fix'd upon the design of Murder, that I was at last, as the lightest Evil, obliged to consent to her selling it to a Company of *Gypsies*; but with the greatest Reluctance in the World; which was executed this Morning. But we had dispos'd of every thing before hand, with Intention to have gone for *Bristol* two Days hence; for we were assur'd the Lady would not come again for some time.

When he had done, I inform'd him how I came to meet with the Child. I then began to examine if he did not know where the Lady liv'd; and at last he confess'd he dogg'd her to her House one Day, set on by his Wife, but would never discover it to her, for fear of her playing some Trick. I prevail'd with him to go with me, and shew me the House, with the promise of a Reward, and letting him go afterwards. We set out (after he had got a Horse) and in two Hours arriv'd at a pleasant House, surrounded by a small River, and almost cover'd with Trees. I stopp'd some time to view it, and through a little Avenue saw two Women gathering Flowers; one had her Face turn'd towards us, which the Man said was the Woman that us'd us'd to come to see the Child, and that was the Place she carry'd it to. I order'd my Man to take the Horses to the next Town, about half a Mile off, and come to me again. But I needed not have bid mine Host to have gone about his Business; for he being fearful of the Event, got away without our perceiving it.

When my Man was gone, I walk'd about to view the House, but I had lost sight of the Women, and it began to rain again. I stood up for Shelter from the Weather under a large Oak; and had but just got there, when a Woman came out of the Gate, with her Mistress's Service, to invite me in. I was very well pleas'd with the Invitation, and went into the House, where I was met by the Gentlewoman, a very handsome Lady. She told me, as I look'd like a Gentleman, she desir'd I would take Shelter there till the Storm was over. I return'd her the Thanks her Civility deserv'd, and we sat down, but were immediately interrupted with ringing at the Gate; and I perceiv'd, through a small Window, a Gentleman in a Scarlet-cloak a-light from his Horse, and go in quite through the House. The Lady begg'd my Pardon, and told me, she was obliged to go keep another Lady Company while that Person was there, but would wait on me as soon as possible again. As my Curiosity had brought me there, I had no Thoughts of going away till I had satisfy'd it in some measure. I could hear the Man's Voice very plain, who seem'd to threaten a Lady with a great many Hardships as to her Fortune, if she would not consent to his Love. The Lady answer'd in so low a Voice, that I could not hear what she said, but I found her Answers did but inrage him the more. They talk'd a great while, and at last they seem'd to be silent. I hearing the Door open, ftep'd back into the Room where the Lady left me. She came to me again, and fat down. I hope, Sir, (faid fhe) you'll pardon my Rudenefs, but I could not wait on you before. Madam, (return'd I) I ought to beg your Pardon for taking Poffeffion of your Houfe here, who am an utter Stranger to you. We were interrupted in our Compliments, by the Voice of a Perfon that fcream'd out Murder! Murder!——We both ran out, and fhe coming to the Door where the Noife was, we found it fhut, and the Voice ftill calling out for Help. I burft it open with my Foot, and, with my Sword in my Hand, ran into the Room, where I found the Gentleman that came in the Cloak, endeavouring to force a Lady. I gave him a Stroke upon the Head, and bid him turn about and defend himfelf; which he did, with many bitter Exclamations. But after feveral Paffes, I had the good Fortune to difarm him; and he having receiv'd feveral Wounds, drop'd down with lofs of Blood. The Lady he had attempted, was ftill in a Swoon; and the Buftle had brought feveral Women Servants into the Room. I retir'd into the Chamber I came from, but defir'd the Lady to take fome care of the Wretch, who deferv'd Death; but I wifh'd might furvive, to prevent farther Trouble. She took my Advice, and fent to the next Town for a Surgeon, who foon came, and my Man along with him by Accident. Perceiving his Wounds were not dangerous, (for I ftood by while the Surgeon drefs'd him) and finding the Houfe in too much Confufion to be better inform'd concerning the Child, I was about to take my Leave. But the Lady I had fo timely refcu'd, having recover'd her Fright, defir'd fhe might thank me for fo great a Providence. I was eafily perfuaded to ftay, and immediately a Lady came into the Room.

Room. But, good God! what Transports did I feel, when in that Lady, I beheld every Feature of my dear Mrs. *Villars*. Our Eyes were fix'd upon each other, and the Sight of me rais'd such a tumult of Joy in her Breast, that combating with her unsettled Heart, she fell down in a Swoon again. The other Lady at first knew not the Meaning of our Disorder: But when I call'd her my dear Wife, and other extravagant Expressions of my Love, she soon guess'd the Truth, and seem'd as much transported as we were. Words would but wrong the Sentiments we felt for each other. Therefore, let the Reader (if possible) guess the Joy of two Lovers meeting, after imagining each other no longer in this World. We thought it was all a Dream; but at last being convinc'd of the Reality, we sent privately for the Parson, and were ty'd by the outward Ceremony of the Church, whose Hearts had been divinely united long before; and that Night I took once more Possession of what I valu'd above all the World could give.

The next Day, I sent for *Don Ferdinand* to partake in our Joy, but was inform'd his Indisposition had increas'd upon him so much, that it was dangerous to remove him. This was some allay to my Joy, for I had a real Friendship for him. I told my dear Wife, the Obligation I had to his Father. I now desir'd to know the Particulars of her wonderful Escape, which she related to me after the following manner.

You know, said she, when we parted at *Mequinez*, our Hearts foreboded something would follow prejudicial to our Loves. I was not acquainted with *Mustapha*'s Escape; if I had, it is very probable I might have avoided the Misfortune that befell me: But he got a Vessel to carry him to *Sallee*, (as he inform'd me, when I was

their

their Prisoner again) and by the Way, met with his Master *Hamet*; who wrote a Letter to the Governor of *Mammora*, and sent *Mustapha* with it, while he intended to wait near the Coast to guard us back. When they had seiz'd me, they hurry'd me away immediately on board a Vessel, and sail'd upon the Instant; and before Night met with *Hamet*, where I was carry'd on Board. He upbraided me in Terms, that gave me to expect worse Treatment from him; but I told him, rather than submit to his nauseous Love, I would starve my self to Death, if I could find no other means to rid me of Life. The next Day a Storm arising of a sudden, blew down one of their Masts, and drove 'em back again, within Sight of the Port of *Mammora*; but to avoid it, they ran beyond it, and the Storm continu'd. In the Evening it began to abate, and he steer'd his Course back again; but before it was dark a Ship appear'd in View. And notwithstanding he had lost several Men in a former Engagement, he resolv'd to set upon this Vessel; and it growing Calm he got up to her with rowing. The other Vessel knowing what she was, began with us first, and fir'd very briskly.

The Fight continu'd about an Hour, as near as I could guess; for all my Employment was to pray, that some lucky Shot would end that Life, which was so burthensome to me. When the Noise of the Ordnance ceas'd, I had not Curiosity enough to go to see how Affairs stood. But judge my Surprize and Pleasure, when I tell you the first Man that enter'd the Cabin, was the Mate that I had made Captain, as I mention'd to you in the Relation of my first Misfortune.

How Madam! cry'd he, is it you! thank Heav'n my Voyage is at End. Come Madam, (continu'd he) I'll carry you to one that thinks
her

her Life a Burden till you are fafe, being your Danger is owing to her. I had not Power to return him an Anfwer, or ask him who it was he meant, I was fo confounded with Thought. He carry'd me on board of his own Ship, where he brought Mrs. *Sufan* to me. My Heart was fo full of Content, that for a Moment you had flipt out of my Memory.

The Ship of *Hamet*'s was juft finking, for they had fhot her between Wind and Water, and could not come to ftop it. They had taken out as many of their Goods as the time would permit, and all the Men that were wounded (before fhe Sunk). I let 'em into your Story, and the mutual Affection we had; and in Return the Captain gave me the following Account of their getting away from *Sallee*.

You know, Madam, (faid he) the *Moors* were not very ftrict in fearching us; and I had at the firft Sight of 'em (judging what they were) fecur'd all the Merchants Money defign'd for Trade, as well as what I had of my own about my Cloaths, and in a great Fur Cap, which I wore upon my Head.

Hamet being fatisfy'd with you, and what he found befides, would not fell us for Slaves, but gave us the Liberty of walking about the Town, with a fmall Allowance of Provifion, till we could fend a Perfon to *England* for a thoufand Pounds, which was the Ranfom of both Ship and Men. In a little time, I became acquainted with one of the *Jews* of *Sallee*, whom I prevail'd upon by the force of Money to buy the Ship, and pay for our Ranfom; which he did, without any one's concerning themfelves about it. We did all we could to find you out, but to no purpofe; fo we were obliged to fet Sail for *England*.

In

In our Voyage home, Mrs. *Susan* inform'd we with your Story, not concealing even her own Part in't; and I found her so sincere in her Repentance, that I could not help pitying her, which soon rose a softer Passion; and assoon as we arriv'd in *England*, the Ceremony of the Church compleated my Happiness. We acquainted Mr *Kendrick*, your Ladyship's Guardian and Steward, with your Misfortune; who, with the Advice of us, fitted the Ship out in your Name, with a sufficient Quantity of Money for your Ransom, if it were possible for us to hear of you; and by meeting with you now, we have compass'd what we intended. I return'd 'em many Thanks, (especially Mrs. *Susan*, who would accompany her Husband, in hopes to meet with me.) I desir'd Captain *Morrice*, (which is the Name of Mrs. *Susan*'s Husband) to steer towards *Mammora*, but he told me it was not safe: For as there was a War proclaim'd between *France* and *England*, the Ambassador could not answer it if he did not make us Prize; and we were further inform'd by one of the *Renegado* Prisoners, that he was very well assur'd they were sail'd for *France*.

Upon this Notice we directed our Course, with this Hope, that you would soon arrive in *England*, and find me out; for I remember'd in the Story of my Misfortunes, I gave you Marks enough to let you know where I was to be found. Before we made the *English* Coast, I found my self with Child, and the very Imagination had like to have cost me my Life, for fear the Father of the unborn Infant would not come time enough to save my Credit; for though I was well assur'd of your Honour, yet I knew the censuring World would be apt to blame my Conduct. I

could

could hide nothing from the faithful *Susan*, who join'd her Fears with mine.

When we came into *Bristol* Channel, I consulted with *Susan* about my Management, and I at last resolv'd to live Private, till I could hear some News of you. But I was obliged to let Mr. *Kenderick* my Steward into the Knowledge of my Arrival, tho' he was a Stranger to my Condition.

I sent to. *London*, in hopes of hearing some News of you; but having kept the Name of your Uncle a Secret in your Relation, our Endeavours prov'd fruitless.

My Melancholy encreas'd with my Condition; and for fear of a Discovery, I went into *Wales*, with a Relation of Mrs. *Susan*'s, and was deliver'd of a Boy, that prov'd the greatest Comfort to my sinking Heart; for in his Face was every Feature of his dear Father. I brought him back again here, and had him put to Nurse, as a Child to a Relation of Mrs. *Susan*'s, and had resolv'd but this very Day to have sent for him home, that I might always have the Satisfaction of having him in my Sight.

My Steward, finding I was under a Necessity of living Private, began to talk to me of Love; and often proceeded so far (after finding I disdain'd his Passion) to tell me, if I would not consent to make him my Husband, he would take care my Estate should come into his Hands. Though I could have soon broke his Designs as to my Fortune, yet my solitary Dwelling pleas'd me so well, that I gave him good Words, which did but more encourage his Insolence, till it arriv'd to that Pitch you so happily deliver'd me from.

I

I soon found, by my Wife's Relation, that the Infant I had so marvellously sav'd, was our own Child. When I related the Accident of meeting with the Child, my Wife express'd so much Fear, Terror, Tenderness and Joy, that I thought the different Passions would have taken away her Understanding. By this we may learn, there is a ruling Providence that regulates every Action of our Lives, when they tend to Virtue.

Mr. *Kendrick*, (the Person that made the Attempt upon my Wife) was soon inform'd of our happy Meeting; and his Wounds mending every Day, he begg'd we would favour him with a Visit, (which we comply'd with) where he ask'd Pardon for all past Offences in such a sincere Manner, that we were easily prevail'd upon to forgive him.

He sent for all the Books of Accounts and Writings, that belong'd to my Wife's Estate, and deliver'd 'em up to us.

The same Day Captain *Morrice* arriv'd from *France*; where he went by the Desire of my Wife, as her last Hope, to know if he could gain any Intelligence of me. He was so very diligent in his Commission, that he got to the Speech of Monsieur *de St. Olon*, who inform'd him of my pursuing the Vessel, and returning, and of my Voyage to *Italy*. I rewarded him by several handsome Presents for his Trouble, and found in all his Actions, a downright blunt sincere Honesty, which drew me into a Friendship for him. I now began to think of *Don Ferdinand*'s Illness, and resolv'd to go with my Wife to make him a Visit; and my dear Wife was so impatient to embrace the Child, she would not let me stay to finish my Affairs with Mr. *Kendrick*.

As we were upon our Journey, we were met by a Relation of mine, Son to that barbarous
Uncle

Uncle that had Kidnap'd me. He was in the Country when I arriv'd at *London*. Notwithstanding the Injury I had suffer'd from his Father, I could not help receiving him with the utmost Affection; for we were both of an Age, and very like as to our Persons, being brought up together till the Death of my Father, which created a Friendship for each other.

He brought me a Packet from *Italy*, and in it one inclos'd from *Don Jaques*, sent from St. Salvaldor. I broke open that first, which was as follows.

I *Hope the Distance of Climates has had no Force upon your Friendship; mine here has rather receiv'd an Addition, tho' I am overwhelm'd with a very great Misfortune. My Daughter (in whom all my Hopes center'd) is (I fear) intirely lost; for the very Day you left us, was the last time my Eyes beheld her. We have some reason to fear the Relations of the Person, who dy'd by your Sword, have us'd some clandestine Means, and perhaps have privately murder'd her, to be reveng'd on us for that Accident, tho' of their own seeking. In short, I am weary of the hateful Place, and shall do my Endeavour to seek Repose in some other Part of the World; and relying upon your good-natur'd Friendship, I hope to have the Honour very shortly after your receiving this, to embrace you in* England, *for I am preparing to leave* St. Salvador *with the soonest. I receiv'd your obliging Letter, and the Bales of Goods, all in good Condition. But there is something Dark in it, or at least my Understanding can't reach this Paragraph; and be assur'd, whatever you gave me in Charge, &c. I sent you nothing but what I hope you will accept as your own; and I took the manner of leaving 'em with you, knowing your generous Temper would*

not

not have been eafily perfuaded to have accepted 'em, from one that fhall ever fubfcribe himfelf,

Your fincere Friend and Servant,

Jaques de Ramires.

P. S. *My Wife (who is inconfolable) throws in her Love and Service; and all the Hopes fhe has left, is the Expectation of telling you Face to Face, the Grief fhe lies under at her fatal Lofs; and to bring us farther in your Debt, we beg you will leave us fufficient Direction among our Countrymen at your* Exchange, *where we may find you.*

I was very much concern'd at my Friend's Misfortune, efpecially in believing I was in fome fort the miftaken Caufe of it. I had inform'd my Wife of the Adventure before, and fhe condol'd with me; and the Thoughts of being fo near the fame Diftrefs in her own Child, redoubled her Grief. When we had given up fome time to thofe Melancholy Reflections, I broke open the following Letter from *Don Antonio.*

My Dear Friend,

WE received yours with the utmoft Tranfports; but as I am an *Italian,* I ought to be jealous at the Joy my Wife exprefs'd when fhe read it; and much more, when fhe now declares that fhe will come to England, *to reproach you for the little Care you took of her Commiffion. She will (farther to encreafe my Jealoufy) write you her Sentiments her felf; but let her fay what fhe will there, I am refolv'd to efteem you as the only Friend that's dear to*

Antonio de Alvares.

The

The other Letter from *Isabella* contain'd these Words.

SIR,

I'LL suspend my Reproaches till I see you, (which I hope will be soon.) I had no Commission to be executed in those Papers you lost, but that of having clear'd the Aspersion you cast on our Sex of Inconstancy, which you had some Grounds for, in the sudden Marriage of Don Pedro and Donna Felicia, after her violent Passion for Don Ferdinand. When I found the Cause of her Distemper, I (as having felt the keenest Dart of Love) pity'd her Pain, and therefore tax'd Don Ferdinand often with his wearing an obdurate Heart in his Bosom. I press'd him so often, that he desir'd to meet Donna Felicia and my self in my Closet. We came according to Appointment, where he spoke to this Effect: Madam, tax me no more with Hardness of Heart, for if I had not a very tender one, I had never arriv'd here; and to discover my Frailty at once, know, I am a Woman: And upon that undiscovering her Bosom, gave us Evident Tokens. We were both so very much surpriz'd that she went on with her Discourse; I beg, Ladies, you will never open your Mouth to my Captain concerning this; for the Moment I am sensible he knows my Weakness, shall be the last of my Life. But notwithstanding this Injunction, I can't help informing you, in Pity to her; and I am well assur'd, (as your Passion is hopeless) you have Humanity enough not to destroy one who dies for you; and nothing in this World can equal my Joy, if I find, when I arrive, Don Ferdinand *the Wife to one who shall ever have the Friendship of*

Isabella de Alvares.

What Words can express the Amazement I felt, at the reading this last Letter! My Thoughts were confounded in Thought, and a Chaos of Ideas possess'd my Brain. I was in so much Confusion, that I thought of returning home again, to consider of this strange Turn. Recollected Circumstances convinc'd me, how blind I was in not discovering it sooner. My Soul was immediately fill'd with the most tender Pity; and I had not the use of Words to declare my Sentiments to my Wife and Cousin. Sometimes I would imagine it was all a fictitious Dream; yet at last I was not displeas'd, that I had it in my Power to restore to *Don Jaques* his long lost Daughter. My Wife was as much concern'd as I was, and my Cousin could hardly believe it. I soon found that she had taken care the Packet should not fall into my Hands; and that convinc'd me she would not have her Disguise discover'd. The next Day we resolv'd to visit her, and form my Resolution from my Observation.

When we arriv'd at the Inn, we found her dress'd at a Table, with Paper, Pens and Ink before her, but very weak. I presented my Wife and Cousin to her. She saluted 'em, and seem'd mightily pleas'd with my good Fortune, and was very much concern'd her Indisposition would not admit her waiting on me, to partake in my Contentment. Her Weakness was so prevalent, that she could hardly utter her Words. She knew nothing of receiving the Packet from my Cousin, but after we had sat some time, I gave her the Letter from her Father; which, assoon as she had read, she fell backward upon the Bed in a Swoon.

The Noise we made at this Accident brought several People into the Room; and among the rest my Landlady, who it seems had fell desperately in Love with her, as imagining her to be a Man. She made such aukward Complainings, that, if our Minds had been at ease, would have produc'd much Mirth; but among her Actions, she unbutton'd her Cloaths, to give her Breath, and soon discover'd her Mistake in the Object of her Wishes. When she found by her Breasts that she was a Woman, she ran down Stairs with the utmost Precipitation, and left us alone to recover her. When we had brought her to her Senses again, she soon found that we had discover'd her Sex; and the Grief and Shame at the Accident had like to have thrown her again into her Swooning. It was some time before we could bring her to her self: But, she found by my Discourse, that I understood the whole Secret.

After a long Pause, said she, I did not intend to let my Frailty be known to you till after my Death; but since it is discover'd, I beg you will have some Regard to my Memory, and I shall die contented. I begg'd her not to talk of Death, but live to comfort her griev'd Parents. It is too late, said she, to talk of any Comfort, for I have call'd my greatest Friend Death to my Aid, who is just now arriv'd. Upon uttering these Words, a deadly Paleness possess'd her Face, and Trembling seiz'd her Limbs: She had just Strength enough to declare to us that she had taken a Dose of Poison, provided for the Occasion, bought of an Apothecary of the Town; and that she was just going to write a Letter to me, but was prevented by our sudden Appearance, whose Contents were only to see her secretly bury'd, and if possible to have conceal'd her Sex and Story from the World. She had hardly made an End, before her Speech forsook her, and Life in all Appearance fled the beauteous Dwelling. My Wife was not present at this Accident, being her eager Desire had carry'd her to her Child; but she came in before it was over. My Cousin seem'd more oppress'd with Grief than any of us, for Love had taken full Possession of his Heart.

While Sorrow had lock'd up all our Tongues, the Apothecary came in, in a strange Confusion; for the Report had soon dispers'd it self all over that little Village. Sir, said he to me, don't be concern'd at the Condition you see the Gentleman in, for he is not dead, he has only took a sleeping Potion. I partly guess'd his Design, when he apply'd to me for Poison; and the extraordinary Price he paid for it, convinc'd me it was for some sinister Design; and therefore I happily impos'd upon him.

This News reviv'd us all again, especially my Cousin, who I thought would have gone distracted for Joy; and to see his impatient watching for her Life's return, (if we may call it so) only gave me further Proof, that one Look is sufficient to fix Love for ever in the Soul. The Apothecary, during this interval of Life and Death, pour'd Cordials into her Mouth to help the Operation; and at last she open'd her unwilling Eyes, and gaz'd around her, as if she had been in another World: But we soon convinc'd her of the Apothecary's Deceit, at which she seem'd in the utmost Confusion, and gave us to understand that Life was forc'd upon her against her Inclination, and she would shake it off.

We gave her all the Comfort we were capable of; and my Wife told her if she talk'd any longer of Death, it was only that she could not bear to see us happy. This as it were rous'd her from her Lethargy. Well then, said she, I will live,

live, if it be only to convince you, that I am pleas'd to fee my Captain bleſs'd (for ſhe would always call me ſo.) After we had a little compos'd her, we left her with my Couſin, to look after our Child, who was in the ſame Place; which had prov'd the ſecret Inſtinct of Nature; for at the firſt Sight in the Houſe of his unnatural Nurſe, I could not help feeling a tender Regard for him. When we had ſatisfy'd our Inn, we prevail'd upon *Donna Bianca* (now no longer *Ferdinand*) to come into the Coach with us, and we arriv'd that Evening at *Briſtol*; where we took Poſſeſſion of the Houſe (which Captain *Kendrick* had liv'd in) that belong'd to my Wife. We ſtaid ſome time there to ſettle my Wife's Affairs, and as much to recover *Donna Bianca*'s Indiſpoſition.

My Couſin by his Aſſiduity gain'd very much of her Eſteem, but ſhe freely declar'd ſhe had no Room in her Heart for Love: But notwithſtanding, with much Importunity, we prevail'd upon her to accept him for a Husband; and her Eſteem ſoon came up to a more tender Paſſion. Aſſoon as the Ceremony was over, we took a Journey to *London* to ſettle our Affairs there, and provide for my expected Gueſts.

One Morning as we were purſuing our Journey, coming near the Skirts of a Wood, we heard ſeveral Groans, which alarm'd us; but as we had too many People about us arm'd, to fear any thing, we came out of the Coach to know the Reaſon: Where we found a Woman weltring in Blood, being ſtabb'd in ſeveral Places with a Sword. When I came to take a nearer View, I found it was my former Maſter (the Watch-maker's) Wife. I could not help having Compaſſion for any Perſon in that Condition, therefore order'd her to be taken up and put

put in the Coach. *Donna Bianca* open'd her Breast, and stopp'd her Wounds as well as she could, till we could get a Surgeon that I had order'd to be sent for. She soon knew me, and cry'd out, Sure Heaven has sent you that know my Guilt to be Witness of my Repentance: The Wrongs I have done my Husband have pursu'd me to my Grave. When I had robb'd him of all I could lay my Hands on, I made my Escape to *Ireland*, chang'd my Name, and set up for a greater Fortune than I really was. I had many Suitors, but Heaven, to punish me, made me place my Affections on a Person that courted me for my Money: And tho' I soon understood he had but very little Estate, yet Love prevail'd with me to make him my Husband. He soon spent both his own and my Fortune, and by contracting many Debts was forc'd to fly for *England*; and finding no Relief, took to the Highway, where he has committed many Robberies. He lodg'd me in a neighbouring Village; but our Place of Meeting was generally in this Wood, for fear of a Discovery. This Morning he came, according to Appointment, where he began his Discourse after this Manner. I had no Inclination for you when I first marry'd you, but now I utterly abhor you, therefore am resolv'd to part with you: But I have another Reason besides my Hatred to you, which is this; I have it in my Power to marry an old Woman, very rich; and therefore it is necessary to send you out of the World, for fear our Marriage should come to her Ears, and spoil my Fortune. He follow'd his Discourse with these Wounds, which he gave me, and rode into the Wood, without my once offering to open my Mouth; for Astonishment had ty'd up my Tongue. I told her, I hop'd

Heaven

Heaven had given her all its Punishment in this World. That's all the Hope I have, said she, and in my unfeigned Repentance; for I feel Death approaching. We observ'd she was just expiring; and before the Surgeon came, she gave up her last Breath, calling upon Heaven for Mercy. I gave Orders for her Funeral, and sent after her Murderer, but to no Purpose. But I heard he was taken for the High-way, some time after, and executed at *Worcester*; where he confess'd the Murder of his Wife. Thus we see the Hand of Heaven, though slow in Punishments, yet always overtakes the Guilty. When I had given Directions for her Funeral, we pursu'd our Journey, and arriv'd safe at *London*.

Don Antonio and his Lady arriv'd first, in a private Capacity; not caring to make a Show according to their Birth, to be taken Notice of. And in a few Days after came *Don Jaques* and his Lady, in a Ship of their own, in Company with the *Isabella* which my Lieutenant commanded, that had sprung a Leak which oblig'd her to put into *Lisbon* to refit, where *Don Jaques* joyfully met with her.

I had desir'd *Donna Bianca* once more to put on her Boy's Cloaths; for I intended agreeably to surprize her Parents.

I was oblig'd to take Lodgings for *Don Jaques*'s Family, being they intended to take a convenient House in the City. Assoon as mutual Caresses were over, Grief again took Possession of their Souls for the Loss of their Child. After condoling with 'em some time, I begg'd 'em to hope for the best, and that it was possible to hear of her again. They shook their Heads, and told me that Thought was long given over, and they had no Hope but in Time to wear away their unhappy Loss.

I told 'em I had a Kinsman, as much as I could remember the Features of their beautiful Daughter, as like her as a Man could be like a Woman. They express'd a great Desire to see him. I told 'em I had invited him with another Relation to sup with us on purpose. We had taken care before, that *Donna Bianca* should Ombre her Face, and speak nothing but *English*, on purpose to carry on the Deceit. 'Till the time of their coming, we spent in relating our Accidents in the Voyage. I told 'em how much I was surpriz'd at the Likeness of my Cousin to their Daughter: for I had given 'em to understand it was a Relation I had never seen before I left *England*: which was Truth.

When the Time I had appointed came, *Donna Bianca* and my Cousin enter'd. I presented 'em to *Don Jaques* and his Wife, as my Relations, and they saluted 'em as utter Strangers. But when they saw and heard *Donna Bianca*, they burst into Tears at the great Resemblance in both Voice and Features, as they said, to their Daughter. She carry'd it on as long as she could, speaking *English* all the while; but at last their Tears prevail'd so much upon her Tenderness, that she begg'd leave to retire, but would return immediately. I made an Apology for my Kinsman to *Don Jaques* and his Wife, and told 'em he would return in a very little time. The Space of their Absence was fill'd with Sighs and Tears; and as I knew their Grief would soon be over, I never attempted to comfort 'em.

When they were ready, they sent a Servant to tell me a Gentleman wanted to speak with me.

me. I retir'd, and came in again immediately, and told 'em our Company would be encreas'd, for another Relation and his Wife were juſt coming in to ſup with us; and upon the Inſtant my Couſin enter'd, leading by the Hand *Donna Bianca.* They both ran and kneel'd down before *Don Jaques* and his Wife. At the Sight of their Daughter, the Mother fell backward in the Chair in a Swoon; and *Don Jaques* was in ſuch a Surprize that he could not open his Mouth, but expreſs'd his Joy by Tears, Kiſſes, and Embraces; and his Lady coming to her ſelf, had like to have ſtifled her with her Tranſports.

They did not ask any reaſonable Queſtions till the Torrent of their Joy was poured out. After the firſt Tranſports were over, *Donna Bianca* told her own Story. She ſaid, the firſt time I din'd at their Houſe in St. *Salvador,* Love flew into her Heart; and knowing the Modeſty due to her Sex, ſhe was reſolv'd never to diſcover it till ſhe found the State of mine: Yet finding her Paſſion daily increaſe, and underſtanding the Day of my Departure, ſhe procured ſecretly the Habit of a Man, with all other Neceſſaries, and convey'd herſelf on Board in the Boat that carry'd the Preſents her Father had ſent me; and counterfeited the Letter ſhe gave me as from her Father. Every thing anſwered my Wiſh, ſaid ſhe; but I ſoon found my Captain had no Heart to beſtow. It is needleſs to tell how many bitter Sighs and Tears that Knowledge coſt me: But it is now buried in Oblivion. Then ſhe proceeded to beg their Pardon for her raſh Folly, as ſhe call'd it; and they were too much overjoy'd not to forgive her every thing; and they expreſt a great deal
of

of Satisfaction in that they could now call me their Relation. We liv'd in all the Contentment imaginable, returning Heaven our grateful Thanks for its bounteous Mercy. And now I am settled, I'll take Leave of my Reader with this Couplet of the Poet:

O never let a virtuous Mind despair,
For constant Hearts are Love's peculiar Care.

THE
VOYAGE,
SHIPWRACK,
AND
Miraculous ESCAPE
OF
Richard Caſtelman, Gent.

With a Deſcription of *Penſylvania*, and the City *Philadelphia*, &c.

Printed in the Year MDCCXXVI.

THE
VOYAGE, &c.
OF
Richard Castelman, Gent.

HE Dangers at Sea are certainly more imminent than those on Shore; even in the fairest Weather, the Space is very small betwen this World and the next.

A *Grecian* Philosopher was, in my Opinion, much in the right, when ask'd by a Friend if he would go to a neighbouring Island in the *Hellespont* to hunt, answer'd, if he should be guilty of so much Folly, he should have no other Hope but of returning safe back, for those that trusted their Lives to the Sea ventur'd with a changing Mistress.

I embark'd on Board Captain *Cox*, bound for *Charles-town* in *Carolina*, with Mr. *Jones* and his Family, and arriv'd safe there without any
great

great Hazard, juſt when Captain *Moor* had made a Deſcent upon the *Spaniards* of St. *Auguſtine*, a Plantation to the Southward of *Carolina*, and return'd with confiderable Booty. By ſome of the *Colony* his Proceedings were cenſur'd with Injuſtice, being the *Spaniards* had not any Notice of the Rupture between *England* and *Spain*; but all Stratagems are lawful in War.

Some time after, the *Spaniards*, reſenting the Uſage of the *Engliſh*, fitted out five Sail of Men of War, and ſeveral Tranſports, to repay them in their own Coin.

They landed eight hundred Men in the Bay, and ſent two Trumpeters to Sir *Nathaniel Johnſon*, at that time Governour of *Charles-town*, to ſurrender; but he ſent 'em word back, as the Place was intruſted to him by the Queen his Miſtreſs, he was reſolv'd to hold it out to the laſt. The Meſſengers inform'd their Admiral of Sir *Nathaniel*'s Reſolution, and likewiſe added, that the Town was too well Mann'd to be eaſily taken. He thought better on't, recall'd his Men, and ſail'd away.

This Attempt very much alarm'd the Country, and put 'em upon fortifying *Charles-town*, which at preſent may laugh at all Attempts from a Foreign Foe, or the native *Indians*, who us'd before to infeſt 'em daily.

Charles-town, or *Charles* City, the Capital of *Carolina*, is ſituated upon a Neck of Land form'd by a River on each ſide, (nam'd *Aſhley* and *Cooper* Rivers, from the firſt Plantations) well ſtor'd with Fiſh. There was when I was there but an indifferent wooden Church; but before I left the Place, Subſcriptions were taken in to build a regular Stone Building. There are upwards of a thouſand Houſes, very neatly built, with Gardens almoſt to every Houſe. There is Plenty of every Thing for the Life of Man to be

found

found at *Charles-town*. It lies in 32 deg. 40 min. Northern Latitude. The Trade of this Place is more confiderable for its Bignefs than any other Plantation in *America*; it being the Southermoft Settlement belonging to the Crown of *England* upon the Continent; and I have been inform'd they have Dealings three hundred Leagues up the Country, which is very much facilitated by the numerous navigable Rivers that come from the Mountains. The Climate is very wholefome. Tho' moft *Europeans* have at their firft Arrival the Diftemper of the Country, which proceeds from Change of Air and Diet; yet I had the good Fortune to efcape with a fwell'd Arm, which had like to have ended in the Mortification of a Finger; but I was happily cur'd by the Care and Advice of Madam *Rhett*, the only good Surgeon on the Place: Tho' were I to enumerate her other good Qualities, my fmall Tract would exceed in Bulk my Intentions: I fhall only fay, another *Dacier* may be found in *America*.

I ftaid at *Charles-town* upwards of eight Months, and was well entertain'd by the courteous Inhabitants; for I muft own Pleafure as well as Profit induc'd me to travel, though I have no Inclination that way now.

Mr. *Jones*, the Perfon concern'd with me in Trade, was oblig'd to go to *Bermuda*, being Secretary and Provoft-Marfhal of the *Summer-Iflands*; and in a fhort time after I follow'd with his Family. We met with no other Accident than a large Shark that follow'd our Veffel feveral Days together, and the Mafter told me he was well affur'd fome One on Board would die. I laugh'd at his Superftition, and endeavour'd to rally him out of it, but he ftill perfifted in his Opinion. When the Shark appear'd firft,

every

every Body was in good Health, but in three Days time a Woman Paſſenger expir'd of a Fever; whom we committed to the Waves, and was probably entombed in the Bowels of the Shark, for he took his leave of us the ſame Day. The Maſter told me he had made it his Obſervation for ſeveral Years, and was never once out. 'Tis not impoſſible but the Shark at Sea has the ſame Inſtinct as the Vulture at Land.

When I arriv'd at St. *George*'s, the Capital of *Bermudas*, I was as well pleas'd with the Climate and Inhabitants as I was at *Carolina*.

St. *George*'s Town is ſeated in the Bottom of a Bay of the ſame Name, and is very well fortify'd. It contains about two hundred Houſes, with a Church ſomething handſomer than that of *Charles-town*. The Incumbent was the Reverend Mr. *Holland*, a Perſon of a good Underſtanding. I had a Preſent, an *Antelope*'s Foot ſet in Gold, for a Tobacco-Stopper, which I was to deliver to the Biſhop of *Bangor*, his Patron; but it was loſt among my other Things in my Shipwrack.

There is a perpetual Spring to be obſerv'd in theſe Iſlands, and the old Leaves never drop before they are thruſt out by new ones. Their Fruit is in Bloſſoms, Buds, and Ripe at the ſame time. The Air is generally temperate and innubilous, but now and then troubled with violent Thunder and Lightning; and I have been ſhown ſeveral Rocks that they ſay were ſplit by Lightning.

I was informed by a Gentleman that had coaſted along theſe Iſlands, that their Number amounts to 378, but above 300 of them deſerve no other Name than Rocks; and moſt of the others that are inhabited have not above half a dozen Houſes upon them.

Mr. Richard Castelman.

The Soil of all the cultivated Islands is alike, being very fruitful; and some People imagine they were once join'd, making one intire Island, but were divided as they are now by the Innovation of the Sea: And what gives them ground for this Opinion is, that the Waves daily lessen the small ones. But this is only Conjecture.

I am sorry to say that the former Inhabitants gain'd much by Pirates; and even some that had large Plantations when I was there, were little better at first than Sea-Robbers.

The late Queen being inform'd of it, order'd Mr. *Larkins* with a Commission to try Pirates, where-ever they resorted in her Dominions in *America*. I happen'd to be at *Bermuda* when he arriv'd there. He acquainted the People in Power with his Commission, but met with a very cold Reception from 'em: But however, he proceeded in his Design, and issu'd out Warrants to seize the suspected Persons. Mr. *Jones*, as Provost-Marshal, was oblig'd to execute the Warrants; but he met with Resistance every where, and was very ill us'd by some of them, even to the Hazard of his Life.

The Governour, whose Name was *Bennet*, as he represented the Monarch of *England*, should have assisted Mr. *Jones* and Mr. *Larkins*; but whether he was afraid of offending the Inhabitants, or not enquiring truly into the Matter, Mr. *Jones* and Mr. *Larkins* were seiz'd and committed to Prison. Mr. *Jones* first made his Escape, and arriv'd safe in *England*; where he set forth his Case, and had all the Redress he desir'd: He was order'd back, and re-instated in his former Post.

Those that oppos'd him, I am inform'd, had reprimanding Letters from *England*, upon his Account;

but when Hate is fix'd in the Minds of some Men, 'tis never to be rooted out: Their Animosities rose as high as ever, and he was once more oblig'd to abandon the Island. There is now depending a Suit in Law between the Governour and Mr. *Jones*, who are both in *England*; and there is no doubt but Justice will take Place.

Mr. *Larkins* was put into the Dungeon of the Prison, and it was the common Report, he was deny'd even Food to sustain Life; and would have certainly expir'd for Want, if he had not made his Escape in the Habit of a Woman, with the Assistance of a true Friend; which is hard to find any where, but more especially among the Men of Power in *America*: But his Confinement had so worn him, and he had contracted so many Distempers by his Ill-Usage, that he expir'd in his Voyage home.

As I said before, this Island was in former Times the common Receptacle for Pirates, and indeed their chiefest Gain proceeded from trading with them. Here they came to spend what Money they got, and recreate themselves; it lying very convenient for 'em, between 32 and 33 Degrees of N. Latitude, and 300 Leagues from the Continent or any other Island.

Among their Trees, the *Cedar* is the most plentiful, which they use even for Firing. I have seen Vessels of a hundred Ton built with Cedar; and most of the Houses are compos'd of the same.

The Laws *should* be the same as those in *England*; but Power is generally Chief Judge in *America*: Yet if a Person never comes under the Lash of the Superior, there is very comfortable Living at *Bermuda*.

Mr.

Mr. Jones, Capt. Bayley, and my self, had jointly bought a Vessel of about 140 Ton, and we had got in all our Freight but Tobacco, which we were to take in at *Virginia*, and then make up with the Fleet for *England*. While we were fitting out our Vessel, Mr. *Jones* was employ'd in his own Affairs, therefore the Care of his Share was committed to me.

We set Sail from *Bermuda*, *April* 5, 1710, with a fair Gale, which continu'd till we lost Sight of the Islands; but in the Night a contrary Wind sprang up, and blowing very fresh at N. N. E. carry'd us to the Southward of the *Bermudas*; and it was the greatest Providence in the World we were not stav'd upon the Rocks; but with great Difficulty we got clear of them, being oblig'd to ply it to Windward three Days.

We had the Misfortune to find our Ship none of the best Sailors; yet in four Days we got in our proper Latitude; and the Wind continuing pretty fair, we made very good Way. We had no other Diversion than taking Dolphins with our Fizgig; but in my Opinion it is but indifferent Food.

We were forty one, including Passengers; and many of those being sick with the Rocking of the Ship, made it uncomfortable living among them; and I wish'd my self once more on Shore.

April 12 we were alarm'd at Sight of a Vessel we discover'd, which we imagin'd to be a *Spanish* Privateer. We crouded all the Sail we could to avoid her, which would have been very hard to do, if immediately after the Wind had not chang'd to S. S. E. a very strong Gale. We bore away before it, and ere Night lost Sight of her.

As we were at Supper in the Cabin, a Son of Capt. *Bayley*'s came and told his Father that the Colour of the Water was chang'd; but his Father reprimanded him, and told him he had lost his Senses, for it was impossible to be near any Shore. When the Sea changes its Colour, 'tis an evident Token Land is not far off. We continu'd the same Course under a Foresail; but our Terror and Surprize was not to be exprest, when in the Morning Watch, the Captain, who being upon Deck discover'd Land right a-head, came down into my Cabin, and with Tears in his Eyes desir'd I would rise. I knew by his Looks something extraordinary was the Matter, and got upon Deck to be resolv'd, for Capt. *Bayley* had not Power to utter a Word. I soon found the Danger, for I perceiv'd we were in View of *Virginia*, near *Ronoke* Sand-Banks. We did all that was in our Power to weather 'em, but our Ship having a round Head, she would not obey the Helm; therefore we all agreed to make in for the Land, hoping, as it seem'd a bold Shore, it was Tide of Flood, and then we might through Providence land safe. But it proving Tide of Ebb, we bulg'd upon the *Ronoke* Sand-Banks, but by lightning the Ship, and cutting our Masts by the Board, we got clear of that; but keeping still in for the Shore, we struck upon the second Sand-Bank, but not very violently, so we threw out our Anchors in hopes we might ride out the Tide; but the Wind increasing, we dragg'd 'em, and were violently thrown upon another Sand-Bank, where our Ship stuck, and the Waves dash'd over us. We had several Women with Children on Board, and their dismal Cries pierc'd my very Heart. We order'd the Boat out, to see if we could gain the Shore that way. I jump'd into her one of the

the firſt, but ere we could leave the Side of the Ship, ſhe was ſtav'd in Pieces. All we could do in this Exigence was get into the Ship again; and with much difficulty we compaſs'd it, being dragg'd in by main Force; yet if I had not held faſt hold by the Coat of one that was in the Water with me, and the Foot of another, I muſt have inevitably periſh'd, for I was under the Keel. When I had got Footing upon Deck, I fetch'd my Box out of my Cabin, and was for ſecuring my Money, which amounted to Fifty Pound. While I was buſying my ſelf with uncording my Box, the Captain's Siſter reprimanded me for thinking on my Money, when all their Lives were in Danger. I muſt own, other Thoughts had been more ſuitable to my Condition, therefore I was aſham'd of what I was about, and had no other Regard than to aſſiſt in ſaving our ſelves. It prov'd a fruitleſs Labour in endeavouring to get off the Veſſel, therefore we laid aſide all Hopes of ſaving the Cargo.

We had two Blacks on Board that belong'd to Capt. *Bayley*, that were excellent Divers (for the Surge was ſo violent no one could ſtem the Billows but by diving) who offer'd to get with a Rope on Shore, and faſten it from the Ship to a Stump of a Tree; and divine Providence had ſo order'd it, there was not any Thing like a Tree for half a Mile on each Side of us. I told the Captain it look'd like a good Omen, and, by the Help of God, I did not doubt but we ſhould get ſafe on Shore.

The *Negroes* with much Difficulty did as they had intended, and by the Help of the Rope came back to the Ship. Capt. *Bayley*, his Wife, and Mate, ventur'd into the Water firſt, upon the Awning of the Ship, and got ſafe on Shore; tho' it broke aſſoon as they were landed. But my my Ears are even pierc'd this Moment with the Cries of his poor Children that were in the Ship, which was more terrible to me than the Storm. I offer'd to help 'em upon the Rope, but they were in such Frights and Terrors that I could not prevail upon 'em to venture.

Two of the Sailors got upon the Rope just as I was going to venture, and with their Bustling had very near thrown me once more into the Sea. I offer'd my Assistance to the Capain's Sister, but she was as timorous as the Children, and fed her self with vain Hopes that the Waves would leave 'em by degrees, and they might with less Danger get on Shore. I took my Leave of all that were on Board, and recommending them and my self to the Care of Heaven, I got into the Water and laid fast hold on the Rope, and, with the Assistance of one of the *Negroes*, got some Distance from the Ship; but the Waves drove back with such an Impetuosity that I was many times in Danger of losing my Hold, and so be carried into the main Sea; which had certainly came to pass, if I had not been assisted by the Black; for every time a great Sea was coming to break over us, he would cry out, *For the Lord's Sake, Master, hold fast*: And whenever he call'd to me, I settled my self to receive the Force of the Waves, which would as oft overwhelm me; and I poured out my Prayers to God for his Assistance. At last, with much Struggling, I could feel my Feet touch the Ground sometimes, and by degrees, with the utmost Difficulty, got Footing; and at every Retire of the Waves set my self to running. When they drove back upon the Shore, I seiz'd upon the Rope, or otherwise I had been dash'd to pieces on the Sand. But at last my Strength began to fail me, with the violent Fatigue I had undergone;

gone; and if the *Negro* had not dragg'd me on the Sands, (whose Strength also was almost gone) I must, after all my Strugglings for Life, have resign'd my self to the Waves.

Assoon as I could recover my Spirits, I gave the divine Creator of all things, Thanks for my wonderful Delivery from the Jaws of Death; which was still more wonderful, for assoon as I had let go the Rope (some other Persons venturing the same way) it broke, so that not one of the unfortunate Wretches came on Shore, but were swallow'd up by the Waves.

A-while after I had got on Shore, Captain *Bayley*, his Wife, and the Mate came down to me, and inform'd me that they could find no Road, nor any Inhabitants. This News renew'd our Griefs, for we seem'd to be in as much Danger of Starving now, as of Drowning before: And to increase our Dread, it was not above three Hours to Night, and then we had the wild Bears to fear.

While we were lamenting our Condition, we heard somebody hollow up in the Woods, which reviv'd our drooping Senses: But running to see who it was, we, much to our Grief, found it to be one of the Sailors that escap'd, who was hollowing to his Companion; and they were both as drunk as 'twas possible for them to be, with Rum, before they left the Ship. Such Beasts are some Sailors, that even the greatest Dangers will not deter them from Drinking, if they have an Opportunity.

When we were all together, (that is, the Captain, his Wife, and Mate, two white Sailors, two *Negroes*, and my self,) we resolv'd to walk to the Southward, to see if it were possible to find any Habitations; but in less than an Hour, our

Journey was stopp'd by an impenetrable Wood, and we were obliged to return.

We then went Northward, but were interrupted by large Swamps, and not the least Mark of any Plantation. Thus, maroon'd as we were, we went back again, and could perceive the poor Wretches in the Vessel, lifting up their Hands to us for Succour; but we could neither give 'em Assistance or Comfort. I made 'em Signs to let 'em know our Condition was as bad as theirs, and that they had nothing to think on but Heaven.

It growing near Night, some of the poor Creatures ventur'd into the Water, but were soon drown'd. In short, every Object we beheld increas'd our Horror. None of us had eat or drank for two Days, besides our Fatigue. Tho' quite cast down my self, I endeavour'd to chear my Fellow-Sufferers; and that we might be shelter'd from the Inclemency of the Night (which, to add to our wretched Condition, prov'd a rainy one) we by joint Consent and Labour, while the Day lasted, pluck'd down a good Number of *Palmetoe* Leaves; and with Pieces of Trees (which we tore, for we had never a Knife among us) built us up a Hut, and shelter'd it from the Weather as well as we could.

The *Palmetoe* Leaf is very large, and the same that they make the plaited Straw of, which forms the finest Hats, that come from *Bermuda* and *Carolina*. It was a very melancholy Reflection to think of our Condition: Nothing to lie upon but the bare wet Ground, and our Cloaths that cover'd us were those upon our Backs, dropping with Rain and Salt-Water; no Food, nor Hopes of getting any; and I was even ready to expire with Thirst. While the Hut was preparing,

paring, to allay my Drouth, I stole by my self, urin'd in my Tobacco-Box, and drank it with as great a Gusto as ever I have done *French* Claret before or since.

When I came to lie down in our wretched Tenement, the Place was full; but I e'en laid my self down upon 'em, (and tho' a Woman was among us, had no Thoughts of different Sexes) and by degrees made Room for my self. Notwithstanding their complaining of Legs and Arms, I held my Tongue, and, maugre all my Wants and Misfortunes, slept soundly till Morning: But with the Day Reflection return'd, sharpen'd with the extreamest Hunger.

When we had got all together again, (that is, seven of us, for one of the drunken Sailors was found dead some Distance from our Cabin, as we might well imagine, with Cold and Want, and spoil'd an excellent Proverb, *That drunken Men never get any Harm*) by my Advice we address'd our selves to the All-seeing Power for Succour; all but the Mate, who told us that Praying alone would not do, therefore while we *pray'd*, he would go *seek*. After our extempore Orisons were over, we rose up, and resolv'd to go into the Woods, to gather, if it was possible, something to kill our Hunger. But as we turn'd toward the Beach, we saw the Mate with another Man, a Stranger to us, coming towards us. The Dove could not be a more pleasing Sight to the Patriarch *Noah*, when he return'd with the Olive-Branch in his Mouth, than that Stranger was to us. We ran with all the Speed which our weak Condition would admit of, to meet him. Under his Arm he had got a little Tub of Butter that the Sea had thrown up; and though mixt with Sand and Gravel, we as greedily devour'd it as if it had been Partridge or Pheasant; but our Misfortune was, when we had tir'd our selves with Eating, for I can't say we were satisfy'd, we all of us grew Sick, and cast it up again.

The Stranger, to relieve us, gave us a Couple of Limes among us, which we greedily devour'd, and to the Butter again. But what was a pleasing Surprize to us, our Mate inform'd us a Puncheon of fresh Water was thrown on Shore. We eagerly ran, and my Tobacco-Box serv'd us instead of a Cup. The Mate, who had slak'd his Thirst before, would not let us drink too much, for fear of endangering our Lives; but with this indifferent Repast we recover'd our fainting Spirits, and were more able to bear the Fatigue of the Day.

Our Vessel was drove close on Shore, but broke in many Pieces; and it was a melancholy Sight to behold the dead Bodies covering the Sand: But what had almost kill'd Capt. *Bayley* and his Wife with Sorrow, were the Bodies of his Sister and one of his Children half buried in the Sands. For my own part, I had no other thing to grieve for but the Loss of my Cargo, which consisted of *Cotton*, *Indigo*, and Straw Ware; which, if it had arriv'd safe to *England*, would have yielded to my own Share fifteen hundred Pound: Tho' the Loss of my *Harpsichord* and *Italian Timbrel* I most regretted, whose Remains I discover'd upon the Shore; and the whole Strand was cover'd with *Bermuda* Hats. Some we pick'd up; and among other pieces of the Wreck, the Mate discover'd my Box floating on the Surface, which by good Fortune he dragg'd on Shore. In it was my Money, Linnen, and Books of Accounts. We kept this private from the

Stranger,

Stranger, and bury'd it in a Place I had mark'd by several Observations: For he had given us to understand, it was his usual Custom, after a violent Storm, to come to the Sand-Banks in Expectation of Shipwrecks; therefore we were not assur'd he might not find Means to destroy us in Hopes of what we had on Shore, or leave us without assisting us to some Plantation.

When we had done all we could about our Wreck, we took leave of the miserable Sight, and set forward to the Stranger's Plantation, which was about ten Miles off. He led us along the Woods by certain Marks on Trees, which we were ignorant of; but the Inhabitants know how to find one another's Plantations by those Marks; and in four Hours (for I had my Watch in my Pocket when I was shipwreck'd) we once more beheld the pleasing Sight of a Chimney smoaking, which was the Habitation of our Guide. You may imagine the Joy we had to enter once more into a House, after our miserable Hardships. But when we came there, we found but indifferent Accommodation. There were no other Eatables to be got, but a little hung Beef, and *Humminy*, (that is, *Indian* Corn ground, mix'd with Milk, and dry'd before the Fire:) but this was Feasting to us; for Hunger is the best Sauce.

There were but two Beds in the House, which the Family complimented us with. The Captain and his Wife had one, and Mr. *Burnam* and I had the other.

I deferr'd going for my Box till the second Day after our Arrival; for I was very much out of Order with the Fatigue I had underwent; and by lying on the wet Ground I had lost my Hearing, which I did not recover throughly till my Arrival in *England*.

The

The Mate, two *Negroes*, and my felf, fet out with one to guide us to the Place of our Shipwreck; but we were fo long in looking for my Box, that we were ready to give over all Search: But juft as we were thinking of returning, the Mate happily found it out.

The *Negroes* took it by Turns, and we brought it fafe to the Plantation.

I had a good Parcel of Linnen in it, which I lent to my Fellow-Sufferers: But it was an odd Sight to difcover fo many Scare-crows, with tatter'd Coats and fine ruffled Shirts on.

Our Hoft was very well fatisfy'd for our Entertainment with what he found of the Wreck.

We ftaid here five Days to refrefh our felves, and then refolv'd to go up the River to wait on Colonel *Carew*, Deputy-Governor of *North-Carolina*; a Gentleman I had the Honour of being acquainted with. We hir'd a Canoo with two Sails, and embark'd, Capt. *Baily*, his Wife, the Mate, two Blacks and the Sailor, with another from the Plantation to affift us. We fail'd up *Ronoke* Sound with a frefh Gale, and at feven a-clock the next Morning ftopp'd at Colonel *Carew*'s Plantation, who out of his known Courtefy entertained us very handfomely. We took our leaves, and at eight a-clock the fame Evening came before the Governour's Houfe, fituate on the River *Notaway*, which runs into the *Ronoke* about fifty Leagues from the Sea.

I fent up one of the Men to acquaint the Governour I was come to wait on him; and upon the Inftant he came down to the Shore, accompany'd by Capt. *Cratbach*, a Native of *Bermuda* Ifland, and one I had long been acquainted with. He had left *Bermuda* fince we came away, and the Governour and he had juft been wifhing I had efcap'd the Storm as the Meffenger came to him.

Affoon

Mr. Richard Caftelman.

Affoon as ever he faw me, he cry'd out, I am forry for your Misfortune, I can eafily perceive an ill Wind drove you hither. He would not fuffer us to talk much, but hurry'd the whole Company into his Dining-Room, where ftood a Supper and a Bowl of Punch, with feveral Genlemen his Guefts. He begg'd their Pardon, but told 'em they fhould neither eat nor drink before we had fatisfy'd our felves; and we foon clear'd what was put before us: and then another Supper was provided for the whole Company, which we had our Shares of, notwithftanding what we had eaten before.

The Governour was but ill provided with Beds, therefore Capt. *Bayley* and his Wife went to Mr. *Glover*'s, a neighbouring Gentleman; and the Secretary would have me home with him, about a Mile from the Governour's. When we came to his Houfe, we found a Quarter of a *Shote* (a young Hog) and a Turkey on the Table. I fat down once more, and made a hearty Supper; and I muft own, I never thought I fhould bring my Stomach to its proper Tone again. After we had drank very heartily, we went to Bed. The next Morning we breakfafted upon broil'd Fowls and Chocolate. (*My Readers, if any, I hope will not ridicule my taking Notice fo often of Eating, till they put themfelves in my ftarv'd Condition.*)

The next Day we went to dine with a Friend of the Secretary's; and as we were at Dinner, a Meffenger came from the Governour and Capt. *Bayley*, to inform me a Veffel was going that Inftant for *Kakatan*, (a Harbour where the *Virginia* Fleet make up, and with the Convoy fet fail all together for *England*) and that Capt. *Bayley* and the reft of my unfortunate Company waited on Board for me. Notwithftanding my Stomach,

I was oblig'd to make all the Dispatch I could to the Place where the Vessel lay; but to my great Misfortune, the Wind proving fair for them, they were oblig'd to take the Advantage; and when I arriv'd at the Port they were almost out of Sight. I was very much concern'd at this Loss of my Passage, for it was very probable I might not get such another Opportunity till the Fleet was gone, and then I should be oblig'd to stay till next Year.

The Governour seeing me so much concern'd, offer'd me his Horse to go to *Kakatan* by Land, about 120 Leagues from the Place where we were; and he procured me a Guide, an honest *Quaker*, who for ten Pieces of Eight agreed to accompany me, and bring the Governour's Horse back again.

We set out immediately; for I had no Luggage to carry: because Capt. *Bayley*, as imagining I would come time enough, had got all my Things on Board.

We rode that Day about twenty Mile, thro' unfrequented Woods; but my Guide knew the Way by the above-mention'd Marks upon Trees. We came to a Quaker's Plantation; and all the Compliments my Guide us'd to him was only this, *Friend, I have brought along with me a ship-wreck'd Gentleman, who is going to* Kakatan, *and desires a Lodging to-night*; who was answer'd by our new Host, *Friend, come in; thou art welcome.* And indeed he made his Words good, for we had plenty of every thing, and a handsome Apartment to lie in, the best in the House. I was very much pleas'd with his Conversation, for I found him a Man of a sound Understanding.

In the Morning when I was going, I offer'd to pay him for what I had; but he seem'd much offended at my Proposition. Said he, *My House is*

Mr. Richard Castelman.

is no Inn, and we see Strangers so very seldom, that they are always welcome when they come; and God forbid that I should lessen the Store of an unfortunate Man, like thy self. In short, this is the Treatment I met with in my six Days Travel. Hospitality is commendable in all Countries, and *England* was once famous for it, but it seems at present banish'd to *America*. The third Day my Horse tumbled with me into a deep Swamp, and I was not only in danger of drowning, but of having my Brains dash'd out with his Hoofs in his Floundering. I continu'd so long in this Condition, that I gave my self up for lost; for my Guide could not come to assist me, without being in the same Danger. At last, my Horse, with much struggling, got Foot on firm Ground; by good Fortune I had got hold of the Stirrup, and he drew me up with him, to the great Joy of my Guide, who gave me for gone.

You must imagine I was not very easy in the rest of my Day's Journey, which I was oblig'd to ride all cover'd with Water and Mud. But our Host, where we lay at Night, got all my Things clean and dry by the time I rose in the Morning.

Our first four Days we travell'd through vast Woods, without seeing any humane Creature, but at the Plantations where we din'd and supp'd; and our Stages were very different, sometimes more than twenty Mile asunder, and at other times not above seven. Monstrous Snakes I saw of different Kinds, but none attempted to come near us till the fifth Day; when, as we were riding along, my Horse gave a Start, and ran on with me five hundred Yards before I could stop him. I turn'd about, and saw a *Rattle-Snake*, of a monstrous Bulk, spring at my Guide, who happen'd at that time to be behind me;

and

and it was very well he was, for if I had been in his Place, I should certainly have met with Death, in not knowing how to avoid it.

Their manner of springing upon any thing is this; they fold themselves up in Rings, then clap their Tail to the Ground, and dart upon their Prey: But as they are some time in doing it, a Person may avoid 'em, who knows their Manner.

There is but one Way to cure the Bite of these venomous Creatures, and that is to apply immediately the Fundament of a Fowl to the Wound, and keep it there till it be dead; which does not always happen. If the Fowl dies, there is Hope of a Cure; but if it does not, all the Physicians in the World can't help you. My Guide told me, this was one of the largest he had ever seen. I believe it was near six Yards in Length, and as thick as a lusty Man's Thigh. It is very rare for 'em to come so near the Roads, but this being little frequented perhaps was the Reason of it. The Rattle, which is in their Tail, makes an odd Sort of a Noise. When I was at *Philadelphia*, a Gentleman show'd me the Rattle. It was about a Yard and a half long, in small Joints, cover'd with a thin transparent Skin, like your white Gold-beater's Skin. They say they have a Joint grows every Year; but I can't tell who can prove it. The Rattle, as it lay folded in my Hand, seem'd so light that if I had not seen it there I could not have perceiv'd it by the Weight.

The last Day's Journey was one of the pleasantest I had ever travell'd in my Life, in a fine sweet Road, shaded by Trees for many Miles together, and through 'em on each side, numerous Plantations, with a well cultivated Glebe.

The whole Prospect put me in Mind of the Vale of *Evesham* in *England*.

The sixth Night I lay at the Father's of my Guide, having one Day's Journey more to reach *Kakatan*. Mr. *Ratcliff*, the Name of my Guide's Father, was Owner of a handsome Plantation upon *James* River; and there were so many about it that it look'd like a little Town.

The next Day after my Arrival, being *Sunday*, there was a general Assembly of the Brethren, and most of the Elders din'd with Mr. *Ratcliff*. When Dinner was serv'd, they began in their usual manner with their long Graces, and when one had made an end, another rose up to begin; but Mr. *Ratcliff* begg'd, upon my Account, that they would for once abridge the Motion of the Spirit, and let it take its full Scope for an After-Grace.

We had Notice from *Kakatan*, that the Fleet would not sail for some time; so I staid with my friendly Quaker four Days, who treated me very generously. I call'd for his Son to dismiss him back to the Governor, with the Horses: As I was paying him the Money I agreed for, his Father coming in by Accident, was very angry with him, and declared he would disown him for his Child if he took a Penny. I was not at all pleas'd with the Refusal, for the poor Man had taken a great deal of Pains with me; wherefore meeting by Chance with four Yards of Muslin to be sold, I bought it, and made him a Present of it unknown to his Father; tho' I had some Difficulty to make him accept of it, after what his Father had said to him.

The fourth Day after my Arrival, we had Notice the Fleet would sail in a few Days. This gave me a great deal of Uneasiness; for I could not get to *Kakatan* without a Boat, and Mr.

A a *Ratcliff*'s

Ratcliff's was broke to Pieces some time before I came there. But he seeing the Uneasiness I labour'd under, procur'd one: Yet another Difficulty arose, we could not gain, even for Money, any Body to row us. Well, said Mr. *Ratcliff*, since we have got a Boat, thou shalt not be made uneasie for want of People to work it, I and my Children will go along with thee. Accordingly we set out, and arrived at *Kakatan*: But we were surpriz'd not to find above five Sail there, and one of 'em that Vessel that Capt. *Bayley* went in; so I had the Satisfaction of getting my Things again.

Notwithstanding the Fleet's not being there, the Place was so full of People in Expectation of it, that there was no Lodging to be had. I was not so much concern'd for my self as for my generous Quaker, who was to meet with such bad Accommodation for his good Nature in accompanying me.

I met with a Gentleman bound for *England*, one Mr. *Le Cruce*, at present a Wine-Merchant in St. *Martin*'s Lane, who seeing the Shifts we were put to, offer'd me half his Bed, which I accepted of for my Friendly Quaker, but I could not prevail upon him to take it: therefore I lay with Mr. *Le Cruce* my self, and Mr. *Ratcliff* with his Sons made what Shift they could upon the Ground.

It was the Report of every one, that the Fleet would not get together in four Months, so I resolved to take a Trip to *Philadelphia* in the mean time.

I did not know how to fasten a Present upon Mr. *Ratcliff* for his Civility, for he would not hear of any thing like it; but at last I found out this Method. I bought a Runlet of Rum, a Thing very much in Esteem among the Planters,

ters, and I begg'd Mr. *Ratcliff* to add to the Obligations I had already received from him, by taking Charge of it and a Letter to one Mr. *Randal*, a Planter in his Neighbourhood. In the Letter I sent to Mr. *Randal*, was one inclos'd for Mr. *Ratcliff*, where I inform'd him the Rum was to him, only as a small Acknowledgment for the many Obligations he had laid me under.

The next Day he and his Sons took their leave of me, even without taking any thing for the Hire of the Boat, tho' I had bargain'd for it before I left the Place.

The Vessel that was to carry me to *Philadelphia* was not clear'd of her Lading, therefore I was oblig'd to stay seven Days at *Kakatan*, which is no Place of Resort but only once a Year, at the Time the Fleet makes up for *England*; so there are not many Conveniences expected there.

The Day before I sail'd for *Philadelphia*, I receiv'd a Letter from my Friendly Quaker, with a Present of a powder'd *Shote* and several Turkies, which he sent me by Water.

The Letter was as follows.

Friend *Castelman*,

I Receiv'd thy Present in a very particular manner; and tho' I am not very easy about it, yet I give thee my Thanks, with a Promise of a grateful Remembrance from me and mine. I pray thee to accept what I send thee as from a real Friend; and I commit thee to God.

J. Ratcliff.

The Vessel had but one Cabin in it, which was taken up by a Woman-Passenger; so that I was oblig'd to make shift to wrap my self up in the Sail; and the Spray of the Waves beating over us now and then, I had but a wet Lodging; and tho' it was nothing to what I underwent before, yet I got more Cold by it. We made so good Way that we got up to *New-Castle* in *Delaware* River the second Evening; and we prevail'd upon the Master to stay there all Night, where I got a good Lodging at a publick House, being the first time I had paid for any thing since my Shipwreck.

New-Castle, the Capital of the County of *New-Castle*, is a handsome well-built Town, standing upon an Eminence, which gives you a pleasant View from the River *Delaware*. The *Dutch* were the first Founders, but did not possess it long. There are now above 500 handsome Houses, and Foundations for several more. As it is daily increasing in Wealth by Trade, we may imagine it will increase in Buildings and Inhabitants. I have been inform'd they have discover'd in the Neighbourhood of this Town a fine Iron Mine.

The Day following we din'd at *Chester*, a little neat Town on the same River, consisting of near three hundred Houses. We were very handsomely entertain'd there by a Gentleman of the Place, who would accompany us to *Philadelphia*. We had a pleasant Voyage, with many delightful Prospects of Towns, Villages, and Plantations, on both sides of the River; and in the Evening we landed at *Philadelphia*, the Capital of *Pensylvania*.

Pensylvania takes its Name from *William Penn*, Esq; Son to Sir *William Penn*, Admiral of a Squadron in the *Dutch* War, where he behav'd like a Man of Courage and Conduct. His Son, the present Proprietor, met with some Difficulty in obtaining his Patent, by reason he had

Mr. Richard Castelman.

had declar'd himself Head of the People call'd Quakers.

Pensylvania is compos'd of all that Tract of Land, with its Islands, Rivers, Coasts, and Bays, which lies from forty to forty-five Degrees of North Latitude, and is one of the richest Countries in his Majesty's foreign Dominions.

The Air is pleasant, wholesome, and unclouded, or very rarely overcast. Tho' the Winter is something colder, and the Summer hotter than in *England*, yet the Inhabitants have known several Winters together without Frosts. The Day in the Summer is two Hours shorter than ours, and in Winter two Hours longer; which is really better for Business of all kinds. And certainly this is a Tract of Ground as well seated as any in the World, for Pleasure and Profit. It is bounded on the East by *West-Jersey*, on the West by *Virginia*, *Canada* on the North, and *Maryland* on the South; all, except *Canada*, fine *English* Settlements.

The original Inhabitants of all these Places are suppos'd to be the ten Tribes of the *Jews* that were scatter'd; but from whence they derive their Authority, even for this Supposition, I can't imagine. 'Tis true, some of the ancient *Jewish* Customs are among the *Indians*; but as every Nation and People have Customs peculiar to themselves, in my Opinion there is nothing to be gather'd from thence. 'Tis certain they have something of the Countenance of the *Jews*, they observe New Moons, and offer their First-Fruits to their Idols. They are most of 'em well made, and exactly proportion'd in their Features, without the thick Lips and flat Noses of the *Negroes*. They are generally good-natur'd and inoffensive, flow to Anger, but hard to be appeas'd; a courteous and humane Behaviour will gain upon 'em more than Severity: It is very seldom they wrong a good Master, but I have known 'em frequently venture their Lives for 'em. Their Language is very lofty and high sounding, but not copious, for one Word hath several Meanings. I'll give you, from my Friend Mr. *Thomas*, a short Specimen.

Hodi hita nee huska apeechi, nee machi Pensylvania *huska dogwachi keshow apeechi nowa, huska hayly chetena koon peo.*

Thus in *English*:
Farewell, my Friend. I shall go shortly to Pensylvania. We shall have a cold Moon presently, and hard Frosts will soon follow.

They throw their Children into the Water assoon as born, to harden their Bodies. The Business of the Men is to fish or hunt, and the Women to Till their Ground, and look after their Children, who commonly go alone at nine Months. They are most of them knowing in Botany; and if at any time visited with Sickness, cure themselves by their Knowledge in Herbs and Roots. They are exceeding charitable; and if any among 'em have the Misfortune to be lame or blind, they take care they shall want for nothing. The Boys go a hunting or fishing with the Father at six Years old; and when they are experienced in both, and arrive to their sixteenth Year, they may marry. The Girls stay at home with their Mother, who instructs them in her Business. The Women are very modest and chaste, and you can't affront them more than by saying any thing to the contrary of either. Adultery is punish'd with Death among 'em.

Their

Their Habitations are generally mean and small, and their Utensils a Pot, and two or three Calabashes, with a Bowl; and when they travel, they lie in the Woods about a Fire, to keep the wild Beasts from them. They are People of a merry Disposition, continually laughing and singing, even at their Work. They have some particular Songs among 'em, though but indifferent Tunes, and their Instruments of Musick are as poor. They are generally given to Sobriety; but if they once get Liquor of the *Europeans*, they never give over till dead drunk; and I have seen 'em lye in the middle of the Roads and Streets, like so many Dogs. Assoon as ever they come to themselves, they plunge into the Water, and gather some Herbs, squeeze 'em into a Calabash, which they drink; by which Means they are recover'd, and are never sick after their Debauches. Their Age generally comes up to seventy, and very few to eighty. I have heard one *Indian* speaking to another, when on his Death-Bed, of the Uncertainty of this Life, and how happy he should be in the Company of their God, where would be no want of Corn, or Wood, or any Thing that was needful for him. But there is a great Number instructed in the Christian Faith. There are *Indian* Schools to teach 'em Writing as well as Reading; and most of 'em are very docile.

The Country of *Pensylvania* abounds with every thing necessary for the Life of Man, even for the most luxurious.

The Woods afford fine Pidgeons, Pheasants, Quails, Partridges, Woodcocks, Snipes, wild Turkies, and various other Birds. About the Rivers, Geese, Ducks, Swans, Teal, Divers, Brands, &c. In the Rivers (generally a gravelly Bottom) are to be found Herrings, Smelts, Roach,

Roach, Dace, Eels, Perch, Salmon, Trout, Gurnets, Shadds, Cats-heads, Sheeps-heads, and many more; with fine large Oysters, preferable to any I ever tasted in *England*; and when any of these are brought to Market, you may buy 'em very reasonably.

The Woods produce Cedar, Mulberry, Vines, Walnut, Beech, Ash, Chesnut, and the finest Oak for building Ships. I am inform'd some of the Inhabitants have made Wine with Grapes of their own Growth; but I have heard nothing in Commendation of it.

The *Dutch* were the first Foreigners that came to these Parts; but they made but few Settlements; their chief Business was to trade with the *Indians* for Skins, Furrs, &c. and give them in Exchange, Rum, Beer, and Sugar. The next that appear'd was a Colony from *Sweden*, who began to plant and manure the Ground. The *Dutch* were offended at these Interlopers, as they call'd 'em, and threaten'd to make War upon 'em; which was prevented by the *Swedes* surrendring the Plantations to 'em, who return'd home.

In the *Dutch* War, Sir *Robert Carr* made a Descent upon 'em, outed 'em quite, and took Possession of it for the Crown of *England* in the Year 1666, and left a Relation of his, of the same Name, as Governour; but the next Year the *Dutch* got the Mastery again; and the few *English* that were there, settled themselves in the other *English* Colonies, better provided with Defence against an Invader.

The *Dutch* remain'd Possessors of this pleasant Country till the Peace was concluded between *England* and *Holland*, and then it was deliver'd once again to the *English*; but no great Progress was made there till 1682, the Year after

ter Mr. *Penn* had gain'd the Patent for it. In less than a Year there were a hundred Houses built, and form'd into a Town, to which Mr. *Penn* gave the Name of *Philadelphia*, (or Brotherly Love.) A Place for its Situation very agreeable, seated high upon a Neck of Land, form'd by two fine navigable Rivers, two hundred Miles from the Sea; yet Ships of five hundred Ton can unlade on the Key.

The Country about it is rich, well water'd and wooded; the Earth producing a vast Increase. They reap their Corn about the Beginning of *July*.

The Gardens and Orchards yield all Roots, Fruits and Flowers we have in *England*, and several peculiar only to the Country. The Air is so healthy that there is no Occasion for Physicians, being they find Cures for their accidental Diseases by Simples; and the People so peaceful, there's no want of a Lawyer among them; and if any Difference happens, a third Person makes up the Matter, without the Charge of a Law-Suit. This Country is divided into six Counties or Divisions, and each County sends six Members to the Assembly at *Philadelphia*. *Chester* 6; *New-Castle* 6; *Kent* 6; *Bucks* 6; *Sussex* 6; and *Philadelphia* 6. All these mention'd Places have Yearly Fairs, and Weekly Markets, being very conveniently situated for Commerce with the Country about 'em.

They have excellent Copper Mines, which produce better Copper than any in *England*, both for Colour and Fineness. Coal Mines have been lately found; and several mineral Waters that perform the same Office as *Bath*, *Tunbridge*, or *Epsom*. There is also found good Stone for Building, that proves handsome and lasting, and another thin Stone which they Tile their Houses with, being much neater than our
English

English Tile. Also Loadstones, and the *Salamander* Stone, having a Substance like Cotton in the Veins, which will not consume in the Fire.

The Woods produce Wolves, Panthers, Bears, Deer, Hares, Antelopes, Foxes, Rackoons, Rabbets, Squirrels, Bevers, &c. whose Skins yield great Profit to the Taker; and a Creature call'd a *Possum*, that has a false Belly into which the young ones retire in time of Danger: Also the Flying-Squirrel, with Wings like those of a Bat; and I have often seen it fly from Tree to Tree.

Red Deer, Buffalos, and *Elks* are common in the Woods, and delicious Food; but they are generally purchas'd from the *Indians*, (tho' at a very reasonable Rate) they being the People that best know how to hunt them. There is a Reward given 'em for killing a Bear or Wolf, which has very much lessen'd the Number of both; though any Person has the Liberty to hunt, fish, or fowl, without being molested. There's also Plenty of Otters about the Rivers, and such a multitude of Frogs in the *Swamps** that they disturb you with their Croaking; especially the *Bull-Frog*, that makes a Noise something like that Beast, and is the Base to all the others.

If the distress'd People of *England* knew the Comforts of *Pensylvania*, and the easy Means there is of a Livelihood, they would never stay where they are, in a continual Scene of Want and Misery. Even the meanest Servant has better Wages than those in *England*. If criminal Persons were sent over there, they would find Employment, and yet be restrain'd in the Vices for which they were punish'd: For a Thief there is to return Four-fold what he has stole; and if he has not wherewithal to do that, he's compell'd to work it out. But every thing is in

---

* A Swamp is much of the same kind as the Boggs in Ireland.

such Plenty there, they would have no Occasion to exercise their Talents that Way.

Their Beef, Mutton, Pork, Lamb, Veal, &c. is equal to our Meat in *England*, with which they trade to the *Leeward-Islands*, and bring in Return, Rum, Sugar, Moloffos, and Pieces of Eight. Their Horses are strong, handsome, and hardy, and seldom feed on any thing but Grass; and after the hardest Day's Work, are turn'd out hot into the Fields, yet get no Harm.

The Country produces great Numbers of Apple and Pear Trees, with which they make great Quantities of Cyder and Perry, that is very wholesome and well tasted.

There are many large, beautiful, well-built Towns in the Province of *Pensylvania*, of which, as I said before, *Philadelphia* is the chief. It is a noble, large, and populous City, standing on as much Ground as our *English* City of *Bristol*, seated upon a Neck of Land form'd by the Rivers *Delaware* and the *Schuylkill*, both navigable many Leagues above the City. It is built square in Form of a Chess-Board, with each Front facing one of the Rivers.

There are several Streets near two Mile long, as wide as *Holborn*, and better built, after the *English* Manner. The chief are *Broad-street*, *King-street*, and *High-street*, tho' there are several other handsome Streets that take their Names from the Productions of the Country; as *Mulberry*, *Walnut*, *Beech*, *Sassafras*, *Cedar*, *Vine*, *Ash*, and *Chesnut Streets*. From these Streets run great Numbers of Courts, Yards, and Allies, with well-built Houses in 'em. There are several Coves and Docks where large Ships are built; and by a moderate Computation, there has been launch'd from the Stocks of this City in forty Year, near 300 Sail of Ships, besides Small-Craft, which may in some sort give us an Idea of the Opulency of the Place. Many of their Merchants keep their Coaches, and the Tradesmens Shops and Streets are well frequented. All Religions are tolerated here, which is one Means to increase the Riches of the Place. The People of the Church of *England* as by Law establish'd, have a neat, well-built Church, founded in the Year 1695, and I am inform'd the Foundation is laid for another. The *Quakers* (who are the major Part of the Inhabitants) have several Meetings. There is a *Swedish* reform'd Church, Mr. *Rudman* the Incumbent, a Man of singular Learning and Piety; who is as much follow'd by the *Quakers*, when he preaches, as the *Protestants*. I shall beg leave to give one Instance of his Humility and Piety. When Subscriptions were taking in to build the Church, he subscrib'd a considerable Sum; but when call'd upon for the Money, he had it not in his Power to pay it; yet to keep his Word, he contracted with the Master-Builder for so much a-day, to carry the Hod, till he had work'd his Subscription-Money out. This was an Instance of his Piety and Zeal for Religion; and I fancy if Churches were to be built after the same Manner in a certain Island, the Work would go but slowly on. There are single Houses upon the Key that have cost 6000 *l*. the Building. Mr. *Badcock*'s Brewhouse is a noble, large Building, and has in it one single Vessel that will hold eight Ton of Liquor.

In this City is held the Courts of the Province, and the Assembly meet here, which is in the nature of a dependant Parliament, as in those Cities of *France* that are distant from the Capital. There are three Fairs in the Year, and every Week two Markets. In time of the Fairs the City is so throng'd, as well as the adjacent Plantations, that it is hard to find a Lodging.

The

The Government and Constitutions are the same as in *England*.

Their Council is compos'd of the Protestants and Quakers, but the Publick Officers are taken out of the former. The Governour is nominated by the King of *England*, and the rest of the civil Officers are, Master of the Rolls, four Judges, a Judge of the Admiralty, Secretary, Attorney-General, Treasurer, Publick Register, Clerk of the Peace, as also a Commissary, and a Surveyor-General. These, with eight Members of the Council, form the Government of the City. The Number of the Inhabitants is generally suppos'd to be upwards of 15000, besides Slaves. There is hardly any Trade in *England* but the same may be met with in *Philadelphia*; and every Mechanick has better Wages; a Journeyman Taylor has twelve Shillings a Week, besides his Board; and every other Trade in Proportion has the same Advantage.

There is a Post-Office lately erected, which goes to *Boston* in *New-England*, *Charles-town* in *Carolina*, and the other neighbouring Places. The uncultivated Ground, which is not grubb'd, sells for ten times the Value it did at first; though there is none of that sort within ten Miles round the City: And that within the Neighbourhood that was sold for ten Pound at first, will fetch above three hundred now. All Women's Work is very dear there, and that proceeds from the smallness of the Number, and the Scarcity of Workers; for even the meanest single Women marry well there, and being above Want are above Work. The Proprietor of this fine Country (as I said before) is *William Pen*, Esq; who has a fine Seat call'd *Pensbury*, built on three Islets, if I may so call 'em; for a Branch of the River *Delaware* runs thrice round it. In his Orchards and Gardens may be found all the
Fruits,

Fruits, Roots, and Herbs that are in *England*, and many more peculiar to the Country. There is very good Paper made in *Penſylvania*, Linen, Druggets, Crapes, Camblets, and Serges, with which they trade. Moſt of the Merchants, and ſome Tradeſmen, have handſome Country Houſes, well and conveniently furniſh'd. No Inſults from the *Indians* were ever heard of here, which is more than any of our other Plantations upon the Continent can ſay; neither are there any of them us'd as Slaves, but they are paid as well as the *Europeans* for their Commodities or Labour; and there are more Chriſtians among 'em than in any other Nation in *America*, for their Number. Moſt of them bring up their Children to read and write, and ſome of them are bound Apprentice to the *Europeans*, who prove as good Workmen at the Buſineſs they follow as their Maſters. In ſhort, in the midſt of War they enjoy the Tranquility of Peace. They are too far diſtant from the Sea to fear the Invaſion of a foreign Enemy, and there are ſeveral Places of Strength upon the River of *Delaware*, before they can arrive at *Philadelphia*. Yet when I was there, the Town was alarm'd with a falſe Report that the *French* had landed within the Bay, and committed ſeveral Acts of Hoſtility. It was judg'd by ſome, that this Report was ſpread abroad, on purpoſe to ſee how active the People would be to defend themſelves, and whether the *Quakers* were to be depended upon in caſe of an Invaſion. The Governor got at the Head of about 700 Men, and exhorted the *Brethren* to ſtand up for the Defence of their Lives and Eſtates; but they declar'd the carnal Weapon did not belong to them, yet they would retire and pray for us. The People of the Town brought out their Proviſion and Liquor, and freely

freely gave it among the Soldiers, who made as free with it. Before Night, News came that it was a false Alarm, which I believe did not displease any of us.

In the Heat of the Day I sometimes took a Walk with some of the Town to *Fair Mount*, a pleasant Place shaded with Trees on the River *Schuylkill*. As we were coming home one Day, deep in Discourse with one another, as I was stepping over a Stile, I saw stretch'd on the Ground before me a Snake, as I suppose asleep. I had not Power to draw my Leg back again, but my Foot fell just upon the Head and part of the Neck of the Reptile, more by the particular Direction of Providence, than my Design. It sprung up so quick, and twisted round my Right Leg and Body with such Force that I was in Fear of being strangled; however, I kept my Foot fix'd fast upon its Head, and in a little time it fell down dead. It is almost impossible for Words to describe what I felt at this Accident; the very Touch of it about my Leg and Body had very near taken away my Breath; and it was the greatest Providence in the World I did not take my Foot from the Head of the Snake; for if I had, it would certainly have bit me. It was a considerable time before I could shake off my Apprehension, and I was downright sick with the Fright the whole Day after. Some of my Companions had the Curiosity to measure it: It was in Length two Yards nine Inches, and ten Inches about from the Neck to within a Yard of the Tail. I remember very well, after this Accident, whenever I had Occasion to cross a Stile, in *Penſylvania* or *Old England*, I ever took Care to look before me; so lasting is the Impression of Fear and Danger upon the Minds of Men.

I

I continu'd at *Philadelphia* near four Months, and was very well entertain'd by the Gentlemen of the Place: I am pleas'd I have it in my Power to pay 'em my publick Acknowledgment of Thanks for all their Favours; particularly the Reverend Mr. *Brooks*, whom I met with by Chance at *Philadelphia*: His Business there was to raise Subscriptions for a new Church near *New-York*: When he heard of my Misfortunes, he was so generous and charitable as to offer to lend me a Sum of Money he had in his Hands, upon my bare Word only, which I was to return to him from *England* by the Society for Propagating the Gospel in Foreign Parts. As I was not in want of it, I did not accept his intended Favour, but I shall ever gratefully remember his kind Intentions.

I must not forget the many Obligations I had the Honour to receive from his Excellency Governor *Evans*, nor Mr. *Evans* the Commissary, who was particularly civil to me. These Gentlemen, tho' of the same Name, are no otherwise related than by marrying the Daughters of Mr. *Moor*, the Collector of the King's Customs. The Commissary is just gone for *Philadelphia* again, having been in *England* near a Twelvemonth, about an Affair between the present Governor Sir *William Keith* and him, relating to the King's Customs. Among the rest of my Friends, I must not forget the facetious Mr. *Staples*, Dancing-Master, who was the first Stranger of *Philadelphia* that did me the Honour of a Visit, and to his merry Company I owe the passing of many a dull Hour, that probably might have lain heavy upon the Hands of a Man under my Circumstances, depriv'd of Fortune, in a strange Country, having no Friends, in whose Power it was to assist me, nearer than
England;

England; for Mr. *Jones* was too much involv'd in his own troublesome Affairs at *Bermuda*, to expect any thing from him. But the Generosity of the *Philadelphians* is rooted in their Natures; for it is the greatest Crime among them not to show the utmost Civility to Strangers: And if I were oblig'd to live out of my native Country, I should not be long puzzled in finding a Place of Retirement, which should be *Philadelphia*. There the oppress'd in Fortune or Principles may find a happy *Asylum*, and drop quietly to their Graves without Fear or Want.

In the Beginning of *August*, News arriv'd that the Fleet would be ready to sail from *Kakatan* the latter End of the Month, so that I now began to bend my Thoughts towards my native Country. I pick'd up at *Philadelphia* four more Companions that intended the same Voyage; and *August* 5 we took leave of our Friends, and the lovely City of *Philadelphia*, which I shall always remember with the utmost Satisfaction. We hir'd a Boat to carry us down the *Delaware*, and lay the first Night at a Planter's, an Acquaintance of one of my Companions, who treated us with the usual Civilities of the Country. The next Day we din'd on Board our Boat, and at Night arriv'd at *Lewis*, about 50 Leagues from *Philadelphia*, and 20 from the Sea. We staid here three Days. This Town is the Capital of *Suffex* County, and is built upon the *Hoorkill*, a River that runs into the *Delaware*. A little below begins the Bay of *Delaware*, which is form'd by Cape *William* and Cape *James*, this last is the utmost Bounds of *Pensylvania*. While we staid here, I had the Curiosity to go into the Woods to see 'em gather Honey, it being free for any one, which proceeds

ceeds from its great Plenty; and you may buy the best Bees-wax at *Philadelphia* for four Pence a Pound. At *Lewis* we had some of the largest Oysters and Cockles I ever saw in my Life; some of the former were six Inches Diameter out of the Shell, and very well tasted. At this Place they make a rich Soup, compos'd of these, and other Shell-fish, which is very nourishing and palatable. From *Lewis* we were to walk over an Isthmus of eight Mile, that parts *Delaware* River, and *Chesapeak* Bay, which would save us three or four Days Sailing, for we had Notice of a Ship call'd the *Globe*, a new Vessel of near five hundred Ton, and twenty-four Guns, that was at *Kakatan*, and would be willing to receive Passengers. We set out from *Lewis* with Horses to carry what little Baggage we had, but we chose to walk it on Foot our selves. We din'd at a pleasant Plantation about the mid-way of our Journey, but found it a difficult matter to prevail upon a Couple of young Girls to come near us at first, for they took us for Privateers; but at last we prevail'd upon 'em, and they call'd their Father, &c. who made very much of us. One of the Girls perceiving I had a Watch in my Hand to see what time of Day it was, begg'd to look upon it; but it was very pleasant to see her Fear, when she touch'd it, and would not be persuaded but it was alive, from its going and the Noise it made. I ask'd her if she had never seen or heard of a Watch before. She told me she had never seen one, but her Sister had read of 'em. I only mention this to shew the Simplicity and Innocence of those Inhabitants of *America*, that live retir'd in the Country; for they told me they had neither of 'em been four

Mile

Mile from their own House in their Lives.

We took Leave of our Planter and his Family, and got that Night to a Plantation on *Chesapeak* Bay, where we lay all Night, and were well entertain'd. The next Day we set about getting a Boat to carry us to *Kakatan*; but we met with a great deal of Difficulty in procuring one, and were three Days before we could succeed; but at last we got one by Accident, that was coming up the Bay. We got on Board, and arriv'd at *Kakatan* the same Evening. *Kakatan* is no more than a large Cove, where all the Fleet rendezvous in order to set Sail for *England*. There are some few Houses scatter'd up and down the Bay, which go at great Rates upon this Occasion. It lies about ten Leagues up the River of *Chesapeak*; which River divides *Virginia* and *Maryland*. It is the greatest River upon the Continent in the *English* Dominions, and the farthest navigable up in the Country; and many other Rivers fall into it. We enquir'd for the *Globe*, and soon agreed with the Captain for his great Cabin, at a reasonable Rate, and he seem'd pleas'd with his Company. We provided what little Necessaries we wanted, as some fresh Provisions, Liquor, &c. and on *Sept.* 4. the Commadore hung out the Signal for Sailing.

I thought it was a noble Sight to see so many Ships under Sail all together. There were upwards of two hundred Sail of Merchant-Men, besides four Sail of Men of War for our Convoy.

We drove down the River, and at Night got over-against the *Virginia* Capes, Cape *Henry* and Cape *Charles*, which form the Mouth of *Chesapeak* Bay. The next Day we left the main Land aftern, and we had Orders from the Commadore to spread our selves, for fear we should fall foul of each other in the Night. We continu'd sailing several Days together with a prosperous Gale. *Sept.* 28, the Skies threaten'd us with a Storm; we reev'd our Sails in Expectation of it, but it blew so violently at last that we were oblig'd to lie under a reeft Foresail; and it was well we had a good stout Ship under us, or we had perish'd. Our Fleet was soon scatter'd, and we saw several of them sink in View, with their whole Crew; and it was not in the Power of the other Ships to succour 'em. I now began to think I should be bury'd in the Deep, tho' our Captain always gave us great Hopes in the Goodness and Strength of the Ship; for she was well rigg'd and fitted, it being her first Voyage. We were terribly toss'd all Night, and when the Morning dawn'd, we could not perceive one of the Fleet; so we were oblig'd to sail alone, which gave me many melancholy Reflections: However, we had this to comfort us, that the Storm was abated; and the next Day, to my great Joy, we discover'd forty of our scatter'd Fleet, and one Man of War. When we could come within Hailing, we receiv'd a dismal Account of the Loss of above thirty of the Fleet, that founder'd at Sea. Some of the Men were sav'd, as also part of the Cargo of seven or eight, but the rest went to the Bottom.

One Reason of the Weakness of the Ships was their being unsheath'd; and staying four Months beyond their usual Time, the Worms had got into their Bottoms.

We sail'd together with a fair Wind till we came upon the Coast of *France*, and then we had

the

the Misfortune of being dispers'd in the Night; and our Danger was the greater in being so near an Enemy's Country. The next Day we perceiv'd a Sail making up to us: We soon discover'd it was a *French* Privateer. There were three Ships of us in Company: we got together to consult, and at last it was agreed to prepare for the Fight, though in a very poor Condition for an Engagement. Some of the Sailors advis'd us to meet 'em, which Advice was taken. We immediately crouded all the Sail we could, and got our Hands upon Deck, Passengers and all; and having the Wind of 'em, we bore down upon 'em, which had the desired Effect; for assoon as they perceiv'd us chasing 'em, they made all the Sail they could to get from us, and in a little time got out of our Sight. We were very well pleas'd with our Stratagem, and continu'd our Course.

November 3, we discover'd *England*, whose Chalky Cliffs gave us all a vast Delight. We coasted along the Channel with the pleasing Hopes of once more setting our Feet upon our native Country; and *Nov.* 7. we got safe into *Deal* Harbour. We staid there but one Night, and hir'd Horses to go to *Canterbury*; from whence we took a Coach to *Gravesend*, and the next Day went in the Passage-Boat to *London*. As we were going up the River, a Ship outward-bound came so suddenly upon us, that we were in the utmost Danger of being run over. Most of the Passengers got up, ready to lay hold of the Tackling of the Ship to save themselves; but by Providence, she mist us by about two Inches. This put me in Mind of the Uncertainty of Human Life, and that a Man may

meet

meet with Death, when he imagines himself paſt all Danger.

I landed at *London, Nov.* 15, 1710. I gave God Thanks for his many and ſignal Mercies, where I hope I am ſettled for the Remnant of my Life, without truſting my ſelf any more to the Dangers of the tempeſtuous Sea.

F I N I S.